LUNA'S EDGE

Roxana Macias

Copyright © 2024 by Roxana Macias

All rights reserved.

No part of this publication may be reproduced, distributed, or transmitted in any form or by any means, including photocopying, recording, or other electronic or mechanical methods, without the prior written permission of the publisher, except as permitted by U.S. copyright law.

The story, all names, characters, and incidents portrayed in this production are fictitious. No identification with actual persons (living or deceased), places, buildings, and products is intended or should be inferred.

ISBN-13: 979-8-9913240-0-7 (Print Paperback)

Book Cover Illustration by Yaesool Jeong

First edition 2024

A man can trade humanity for technology and be doomed to the coldness of that void.

-ILEX REGEN

This book is dedicated to the loves of my life: Daniel, whose endless encouragement and patience sustained me through countless late nights; Joshua, Julian, and Leo, you are my motivation, and my heart.

CONTENTS

Chapter 1

PARKVILLE

Eveley's 20th Birthday

Normally, [1] Eveley Luna would never walk alone at night, even in the cozy familiarity of this small town, but tonight was different. She had an unusually busy shift at the local pub in town, waiting on more tables than she normally did on a late Friday night. The energy was draining from her body as the clock turned 10:30 pm. When the last table stood to leave, she started helping to tidy up, sweep, and count her tips quickly with the goal to set off toward home within the next half hour. Usually the waitresses tried to walk to their cars in groups of two or three. However, by 11 pm, Eveley was the only waitress left. Her manager offered to escort her out, but not wanting to wait for her boss to finish his tasks, she declined. Since her car was parked less than 100 feet from the pub entrance, she didn't think there was a reason to be overly cautious.

It was a brisk November night in downtown Parkville, a little riverside city in Missouri that was the quintessential All-American town. Though it felt like it was tucked away in some hill enclave faraway from the bustle of the city, Parkville was only 10 minutes away from the downtown area of Kansas City. The zenith of Kansas City's skyline barely peaked out of the foggy

---

1. Eveley (Ev-uh-lee)

shadows for those lucky enough, or affluent enough, to afford a mansion on a hill, which there were many in the hills of Parkville.

Eveley paused as she stepped out onto the sidewalk in front of the pub, the weather had been dreary and rainy all day, typical November weather for the Midwest. It had died down to a slow but chilly drizzle. Eveley shivered and wrapped her arms around herself. She dropped her keys accidentally and kneeled down to pick them up, in a millisecond she felt a chill go through her body like a bolt of lightning. She jumped up instinctively and looked around her.

The streets were lit with vintage street lamps that let off a soft glow in the drizzle. Up the inclined street leading to the hills of Parkville, she could see the glistening of the wet pavement and the wind rustling the leaves in the small trees lining Main Street. To the other side of her were the train tracks, where she was barely 100 feet away to cross and make it to the large expansive parking lot that was part of English Landing Park. She'd often come to English Landing Park to play pickleball, read a book by the riverside, browse the farmers market, or take in the sights walking alongside the Missouri river. Tonight was different, the usually warm and inviting aura of English Landing was missing, in its place, heavy fog, laced with unsettling quiet and eeriness. Despite feeling a strangeness inside her she told herself she was being paranoid.

Eveley took a deep breath and started walking toward the train tracks, her car was parked only a short distance past the tracks. She glanced behind her and saw no one, everything seemed quiet. As she reached the edge of the train tracks she turned her face to the left to make sure the track was clear, as she did so, she felt the same bolt of electricity run through her body again, this time more potent and frenzied. Her whole body ached, her knees became weak, she felt a warmth running through her veins and a distinct caress of hot air on the arch of her neck. A sweet smell in the air further perplexed her, her entire senses were confused at this point and she managed to turn her head to the right, and that's when she saw *it*.

In the total darkness, a beam of white light connected sky to earth. In the middle of the tracks, 200 feet from her, was the silhouette of what she could only describe as a man. She couldn't see any of his features, he was a black void in the shape of a man, and although everything in her body told her to run, she was frozen in her spot.

In a fraction of a second her mind tried to comprehend what she was seeing but it was unable to compute. Behind this tall man, a large ball of blinding light grew larger, hypnotizing her. She saw the silhouette raise and reach out his hand toward her as if to plead she come closer. In that moment she panicked as she realized he'd seen her. She frantically looked around her, thinking surely someone else must be seeing this light, or hearing the commotion surrounding her. There was a sound that was completely deafening in her ears like a roar from a jet engine. The light got brighter and closer letting off a high-pitched whir, she could no longer see the silhouette as the light completely blinded her. Her stomach dropped as the lights accelerated toward her in a flurry, she instinctively shut her eyes, put her hands in front of her face, and let out the most ear-piercing scream she'd ever screamed. She felt herself falling and her body crumpled to the ground, right in the middle of the train tracks.

The blood moon is all I can see. If I can just extend my hands an inch more I know I can reach the moon's dusty craters and dips. Somehow my senses relay I'm not on earth but somewhere far away, but where? Is this a dream? I look down at my legs. I'm sitting on a cliff's edge, overlooking a clearing of pine forest below. I sway my feet casually like a child, admiring the dramatic aura of light the moon casts on

the scene before me. Static is running along the contour of my neck. I can't remember how I got here, but I never want to leave. A warm breeze caresses my face as I look up at the expansive sky, the stars are in large dramatic clusters, a beauty to behold. I feel lucky to be in the presence of this work of art. In total awe of nature's painting, I suddenly want to cry. I want to get lost in this scene and never look away. Just when I feel my body melt into this panorama, a chilling fear grips my insides, my skin turns cold and my breathing stops. The most terrifying and deafening roar, the moon, fractures into millions of pieces. The outburst of all those pieces hurl violently toward every corner of the sky, and I scream till I can't utter any more sounds. I place my hands in front of my face as the rocks hurl toward me. My body plummets in free fall, my stomach lurches as the ground inches closer. I fall through the ground and suddenly I am floating among the moon debris. I have no physical body. I am only consciousness, lost and alone in space.

Saturday 6:05 am

"Miss! Hello! Are you okay!?" Mr. Collins shouted from his front door on the balcony next to the train tracks. Mr. Collins, a gentleman of 70 years about to take his early morning walk, noticed the crumpled woman's body on the train tracks. He couldn't come up with any idea on what happened to the young lady but she wasn't moving. There was also another reason he was alarmed. The train that passed through town usually made its way through Parkville around 6:08 am, as he usually made sure to cross before it passed.

Stanford, an astute dog, was alert and extremely agitated all morning from the time he woke up to get ready for the day.

He was so agitated he scratched on the front door to be let out which was unlike Stanford and perplexed Mr. Collins.

Today was especially foggy, a thick blanket covered Parkville due to the proximity to the river. As soon as Mr. Collins closed the front door, Stanford whimpered and pulled lightly to the edge of the balcony closest to the street. Mr. Collins would probably have missed seeing the young lady if it wasn't for Stanford, as he usually crossed in the opposite direction. Mr. Collins hurried down his stairs, even with his slight limp he made it quickly down the 2 flights. He released Stanford as his whimpering increased to a fever pitch and Stanford raced to the silhouette. Stanford nuzzled the young girl's face while whimpering in concern.

When Mr. Collins saw the young lady, he couldn't help feeling anxious...she looked lifeless. It'd been drizzling all night and into the morning so she was soaked. Her body laid in the fetal position. Her hands laid limp covering her face, her fingertips were blue, her clothing tattered and burned, down to her one remaining boot. Her remaining boot was stuck in the rail of the train tracks. Her blouse was burned partially off her body, exposing a bright red burn in the shape of a fern close to her collarbone.

"Miss can you hear me?! My goodness! what happened to you miss?!" Mr. Collins grabbed her shoulders firmly to wake her, her skin felt ice cold. Her face tucked into her shoulder, he brushed away her long chestnut hair, matted to her cheeks from the rain. Her face was bruised on the side that touched the train track, black soot marks covered her face, neck, and chest area as well as the areas exposed from her tattered clothing. He squeezed her wrist and felt a faint pulse.

Last night it was raining but peaceful. He recalled one particularly strong and random lightning strike that woke him and Stanford. Till that moment he thought it was a dream, but maybe not? Could this mean she was hit by lightning? It was the only explanation for the burn marks and tattered clothing on this young lady he thought. As soon as Mr. Collins made this conclusion he tried to move her. He needed to move her off the tracks to safety and get help.

"Help! Someone call 911! Help!"

Mr. Collins shouted over and over again as he tried to pry her boot free. He realized it was useless so he unzipped the ankle boot. He saw swelling in her ankle which confirmed it was severely sprained or broken. He took her foot out of the shoe when he heard the train. First, he felt the vibrations in the ground, then, the low rumble of it approaching from a distance. He knew the train would be there in less than a minute. Once he heard the horn of the train, he would only have seconds before both their lives were in jeopardy.

By now, several other residents heard Mr. Collin's loud pleas for help and peeked out from their apartment and shop windows. Two men and a woman ran frantically to his aid. Stanford was already tugging on her pant leg trying to pull her to safety. The train bellowed its horn as it turned around the bend in full view. Everyone worked together to pick up the young lady and quickly move her beyond the train track onto the sidewalk with only seconds to spare.

"Oh my goodness, what happened?!" Mrs. Kennedy, who lived in the apartment next to Mr. Collins asked frantically.

No one answered her as Mr. Collins was already dialing 911 and the stranger laid on the sidewalk. Fortunately, Mrs. Kennedy was a registered nurse and she quickly recognized the burns and tattered clothing.

"Oh my! Lightning?!" She kneeled down and took her pulse and put her ear close to the young girl's nose and lips to hear if she was breathing.

"They're 5 minutes away! Is she breathing?!" Mr. Collins asked.

"Yes, she's breathing," Mrs. Kennedy said as she went into autopilot. She was used to patients coding at the busy ER she worked at downtown. Mrs. Kennedy took note of her heart rate, breathing rate, and pulse strength. She concluded she was showing signs of moderate hypothermia, teetering on severe, they'd found her in the nick of time. She gently inspected her body for injuries, as she ran her hands with care over her injured foot, she heard a faint moan and she saw a flutter from the young girl's eyes.

"Can you hear me? Stay with me, we need you awake, help is on the way. I know you're in a lot of pain but you must stay awake," Mrs. Kennedy said firmly and calmly.

"Is there anything you need us to get you?" Mr. Suarez asked, a local shop owner who was taking inventory in his shop when he heard Mr. Collin's pleas for help.

"If you could cover her up with your jackets, that would help her warm up," Mrs. Kennedy replied.

"Of course!" Mr. Suarez placed his insulated jacket over her top half.

Mr. Long took off his jacket as well and placed it on her lower half.

She moaned louder, her eyes fluttered but never opened. Her face scrunched up in agony and her moans stopped suddenly as she went in and out of consciousness. Her pulse sounded stronger but was still weak by the time they saw the ambulance approaching from the hill. By now a small crowd had formed from afar, local residents who didn't want to interfere, but still felt concern for the young lady who not only cheated death by lightning, but was still fighting for her life. Everyone was in awe she survived all night soaked to the bone, with a failing heart, severe burns, all in 40-degree weather.

The EMTs quickly took control of the situation and within a minute loaded her onto the ambulance. Mr. Collins recounted what he had encountered on the train tracks minutes prior and her condition. No one knew her identity so two Parkville police cars pulled up to get statements from witnesses and possible clues to her identity.

After speaking to everyone they scoured the area for clues. In a bush nearby they found her purse which contained her wallet with her driver's license. A mere foot from the track they found her phone. It was completely fried so they assumed it was in her hand at the time of the lightning strike.

Mr. Collins took a seat on the edge of the sidewalk, Stanford sat quietly by his side. Mr. Collins, a man of few words and little emotion placed his face in his hands and felt a wave of emotion hit him like a pile of bricks. He was reliving the death of his daughter all over again and it hit him all at once when the young lady was being carted away into the ambulance. He wanted to believe and he quietly prayed she'd make it through. Mr. Suarez and Mr. Long sat down next to him and placed their hand on either one of his shoulders, quietly offering their support.

The whole town had felt the death of Mr. Collin's daughter. It was a tragedy still affecting lives in Parkville today. Residents still spoke of the sweet young lady intent on changing the world and her dreams cut short. Everyone loved Willow Collins. After her death, Mr. Collins could've moved far away from her memory. Instead, Mr. Collins continued to live in the town that regularly kept her memory alive, adorning their businesses with pictures on its walls of the daughter he loved more than anything in this world. Parkville had been his home for 30 years, and his daughter's death and the solidarity and support from his neighbors, made him adamant to live and die in a little piece of the world called Parkville.

I don't know if everything I saw, heard, and felt that night was a dream. I still don't know what exactly happened to me or if my path diverged on that very night to something I will never be able to comprehend. The only thing I know for sure is something changed inside of me that

night and I am on the verge of breaking the code, solving the enigma of my memories. Somewhere there has to be a clue to who I became that night.

Sunday 11:00 am

My eyes felt heavy as if I hadn't slept for days. I could see a shimmering orange light filtering through my eyelids and for once in my life I felt scared to open them. I heard the clear beeping of a machine nearby. I felt as if my body weighed a 1,000 pounds and couldn't move. I felt a searing pain in my elbow and ankle. I slowly opened my eyes and saw a sterile hospital room. I was propped half sitting in a hospital bed. I looked down and saw my arm hooked to an IV, the reason I felt pain in my arm. My window shades were wide open, bright rays of sunshine covered my entire face. I felt a throbbing pain near my chest, there was a bandage visible from the edge of my hospital gown's neckline. I tried to move my arm to move my hospital gown out of the way but I couldn't move my arm.

"It's better if you don't move for now, you're still weak," a deep voice bellowed out from the corner.

It startled me and I jerked my head in the direction of the voice. My head felt like it was going to explode and I scowled in pain. There was no one in the corner of the room from where I thought I heard the voice. Perhaps my drowsiness was getting the best of me? I looked intently at the corner of the room, and for a brief second I felt static on the back of my neck and the pain in my chest throbbed quicker than before. The pain increased in intensity until I felt like I was going to pass out and I realized I was holding my breath. Then I saw something...I could have sworn I saw a silhouette of a person flash before my eyes. I must be dreaming...definitely dreaming, and then a nurse casually walked in.

"Hello Miss Luna, I'm so glad to see you are awake, how are you feeling?"

Her voice was gentle and calming. She walked to my window and pulled the shade down to block the sun from my face. She looked at me with an inquisitive look on her face.

"My name is Nurse Downs but you may call me by my first name, Janet. I'm your nurse for the day, your doctor will be in shortly to see you, you just rest and don't worry about a thing, I'll take good care of you."

I simply nodded, still confused. Was I in a dream or not? The heaviness on my body started to feel uncomfortable, to the point I started struggling to breathe.

"What's wrong?" Janet asked.

Darn it! Why couldn't I move? And why was I feeling this aggravating static on the back of my neck? Could it be...I was paralyzed? No! I mean I wasn't even sure what happened to me but something bad had happened, I knew it. I panicked and Janet noticed the terrified look on my face. I heard the machine I was hooked to start beeping like crazy. Janet glanced at it and looked at the pained expression on my face.

"Okay, breathe for me, try to take deep breaths, I think you might be having a panic attack."

I tried to move my diaphragm, I really tried, but my body wouldn't listen. I started trying to move my arms in an attempt to move my position, I couldn't even speak for goodness sake!

"Okay, I'm going to move you to your side and lay you down and you tell me if it helps, I need you to try your hardest to take a breath or you're going to pass out."

Janet quickly lowered the head of my bed, when she placed her hands on my arm I felt the most painful shock of my life, I managed to get out a muffled groan through my clenched teeth.

"Alright I'm almost done."

She managed to push me to my side and I heard it again.

"Close your eyes and clear your mind, you'll be able to breathe," the deep voice bellowed. This time the voice was near my ear as if the person's lips were mere centimeters from my ear.

I closed my eyes, my diaphragm snapped and my lungs filled with air. I burst into tears as I took frenzied breaths in, an embarrassing and unusual way to learn to breathe again. My hands were all of a sudden working and the heaviness I felt earlier dissipated. I covered my face with my hands in embarrassment.

"That's it, slow it down, try to take in air slowly, take your time." Janet looked relieved and the machines stopped their incessant beeping.

"You were turning blue there, it's completely normal to have panic attacks after such an experience, do you remember anything from the last couple of days?"

"No...everything is so muddled in my head, I...I-" I clasped my lips shut and stared at the window, trying to bring my emotions back in check.

"What was the last thing you remember dear?" Janet continued.

"I don't know, I remember getting ready for work, what happened to me?"

"Well," she took a long pause, "You were found on the train tracks in Parkville. We think you were struck by lightning at some point during the night...an elderly man and his dog found you in the early morning according to the EMTs."

My jaw dropped, lightning? How was so much of my memory gone? How could I not remember anything after getting ready for work?

"I know, it's a lot to take in sweetie, you were very lucky," she said with a gentle smile on her face.

"Yeah..." I let out a tired sigh. I looked down at my hands as my eyes felt hot and welled up with more tears. I was definitely confused and the feeling of uncertainty worried me. I felt I was going insane but at the same time I should be grateful to be alive.

"You ready to try again and sit up a bit?" Janet asked.

"Yeah," I said softly as I tried to move my body and help as much as I could. Janet moved my body upright to a slight sitting position.

"Now you're going to be super sore for a while, we've given you pain medication for that. We've also ran tests on your heart and everything seems stable for now. We'll be keeping you in the hospital for a couple more days to monitor you and help you recover."

"Okay," was all I could muster.

"You'll also need more tests to confirm you haven't suffered any serious damage, but you're already a miracle. To be awake and conscious after such a violent strike, you must really have a guardian angel sweetie."

"I just wish I could remember." I must have sounded like a lost child.

"Don't you worry, it's totally normal to have some temporary amnesia after a lightning strike, you'll improve little by little. Your mother was contacted and she's on her way, she let us know her plane would touch down today around noon, just wanted to let you know."

"I don't want her to see me this way."

"The important thing is you're alive and that's what your loved ones are thankful for. Your mother called to check on you every hour, she's been so worried for you. I've also taken some messages for you from other people calling for you, I've written them down and set them there on the table." Janet signaled to a small notepad on my table.

"Thank you." More tears streamed down my face.

Janet squeezed my hand gently, "Hey, hey now, everything will be okay, you'll see, easy does it, one step at a time."

I nodded my head and tried to make the tears stop. I hated crying.

"I'll be back to check on you in a few, if you need anything before then, just push that button on your bed and I'll be back in a jiffy, okay?"

"Okay, thank you," I said and closed my eyes after she left the room. I took a deep breath. I looked down at my chest, my gown had slid down off one shoulder. I saw a raised ridge below my collarbone peeking out from under the bandage, shiny with some kind of ointment. I took my hand to the ridge and traced it under my bandage. I pulled my gown and bandage down further and saw burn marks, raised and angry, in the shape of an intricate fern starting from my collarbone to the middle of my cleavage near my heart. The pain was searing but I couldn't stop tracing it lightly with my fingers. I had survived this? I should be dead. I felt static electricity on one side of my cheek.

"You are stronger than you think...than I thought you were," the mysterious voice bellowed again next to my ear.

I intended to ignore the voice. Whatever it was or whoever my mind was conjuring it was going to go unseen and tucked away in the deepest recesses of my mind. It wasn't like I was scared, but after all the trauma of the last couple of days, I just couldn't muster any energy to entertain the idea of me going crazy. Whatever it was, it would have to wait.

"We don't have a lot of time-"

I grabbed the remote Janet left on my bed and turned on the TV, raising the volume to something louder than I would normally. An instant frustration came over me—slight, yet trying to change into something else, a foreign emotion. It was like watching someone else's emotions running through my mind; these emotions felt muted and static, like something repressed I was feeling in my veins. I flipped through the channels, landing on a music video. I closed my eyes and tried to think of anything other than the voice. Maybe if I slept, I could forget everything and let my mind retrieve my lost memories. What an oxymoron, I thought. Or maybe what happened to me and that memory were lost forever?

"I would never allow it," the voice said firmly and imposing, drowning out my loud music in the background as if the volume had been turned down.

I couldn't respond. I could handle knowing I had almost died but to survive just to end up hearing voices in my head? I refused. The phone next to me rang just in time, breaking the tension.

"Hello?" I answered.

"Mi corazon [My heart]! You're awake! Gracias a Dios [Thank God], Como te sientes [How do you feel]!?"

My heart just about broke into pieces when I heard the familiar voice.

"Ama! I don't know what happened! I can't remember anything, I don't know how I'm gonna bring back my memori-" my voice broke and I couldn't continue speaking.

"[2] Mija [My daughter] don't worry, I'm here, I'm here, I just called to check on you and tell you my plane just touched down and I'm getting in my Uber right now. I'll be there in 20 minutes mija, we'll sort it all out when I get there."

"Okay ma...I'm so glad you're here, thank you."

"Of course mi cielo [my sky], I'm here to help you with anything you need...just stay calm and try to rest until I get there okay?"

"Okay ma."

"Okay, te amo [I love you]."

"Te amo ma [I love you mom]."

I hung up the phone, thinking to myself if coming to this place was the right choice. Mom begged me not to leave. Moving away from my mom was the hardest and most bull-headed decision I'd ever made. But in my mind I had a good reason...yet at this moment I regretted ever coming here, maybe what happened to me was karma for breaking my mom's heart?

---

2. Mija/mijo (Me-ha)/(Me-ho)

"It's not your fault, it's mine."

Again with the voice!

"Stop it!" I yelled without thinking first. Argh! At that moment there was a knock on my door and I hoped they hadn't heard my outburst. I tried to look normal, but I probably gave away I was just talking to an imaginary voice in my head.

"I'm not imaginary."

I sighed in frustration.

"Hi Miss Luna, I'm Doctor Kent, is everything okay?"

He looked genuinely concerned and it made me feel ridiculous. I sheepishly looked down at my clasped hands and tried to calm myself and look normal.

"Yes, just a little tired."

"Of course, that's totally normal after what you've been through." He walked closer and stood next to my bed.

"I'm so glad you're conscious, you're making quite a rapid recovery so far, your nurse must have explained what we think happened to you?"

"Yes she did, but I'm still very confused, when will my memories come back? I can't remember any of what she told me happened."

"Oh yes, well that tends to be different for everyone. It could be a matter of weeks or months, it's completely norma l...I know as frustrating as it seems, I'd like for us to focus on all the positives, okay? You're alive, your heart shows no signs of damage, your organs are working normally, your blood work looks great. The burns you received, except for the one where we think the bolt entered your body on your chest didn't leave any 2nd or 3rd degree burns, you have a lot of positives Miss Luna."

"I know, you're right..."

"So let's just keep that positive outlook okay? Can you do that for me Miss Luna?"

He said it in such a way it felt paternal, the way my own father would speak to me with a gentleness and confidence that I never ceased to believe him. I'd been missing that feeling ever since the night my father disappeared.

"Yes I can." For a second I actually believed it.

"Great! Now I'm going to listen to your heart and lungs one more time." He pulled off his stethoscope from around his neck.

"Sure."

"If your vitals and tests continue to be positive we may be able to discharge you in a day or two. Other than the temporary amnesia and burn on your chest area are you experiencing any other discomforts?"

"No, not that I can think of." I wasn't about to expose the voice in my head and open that can of worms.

"Great, that's what I like to hear." He proceeded to listen to my lungs and heart with his stethoscope.

"You sound perfectly normal, very reassuring, you must have a guardian angel, it's not often people recover this well from a lightning strike."

"So I've been told."

"Well, Janet will keep tabs on you throughout the day and I'll touch base with you tomorrow morning during my rounds, okay?"

"Okay, thank you."

"You're welcome Miss Luna."

Dr. Kent left and less than a minute later Janet knocked and peeked her head in. Her expression perplexed me, she looked as if she was concentrating on saying something and paused before speaking.

"Miss Luna, your mother is here, I'm going to let her through in a minute okay?"

"Yes, thank you Janet."

"No problem," Janet said and closed the door.

A minute later I heard a knock on the door.

"Come in," I said.

My mother burst through the door.

"Mija! Dios mio! Mi princesa [My princess]!"

Mom frantically dropped her things on the floor as she ran to my side and we embraced. I couldn't help bawling like a baby. My mom was the only person who I could truly be my vulnerable self. She was the only person that knew how big of a baby I could be. She stroked my hair as we embraced for what seemed ages.

"Ya mija, ya [There there my daughter], everything is okay, don't worry about anything." She kissed the top of my head as she continued to stroke my hair and the tears continued to flow. I felt back as a four year old, running for comfort to my mom with a scraped knee. I looked at her face, her eyes bloodshot and puffy, surely from crying.

"Ma I can't remember *anything*! My last memory was of getting ready for work, how could I've forgotten everything until just now when I woke up?!" My voice shook. I debated telling her about the rest.

"What did the doctor say mija?" she asked.

"He said it's normal, and my memories could take weeks or months to return."

"Then that's reassuring mija, at least you didn't lose more memories or your short-term memory. I'm just happy you're alive and well. I worried so much for you." She hugged me again, tighter than the first time.

"I thought I'd lost you sweetie, eres un milagro [you're a miracle]."

"Mom, there's something else..."

"What mija?"

"Please promise me you won't tell the doctors or nurses."

"Ay Dios mio [Oh my God] Eveley! You're scaring me, what is it?!"

"Promise me?"

"Of course, I would never tell anyone, but why so secretive? You're worrying me."

"I'm hearing voices...well just one voice actually, a man's voice in my head, but it feels so real, like he's speaking into my ear. I've been ignoring it all morning but it hasn't stopped."

I looked at her expression to see if she looked incredulous. I was surprised to see she didn't look unsettled at all.

"Mija, does this voice say bad things to you?"

"Well no, the opposite, it's been kind of an over-protective annoyance so far. I refuse to talk to it. I've never had this happen to me before, I think the lightning strike did something to my brain."

"Don't worry just yet mija, it'll probably go away in time. Plus it's only the beginning of your recovery, yes most likely it's just a temporary after effect..." She sounded like she was trying to convince herself as she said this.

"But it's weird, sometimes the voice starts talking in the middle of my thoughts." She looked worried when I said that.

"In the middle of your thoughts? Are you sure?"

"I'm sure, why? Now you're scaring me."

"Nothing mija, just tell the voice it should ask for permission to speak."

"I don't want to speak to it Ma." I couldn't believe I was talking about voices in my head with my own mother. Perhaps her advice was to not alarm me I was completely crazy and she was trying to find a solution, that there was still hope for me to be normal, but how does one's mother fix voices in their child's head?

"Just set boundaries mija, and if it doesn't go away in a week or two we can let your doctor know. Just make sure you tell me if this voice gets worse or is saying bad things to you okay?"

"Okay ma."

She smiled and hugged me tightly again.

"Ma will you stay here with me a while?"

"Of course, I'll be here until you don't need me," she said smiling faintly. She sat in the chair next to me and gently held my hand.

"Your nurse told me you needed rest, so I want you to take a nap, do you need anything?"

"I'm a bit hungry, but I'm not sure if I'm allowed to eat yet."

Mom agreed to ask one of the nurses and grab me something to eat if I was allowed. She stepped out of my room to go to the nurse's station. A few minutes later, I heard a knock on the door.

"Hi Miss Luna, it's time for some more blood work." Janet stepped inside my room.

"Oh okay..."

"Unfortunately yes, sorry, I'm sure you're tired of people coming in and out of your room."

"Oh it's okay, I'm getting used to it," I said.

Janet smiled and made her way to my side. She set up her supplies on a small cart next to my bed.

"Afraid of needles?" she asked nonchalantly.

As far as I could remember I'd never been afraid of needles but somehow the more I stared at the medical supplies on her tray the more afraid I felt.

"Uh...I don't think so?" I asked in a questioning tone.

"I'm sorry, we just need to run some more blood work to monitor that your organs continue to work normally."

"I understand, go ahead."

She felt in the crease of my elbow with her gloved fingers. She placed a tourniquet on my arm, dabbed my arm with an alcohol swab and skillfully found the vein, she quickly and painlessly inserted the needle, instant blood and nausea. My head felt dizzy and hot as if I'd entered a sauna, the hot feeling in my neck returned, I could feel the hairs on the back of my neck stand up.

"Miss Luna, are you okay?"

"I- I-" and I felt my eyes closing.

Man? Alien? Something in between? I don't even know what you look like, am I standing face to face here with you? Where are you really? All I can feel is your energy, the hairs on my body stand on edge when

you're near, the warm static on my skin the last giveaway you are here, are you running yourself over me? Are you running through my veins and the deepest valleys of my mind? I cannot refuse you, for your mere presence is literally magnetic. Yet in you I feel an icy coldness in contrast to the warmth you make my physical body feel. My mind in endless incertitude when you make yourself known. And somewhere in my most egotistical and prideful self I wanna yell at you, "Stop! I will not yield!" But your response is calm and collected, you can't help it, it simply is. You require no submission, no worship, you simply are, and now I am as well. My destiny to forever be in a state of flux and disequilibrium, my body fighting against the foreign sensation of you bonding yourself to me.

I woke gasping for air and clutching my chest, searing pain all over my skin overwhelmed me.

"Eveley, Gracias a Dios [Thank God]!"

I could see my mother's puffy face, full of desperation, tears streaming down her face.

"Miss Luna, please breathe, take deep long breaths." Janet was by my side, glancing at the machine beeping rapidly. She could see I was agitated.

They would never know what I had *felt*. I still felt the strange sensation running through my veins. I panicked and began to take off my oxygen mask. Janet jumped and tried to stop me but not before it was completely off my face and on the floor.

"Miss Luna! Please, you must remain calm! I need you to stay still."

"Eveley, calmate mija [calm down my daughter]!" Mom yelled as she tried to push my shoulders down to the bed.

I didn't care, I was being held down only by the stupid IV which was still in my arm, as well as the blood pressure monitor. I managed to rip the cuff off as Janet began to grab my hands.

"Please don't Miss Luna, you're gonna seriously hurt yourself!"

"Eveley, stop! You're gonna hurt yourself!" Mom yelled.

Mom tried to grab my other hand but all at once I managed to break free from both of them and grab onto the edge of the tape over my IV. I couldn't completely take off the tape because it was sticky but I simply grabbed the tubing and tore it apart. Blood drained out of my IV tubing. I stood and pushed past my mom. Janet tried to make it in time to grab me but I was already at the door by the time she made it. I opened the door and ran as fast as I could. My body felt like when you try to run underwater, slow and unsteady. I could hear my mother yelling in the background. I looked back, a path of my own blood followed me.

"Miss Luna, come back!" Janet shouted.

Both Mom and Janet were running behind me, trying to catch up. I was running faster than I thought.

I turned a corner, then another, passing a nurse on the way, leaving her with a bemused look on her face. Janet must have called security because I heard an announcement for lock down overhead. I made it to the next door in front of me and entered the stairwell. I made my descent down the stairs unsteadily.

"Eveley, please stop," the voice said calmly.

I reached a landing several floors below mine.

"Be quiet! Don't talk to me, you hear me? I don't ever want to hear your voice again!" I shouted and my head began to spin from the sudden visceral anger I felt toward this voice in my head.

"You have no right to do whatever you are doing! You hear me! You have no right!"

"I know that Eveley."

"I must be going crazy, crazy..." I was facing the corner on the landing and I nestled my forehead against the cool concrete.

My eyes zeroed in below me, blood pooling on the floor as a steady trickle of blood continued from my IV down my arm and dripped from my fingertips. I grabbed the tape and took the time to tear it off and take the catheter out. With my blood trail it wouldn't be long before someone found me. Why was I running? Why had I panicked and acted before thinking? This was so unlike me. I felt unsteady and closed my eyes.

"You must return to your room Eveley, you cannot leave, you need to rest."

I was hearing his voice, yet I was slowly losing focus of the sounds all around me and feeling weak again. I squatted down, wrapped my arms around my knees and rested my head on my knees. I wanted to shrink in that cold concrete corner and disappear into nothingness. Static filled my ears, then ringing, I felt a hand on the nape of my neck. I was too weak to care or lift my head to see who it was.

"Is that you?" For once I didn't care who answered.

"Yes Eveley, I am helping you until you fully heal."

I felt an electrical current running through my body, it didn't hurt, just felt like pressure from within. Within seconds my eyes fluttered open and I felt better.

"What are you?" I mustered brokenly.

"Your friend."

I still felt dizzy and unsteady when I slowly stood. I don't know why I suddenly felt a sliver of trust in this being.

"Please don't let me fall," I said.

"Never."

Chapter 2

PABLO AND ISABEL

Eveley's 2nd Birthday

The creep appeared in their life like a sudden crash, unexpectedly and without warning. Isabel spoke to her husband Pablo over the phone after that first encounter from her mother's house. She recounted the disheveled man that stared at her menacingly upon entering the small café they owned. She told him about the incessant requests asking personal questions such as where she lived, her age, and if she had a boyfriend, even her phone number to the point she mentioned it to her employee Pete who kept a close eye on him the entire time. So much so that at the end of the shift Pete checked around the parking lot to make sure the creep hadn't stuck around and even walked her to her car.

Even though she saw no one following her, Isabel said she felt as if someone was watching her when she drove to her mother's house to pick up little Eveley. Isabel told her mom, Magdalena, about the creep at the café and Magdalena told her it was smart she'd checked no one was following her.

Later, when Isabel and Magdalena were outside and Isabel was buckling Eveley in her car seat, a black car pulled up on the opposite side of the street a few cars back and slightly opened their tinted window. Magdalena observed a hand sticking out with black leather gloves, the windows were so dark nothing could be seen inside the car. Magdalena asked Isabel if she knew the car, Isabel answered no, so Magdalena started walking toward the car to see who it was. As soon as she approached the car, the car quickly backed in reverse to the corner of the street and drove away screeching their tires, Magdalena noticed the car had no license plates.

Magdalena told Isabel she'd better call Pablo's job and let him know what was going on and stay the night with her in case she was being followed home. Isabel decided to stay with her mom which was perfect since the café was closed the next day.

Getting a hold of Pablo via phone was tricky. Pablo couldn't speak on the phone as his job required driving to different job sites throughout Dallas. At the time Pablo was working nights, 12-14 hour shifts because of a staff shortage. Usually, he would arrive home at 6:30 am after his shift ended. He received the written message from the operator when he came into head-quarters close to midnight. The note said Isabel planned to stay the night with her mom and to call her if he could. This alarmed him and he called his mother-in-law's house right away. Despite it being past midnight Isabel picked up the phone, she was sleeping in her old childhood bedroom. Eveley a little past 2 years old, snuggled safely in her mom's arms. She slept peacefully while Isabel spoke on the phone.

Pablo told Isabel not to worry about Bandido, their full grown German Shepherd, he'd fed him and left him plenty of water outdoors before he left. The weather was mellow that night and Bandido would relax in his dog house, which Pablo had painstakingly built him for nights when Bandido refused to come indoors which was occasionally.

Isabel sounded calm and sleepy when Pablo spoke to her, she seemed unfazed by the scumbag from earlier. He told her to make sure she carried her firearm with her. She always carried her firearm, a Colt .38 Police Special after a traumatic incident when she was in college 7 years ago. She told Pablo she'd learned the hard way there was evil ready to devour innocent people everywhere and she refused to be a victim again.

She'd met Pablo 2 years after the incident at college, an experience that almost made her quit. Ultimately, she didn't quit and graduated with a degree in business administration which was a solid foundation for opening her own café a year after graduation. She opened the small breakfast and lunch café with a little financial help from her parents which took her a year to pay back.

It was by chance they met, Pablo having seen the newly opened sign of the small café on his way to work one day. He had accidentally woken up too early, unbeknownst to him, daylight savings time had ended and he had an extra hour to kill.

He still remembered the first time he stepped into the small café, Pablo noticed the beauty of doe-eyed Isabel, the attraction was instant. Pablo quickly made his daily coffee at her café his morning routine. Isabel was a ray of sunshine to start his day. She was kind, funny, and easy-going. It also didn't hurt she was the most beautiful woman he'd ever seen. He considered her a natural beauty, big brown eyes, full lips, big smile, long wavy cinnamon hair, and bare faced except for lipstick. She was the whole package in his eyes.

When he first started going to Isabel's café he quickly realized she had a lot of other admirers captivated by her beauty and charm. He quickly decided to take his shot, he asked her out on a date his third week going to the café.

The rest is history, they were engaged six months later and married six months after that. They tried to start their family right away but after a few miscarriages quickly dampened the happiness they had enjoyed up to that point, they switched focus to their relationship and traveling as much as possible during their free time.

They bought their first little house not far from both their parent's houses and adopted a puppy, Bandido, from their new neighbor down the block. Two years later they found out they were expecting again on Christmas Day.

Since the day she was born, Eveley became the center of their universe. She was the only grandchild, spoiled by both sets of grandparents, and such a joy for both of them to raise. She only made their life and marriage better.

Everything seemed idyllic for a while and although Pablo never let on to Isabel there was anything wrong, in the back of his head he was always waiting for the other shoe to drop. He didn't want to believe happiness such as the one they created with their little family could be tragically ripped away by an evil force but he couldn't help feeling an unease occupy his mind after Isabel told him about the creep at the café.

When Pablo arrived to his neighborhood the next morning at 6:20 am, he couldn't get to his street. There were dozens of police cars blocking the corner of his block, a fire truck barreled past him as he moved over to the side of the street. He stepped out and ran in the direction of his house, several police officers turned their attention to him and held him back.

"Hey! I live down this street! What's going on?!" Pablo shouted.

"Hey! Stay back! We have a psycho in there trying to blow up the whole block!" one of the officers barked at him.

"What?! My dog is in there man, don't shoot my dog!" Pablo was relieved his wife and daughter were safely 10 minutes away at his in-law's house. He was still worried for his dog and his neighbors.

"We're not trying to shoot anyone, we've evacuated everyone on the block, go back to your car and drive away," one of the officers said sternly as they pushed Pablo back.

In that moment, a huge explosion shook the whole neighborhood, screams came from neighbors and car alarms blared. His ears rang and he ran to his truck, he jumped in and sped to his in-law's house.

When he arrived he knocked loudly, it took his mother-in-law a minute to open the door.

"Pablo, que paso [what happened]?!" Magdalena said as she opened the door and saw the concern on Pablo's face.

"Can you turn on the news? I just came from our street, the cops blocked it, there's some psycho down there setting off bombs on our block."

"Ay Dios mio!" Magdalena quickly turned on the TV and put it on the local news.

The news were reporting the incident live, they reported there were calls by residents of a small fire and suspicious man seen in one of the houses on the block. Then a female officer who was the first responder was attacked by someone, that's when the entire police force descended to the area to find the perpetrator and contain the scene. Neighbors were evacuated after a small explosion was heard in the same house minutes later, and an even bigger explosion after that, the one Pablo heard moments earlier.

Isabel was awake by now and walked into the living room, she noticed both her mom and Pablo looked upset.

"Pablo, what are you doing here? What's wrong?" Isabel asked.

Pablo came up to Isabel and hugged her tightly.

"There's something crazy going down on our block, is Eveley okay?"

"Of course, she was just sleeping next to me when I heard the TV...What's going on in our neigh-"

They heard a loud crash and tires screeching, little Eveley screamed and everyone ran to the bedroom with Pablo making it to the bedroom first. The window next to the bed was shattered, a large rock was on the tile floor. Pablo and Magdalena looked out the window, a dark car drove away with no tags. He looked at Eveley crying in Isabel's arms.

"Did it hit her, is she okay?!"

"No, she's okay, just scared, it's okay mija, mommy and daddy are here, Pablo call the cops!"

"That was the car we saw on the street earlier!" Magdalena blurted.

"I have a better idea, wait here and tell Cesar to keep an eye out," Pablo said.

His father-in-law, Cesar was just running into the room.

"Stay away from the windows, if I'm not back in an hour call the cops," Pablo said as he ran out.

Pablo jumped into his white truck and floored it. He needed to get to the car before it made it on the freeway or else it'd be nearly impossible to find him. Luckily, he saw the car ahead, the same tagless black car with ultra dark tint. He wasn't going to let him get away Pablo thought, not after he'd just tried to terrorize his family. He had his trusty Beretta with him so he wasn't without back up.

He caught up to him, once he was two car spaces behind him he knew it was only a matter of time before he'd realize he was being followed and try to get away. They were only blocks from a long stretch of industrial road that didn't usually have much traffic and at the end of that road was the freeway entrance, he was gonna make sure he didn't make it that far. They were already going 70 in a 35, the black car swerved suddenly into the lane next to them accelerating further, Pablo kept matching the car's speed.

"You're not getting away!" Pablo yelled as he pushed his truck past 80 miles and accelerating, he needed to inch his way past the car. As Pablo came closer the car swerved across the lanes into oncoming traffic. A semi almost hit the car before he swerved back into the left lane. Pablo could hear sirens far away and the sound of a helicopter nearby.

They were almost doing 90 mph when he was able to inch past the back bumper and tap the side of the car, the car fishtailed and almost lost control, but it made a full 180 without crashing, stopping facing Pablo's truck. Pablo slammed on his brakes to stop his truck from crashing into the front of the car, for a few seconds they were both still.

Everything was quiet with no other cars around. They faced each other 100 feet apart, the car's tires screeched alive and Pablo saw the car barreling toward him. Pablo swerved to avoid him and turned his truck around to pursue. The car hit his brakes and Pablo almost slammed into him, swerving and passing him halfway, the car slammed into the side of Pablo's truck and sent it into oncoming traffic, he brought his truck back into his lane and slowed down slightly behind and to the side of the car. Ahead, Pablo saw a ditch that was hard to see, he'd passed by it many times on late nights and knew this guy most likely didn't know it was there. As soon as they made it to the spot, Pablo gave him a nudge, the car couldn't help going into the ditch as otherwise a guardrail would have been in his front bumper. He careened into the ditch, flew into the air at least 15 feet, then rolled over several times before landing on its side in a big cloud of smoke and debris.

Pablo pulled over to the shoulder of the road. They were the only cars on the road. He pulled out his gun from its holster; he wasn't taking any chances. He could barely see with all the smoke in the air, but he aimed his headlights at the car. He walked cautiously to the side. The car's driver door flew off its hinges and into the street. Pablo saw a dark figure emerge. He heard weird growling noises emanating in large waves, each one increasing in rage. It sounded like demons growling, it didn't sound human. Pablo pulled the trigger and a loud scream like an Aztec whistle came from the figure. He saw the dark figure sulk, the light from his headlights caught its face momentarily. Its face half frozen into a stiff, emotionless gray mask, as if made of plaster. The other side of its face grotesque, with large pieces of gray skin melting from its jowl, and eyes as dark as black holes.

"Don't move or I'll shoot again!" Pablo yelled, feeling the hairs on his neck raise up.

He heard a maniacal laugh, the figure leaped toward him and Pablo managed to pull the trigger twice before he landed on his back. The figure leaped into the overgrown brush behind him.

Pablo knew he'd gotten all three shots into that thing. He knew it wasn't human or at least not fully. It didn't look, sound, or move like a human. Whatever it was, it was the definition of a monster, and he hoped the three bullets he got into its body would be enough to take it down.

He could hear sirens getting close, he looked around for his shells, luckily he found all three. He picked them up, jumped into his truck and drove off. Pablo turned the corner just as cop cars emerged from the opposite end of the street without seeing Pablo's truck. The black car was now in flames from the small fire that started in the engine compartment.

Pablo touched his shoulder as it throbbed, there was a gash in his shoulder where the monster pushed him during his escape. A strange blue substance stained his shirt. The stain looked like splatters of liquid but when he touched it, it pulverized like sand.

As he made it back to his in-law's house, he felt a weird sensation inside his gash wound, like something burrowing itself and causing a sharp stabbing pain. He grabbed his shoulder as he stumbled to the front door and knocked, overcome with a feverish feeling. By now the sun was starting to come up. Magdalena and Cesar were both at the front door within seconds.

"Mijo, what happened?!" Magdalena exclaimed as they grabbed him and helped him walk to the couch.

Isabel came in carrying Eveley.

"Oh my god Pablo, what happened?! You're hurt! Here ma, can you hold Eveley?" Isabel handed off sleepy Eveley to her mother. She kneeled down in front of Pablo.

"What happened baby?" she plead.

She noticed Pablo holding his shoulder tightly, he looked dazed and confused.

"Baby is this where you're hurt?" She pulled his hand aside, revealing the bloody gash wound, blood dripped everywhere.

"Don't touch it!" Pablo said loudly and she flinched, he was acting unlike himself.

"Que te paso mijo [What happened to you son]?" Cesar asked sternly.

"Cesar, you still have your guns?" Pablo asked avoiding answering the question.

"Always mijo, what kind of question is that?"

"Good, keep an eye out on the house. I need to speak to Isabel alone, come on Isabel." Pablo grabbed Isabel's hand and led her into the bedroom closing the door behind them. She looked perplexed.

"Pablo, don't you need to see a doctor for that?"

"No, it's fine, I'll be fine, it's just a scratch."

"It doesn't look like a scratch baby, it looks bad."

"I shot him Isabel."

Isabel's eyes grew wide. She spoke in a whisper.

"Who?"

"I don't know Isabel, but I'm gonna tell you something that's gonna sound crazy..."

"Crazier than you shooting a man?"

"Yeah, except this wasn't a man."

"Okay..."

"The creep at the café? Did you see his face?"

"Yes."

"Did he look normal?"

"I mean other than the creepy stare, I guess so."

"Was his skin gray?"

"What?" she paused for a second to think, "You know when I was there I do remember thinking to myself this man looked ghastly, so maybe."

"Did you see his car?"

"No I didn't, I think he parked in the back or walked."

"Okay, that *thing*...or monster that just attacked me, was not a man."

Pablo described everything to Isabel, from the shrieks he heard to the ugly, flabby, melted face of this monster and the way he leaped into the brush like an animal. She looked more and more worried until he finished.

"Do you think he'll come back?" her voice trembled slightly, giving away her fear.

"Don't worry about that baby," Pablo said as he took her face into his hands and brought her face close, he kissed her forehead.

"I will never let anyone hurt you or Eveley," he meant it with every fiber of his being. The problem remained they needed to go back home and find out what had been of their house and dog.

Chapter 3

FALLOUT

When Pablo came out of the bedroom, Cesar looked upset.

"Whatever just happened you better fess up Pablo, we're family and if anyone is targeting our family I deserve to know."

Pablo looked at Magdalena pleadingly.

"I know I know, but I can't be affecting your health like that Cesar, I got this," Pablo tried to deflect.

"Doesn't look like it," Cesar said as he pointed to Pablo's injured shoulder.

"Looks like you might need another gun in this fight."

Pablo looked at Isabel as she stepped out.

"Pa por favor [Dad, please], ma?" Isabel looked at her mom for support.

"I tried to tell your father mija, but you know how he is," Magdalena said softly, carrying Eveley in her arms.

"Fine, I'll tell you but you promise you'll let me worry about this and handle this unless I absolutely need your help?" Pablo asked.

"I can't promise you that, you're talking about my daughter and granddaughter, but, I tell you what, if you tell me what went down, we can figure out how to fix this."

"Fine."

Pablo wasn't pleased but he had no choice. His father-in-law was in poor health, he'd been like this for the last six months, having a mini heart attack that made it hard for him to recover his strength. He'd been a completely healthy man up to that point so he was stubborn and strong-willed, unable to see himself as a weak man. Pablo didn't want to make his father-in-law worse or cause him to have a major heart attack from the stress of what was happening.

They sat down on the couch as Magdalena and Isabel walked to the kitchen in the back of the house.

"Pablo, I'm going to get my supplies and bandages to help you with that gash," Magdalena said as she walked away.

"Okay, gracias suegra [mother-in-law]."

Cesar waited till Isabel was out of sight.

"Look, this isn't my first rodeo, you know when Isabel had that stalker seven years ago? Well let's just say that me and Magdalena took care of it...but don't tell Isabel," he said in a low tone.

Pablo had always wondered what happened, all he knew was what Isabel told him. She received an anonymous letter apologizing, telling her that whoever he was, he was sorry for all the pain he caused her and she'd never see or hear from him again. The letter turned out to be true, she never heard from this individual again.

"Cesar, do you believe in the supernatural?"

Cesar chuckled. "You mean like aliens, monsters, ghosts?"

"Something like that."

"All I know is if they target my family, whatever it is, it'll be called dead." His eyes looked deathly serious.

Pablo knew Cesar's violent past so he knew he meant it. He'd been warned by Isabel when they first started dating that her dad had a controversial past. Pablo found her characterization of him a bit intimidating and treaded lightly when he first met him.

Especially now that Cesar was starting to age and have health problems, you'd never guess the unassuming old man hid a stormy past. It was peculiar to Pablo how witty and easy-going Cesar could be especially with his family and how serious and willing to go to extremes he was the next minute when someone threatened his family. Pablo however, was starting to understand his methods after today and his own brush with evil.

Cesar was a man who'd teetered a fine line between villain and hero. Even if his past could be seen as righteous in many ways, some would disapprove of his ability to sleep at night after the things he did in the name of protecting those he loved.

Very few people actually knew those events. From the tidbits Isabel told Pablo, Cesar worked for an international organization that helped expose and bring to justice head figures around the world for human trafficking, a sordid and gut-wrenching job. When he found a traitor within the organization, one that was placing all of their secret identities at risk, and even worse participating in the trafficking himself, Cesar had no qualms in getting rid of him. This prompted an all out war within the organization that almost killed him and placed his family at risk. He had to claw himself out of the hole they threw him in figuratively. Along the way he had no misgivings in getting rid of every single person that threatened him and his family, for he knew that anyone on the side of the traitor he killed was likely corrupted as well.

When Cesar was finally able to bring his family to Dallas from their previous location safely, everyone was given new identities. Guerrero was a last name that existed many generations back in their family, and so they became the Guerrero family.

Isabel grew up only learning limited pieces but over the years she was able to piece them all together. So when the stalker showed up in Isabel's life in college, for Cesar it was as easy as flipping on a switch to get rid of him.

"We need to find him, and set a trap," Cesar said.

"I got three shots in him Cesar, he's either dead or he'll be dead soon."

"Unless one of those shots was here…" Cesar pointed to his forehead, "There's no guarantee, better finish the job and make sure he's never coming back."

"I know I know, I just have so much on my mind right now."

"Don't let the noise cloud your mind, follow your instinct. There's something about this thing that told you it needed to be dead, something evil in this thing, and the quicker he reaches his destination the better."

"I know, but I don't know how I'm going to do this without putting Eveley and Isabel at risk."

"What do they have me for then? Isabel already knows how to shoot, and Eveley will be home with us while she works. Nothing is going to hurt our princesa [princess] while me and Magdalena are around. I need you to take a trip back to where all this went down once things quiet down and track this thing, there will either be a body or clues to where it is."

"Alright," Pablo replied.

"And Pablo, don't tell the cops anymore than they need to know if they are still there asking questions on your block."

"Roger that."

After their discussion, Cesar and Pablo boarded up the window with plywood. The rest of the day everyone kept tabs on the news report of the craziness on their block which was fully contained by noon. The fires were put out and all the areas around the houses cleared but now there was a statewide man hunt for the perpetrator. They also reported on the car in flames Pablo chased down. The cops didn't have a clue who it belonged to.

Magdalena took out some of her nursing supplies and took a look at Pablo's wound. It wasn't very deep, but it bled a lot and looked like it started getting infected which was strange since an infection wouldn't have been apparent so quickly. She helped stop the bleeding, washed out the wound, and bandaged it up. Later Isabel and Magdalena played with little Eveley and in between play sessions, cooked the meals for the day.

Later that night Pablo, Isabel, and little Eveley slept for the night in Isabel's old bed, little Eveley snuggled in between them. Cesar volunteered to keep watch in the living room, every half hour he would peek out the blinders in his front and back window. Cesar had a talent for feeling out the air when something bad was nearby. Years of working in a job that required him to be under intense danger and secrecy had taught him to trust his gut every time. He had his shotgun by his side, and in between quick micro naps, he felt the air getting heavier.

That night, Pablo had a maddening nightmare. His dream was of him watching the monster devour him, but not devour him in the way a predator devours his prey. He saw as light entered his body through the gash in his shoulder. His mind shattered into millions of fragments. He saw himself from outer space, he couldn't move his real body to save himself as this sickness invaded his body and turned him into a monster just like the one he'd encountered. His blood turned blue, and he finally understood.

He woke up drenched in sweat. His mind racing, his eyes bloodshot, and his nose bleeding, the throbbing in his wound worse than before. He felt like he was burning from the inside out. In his mind he needed to get whatever it was out of his body. He grabbed his pocket knife and went into the bathroom attached to the bedroom, shutting the door quietly. He tore off the bandage and opened the gash with his fingers. The throbbing intensified and he pushed the knife into the wound. At first it hurt as expected but then he couldn't feel anything. Then he poked *it*, as soon as his knife cut through *it*, violent flashes of light, like that of his dream began in his head, but he felt no pain. The flashes became more and more disorienting, he twisted the knife and pulled with a lot of resistance but still no pain. Finally, his knife pulled all the way out, on the tip of the knife a large clot, not of his own blood but of that blue color he had on his shirt on his way home. He threw the palm sized clot in the sink, grabbed his lighter and burned it until it was nothing but black soot and washed it down the sink.

Pablo looked at his face in the mirror, the redness in his eyes began to fade, his skin returned to a neutral color, the bleeding in his nose finally stopped, he felt centered and clear headed again. He finally saw himself in that reflection, feeling the recognition return as he scanned all his features.

The next morning, Isabel and Pablo left Eveley with her grandparents and made their way to see the damage on their block. When they arrived everything seemed relatively normal except for the burned out house next to theirs. There were 2 cop cars on either end of the street. One of the cops blocking the entrance stepped out of his cruiser and approached them when they pulled up.

"Can I help you?"

"Yes, we live in the blue house there," Pablo said as he pointed to their house.

"Okay, I'll need some ID from both of you. We just completed the scene investigation but for today we will need to keep vetting everyone."

"Sure," Pablo said.

Both Pablo and Isabel handed over their IDs.

"Is it safe officer?" Isabel asked.

"Yeah, everything has been cleared, we'll need statements from you if you were a witness."

"Neither of us were home during the entire day," Pablo said.

"Okay then, I'll write your info down but a detective will probably still contact you to do his due diligence."

"Sure of course," Pablo replied.

The officer wrote down their info and phone number. "Ok, you may go into your house."

"Okay, thank you." Pablo drove in slowly to their driveway, from the outside their house looked like the day before when he left for work. But he had a feeling the inside would be different.

"Stay behind me Isabel, keep your eyes peeled for anything suspicious." Pablo placed his hand on his weapon still holstered.

They walked slowly to the back of the house, opened and closed the gate and walked toward the back door. Pablo whistled softly, like he usually did, Bandido was nowhere in sight. Pablo placed his hand on Isabel's shoulder to stop her from walking further. The back screen door was mangled beyond recognition and the hinges torn from the frame. The back door glass was broken and the door halfway open. Pablo pulled out his weapon and so did Isabel. He slowly pushed the door open with his foot. There was a large rock in front of the door, and he noticed the blue splatters on the floor.

"Don't touch any of the blue stains," Pablo said.

"Okay."

They made their way through each room, they found nothing was inside their house. The blue stains made their way all the way to the opposite side of the house, and ended abruptly in front of an open window on the side of the house. They heard a whimper coming from the corner.

"Bandido!" Isabel exclaimed.

Bandido had entered the house, limping behind them.

"Dammit! You're hurt buddy." Pablo could see blue stains all along Bandido's muzzle and teeth, he'd gotten a bite of the creep who'd broken into their house. He went up to him and inspected his paws, he whimpered when he raised one of his front paws, there was a puncture wound on it and Pablo suspected the creep must have bit Bandido back.

"Make sure you don't touch any of the blue," he said to Isabel.

"Okay, what should we do?"

"Let's fill the tub with warm water and a bit of salt to help disinfect the wound," Pablo said.

Isabel filled the tub and Bandido slowly followed them. They helped him into the tub and Bandido just laid there, exhausted.

"I'm gonna get his water and food ready amor [my love]," Pablo said as he walked to the kitchen.

"Okay."

Pablo walked to the kitchen, grabbed the kitchen gloves, and walked back to the bathroom.

"Here, wear these so you don't get any of that blue stuff on you."

"Okay, does that mean this is the same thing you shot?"

"Yeah it looks like it," he said.

"I had a dream last night that I lost you," Isabel blurted as she hung her head and looked down at the floor.

"I'm not going anywhere baby, you know that."

Isabel looked up at him, her big eyes welled up with tears. "I can't lose you."

She stood and hugged him with the intensity of a final goodbye.

"Promise me you'll never leave me," Isabel pleaded.

"I'll never leave you, promise."

He knew he was going to do everything in his power to keep that promise.

He gave her a kiss on the lips, her eyes searched his and for a moment he felt as if she was reading his mind.

"In my dream you sacrificed yourself for me and Eveley."

"Cielo, no te preocupes, nada me va a pasar [My sky, don't worry, nothing is going to happen to me]."

He held her closer and ran his hands through her hair, resting his fingers on the back of her neck, bringing her closer. He brought his forehead to hers for a moment.

"You looked hot holding that gun," he whispered in her ear to try to distract her.

Isabel chuckled. "You always say that."

He smiled. "Because it's true."

He grabbed her chin softly and kissed her once more. She wiped the tears off with her hands and took a deep breath.

They washed Bandido, bandaged his paw, and fed him. He was ravenous and after eating his food he laid in his dog bed and quickly fell asleep. While he slept, Isabel cleaned up all the stains on the floor with bleach and threw away the mop. Meanwhile Pablo boarded up the back window with plywood until they could get new glass for it. They double checked all the windows were closed and reset their tripped house alarm.

It almost felt like everything was fairly normal except when they looked out the window and saw the charred remains of their next door neighbor's house. Isabel walked out the front door, the cop cars were still there, she recognized her next door neighbor's car pull up, she felt a pit in her stomach. Their next door neighbors were a young couple with two small children that had been there since they purchased their home. They were such great neighbors, always looking out for each other, she couldn't stomach seeing them going through the loss of their entire house.

As soon as they pulled up, Stella ran out, her face said it all, she looked devastated. Jason, her husband, stepped out and hugged her as she sobbed.

"Why! This can't be happening!" she exclaimed with a desperate edge in her voice.

"Why! Why! Why!" she shouted at the sky as if demanding a response from above.

"It's gonna be okay baby, we'll make it through this," Jason said as he hugged her tightly and she buried her sobs in his chest.

Isabel couldn't help but start crying for them, she knew this was devastating for their family. They'd become like family to them, often having their kids playing together in both of their backyards and spending time with them on occasion. They also had a cute golden retriever named Rally that would play with Bandido. They had twins, a boy and girl, about a year older than Eveley. The O'Brien family were on vacation so neither they nor Rally were home during the mayhem. Isabel started walking toward Stella and Jason, Stella lifted her head and saw Isabel and walked up to her and hugged her.

"I'm so sorry Stella," Isabel mustered as they both cried.

Pablo went up to Jason and gave him the typical bro hug.

"I'm so sorry man," Pablo said.

"Thanks, I'm just thankful we weren't home, we're safe, that's the important thing, everything else is replaceable."

"True, well, we are here to help out, anything you guys need let us know."

"Thanks I appreciate it, I think we're going to meet the insurance company tomorrow and we're going to stay a few days with my in-laws till we figure out what's going to happen."

"Alright, well we'll keep an eye out on things while you guys are gone." Pablo assured him.

"Thanks man, I appreciate it."

"No problem."

"Thank you Pablo, you guys are such great neighbors, thank you for everything," Stella said to Pablo as she held on to Isabel.

The families said their goodbyes and Stella gave Isabel the number to her parent's house in case they needed to contact them.

Pablo and Isabel looked as the O'Briens drove away.

"Okay baby, are you ready to head out?" Pablo asked.

"Yeah," Isabel said. She was looking intently at the O'Briens driving away. She let out a big sigh.

"I can't help thinking what if I'd come home with Eveley last night..."

Pablo hugged her.

"You're safe mi amor [my love], Eveley is safe, nothing is going to hurt our family as long as we're around, we're a team remember?"

She nodded, holding onto his hand tightly. She looked down at their hands, their wedding rings, and the matching tattoos they'd gotten on their honeymoon.

He took her hand, still in his, and kissed hers. "C'mon, let's go," Pablo said.

They loaded Bandido onto the back seat and took off toward the desolate industrial road where Pablo encountered the monster. Pablo parked on the side of the road. The tire marks, glass and debris still visible on the road and ditch.

"Okay, I'm going to go into the brush here, wait here. Lock the doors, stay alert. If anyone comes asking questions, tell them your car was acting up and you pulled over but don't get out or open your windows, okay?"

Isabel got out and kissed Pablo.

"Okay baby, be very careful," Isabel said.

Her face gave away her concern for him. Isabel stepped into the drivers side and Bandido moved into the passenger side without prompting. He nestled into the seat and nuzzled his head on her lap, she stroked the top of his head as he looked at her.

"I'm so sorry about last night buddy, you know I didn't want to leave you behind but it wasn't safe for us to come home."

Bandido whimpered as if to say I forgive you.

Meanwhile Pablo pushed through the overgrown bushes, he saw train tracks behind about 200 yards away. He saw large blue puddles leading to the tracks that eventually disappeared. The puddles looked congealed, as if they'd become solid. Every time he saw the splatters his body experienced flashbacks to last night when he pulled out the clot from his shoulder. He walked back to the car, feeling disoriented. His shoulder throbbed and the panic set in again. His body hadn't rid itself of that plague, just slowed it down temporarily. He stood there, looking down at his hands, the veins still human, but for how much longer?

Pablo walked back to the car and stepped into the passenger side.

"What did you find?" Isabel asked.

"There were blue splatters but they disappear by the train tracks behind all the brush. I think he was able to get on a train car, we will need to be very vigilant for a while."

Isabel sighed, "Okay."

"Alright, let's go get Eveley," Pablo said.

"Okay," Isabel said and took off toward her parent's house.

CHAPTER 4

THREE MUSKETEERS

Eveley's 10th Birthday

For the first couple of months after the incident with the monster in 1999, Pablo and the whole family remained vigilant and alert to anything suspicious. Fortunately, nothing came of it and for the next eight years they didn't experience any further incidents. Pablo naturally assumed the three bullets he shot into the monster got the job done.

Pablo never did develop anything from the wound in his shoulder, though it still bothered him occasionally, and he still dreamed nightmares of his mind being devoured by the monster. He still hadn't told Isabel about any of it as he didn't want to worry her. The cops never found the guy who blew up the houses on their street, although Pablo knew it was the monster he encountered that fateful night eight years ago.

Their neighbors, the O'Briens, rebuilt their house over the course of a year. Pablo and Isabel helped them with several projects around their house and threw them a housewarming party that everyone in the neighborhood attended. Life after that became as normal as it had ever been.

Eveley grew to be an intelligent 10 year old, she was equally a daddy's girl and mom's helper. She loved helping Pablo with projects around the house and on his truck, and loved to help Isabel cook and bake whenever Isabel offered.

Eveley spent her evenings playing with Bandido, Rally, and her neighbors the twins, Aidan and Eileen. They were like the three musketeers, they went to the same school, and were the best of friends along with a few other neighborhood kids that completed their circle. Eveley, always inquisitive and curious, became obsessed with anything science, especially space exploration. It wasn't long before Pablo bought her a telescope, and the group of friends would spend almost every evening after dinner in Eveley's treehouse. Despite the light pollution in their large city, they loved looking for the planets and moon through the telescope.

Eveley slowly developed her first crush on Aidan. She felt shy around him at times, and would sometimes daydream about his cute freckles, light blue eyes, and messy dark auburn hair. Isabel and Pablo noticed the change and put two and two together. They were surprised how quickly time had passed and how they were now raising a little girl on the brink of young womanhood with girlish crushes. Isabel thought it was cute but hadn't mentioned it to Aidan's mom, Stella, for fear of embarrassing either of their kids.

That evening right around sunset, Eveley played in her backyard waiting for the twins to come to the side gate and do their secret knock, which was always ironic because the gate was unlocked. Bandido was always there first to greet the twins and Rally. Eveley was surprised to see only Aidan and Rally at the gate. Rally happily chased after Bandido and both dogs ran across the yard.

"Sup?" Aidan said.

"Sup with you? Where's Eileen?"

"Oh she didn't feel good, she told me to tell you," Aidan said shrugging his shoulders.

"Oh..." Eveley froze for a second, "Well do you still want to loo-"

"Race ya!" Aidan shouted as he ran toward the large oak tree and started climbing the ladder.

Eveley smiled with joy and ran after him. "Wait up! That's cheating!" she shouted.

Both dogs ran after the kids and jumped up toward the canopy as they climbed higher and higher above them. When Eveley reached the top after Aidan, she saw him already taking something out of his pocket.

"Beat ya!" Aidan said.

"Only cause you got a head start!"

"Okay okay, but I am pretty fast huh?" he boasted.

"Yeah I guess, what's that?"

"Just a popsicle, wanna share?" Aidan asked.

"Uh yeah, of course!" Eveley said.

Aidan opened the wrapper of the bright red Popsicle, the kind with 2 sticks. He pulled it apart but it broke off uneven, one of the pieces a bit bigger.

"Here, you can have the bigger one," Aidan said.

"Thanks!" Eveley bit the large chunk of extra Popsicle in her mouth.

"How do you do that?" Aidan said as he observed her chew the Popsicle like it was gum.

"I don't get brain freeze I guess," she said and shrugged.

"Wow," he said and then plopped down on the floor and began to pry open a secret compartment in the floor he'd cut out.

"Hey, wanna try to find Mercury? My dad said it might be visible tonight," Eveley said.

"Sure."

Eveley noticed Aidan quickly hid something behind his back.

"What's that behind your back?"

"Nuthin," he said slowly and suspiciously.

Eveley narrowed her eyes at him to thin slits. "It better not be another prank."

"It's not, look, nuthin,"

He pulled his hands in front of him and opened them to show her his palms.

She gave him a look that only communicated she was still skeptical.

"Alright, if you say so..."

They adjusted the telescope now that the sunset had completed its course. They turned on a small battery operated lamp that they dimmed just enough to see around the treehouse. They'd become pros over the last six months so it didn't take them long. Eveley was the first to zero in on Mercury.

"I see it, here look!" she said as she moved and motioned to Aidan to come closer. He came up to the eyepiece and brought his face close, meanwhile Eveley waited with anticipation as he looked.

"Impressive," he said slowly. He continued to look through the eyepiece then stopped and turned to Eveley.

"How do you say Mercury in Spanish?" Aidan asked.

"Mercurio."

"Mehrcurioh," Aidan repeated back with a softening of the r sound.

Eveley grinned. "Pretty good, rrrrr," She rolled the r sound.

"Merrrrrcurrrrio," Aidan said as he exaggerated the sound this time.

Eveley laughed. "Yup, just like that."

They spent the better part of an hour looking at other stars through the telescope. When they were finally exhausted, they laid down side by side, a small gap between them. They gazed at the sky, while joking around and laughing loudly.

"Hey look! Did you see that?" Aidan said as he pointed at the sky.

"What?"

"It looks like a bird flying made of those stars." He pointed with his finger.

"Oh yeah! That's supposed to look like an owl flying, but I see more of a dragonfly."

"I see that too, how do you call that in Spanish?"

"Owl or dragonfly?"

"Both."

"Owl is buo and dragonfly is libelula."

"libelu-lah, I like that one," Aidan said.

He laid his hand down to his side, his pinky finger slightly brushed Eveley's and she felt a little shock go through her pinky.

"Eveley!" Pablo shouted.

Eveley heard her dad call out to come inside for the night.

"Time to go!" Eveley said as she jumped up and ran first to the ladder.

They both climbed down and Eveley ran toward her back door.

"Hey, wait up Eveley!" Aidan ran after her, grabbed her hand, and placed something in it.

"I found it in the ground the other day and thought you'd like it."

Eveley opened her hand and looked at the most beautiful rock she'd ever seen laying on her palm. Her mouth fell open, followed by a smile.

"I love it! Thank you!" she said.

She gave Aidan a hug, he smiled sheepishly and his face flushed red.

"Glad you liked it, okay, goodnight, bye Mr. Luna!" Aidan shouted as loudly as he could.

"Goodnight Aidan!" they both heard through the screen door.

"See you in school tomorrow, tell Eileen I hope she feels better," Eveley said.

"Will do, bye, c'mon boy, let's go." Aidan motioned at Rally to follow him as he ran to the gate and closed it behind him.

Eveley ran inside, overcome with the euphoria of receiving a gift.

"Mom! Mom!"

"What!? what mija?!" Isabel turned around from the kitchen where she was rinsing some dishes.

"Look! Aidan found this and gave it to me," Eveley said.

Eveley showed Isabel the oval shaped rock, the size of a quarter, translucent with shades of blues, pinks, and purples and a powdery cloud-like inclusion in the middle.

"Wow this is very pretty, the inside looks like something I've seen before but I can't put my finger on-"

"A nebula mom!"

"That's it! It does, doesn't it? Wow it's so unique, did you tell Aidan thank you?"

"Of course!"

"What's that?" Pablo came into the kitchen and peeked over their shoulder.

"Nice, that's a cool rock, want me to make it into a necklace?" Pablo offered.

"Yes, could you pa?!" Eveley jumped up with enthusiasm as she grabbed Pablo's arm.

"Okay okay, leave it on the countertop for me tomorrow morning and I'll work on it."

"Okay! Gracias pa!"

"De nada [you're welcome], get ready for bed mija."

"Okay." Eveley turned around and ran to her room.

Isabel and Pablo shook their heads at each other.

That night Eveley used her hidden flashlight to admire all the details of her rock under the covers. She smiled when she thought that Aidan had given her something so precious. As her mind finally quieted down and she slowly drifted closer to the edge of sleep, she felt like she was in a dream. A beautiful, full color dream like in the rock she held gently in her hand.

The next day was a day like any other, Eveley, Aidan and Eileen walked the half block to their bus stop and rode the bus to their elementary school. The twins shared the same classroom,

Eveley only shared lunch and recess with them. That day Aidan was very quiet around Eveley and she wondered if perhaps it was because Aidan regretted giving her such a cool rock. But during recess things were normal as usual and they played with several of their classmates. Later that day on their walk home from their bus stop Eveley brought up the rock.

"Hey guess what?" Eveley motioned to Aidan as she grabbed another piece of candy from Aidan's hand who was sharing it with both his sister and Eveley. Eveley plopped the candy in her mouth.

"What?" Aidan asked.

"My dad said he's going to make the rock you gave me into a necklace for me," Eveley said.

Eileen who was on the other side of Eveley opened her emerald green eyes wide and smiled toward her brother.

"You gave Eveley the rock you found?!" she said with excitement and pushed herself in between her brother and Eveley.

"I knew it!" she said at her brother.

"What? I thought Eveley would like it," he said turning red and looking down at his feet.

Eileen grabbed Eveley's arm and pulled her ahead of her brother while looking at her brother with a mischievous smile. She whispered in Eveley's ear, "He's got a crush on you."

Eveley smiled slightly and looked back at Aidan who looked embarrassed. She felt embarrassed too.

"No he doesn't," Eveley whispered back in Eileen's ear and pulled her back toward Aidan.

"Hey, want me to bring you guys some dessert after dinner? My mom said she's making some churros," Eveley said changing the subject.

"Uh yeah, duh!" Eileen chimed.

"Yes, is that even a question?" Aidan said, relieved they were finally talking about something else. His sister could be such an instigator sometimes but he still loved her.

"Okay guys, I'll see you at the usual spot after dinner!" Eveley said.

"Okay, bye chica!" Eileen waved at her as Eveley ran to her back gate first.

"Bye Eveley!" Aidan said smiling.

When Eveley entered the back, Bandido greeted her, he was not as fast as he once was. Eveley kneeled down and stroked the top of his fluffy head.

"Hey buddy, whatcha doin? Did you miss me?" she said as she picked up a tennis ball next to her foot and threw it in the middle of the yard. Bandido ran after it and brought it back.

"C'mon let's go!" Eveley motioned to Bandido. She opened the back screen door, Isabel always kept the back door open when she was in the kitchen. She found her mom organizing groceries in the pantry.

"Hola mija, how was school?" Isabel turned around to face her.

Eveley hugged her mom quickly. "It was good, I'm tired."

"Oh yeah? Did you do a lot of running today at recess?"

"Soo much mom! I thought I was going to die of thirst!"

"Oh, I made some agua fresca if you'd like some."

"Yes! what flavor?"

"Your favorite, limon [lime]."

"Yum, I'm gonna grab some." Eveley grabbed a glass from an upper cabinet and set it on the countertop, she opened the fridge and found the pitcher.

"Ma? Are you still making the churros tonight after dinner?"

"Yes, why?"

"I asked Aidan and Eileen if they wanted me to bring them some after to share, is that okay?"

"Of course mija, you can take some to Stella and Jason too if you'd like."

"Awesome, can I help you make them too?"

"Si mija."

"Okay, cool, when is dad gonna be home?"

"He should be here by 5:30 today."

Eveley drank a whole glass and took some cookies from the cookie jar and munched on them.

"I'm gonna do my homework in my room after I'm done eating."

"Okay mija, I'll be in the kitchen."

Eveley went to her room and set her backpack on the tile floor. She began to set her books and homework on her desk. Bandido took his usual spot underneath her desk, he laid his head on top of her criss-crossed feet. She worked diligently on her homework, but every once in a while she would look at her window and look at the oak tree with her treehouse and smile at the thought of what transpired since yesterday. She heard the sound of her dad's truck and jumped up in excitement. Bandido came to attention as well.

"C'mon boy! Dad is home!" She ran to the front door and opened it. Pablo was barely stepping out of his truck when she ran toward him.

"Pa!" she gave him a hug and he hugged her back picking her slightly off the ground.

"Hola mija, muy feliz en verme [someone's happy to see me]," he said since it was unusual for Eveley to run up to him when he arrived from work. Usually she would wait by the door smiling until he got to it then she'd talk his ear off.

"How was your day?" she managed to ask in her excitement.

"Very good mija, I was hoping to get your necklace done by the morning but things started getting busy and we started to fall behind..." Pablo could see Eveley's face start to fall in disappointment.

"So I finished your necklace at the end of the day," he said with a smirk as he dangled it in front of her face. She smiled and grabbed it slowly, mesmerized by it.

"It's beautiful!" The necklace hung from a simple leather string, the rock surrounded snugly by silver wire holding it in place. Pablo didn't want to drill into it and risk breaking it so instead he thought of this design which worked perfectly.

"Okay okay, take good care of it, don't lose it," he said as they walked into their house.

"Hey Pablo, you're just in time," Isabel said from the kitchen,

"Oh yeah? It smells good in here, just in time for what amorcito [sweetheart]?" He walked up to Isabel and kissed her on the lips.

"For dinner of course." She smiled as she signaled to a pot on the stove.

"Mmm, what'd you make?"

"Carnitas, arroz, frijoles charros, y tortillas."

He kissed her quickly on the lips again.

"Gracias mi vida [Thank you my life], I'm starving," Pablo said and Isabel smiled. She turned to Eveley who was admiring her necklace.

"Look ma, it's so pretty."

"Let me help you put it on mija."

Isabel motioned for her to come closer and Eveley placed the necklace in her mom's hands. She turned around and Isabel wrapped it around her neck and gently flipped Eveley's long wavy hair to the side and closed the clasp in the back.

"There you go," Isabel said.

Eveley turned around, her face was bright, the joy evident in her eyes.

"How do I look?" Eveley asked.

"Hermosa [Beautiful]!" Isabel said.

"Muy bonita [Very pretty]," Pablo said as well.

"Thank you! I'm going to go look in my mirror!" Eveley ran off to her room.

Later that night, the three friends met up in the treehouse. They sat on the edge of the wooden platform as they always did, all three of them waving their legs over the edge. They all munched happily on the churros Eveley helped her mom make, all of them scarfing them down despite them just eating dinner.

"Those were so good, your mom makes the best Mexican food," Eileen said while eating the last bite of her churro.

"Yeah she should make a cook book," Aidan added.

It wasn't uncommon for all of them to share food from each other's home. Stella, Aidan and Eileen's mom, often shared her delicious Irish dishes with them, while Isabel shared recipes from her childhood that she learned from Magdalena.

Aidan grabbed the sketchbook he brought with him and a charcoal pencil. He started drawing ever since they were encouraged in their art class to draw what they saw out in nature. He'd gotten pretty good at drawing some of the small critters and insects they saw whenever they were outdoors which was a lot of the time.

"Whatcha gonna draw?" Eveley asked.

Aidan signaled back at her. "Don't move please," Aidan said. Eveley looked confused.

Eileen pointed at her as well. "You have a dragonfly on your head!" Eileen whispered excitedly.

"It's so pretty! Hurry up Aidan, it's gonna fly away!" Eileen whispered and tugged on his arm.

"Shhh, stop moving Eileen, it's you who's going to make it fly away if you keep moving," he said slightly annoyed at his "little" sister. He always thought of her as his "little" sister although they were twins since he was born 10 minutes earlier than her. From what his mother told him, Eileen was the smaller, more fragile twin and there were some complications during Eileen's birth. Eileen spent a week in the NICU after she was born which separated them. Meanwhile, Aidan spent that time bonding with his mother. Sometimes Aidan would get an irrational fear that his little sister would not be there when he woke in the mornings. He mentioned this fear to his mom Stella who told him she thought the bond they shared in the womb was disrupted by the separation in the first week of their life. She believed it imprinted a sort of anxiety in both of them where they feared something bad would happen to the other.

Aidan was concentrating deeply now, using his pencil quickly to draw the dragonfly. Luckily it didn't move. Eveley looked straight ahead, focusing her eyes on the leaves on a tree branch behind Aidan, avoiding looking right at him. He would look at her but not connect directly with her eyes. Every once in a while though, their eyes would connect and Eveley would look away as she felt her cheeks flood with warmth.

Meanwhile, Eileen was watching the drawing over his shoulder. She gave Eveley a thumbs up and Eveley smiled. It took Aidan about 5 minutes to finish.

"Okay I'm done, you can move, the dragonfly is still on your head," Aidan said.

"Right or left?" Eveley asked.

"Right, hold on, I'll try to get it." Eileen got up from her spot next to Aidan and kneeled next to Eveley. Eileen slowly moved her hand closer to the dragonfly. She slid her fingers gently over its banded wings, expecting it to fly away but it continued to stay still.

"It likes me!" she exclaimed.

Suddenly the dragonfly flew up in the air, made a loud whirring sound with its wings and landed on Eileen's arm. Eileen looked down and her face bubbled with emotion like she was going to shriek in excitement but she pursed her lips to stop herself.

"Aww, it's so pretty," Eveley said when she finally saw it.

It was a powdery blue color, it finally flew off in the distance and Eileen let out a big sigh.

"Phew! I thought I was gonna explode, I was trying so hard to stay still." She plopped down next to Eveley. She turned to Aidan, ready to peek at his drawing. Aidan had already rolled it up and held it next to him.

"Libelu-lah liked you," Aidan said to Eileen to distract her.

"Who?" Eileen said, burrowing her eyebrows in confusion.

Aidan looked at Eveley with a smirk, Eveley chuckled at their inside joke.

"Libelula means dragonfly in Spanish," Eveley fessed up.

"Oh! Then yes, libelula loved me!" Eileen said cheerfully. She turned her attention to Aidan.

"Can I see?" Eileen asked as she tried to peek around Aidan's body to see the rolled up drawing.

"Uh not yet, I still have more to finish, I'll show it to you tomorrow."

"Fine," Eileen said.

"Should we turn on the lamp?" Eveley asked, the sun was almost down.

"Yeah, I'll do it." Aidan turned on the dim lamp.

They saw the glow of a group of fireflies.

"Wow, there are so many of them," Eveley said.

All three of them caught a few fireflies gently with their hands, then released them. They joked around for a little while longer. Eveley braided a french braid into Eileen's unruly red curly hair. Unlike Aidan, whose wavy hair was a darker shade of red, Eileen had the captivating locks of an Irish gal. Bright red curls framed her small face and bright green eyes to match. She often complained about her hair and how she wanted straight hair and blue eyes like the men in her family, since her mother, Stella, also had curly hair. But in Eveley's eyes, the O'Brien girls had beautiful hair and features.

They soon realized it was getting late and decided to head home. They agreed the next day they were going to ride their bikes after school to the creek at the end of their street. They hadn't ridden their bikes to it in a while. Some of their friends would surely join them as they usually rode their bikes down there in spontaneous groups. Usually as they cruised slowly down the half mile to the creek, other kids would see them on their bikes and join them, it was like a sixth sense.

Sometimes the group would start shouting out their friend's names as they passed by and that worked too. By the time they would make it to the creek sometimes there would be as many as 10 to 15 kids all riding bikes with them. It was unusual and amazing so many kids got along so well in their neighborhood. It made their neighborhood incredibly fun as they never had a shortage of friends to hang out with.

Summer breaks were especially amazing, they tended to get a little crazy, but it was all in good fun. There was usually a lot of friendly competition with the kids and their bikes, a few scrapes and falls, and even a few scuffles but at the end of the day, everyone had a blast.

The residents still looked after one another, especially each other's kids. If anyone tried to come into their quiet middle-class neighborhood to mess with the kids, it wouldn't be long before one of the adults noticed and took care of it. All these factors made it to where the kids enjoyed a lot of independence and would stay out until sunset almost every day during summer break.

Chapter 5

CROOKED CREEK

The next day, Friday, the kids came home excited, the school talent show was the highlight of the day. Their friend, nicknamed Wheels for his obsession with anything with wheels, was part of the show. Wheels presented a 5 minute show, demonstrating all his bike tricks on his bmx bike. He'd not only been dirt road and four wheel riding since he was old enough to walk but was naturally the most skilled with a bicycle out of the group. He was the first to go full speed down a steep hill and take more risks when they were riding on trails around their neighborhood. He lived right by the creek and was always outside, either riding his bike or working on a project in the cul-de-sac at the end of his street. His real name was Marco Aragon. He was basically the coolest kid and the daredevil in their circle.

They also heard their friend Camila Trejo sing a rendition of Bidi Bidi Bom Bom by Selena. She was incredibly talented, with a beautiful singing voice as well as being the tiniest in height in their group. They nicknamed her [1] Chiquis, which stood for small in Spanish.

Their friend Rome James or R.J. as they called him, had everyone in the audience dancing when he came out to Crank That by Soulja Boy with some other kids they knew. The whole auditori-

---

1. Chiquis (Chi-keys)

um erupted into unison, standing up from their seats, they had a blast and left school on a high note. Ultimately the winner of the talent show was R.J. who received a standing ovation from the audience. On the walk home Eileen, Aidan, and Eveley couldn't stop talking about the talent show.

"I almost tripped when I was jumping to the side, I had to catch myself!" Eileen talked while she simultaneously dug into the bag they were sharing, her fingers stained red, she let out little breaths in between her frenzied sentences.

"I always forget how hot these are!" Eileen continued to munch happily. Eileen tended to get extremely excited to the point that sometimes she could annoy those around her. She was a caring and considerate person, but her personality was big and loud, though she was tiny in size. She tended to get her feelings hurt easily when people didn't seem to like her, she definitely was the type of person you either loved or couldn't stand to be around. Fortunately for Eileen, her group of friends loved her but there was a running joke that if they ever wanted to seriously annoy someone all they had do was send Eileen to talk their ear off until they couldn't take it any longer.

"I think they're barely spicy, more like peppery," Aidan said as he munched on them 2 and 3 at a time.

"Yeah, they're not that bad," Eveley concurred.

Eveley and Aidan were always tied for who could endure the spiciest foods. The first time she saw him trying all the salsas at their carne asada, she was impressed he could handle even the spiciest salsas her mom and dad made. She could barely handle the hottest one but she didn't let on she was feeling the pain on her tongue when she sat next to him and plopped a spoonful of the habanero salsa on her carne asada and ate it. The entire time she looked at him for signs he was feeling the heat, redness in the cheeks, sweating, drinking excessive amounts of water, but it never came to be, he looked as calm as a cucumber. Since that day, she would ask her mom to buy her the spiciest candies anytime she went to the Mexican store she frequented for some of their cooking supplies. Aidan and Eveley would share the candy on the bus since no one else would touch it.

"Hey! I have an idea! What if we take our bike ramp and see if we can jump across the creek with our bikes?" Eileen's eyes lit up.

"I don't know Eileen, if you fall, later you're gonna get me in trouble with mom and dad, and say it was my idea." Aidan was speaking from experience.

"No, I promise I won't!" Eileen whined.

"Isn't the ramp really heavy?" Eveley knew that Eileen could come up with some crazy ideas to keep them entertained.

"It's not that heavy! It's portable so it's light, c'mon please?"

She turned to Aidan, the only reason she was pleading was because the ramp technically belonged to Aidan and if she took it without him okaying it, he would tell on her and get her in trouble with their mom and dad.

"Okay, but be careful, only small jumps, got it?" Aidan finally gave in.

"Got it!" Eileen said with a satisfied smile. She had a bad habit of getting her way most of the time with Aidan.

"I'm gonna run and get my bike and put away my things, I'll meet you guys out here in 10 minutes," Eveley said as she started running toward her gate.

"Okay!" Eileen was already running toward her own house, Aidan walked behind her.

Eveley ran in her house, her mom was by the window watering her plants.

"Hola ma! Can I go ride my bike with Aidan and Eileen down to the creek?"

"Hola mija, you're in a rush, do you have any homework?"

"No ma, I finished it at school."

"Okay mija, but be careful, make sure you all stay together and stay in the neighborhood, got it?"

"Si mami."

Eveley ran to her bedroom and plopped her backpack on her bed. She was about to grab her tennis shoes when she noticed a white sheet of paper falling out of the back pocket of her backpack. She grabbed the folded piece of paper and opened it. It was Aidan's drawing of her, he must have slipped it in her backpack when they were walking home. It was a drawing of her entire face with the dragonfly on one side of her face. Everything was in shades of black and gray, except her eyes, which were expertly shaded in light brown and copper, and the dragonfly, with powdery blue on its wings.

The drawing was especially stunning since the reflection of the eyes and the wings made it almost look like a photograph. She had no idea Aidan was so good at drawing. She felt her body flood with a warm feeling, like a warm hug. She couldn't avoid the big smile that formed on her face as she hugged the drawing to her chest. She placed it on her desk and placed a paperweight on it so it wouldn't end up on the floor, she had plans to frame it when she had a chance.

She rushed to put her sneakers on and then ran out the back, grabbing her rally blue bike. Aidan was already sitting on the sidewalk's edge next to the street. Eileen was still inside getting ready.

Eveley sat next to him, close enough that their arms brushed.

"You're sneaky!"

"Huh?" Aidan responded.

"Thank you for my drawing, I like it a lot." She smiled at him.

He turned red. "You're welcome, it's probably the best drawing I've made so far."

"Really? Thank you, it's probably the best gift I've ever gotten beside the rock you gave me." Eveley took the stone necklace in her hand when she said this.

"You're welcome, glad you liked it." Aidan fidgeted with his bike's wheel in front of him.

Eileen came running out shouting. "Don't leave without me!"

"When have we ever left you behind?!" Aidan shouted back at her.

"Never, but don't start now!" Eileen said as she jumped on her bike with gusto.

The friends began to ride slowly down the street, followed by Rally and Bandido. By the time they made it to the cul-de-sac and ran into Wheels, four other kids rode alongside them.

As soon as Wheels saw them, he grabbed his lime green bmx bike and joined them. They started down a small pathway that took them into a small forest for about half a mile. Wheels led in the front, doing tricks with ease every once in a while. They took an unpaved trail to the side of the concrete walkway until they got to the creek. The creek fluctuated from a shallow 25 feet wide channel with small cascading waterfalls to narrow areas three to six feet wide.

The dogs loved to get in the water and the kids would play fetch with them by throwing sticks to them while wading in the knee-deep water. Usually, the rocks were super slippery and there were always a few amusing falls. Today however, they were more interested in jumping over the creek. It was desolate, they hadn't seen anyone else so far, they continued to ride along the edge of the creek till Aidan saw a narrow enough width of about five feet to jump over.

"Here, this should work, I think we can all reach the other side. If it's too easy we can move where it's wider," Aidan said as he took down the ramp he was wearing as a backpack and started to unfold it.

Once he set it up, Wheels was the first to volunteer to jump. He rode his bike all the way up the embankment to pick up speed.

"Clear!" Wheels shouted as he stood up on his bike then pedaled furiously. He got low and smoothly departed from the ramp, higher than everyone expected. He did a bar spin before landing effortlessly. Everyone hooted and shouted.

Aidan was up next, he also made it with no effort.

Eileen went next, she pedaled like crazy to gain enough speed down the small embankment. She barely made it, her back wheel a mere inch from the edge.

Eveley ended up being last, everyone was already at the other side of the creek, she pushed her bike up the embankment.

"You got this!" Aidan shouted.

"Eveley, Eveley!" Eileen shouted, until everyone shouted her name in unison.

Eveley saw the brush behind her friends shake back and forth but didn't realize the wind was calm around them.

She pedaled with all her power; she flew in the air and threw her hands up off the handlebars without falling. Everyone went wild when she landed. Eileen ran to her first, then everyone else surrounded her, giving her high fives and fist bumps.

Eveley was still on the high of her jump when she felt the hairs on the back of her neck stand up. Her stomach felt uneasy. Everyone walked beside the creek to a little wooden bridge to cross to the opposite side. Eveley grabbed a stick and threw it up the creek as Rally splashed in the middle of the creek. Bandido sat next to Eveley observing Rally. Bandido suddenly turned to the brush behind him and snarled loudly.

"What is it boy? There's nothing there," she said as she bent down to his level and looked at the brush. Aidan and Eileen were about 30 feet in front of her when Bandido ran into the thick brush disappearing. Eveley got on her knees to search through the brush.

"Bandido come back boy!" she yelled frantically which grabbed Aidan and Eileen's attention.

"Eveley? Is he okay?" Aidan asked.

They saw Eveley try to push through the thick brush. She looked up above her and she froze, she let out a frenzied scream and jumped back. Aidan saw her back up and fall into the water, landing on her back. She desperately reached up with her hands, splashing water everywhere. The water was knee-deep so it wasn't like she could drown but Eveley looked as if something was holding her down. She couldn't get any breaths in as water filled her nostrils and mouth. Finally, Aidan ran to her, jumped into the creek, grabbed her arm, and pulled her up to a sitting position. Aidan got scared when he saw her face, she looked shell-shocked as if she'd seen something awful.

"Eveley, what's wrong? What happened? What did you see?" Aidan asked confused.

Eileen jumped into the creek and hugged Eveley.

"Eveley, are you okay? What scared you?!" Eileen hugged her while Eveley looked ahead blankly, not saying a word.

"I think we should go back home, we need to find Bandido though." Aidan looked back where Eveley had froze but still didn't see Bandido.

By now everyone else had come back. Wheels, Chiquis, RJ, Julian, and Leo stood surprised by the commotion.

RJ spoke first, "What happened? Is she okay?"

"She fell back into the creek, Bandido ran off after he was snarling at somethi-" Aidan was interrupted mid-sentence by loud snarling which sounded like Bandido. They heard loud growling and demon-like screams. Eileen and Chiquis screamed.

"What the heck was that?!" R.J. asked.

Everyone huddled close. Eveley was now standing in the water next to Eileen. Aidan extended his hands and helped both of them up the embankment. Bandido started yelping and whining as if he was being hurt.

"Stay back everyone!" Aidan shouted as everyone backed away.

"Go! I'm going to try to get him back," Aidan shouted and the girls ran toward their bikes by the bridge. All the boys grabbed rocks from the ground.

Aidan tried to push his body through the brush when Bandido flew into him as if something threw him like a slingshot, making Aidan fall back on his butt. All his friends helped him up when the loud growling began again. They felt the hair raise on their necks. A long gray hand suddenly came out of the brush with dangling, hanging skin, and long pencil-like fingers that took hold of Wheel's leg.

"Guys! my leg, help!" Wheels shouted as R.J. saw the deformed hand, he thought fast and stomped on the arm, it recoiled with a demonic scream.

"Everyone run!" R.J. shouted pointing toward the bridge, they all ran and jumped on their bikes as the low pitched growls followed them along the brush. The girls were already on their bikes pedaling with all their might ahead of them. Eileen was hyperventilating near a panic attack.

"Go! Go! Don't stop!" Aidan shouted at the girls as they caught up to them.

They pedaled like they'd never done before, Eveley pointed to the other side of the creek. The brush beside the creek shook vigorously keeping pace with them as the growling and screams continued.

"No matter what, don't stop!" Aidan shouted.

They pedaled like their life depended on it. When they finally made it to the concrete sidewalk, they continued to pedal without stopping until a black-cloaked figure appeared suddenly in the middle of the sidewalk blocking their path. The kids screeched to a halt.

Everyone was frozen in their place. The only thing they could see was the deep breathing of the figure up ahead. A loud scream emanated from the figure as it started limping toward them. It shook like a leaf, as if its joints were dislocated. The boys remembered the rocks they picked up earlier and threw them at the figure with all their strength. The figure growled and turned around and ran off in front of them, this time leaping like an animal out of their sight.

Everyone looked at each other in disbelief, the girls were crying from fright.

"Stay behind me and R.J., Wheels is in the back, once we get to the street we'll be safe. Just keep pedaling and don't stop,"

Aidan said as they pedaled. They still had a quarter of a mile to go. They pedaled and made it to the cul-de-sac where Wheel's house was the first.

"We need to go home and tell our parents what happened," R.J. said, everyone nodded.

"Everyone needs to stay in a group, Wheels, be careful," Aidan said.

"My dad is home so he'll probably be out here soon," Wheels said.

"Okay, we're all gonna go home to tell our parents, be careful," Aidan said.

Wheels nodded. The kids watched as he walked up to his front door and knocked, his dad opened the door and let him in safely.

"Okay, let's go guys, stay close," Aidan said.

Everyone was dropped off one by one until Eveley, Eileen, and Aidan were the last ones left.

Eveley still looked shell-shocked having said nothing since she fell in the creek. When they arrived at her back gate, she felt the uneasiness return again. Bandido looked exhausted although he didn't look injured.

As they opened the gate to her backyard and stepped in, it felt eerily quiet. Eveley walked toward her back door with Aidan and Eileen following behind her when she heard a scream and a shot rang through the air. She ran into the house, her mom stood facing away from her. Her gun pointed in front of her, a broken window on the side of the house.

"Ma!!"

"Eveley! Mija are you okay?! Did anyone hurt you?!"

"No ma, but something at the creek was trying to hurt us!"

Isabel shook her head in frustration.

"Aidan and Eileen, let's get you guys home, hurry, it's not safe here."

Isabel got in front of the kids as she walked them out the back door and into their own yard. She knocked on the back door and Stella opened and saw the gun.

"Isabel what's going on!?"

"Mom! Something tried to chase us at the creek, there's some guy trying to kidnap us!" Eileen said as she burst into tears.

"Lock all your windows and doors Stella, I'm calling the cops." Isabel grabbed Eveley's arm and pulled her close to her.

"Stay close," Isabel whispered to Eveley as they made it back into their yard. Once inside the house, she called the police, then Pablo.

"Pablo, he's back, hurry home," Isabel said over the phone.

She left the voicemail on his cell phone as he wasn't always available due to the nature of his job. Five minutes later, the phone rang. Isabel picked up,

"Don't put your gun down until I'm there or the cops get there," Pablo said, his voice serious.

Deep down Pablo always knew this day would come. He'd prayed this was all behind them but it wasn't over. He hurried home, when he arrived he observed over a dozen cop cars on his street with kids and parents huddled outside and police officers taking statements.

Isabel saw Pablo's truck pull into their driveway. She ran to the front door with Eveley by her side, setting her gun back in its holster. She ran to him and they all embraced.

"Are you guys hurt?!" Pablo asked.

"No, but I shot him Pablo. He came into the house while Eveley was down in the creek, and this time I saw his face, it was the creep from the café. I saw what you told me, his face looked like it had melted, actually his whole body looked like it was disintegrating," Isabel said.

Pablo looked shocked, he knew what he saw eight years ago was real but it felt weird having it confirmed by Isabel. It felt like a nightmare he tried to forget and couldn't escape.

"Pa, it tried to attack us down at the creek. Bandido went crazy next to the creek, snarling at the brush, then he disappeared in the brush and something growled really loud. Then I saw the face like mom said, it looked like a melted man, he looked so scary. It tried to grab one of my friends and we managed to escape. It followed us, then it stood on the sidewalk blocking our escape. It started coming at us again but my friends threw rocks at it and it ran off." Eveley's words came miles a minute and her eyes filled with tears until they overflowed from the rim of her eyes. Pablo wiped a tear away from her cheek and kissed the top of her head.

"It's okay mija, you're safe now, nothing is going to hurt you, your mom, or your friends."

In his mind, Pablo had already decided he would not rely on the cops to solve this problem. They didn't know how dangerous this thing was and how quickly it could snatch a kid. The monster had gone berserk and it was only a matter of time before it did something worse than tonight. Pablo wasn't planning on waiting to find out what. It was up to him to end this once and for all. It was his responsibility as a father and husband.

The cops took statements from both Isabel and Eveley. The authorities had already gathered a team, and they were in the middle of a search party in the wooded area near the creek to look for the "suspect". The large police presence was visible in their neighborhood, as well as helicopters overhead in the general area around their neighborhood. No one had seen the guy since he broke into their house and tried to attack Isabel.

Pablo called Cesar next, "Cesar, he's back, I need you here, I'm going to leave tonight to take care of it."

When Isabel heard his words it set her in a panic. She walked up to Pablo and grabbed his arms, looking intently at him.

"Pablo, what are you planning on doing? Don't leave please, you know that's not a good idea," she said distraught.

"Isabel, I need you to be strong, I have no other choice, I can't just do nothing." He saw her eyes fill with tears. He embraced her and rested his chin on the top of her head looking ahead.

"Cielo, no llores [My sky, don't cry], I know this is hard, but this has spiraled out of control, this has to end."

"Let the cops take care of it Pablo! You don't have to place yourself in danger."

"And continue to wait for his return to hurt you, Eveley, or the other kids? No tengo otra opcion Isabel, entiende por favor [I have no other choice Isabel, please understand]."

Isabel knew Pablo was right but it didn't make it any easier. She had a premonition she couldn't shake no matter how many times she told herself everything would be okay.

When Cesar and Magdalena arrived, everyone in the room looked somber. Eveley sat next to her dad, hugging him in silence. She wasn't sure what was happening but she was scared for everyone especially her father after she heard him tell her grandfather he was going to "take care of it".

When her grandparents came in Eveley ran to her grandmother Magdalena and hugged her tightly with tears streaming down her face. Cesar hugged Eveley as well then Isabel hugged her parents. Cesar noticed Pablo who was silent and looked on edge.

Pablo was lost in thought, he couldn't focus on anything around him. He was too engulfed in the anxiety of his family being in peril, he knew there was no room for error this time.

Cesar motioned at him and they walked outside to the backyard. They spoke in hushed tones.

"What's the plan?" Cesar carried his Colt 1911.

"I'm leaving once the cops leave our street. I'm going to find him this time." Pablo paused and looked up at the stars, "If anything happens to me, please take care of Isabel and Eveley."

Cesar came in with a poker face as always, but his facial expression changed to that of concern.

"Mijo, you do what you have to do, Isabel and Eveley are going to be safe. If anything wants to get to them, they're going to have to do it over my dead body." Cesar noticed Pablo was looking intently at the sky.

"You just come back okay? You take care of this monster, then you bring yourself right back to us, your wife and daughter need you."

"I have a premonition Cesar, I don't have any doubt I'm going to get rid of this thing, but as far as coming back, something is telling me that isn't in the cards for me."

Pablo continued to look up.

"You don't know that mijo, God is going to be with you. I'm going to pray for you and so is everyone else," Cesar said placing his hand on Pablo's shoulder.

"Save your prayers. I prayed to him these last 8 years, and almost, *almost* grew to believe my prayers were answered, but they weren't," Pablo said with a tinge of resentment in his voice.

"Mijo, God doesn't cause bad things to happen to us, they just happen."

"Yeah well unlike him, I'm not going to stand around and do nothing." Pablo stormed back in the house, to his bedroom and grabbed a backpack from his closet. Isabel came in frantically, her eyes bloodshot from crying. She came up behind Pablo and rested her hands and head on his back. Pablo turned around and felt awful. He kissed her cheeks, wet from the waterfall of tears.

"Cielo, you're the best thing that's ever happened to me. Believe me, if there was another way, I would never leave you." Pablo kissed her lips and felt a part of his soul ache. He could never say goodbye right but this time he couldn't make the mistake of leaving Isabel with a bad memory as her last memory of him, of them, and everything their marriage stood for.

"Please promise me-"

"No, don't even say it," Isabel said, her voice shaking. She placed her finger to his lips to signal him to stop speaking, "I don't want to hear it, please don't."

Pablo grabbed her hand and moved it away gently, he looked at her in silence. He remembered the day he met her, falling in a trance when he looked at her big brown eyes. The ones that were full of sadness and desperation now.

"Promise me if I don't come back, you'll continue on without me, you won't stay stuck in grief, you'll find a way to find happiness for you and Eveley. What happens to me cannot be the end of the road for you and Eveley," Pablo said.

Isabel broke into sobs as she shook her head angrily.

"What you're asking of me is too much, how can you ask me that? I can barely take the thought of never seeing you again, let alone moving on!"

Pablo hugged her. Isabel tried to shake the premonition that he would never return but it was impossible for her to do so at this point. She was desperately trying to hold on to hope above all else.

The thought suddenly crossed her mind that she couldn't control what lay ahead...she needed to let go, she needed to accept it with dignity and make the best of the remaining minutes.

Pablo noticed the calm that suddenly came over Isabel. She looked up at him, then kissed him.

"I promise you...but I need a promise from you as well," Isabel said.

"Yes, anything."

"Promise me you're going to fight like hell to make it back to me and Eveley," Isabel said.

"I promise."

Chapter 6

THE SNAIL AND FLATWORM

There was no turning back for Pablo Luna. As he walked down the desolate streets of downtown Dallas on that fateful night, he knew what he needed to do to keep his family safe. Isabel tried to hide the direness of the situation for Eveley's sake but it was an emotional goodbye nonetheless. Isabel ran out after him on the front lawn as he was leaving, grabbing him by his jacket and kissing him one last time. It was a bittersweet kiss, one with so many emotions rolled into one that Pablo couldn't help but lose it a little when he got in his truck. He punched the dash of his truck several times to stop himself from sobbing like a baby. The tears trickled down his face anyway, his resignation to the hopelessness he felt. He feared this was the last time he would see his family.

As soon as he drove his truck out of the neighborhood, he knew where to go. He found a big blood trail from the monster when he inspected around the house. The monster had a good head start so he wasn't sure how far it would take to find him. Again the blood trail led him to the same train tracks from eight years ago when he escaped. He found the train tracks were full of blue stains leading northbound so he decided to follow the tracks, and stop his truck every mile or so to check.

He made it downtown where the blood trail suddenly disappeared. He decided to look around the large train yard and walk down the streets in search of him. He knew he was near, he could feel it. He figured out the closer he was to the monster, the more intensely his shoulder throbbed in pain.

He walked in front of a large glass storefront, the window reflected the entire street behind him. He saw a dark cloaked figure appear out of nowhere reflected on the glass, standing next to him across the street. He turned around and saw the figure turn the corner into an alley. Pablo ran after him then slowed down and walked slowly down the alleyway in case it was a trap. He was almost at the end of the alleyway when he saw the dark figure dart across the street. The monster was fast, like a panther on the chase.

Pablo ran after him but the cloaked figure was already making headway. Pablo was being led right back to the train tracks at the train yard. Pablo ran as fast as he could, he made it to a large open part of the train yard. The yard contained at least 20 tracks, as he approached the third track, a train passed by and the figure jumped on one of the open cars. Pablo could see the beady reflection of the monster's eyes from where he was standing, bluish black pits challenging him with a dead stare.

Pablo ran to his truck and tried to keep pace with the train. He could see the cloaked figure as he drove beside the train tracks that for now were following closely to the road. He saw the cloaked figure stand in the middle of the train car's open doorway. He looked directly at him and took off the hooded part of his cloak, defiantly fixated on Pablo. Pablo caught the reflection of metal near the monster's side...a knife. Pablo kept pace with the train, he saw the tracks divert away from the road and he looked at the map beside him to confirm where to go next to keep pace with it. Pablo knew it wasn't going to be easy to keep up. He wasn't giving up though, he wasn't resting until this monster was gone from the face of the earth.

Pablo spent all night driving, catching glimpses of the train car. He memorized the large serial number on the side of it. He finally crossed into Oklahoma. He hoped he could get through the journey without stopping for fuel as it would make it difficult to keep up.

Every time he glimpsed the train, his shoulder throbbed. The pulsing sometimes made him dizzy. As he got closer to the train, the flashes of light returned full force, making him disoriented. He pushed on anyway, keeping sight of the promise he made to keep Isabel and Eveley safe.

He eventually made it through Oklahoma into Missouri. The train tracks followed next to a two-lane country road. As he drove next to the train, he could see the monster still there, facing away from him, crouched looking the other way. Pablo was tempted to shoot him right then and there but he couldn't risk attracting the attention of anyone in this small town.

For the time being he felt better knowing he hadn't lost sight of him. Pablo thought the monster had to be injured badly if he was using the train to evade him. He made it through Joplin, Missouri when the train slowed down. Pablo thought maybe he'd finally get his chance. He heard the high-pitched screeching of the wheels slowing down. He parked his car across from the tracks, watching the train car intently with the serial number he memorized. He watched as an engineer disembarked and walked beside the length of the train, inspecting periodically. Pablo had been driving five hours by now, he felt the vibrations of his phone, a text message from Isabel.

Isabel: Where are u? Are u ok?

Pablo: I'm okay, in Missouri.

Pablo put his phone away. When he looked up, he saw the engineer close the doors to the open train car which was strange. Now he couldn't see the monster or if he was inside. All he could do was follow the train again. The only thing giving him hope he was near was the constant throbbing in his shoulder.

He drove several more hours, day break was near. He saw the train slow down as they reached the limits of town after town, eventually reaching the outskirts of Kansas City, then further into the northeast area of the city. The train screeched to a halt in a valley with bluffs on one side, on the opposite side several silos loomed over the train tracks. The area looked working class, small dilapidated houses made up most of the neighborhood. A bridge crossed above them, allowing further passage into the sleeping city.

Pablo parked his truck under the bridge near a street named Guinotte, next to the train tracks. He slowly stepped out of his truck, as he did his phone slipped out onto the seat without his knowledge. He calmly walked along the tracks toward the train he was following. He walked about 500 feet, all the while the pain and throbbing in his shoulder intensified, his flashbacks began and he knew he was near.

To make matters worse, rain started coming down in heavy sheets that made it hard for him to see. He was about a train car away from the one the monster had inhabited the whole journey. As he took his next step, he heard a loud pounding from a train door swing open, a door he couldn't see, he knew it was the monster.

He got on his stomach and dragged himself under the train to get to the other side. He caught a glimpse of the dark figure running and limping across multiple tracks toward the large treed bluff looming above. Thankfully, there were no other trains in Pablo's direct path to slow him down. He ran after him and reached the edge of the steep bluff. Pablo climbed, all the while hearing the maniacal laugh of this monster taunting him, egging him to reach him.

He pushed through the thick brush, the steep climb at times seemed like it would never end. He finally reached the top to a desolate road banked by another steep bluff above it. He pulled out his gun, he knew this monster was near as his pain was near the point of him blacking out. He turned slowly in 360 degrees as he walked down the road. He reached a small man-made waterfall on the side of the bluff when he heard noises above him.

"What do you want from my family!" Pablo shouted.

For a moment it was silent...nothing stirred. Pablo couldn't see much above him, or in front of him, he could only see a glimmer of the moon's light on the pavement. He had the light attached to his gun turned on.

A deep voice bellowed from above, "Your family?"

"Oh so you do talk, what the hell are you?" Pablo asked.

"I don't think your little brain could comprehend..."

"Try me." Pablo tried to catch where his voice was coming from. He continued to search with the light on his gun and finger ready on the trigger.

"You ever heard of the snail and flatworm?" the monster asked.

"Yes."

"Well, I'm sort of like the flatworm, except I have to find a suitable human host. And every time I infect a human, I control their body and their mind is no longer their own."

"Hmm, well you aren't very good at it, with the whole melting skin and all," Pablo said.

At the mention of this, the monster let out a snarl.

"I didn't know the person I took over had a rotten cancer inside them...you humans are so weak, so easily defeated by the simplest things."

"And by the looks of it, so are your kind," Pablo shot back.

"My kind? My kind have always controlled you mindless humans," he said triumphantly.

"Hmm I'm not so convinced...where does your kind come from?"

"Another planet, which you wouldn't know."

"Why are you here?"

"Survival...it was death or exile, earth happened to be an easy hunting ground for hosts...being that you guys are so defense-less."

"So why my family?"

The monster laughed.

"It was by chance eight years ago that I caught the scent of your wife that day at the café. One in a million people match my organism without rejection. I could sense she was the correct host. I needed to rid myself of this useless carcass, preventing me from reaching my full potential."

"And it turns out she wasn't so easily taken huh? You call humans weak but yet a female of our species was too hard for you to defeat...what are we at now? Three bullets from me, and one from my wife?"

The monster thrashed and went berserk. Pablo could see his shadow flash from tree to tree. He didn't want to take a shot he wasn't 100% sure would hit its target, as well as not knowing how close they were to houses.

"You want to know the amazing part?!" the monster shouted.

"Your little girl has the same scent, and after tonight I'm going to turn around and return to that pretty little home of yours, catch her in her sleep, and she's going to be my little unsuspecting snail."

Pablo felt rage wash over him at hearing the parasite's evil plan. He could see him in his sights and he got a clean shot right into his middle section. The monster screamed, thrashed, and managed to leap to the next tree. Despite the alien's limp and deterioration, he leaped quickly onto the road, leaping at full speed toward Pablo who was 50 feet away. Pablo shot him five times in succession as he backed up quickly, getting close to the edge of the bluff.

Finally, when the monster was 10 feet away, Pablo got another shot in his cheek. As they made contact, they both fell back onto the bluff below, but not before Pablo made the last fatal shot, and the alien stabbed Pablo right in the chest with a Mora blade. Pablo rolled down the bluff roughly, the roots of a large tree stopping him halfway down the hill, the alien's lifeless body rolling further down the hill and landing against another tree. He didn't care about the blade in his chest, which he instinctively knew was fatal as he felt his world fading away. He laid there what seemed like hours, but was more like 20 minutes. He was unable to move as he was too badly injured, he was at peace knowing his daughter and wife were safe now. The rain continued to fall, the first rays of sunshine touched his face. He took one last look at the sun, the leaves, and the rain above before he closed his eyes for the last time.

CHAPTER 7

FADING STAR

Two days later, Isabel knew she needed to do something. After Pablo texted he was in Missouri, she texted him again and again with no response. She reported him missing the next morning. Unfortunately, the police were not very helpful knowing he was traveling, which is what Isabel told them instead of the real reason. They told her they would take it upon themselves to look into the case once 48 hours transpired.

In the meantime Isabel obtained his phone records. Luckily what she found in the report was helpful, Pablo's last pinged tower in an area north of downtown Kansas City. Unfortunately, the tower didn't give her a specific place, only a radius which meant thousands of possibilities. Still, she called the detective assigned to her missing person's report but was still advised to wait until the 48 hour mark.

Eveley was feeling utterly unmotivated to go to school on Monday. She knew her mom wasn't telling her the whole story. Her mom made it seem like her dad was just going to be gone for the night, but it was now two days since she'd seen her dad. Eveley's nights were plagued by horrible nightmares since the attempted attack by the melted man and she was super scared of sleeping in her room. Even with Bandido there she'd slept in her parent's bed with Isabel, or with Magdalena who stayed the night.

Magdalena and Cesar helped Isabel those two days, the atmosphere in the house quiet and depressing but they'd done everything possible to keep Eveley distracted.

They informed the school she wasn't feeling good due to the incident at the creek. The media picked up the story so the school was aware of the events that happened on Friday. Isabel was running out of options, she knew she needed to tell Eveley sooner or later her dad was missing.

Monday at school was ridiculously tiring for Eveley, all the friends that were at the creek with her on Friday huddled and passed notes, trying to keep the details of their closely guarded secret safe to no avail. By lunch time, so many students had asked details about the incident. It didn't help that there were tons of police patrolling their neighborhood and now the school was surrounded by police as well, prompting a few parents to call the office and inquire about their child's safety. The curiosity from teachers and other students overwhelmed most of the involved children. Eveley still hadn't told Eileen and Aidan that her dad had been gone for 2 days but she was hoping he'd be home when she made it home from school.

When Eveley arrived home, her mom was sitting silently in the living room. Her grandmother, Magdalena was sitting next to her, hugging Isabel.

"Hola Ma, hola abuelita, are you okay ma?" Eveley walked in front of them on the couch, she hugged and kissed each of them on the cheek. She became concerned when she saw her mother's bloodshot eyes and her trying to wipe away tears.

"Mija sit down, I need to talk to you," her mom motioned for her to sit next to her. Magdalena looked concerned as well.

"Anda mija, sientate [C'mon my daughter, sit down]," her abuelita prompted.

Eveley sat down, it seemed like time was standing still and she felt her stomach tighten with anxiety.

"Mija, what I'm about to say is very hard for me, I want you to remember that we all love you, including your dad," Isabel said.

"Dad?" Eveley knew it was about her dad.

"Mija...your dad is missing. I haven't heard from him since Saturday morning, when he texted from Missouri."

"Missouri?" Eveley continued to speak in one word, as her world stopped.

"Missing?" Eveley sat silently after the words left her lips, "Ma are you sure?!"

"Si mija, he hasn't replied to any more of my messages since then."

"But he could have had something happen to his phone?" Eveley suggested.

"No mija, he would have called me from a pay phone or a different number by now, it isn't like your dad to not respond to messages."

Eveley placed her face in her hands and sobbed. Isabel embraced her, and so did Magdalena. After Eveley calmed down a little, Isabel told her the next bombshell.

"I'm leaving tomorrow morning to look for your dad and his truck. I'm going to leave your abuelita and you in charge of the café for the whole week and come back by Friday or if something new develops."

"I wanna go with you ma!" Eveley wrapped her arms tightly around her mom's waist.

"Mija, you have to stay here and continue going to school. Your abuelitos are going to stay here and take care of you. I have to go up there and try to get this investigation going and look for your father."

Eveley looked dejected.

"But I'm scared Ma! It's because of the melted man isn't it? He's done something to pa, it had to be him, he said he was going to take care of it, I heard him, what if he comes back?!" Eveley's voice raised as her words became more frantic.

"Shhh, shhh now, don't think of that, you'll be safe here with your abuelito and abuelita, they're not going to let anything happen to you, I promise."

Eveley didn't look convinced but she knew her mom was going to leave anyway. Her mom loved her dad too much to stay idly by. She continued holding on tightly to her mom. Her world was already halfway broken and lost, it's as if she was holding on for dear life to the other half still here.

After dinner, where basically everyone barely touched their food, Eveley went to her room and laid in bed. Her mind raced with all the possibilities of what could have happened to her dad, or if he was going to come back. The thought of her mom leaving for the rest of the week filled her with unease.

Eveley heard her mom call her name from the hallway.

"Eveley! Aidan's at the back door, he wants to speak to you," Isabel said from the doorway.

Aidan had snuck out of his house as it hadn't been exactly easy for his parents to get over the fact that a creep tried to hurt the kids. They'd begun driving Aidan and Eileen to school and keeping them in the house.

"Oh, okay." Eveley walked up to her bedroom door. "Ma can we go to the tree house?"

"Okay, but stay within my sight."

"Okay, thanks ma."

Eveley looked at Aidan's face when she opened the back door, he looked sad and tired.

"I need to talk to you," he said seriously and Eveley scowled. She'd quickly learned that phrase never led to anything good. They climbed up to the treehouse and sat side by side.

"Are you okay?" Aidan asked her, it was like him, even though he could be going through the worst, he was always looking out for everyone else first.

"No, not really...my mom just told me my dad is missing," Eveley said.

Aidan's eyes got wide, Eveley tried not to let the tears form in her eyes, but they did and they fell silently down her cheeks.

"I'm sorry Eveley, that's terrible." They were sitting in their usual spot, their legs over the edge of the wood platform. Aidan placed his hand on her upper back.

"I know I can't help with your dad missing but I'm here if you need to talk and I will always help you with anything."

Eveley nodded, she hugged him tightly.

"Thank you."

"You're welcome."

They sat in silence for a minute while Eveley gathered her thoughts and wiped her tears.

"So what did you want to tell me?" Eveley began.

Aidan looked nervous when she asked.

"Well, you know my dad is from Ireland right?"

"Yeah."

"Well he told us today that the company he works for here is transferring him back...to Ireland. We leave in a month."

Eveley was left flabbergasted. She sobbed.

"Eveley, I will come back every summer and holidays to visit my grandparents and we can hang out again, all three of us," Aidan said but Eveley wasn't listening. Her crying was the culmination of everyone she loved leaving her, the pain was too much.

"I don't want to leave either, I don't want to leave my friends," Aidan added.

Eveley continued to sob. Aidan put his arm around her shoulder and she rested her head on his shoulder, her sobs were gentler now but she felt embarrassed by her reaction.

"I'm sorry, I'm going to miss you guys a lot," Aidan said and Eveley nodded in agreement.

"I promise to email you and Eileen, can you write me back?" Eveley asked.

"Yeah, I will. I promise." He forced a faint smile even though inside he was feeling like a heavy pile of bricks on his chest.

The entire week Isabel was gone, Eveley was anxious to the point she felt on the verge of a panic attack several times. It was mostly in the moments when neither one of her grandparents were around, like when she was in school. She kept replaying the awful sight of the melted man in her head, how scared she felt when she first saw him at the creek. Anytime she would think of his grotesque appearance she would shudder and become anxious and paranoid. She imagined his face around every corner of the school. Even with tons of kids around her she couldn't remove the fear from her mind.

Her friends that were at the creek were also on edge, but fortunately for them they never saw the melted man up close. They only thought he was some creep trying to chase them. In a way maybe that was worse, because technically anyone could be the man that chased them.

The only people Eveley confided in about the man's appearance was Aidan and Eileen. They promised not to tell anyone and she trusted them. Eileen was weirded out when she told her, Aidan was concerned. He thought it wasn't possible for someone human to look the way Eveley described him. They then discussed what it could be if not human...an alien, demon, monster? It was unclear but she felt better after talking about it with both of them.

Friday her grandfather and grandmother picked her up from school. They drove straight to the airport to pick up Isabel. Eveley knew as soon as she saw her mother's face, that good news were not in the cards. Isabel was stone-faced, pale, the spark in her eyes had dulled, she'd lost at least 15 lbs since Pablo left. Eveley hated seeing her mom declining so rapidly. Eveley ran to her mom before Isabel could reach them and hugged her mom tightly. They walked up to Magdalena and Cesar and they all embraced. Isabel broke into painful and heart-wrenching sobs. People passing by looked their way in concern and curiosity. Isabel stumbled and looked like she was about to faint. Cesar grabbed her and steadied her.

"Mija, you need to rest, have you been eating?" Magdalena asked. She knew Isabel was not taking care of herself. Isabel didn't answer, in between ragged sobs, all she could do was whisper sorry to Eveley.

"Let's get her home honey," Cesar said as he supported her weight, with Magdalena and Eveley helping to hold her up as well. In the car, Magdalena and Eveley helped Isabel sit in the middle between them, they both held one of her hands, her past and future both beside her. By the time they made it to their house, Isabel had dozed off.

Eveley felt sad for her mom, she felt sad for all of them. She also felt scared for her dad, she was starting to consider perhaps he wasn't even in this world anymore which scared her the most.

Her grandparents helped Isabel out of the car, into the house, and into her bedroom where she collapsed on her bed in sobs. Magdalena sat on the bed beside her, she pulled back Isabel's tear matted hair and caressed her forehead.

"There there mija, let it out, you need to rest, this has been too much," she said gently as she continued to caress her forehead. Eveley stood in the doorway watching her grandmother console her mother.

"Mija, go help your abuelito no? Your mom needs to rest for a little bit okay?," Eveley nodded her head and closed the door and walked to the kitchen. Her abuelo was already taking some things out of the fridge.

"Mija, me ayudas [Could you help me]?" Cesar began setting up some pots and pans.

"Si abuelito [Yes grandpa]," She walked up to Cesar and observed the ingredients on the countertop.

"I'm going to make some caldo de res [beef stew], you're gonna help me with some of the vegetables."

"Okay, abuelito." Eveley helped her grandfather make the caldo, even though she wasn't hungry helping him cook was a good distraction and the house smelled wonderful.

Eventually once they were done and sat down to rest, her grandmother came out of her mom's room to make tea and took it to Isabel's room. Fifteen minutes later, Isabel came out of the bedroom, she came straight to Eveley and hugged her.

"I'm sorry mija, I'm sorry I didn't keep it together back there," Isabel said.

"It's okay ma," Eveley said as she hugged her back.

Isabel took a deep breath, "I'll tell you what happened once we all sit down and have some dinner."

They all shared a small meal, Isabel forced herself to eat, she knew she needed to set a better example for her daughter despite the searing pain in her chest. Losing Pablo was physically causing her pain she didn't know was possible, pain that constantly stole her attention away from the present.

After dinner, Isabel recounted what happened in Kansas City. When she arrived to Kansas City, she went straight to the downtown police station and asked to speak to a detective. Fortunately she got a very sympathetic investigator. She showed him all the evidence that pointed to Pablo's location in Missouri, they requested information from the Dallas Investigative Unit and scheduled a search based on Pablo's last pinned location.

Nevertheless, Isabel searched on her own. She remembered the monster left distinctive blue blood marks and liked to hide in brush. She took it upon herself to start looking through some areas near the pinned cell tower. The official search happened on Thursday. They managed to gather 20 volunteers along with the investigator to comb some neighborhoods near the pinned tower. They distributed flyers and knocked on doors. It was fruitless and exhausting, but Isabel held out hope to an answer to Pablo's whereabouts. Things were looking dire and she was left to accept something bad happened to him.

That night Eveley snuck out once everyone was asleep and climbed up to her treehouse. It was a warm and muggy night, she sat looking at the stars, wondering where her dad was. Hoping wherever he was, he was looking up at the same sky, and she prayed in her heart that if he was no longer with them, he was in a better place. She watched as a falling star zoomed across the dark clear sky. She let the tears fall silently, never taking her eyes off the stars, this was the only way she felt connected to her dad. Wherever he was, he was either under the same sky or in it looking down on her.

Chapter 8

Endless Orbit

Eveley's 11th Birthday

The first six months after Pablo's disappearance, Eveley and Isabel took refuge in each other. Isabel had ups and downs, some days Eveley could tell her mother was having a really hard time living on. Despite this, Isabel tried to hide her despair and tears in order to be a mother to Eveley. Eveley struggled too, she stopped caring as much about her grades. She stopped doing the things she loved, like drawing, writing, and hanging out with friends. There were days both would go through the motions in order to keep their head above water and not drown in their heartbreak. When things got a little too much to bear they would visit Magdalena and Cesar which they did often anyways. Sometimes the release of tears was therapeutic, other times they wondered if the pain would ever end. Slowly over time the pain changed, from a searing stabbing pain, to a constant dull throbbing.

Before they knew it, a year had passed since Pablo's disappearance. His case went cold almost immediately except for the only break in the case which was Pablo's truck being found months after he went missing. Unfortunately, the tow lot didn't record where it was found so it didn't give them many leads in the case.

Life hadn't exactly returned to "normal", but life was still spinning its endless orbit. They survived the pain, it wasn't the same, but they were still hoping to find him. Her mom went back to Kansas City every month, keeping the case fresh in front of the investigators in charge of Pablo's case. Magdalena helped Isabel by helping to run the café in her absence and taking care of Eveley during these trips. Even Eveley would help regularly at the café now that she was growing older. Magdalena supported Isabel with the trips because she knew her daughter needed closure. If she was in Isabel's shoes, she wouldn't stop looking for her husband either.

Two weeks before Aidan and Eileen arrived from Ireland and summer school would begin, Isabel decided to take Eveley with her to Kansas City on a weekend trip. This was the first time Isabel allowed Eveley to come with her. She didn't plan it as a trip to delve into the disappearance of Pablo although she still made plans to talk to the lead investigator while she was there. Isabel saw it more as a chance for both of them to heal. Perhaps going to the last place they knew Pablo was near would help them mend their broken hearts.

They stayed in a small town called Parkville, Missouri. Right away, Eveley fell in love with the picturesque hilly town along the Missouri river. They stayed a few days and hiked through the nature sanctuary, walked along the park by the riverbank, drank coffee (something which Isabel rarely allowed her to have since she said it stunted her growth) and went shopping through the little town's shops. They also went to the small farmer's market on the weekend. She felt a sense of connection knowing her dad had been near this place. It brought her peace that was hard for her to put into words and she could see her mom was also at ease there.

They returned to Dallas after a few days, it was a great mother-daughter bonding trip. The first trip they enjoyed since Pablo's disappearance. They'd been used to taking 3 family trips a year before Pablo disappeared. They usually visited Mexico and picked a new city to visit each year in the States. They would usually go to Merida where her father's family originated from and Chihuahua where her mother's family originated from.

When they returned to Dallas, Eveley received the news that Eileen and Aidan were on their way to stay for the summer, Stella was with them. Stella would return to Ireland in a few weeks but the twins would stay in Dallas with their grandparents until close to the end of summer. It brightened up her whole week, knowing her two best friends would be around all summer. She'd missed them so much and she kept in contact with them regularly throughout the year so they were still very close.

When the O'Briens arrived, their friendships started up right where they left off. Stella and Isabel took the kids to a waterpark during their first week in Dallas, which was quintessential for a hot city like theirs. Aidan and Eileen hadn't changed a bit, just lost their tan a bit and gained a slight accent that Eveley found endearing. Eileen was still the best friend she could tell everything to. Aidan was also her best friend but now that she was close to 12, the little crush she felt for him was growing stronger.

Every summer after was the same routine, the twins would visit their grandparents every summer and hang out with Eveley and their old friends from elementary school.

The summer the three friends turned 13 and 14 years old, Stella and the twins decided to travel with Isabel and Eveley to Merida and Cancun for a shared vacation. They had so much fun on that trip, Stella talked about it for months after they returned to Ireland. She even talked of purchasing a vacation home there as she loved it so much.

Isabel continued to be a dedicated mother to Eveley after Pablo's disappearance. She never gave up on his case. She religiously stayed on top of any developments in the case. She started going less frequently to Kansas City as their life became busier and busier. Eveley could tell her mom's love for her dad never lessened, since she hadn't dated anyone since. Isabel always said she was too busy being a mother to Eveley and keeping her café running. Eveley thought her mom deserved to be happy and felt sad for her mom. She hoped someday she would find another love, even if it hurt to think of her father and all their memories as a family.

CHAPTER 9

WILDFLOWERS

Eveley's 17th Birthday

The summer of Eveley's 17th and Aidan's 18th, the O'Briens visited Dallas as usual. This time, it's as if something broke free. When Eveley saw Aidan she felt the craziest feeling in her stomach...intense butterflies. She grabbed her necklace as she observed him. She had a habit of always fidgeting with the necklace when she was nervous or anxious. Aidan seemed surprised she still wore it. Little did he know she treasured it above any other jewelry and wore it every day. It reminded her of Aidan and her dad since he'd made it into a necklace for her with the rock Aidan gave her.

That summer it seemed like more and more they would find little ways to tell each other they cared about each other as more than a friend. Sometimes they'd sneak away from the group of friends they were with to talk alone. Aidan was a gentleman, he'd always been, but he was especially considerate and genuinely interested in her hobbies and her life in Dallas. He seemed to miss his life in Dallas quite a bit, a place with so many of his friends and old memories.

Eileen noticed some of the mysterious signals between Aidan and Eveley. She thought nothing better than for her best friend to end up with her brother which since they were twins was also like her best friend. It amused her how her brother would look at Eveley, all goo-goo eyed. When she would mention it to

Eveley, Eveley would pretend Eileen was imagining things. She didn't get why they both acted all shy and drew things out so long. When she would try the same approach with her brother, he usually stayed quiet and didn't deny nor confirm what she observed. It sometimes drove her crazy their ability to hide things from each other and her. But she wasn't fooled, she knew they were going to end up together someday. What Eileen didn't know was something had changed that summer, and Aidan and Eveley were indeed keeping a secret.

The second week of the O'Briens being in Dallas, Eileen, Aidan, Eveley, and their group of neighborhood friends went to the mall to hang out. Chiquis had just gotten her driver's license and so Eileen, Eveley, Aidan, and Wheels rode in her car with her. Everyone made lighthearted jokes regarding her driving ability since it took her two times to pass the driving test.

"Hey Chiquis, you sure you can see over the steering wheel?!" Wheels said smirking as he got in the front passenger side. She made a face then stuck her tongue out at him.

"I think so," she finally replied.

"What about the pedals, can you reach?" Aidan piled on the teasing.

"I guess you'll have to hold on and find out," Chiquis said with a sly grin and took off, jerking all of them a bit and stalling the car. She had a manual transmission which wasn't common for a teen driver but they all thought it was cute the way she drove. First of all, she had extenders on her pedals, and a seat cushion to raise her seat. But the funniest part was the way she shifted gears. For the most part, her shifting was smooth once she could get past first gear. Her little hands furiously shifting combined with her facial expressions you'd think she was racing in Nascar, it was so aggressive-looking and funny to them.

"Hey hey, don't listen to these burros [dummies]!" Eveley said from the backseat.

"You take your time and the guys will shut up, let her concentrate," Eileen added as she glared at the boys.

"Ok ok, lo siento [I'm sorry], go ahead, but take your time," Wheels said to Chiquis.

Chiquis took a deep breath. She started the car back up and quickly got it into first gear, off to a great start. Of course the boys actually thought it was cool a girl could drive stick shift since it wasn't common but it was just playful teasing.

They met up with R.J., Julian, and Leo at the movies. The group of friends watched a scary movie, though it wasn't the girls' first choice. After the movies, they went to a local carnival and ate a well-balanced meal of corn dogs, funnel cakes, deep fried Oreos, and washed it all down with soda.

Toward the end of the night Eveley sensed Aidan wanted to tell her something. They snuck away from their group of friends and took a ride on the Ferris wheel together. The lights from the city skyline were captivating at the highest part of the wheel. It had been a muggy day, the breeze along with the slipstream from the ride's speed felt refreshingly cool on their skin. Eveley didn't say much, she simply rested her head on his shoulder and he welcomed the sweet gesture.

She had been on his mind nonstop since they had touched down in Dallas and she welcomed him at the airport. He was astonished by her beauty the moment he saw her. She had gone through a metamorphosis since the last summer he saw her, she no longer looked like the awkward and nerdy girl he remembered the year before. He had also changed quite a bit, he had grown several inches taller and gained muscle as he participated in several sports, soccer being the one he excelled at the most, then boxing. They were both growing and maturing like wildflowers in a field.

For some reason he no longer wanted to hide his feelings. He gently grabbed her hand, she didn't protest nor pull away.

"You know I've been waiting four years for you to do that," Eveley said softly. "But right now, happens to be the perfect time for you to finally hold my hand."

She raised her head and looked up at him. Her honey eyes glowed warmly and he felt mesmerized. He couldn't help but feel under a spell when she looked at him like that, like he was the only person in her world. His eyes were drawn to her full lips, he could smell sweet strawberries as he lowered his head and their lips met. It was small, sweet, and magnetic...the perfect first kiss.

They were hooked, the rest of the summer they were secretly holding hands, and sneaking kisses anytime they could. They would text late into the night, Aidan would send her poetry he wrote in Irish, and they made many promises to each other as their relationship intensified. There was something thrilling and sacred about keeping their relationship secret to others. Not because they were ashamed, but because they were slowly figuring out what it was like to finally express their feelings to each other. They were falling deeply into the wonder and beauty of first love.

CHAPTER 10

MEXICO

The last month they were in Dallas, the twins and Stella traveled with Isabel and Eveley to their rancho [small ranch] in Chihuahua, Mexico. Cesar inherited several properties from his family, he'd grown up on most of the properties at one time or another, as well as going back and forth between Texas and Chihuahua. He gifted Isabel one of the smaller properties he owned in Chihuahua as a wedding present when she married Pablo. Although Cesar called it small it was actually an expansive property of 50 acres, near the cerros [steep hills] that were everywhere in those parts. It was a beautiful rancho, Isabel's uncle and aunt took care of the property while she lived in the US and lived in the guesthouse on the property.

They often rented out the property to vacationers and honeymooners. The property backed onto a large river, the rest of the area was dotted by tall jagged cliffs and dry desert-like agaves and grasses. A big expansive field bent around the start of cerros behind the river. They owned horses and small farm animals, they owned neat rows of pecan trees and fruit trees. When they arrived they had just begun harvesting the fruits and nuts to sell commercially and to local businesses. The scents of apples, pecans, and sotol permeated the air.

When Eveley and Aidan stepped onto this property, it's as if a magical place opened up just for them. They spent two wonderful weeks there. They alternated between crazy days full of non-stop events and days out on the town, dancing late into the night, and lazy days on the property which was an oasis in and of itself. During those 2 weeks they attended several of Isabel's family events, they went to a wedding, a quinceañera, and a huge birthday party which became their most memorable event.

Aidan confessed he'd watched online videos to learn how to dance ahead of time, they'd danced all night at several events and everyone commented on how good he was for being his first time. Some of Eveley's cousins asked Eveley if he was her boyfriend, when she said no, they didn't believe her and gave her the "look".

Some of Eveley's tias [aunts] also mentioned to Isabel they thought there was something going on between Eveley and Aidan, but Isabel didn't think there was anything to discuss. She trusted Eveley was a good girl and if there was something going on, it was sweet and innocent.

Eileen also had a blast, with her super bubbly person- ality and up for anything attitude, by the end of the two weeks, she'd made tons of friends. They would all joke Eileen 'Mexicanized' the most as she bought herself some vaquera [cowboy] boots and a beautiful sombrero [cowboy hat] she would wear every time they'd go out to the plaza grande [main square]. Eileen fell in love with how easy it was to make new friends and her Spanish improved in those two weeks to the point she was saying some Spanish phrases by the end of the trip which amused everyone around her.

They spent a lot of their time outdoors, sometimes swim- ming in the river, sometimes riding horses through the prop- erty. They visited a few local markets with so many expertly hand-made artisan goods the O'Briens were impressed and bought several. And last but not least, every day they could count on drool-worthy food that made them wish they could eat this way the rest of their lives.

The entire time the fresh air was permeated by the fragrance of the big agave-like plants Eveley explained they sold to local distilleries for sotol making. It was a slightly floral and herbal scent. Some of the overripe apples on the ground were also fermenting, so it smelled like apple cider, fresh water from the river, and pecan wood mixed with the grassy brightness of the sotol.

On the night before their last day, Eveley and Aidan snuck out late at night after everyone was fast asleep. They quietly walked to the stables and slowly rode their horses further away toward the edge of the property, following the river. The reflection of the bright moon on the river's water was the only illumination. They sat by the rivers edge, talking, and looking up at the stars.

Eveley and Aidan were faced with the fact that they were going to be apart for a long time, at least till Christmas when the O'Briens would visit Stella's side of the family.

After they returned back to Dallas from Mexico, she couldn't help feeling anxious knowing Aidan would soon be thousands of miles away. When the final day came they were leaving for Ireland, Isabel and Eveley waved the O'Briens goodbye. Eveley couldn't help the tears, really everyone was teary-eyed or crying. It was always such a bittersweet goodbye.

Chapter 11

IRELAND

Over the fall and into the winter, Eveley and Aidan continued their relationship in secret. He'd often have to find time in between his soccer club, part-time job, school, and sneaking away from the prying eyes of Eileen. Eveley was also struggling to find time to keep in touch, she was now helping with the café on the weekends and after school when she didn't have too much homework. They were also in completely different time zones. Before they became a couple they mostly texted regularly in a group chat with Eileen. They would all respond when they could with the understanding they were thousands of miles apart and the response would take a while.

Occasionally they would video chat or communicate through social media. But now Eileen was starting to suspect something was up as the group chat became less and less frequent since they were having their own private conversations. Eileen became so suspicious she asked Aidan if he and Eveley were still cool or if they were mad at each other. They decided to start using the group chat with all three of them more often to placate her suspicions. It eventually worked because she stopped asking probing questions.

Toward the end of the year, as everyone's schedule became crazy, both Eveley and Aidan were taking longer to reply to their texts. It hurt Eveley so much because many times she just wanted to have Aidan in front of her and tell him everything she wanted to say instead of putting it into a long message or waiting till the next time they were both awake. She didn't know what was going to happen to their relationship even though she couldn't fathom not being with him.

Aidan was also going through increased pressure as it was his last year in high school before college. With his job, school, sports, and college admissions, his time was close to nil. He barely had time to eat and sleep, he was always tired, and even though he wanted to see Eveley and talk to her every day it wasn't possible. He felt awful and many times he expressed these thoughts to her. He didn't want to lose her, as she was everything he'd ever wanted in a girl. He was just hoping they could both hold out a little longer till they could find time to reconnect like before.

Many nights when he was overwhelmed with life, no matter what he had going on, he'd lay in his bed, put on his headphones and listen to their song. He would play back the summer when they made the promise of forever. As childish as it may have sounded to a stranger looking in, they both knew it deep down. He would replay the night they snuck out at the rancho in his head. How enchanting it felt to be next to Eveley under the full moon with the sounds of the river and aroma of fruit all around them. What he wouldn't give to be back there again, under the spell of her brown eyes, the warmth of her embrace, and the timid kisses they shared.

Before they knew it, the holidays were upon them. This year the O'Briens were having their family visit them in Ireland the first part of December so they weren't going to the US like they usually did. When Aidan told Eveley, Eveley broke into tears. She was looking forward to him coming to Dallas. She was even planning on telling her mom about their relationship so it wasn't a secret anymore.

Eveley was silent and depressed for a few days after, not re-sponding to Aidan's texts as quickly as usual to the point he asked her if everything was okay. She told him the truth, she was simply sad and didn't know how they were ever going to stop pinning for the days when they would see each other, it was taking a toll on her mentally. He panicked, he didn't want to lose her. That night he told everyone in his family including his mom Stella about their relationship, but asked them to please respect Eveley's wishes if she wanted her mom to know, but he needed to see her. Stella's reaction was happy, she considered Isabel one of her closest friends, she couldn't think of a nicer girl for Aidan than Eveley. She told him she'd be happy to invite them to Ireland, since they couldn't change their plans so late into the season due to work commitments.

The next day, Isabel told Eveley the news, the O'Briens had extended their invitation to come visit them during December in Ireland and she had accepted. Eveley was ecstatic, she texted Aidan right after asking him if he'd had anything to do with this. He replied yes, he needed to see her, he couldn't wait another six months. His words made her heart rejoice.

She was still unsure if she should tell her mom, she didn't want extra scrutiny by her mother who was very conservative about relationships but she also didn't want to feel like her mom was the only one in the dark. She planned to tell her when they were on the plane. Her gut told her that her mother wouldn't necessarily have any issue with their relationship as long as it was proper. Eveley feared an interrogation from her mother, she didn't have anything to hide, but still the thought of being placed on the spot made her anxious.

Two weeks later the day came for them to leave Dallas, Isabel decided she could only go for one week as she didn't want to leave the café to Magdalena for two weeks as it was a big responsibility. They took an early flight out of Dallas, headed for Dublin, Ireland. This was the longest flight they had ever taken, over 8.5 hours long. Eveley felt a bit nervous because she knew she promised she'd tell her mom about Aidan on this trip. Her mother was in a great mood, she'd always wanted to visit

Ireland so the weeks leading up to this trip she spoke often of the places she wanted to see in Ireland.

The O'Briens lived in Galway City, once they reached Dublin, the O'Briens would pick them up and drive the two hours to their home. They owned a beautiful home blocks from the sea. Jason worked near downtown for an architectural firm while Stella worked from home, she was a freelance writer and took time off for the month of December to welcome the Luna family and also for the holidays.

When Isabel and Eveley saw Stella, Aidan, and Eileen they all greeted with enthusiasm. Eveley hugged Eileen tightly, she hugged Aidan next, trying not to be too obvious. In the car they all sat in the back, Eveley purposely sat on the opposite side of Aidan with Eileen in the middle, the entire way to Galway, they all caught up on everything, they didn't stop talking and joking till they arrived to the house.

The O'Briens planned a few special things for them to do while they were there, they wanted to really show them their town and the surrounding area. Isabel was just grateful to have a great family like the O'Briens welcome them and show them around. They had been such good neighbors and friends since the kids were barely old enough to walk and she had missed them greatly.

When they arrived, Isabel and Eveley fell in love with the O'Brien home, they had a beautiful cottage style house, painted a moss green color with a navy blue door. Despite the cloudy weather, the O'Brien home was cheerful and charming with a large yard. It was flanked with stone hedges and bushes as well as being blocks from the ocean.

"I love your house Stella!" Isabel exclaimed when they stepped out of the car.

"Thank you! It's not bad eh?" Stella said as she walked around her car and started to open the front door.

"Jason will be here after he gets off work, he asked me to tell you guys sorry he couldn't take the time off to meet you guys."

"Oh no, we wouldn't expect him to do that," Isabel said as they followed Stella into the house.

"I was hoping you guys were up to go downtown to have dinner with us to celebrate your arrival. Unless you guys are tired, we can go tomorrow..."

"Oh no, we're fine, we would love to go!" Isabel looked at Eveley when she spoke and noticed her staring at Aidan, her mom senses went off.

Eveley looked quickly away and down to the ground.

Eveley and Isabel left their suitcases in the guest bedroom with two single beds, the windows overlooked the side of the house.

Eileen, Eveley, and Aidan walked down the street to the ocean's edge. The weather was cloudy, the air cool but not to the point of discomfort. Halfway through the walk, the sun peaked out from large clouds, bright sunbeams touched everything around them.

Eveley was already enchanted with this place. It was a wild beauty that seemed harsh and untameable, it attached itself to the soul, forever changing those entranced by it.

When they made it to the shoreline, they walked along slowly, climbing carefully on some of the large rocks lining the ocean's edge, the water a dark, cool blue. The ocean breeze tasted salty and it stung when it picked up speed but it also felt refreshing when it was calm. They picked a huge rock to sit on, where there was no risk of the water splashing on their feet.

"How did you guys get used to such a different place?" Eveley asked as she saw gray clouds in the distance.

"At first it was super hard, it's like the complete opposite of Dallas, but after a while I got used to it," Eileen said and shrugged her shoulders.

"Yeah it was harder to make friends here since everyone knew each other from childhood and we didn't know anyone, but now that we've settled in I'm cool with it," Aidan said. He grabbed a small rock and threw it into the dark blue water.

"I think this place seems beautiful, especially next to the ocean, you guys are so lucky, it seems like a page out of a storybook," Eveley added.

"Hmm...more like a scary book, especially when it gets misty—" Eileen said.

"Oh yeah, Eileen is scared of going outdoors after dark on misty days," Aidan interrupted Eileen.

"It's your fault!" Eileen pointed at Aidan and swatted his shoulder as Aidan playfully pulled away and lost his balance. They all laughed.

"What did you do Aidan?" Eveley knew Aidan was a bit of a prankster, especially with his sister who took the brunt of the pranks.

"All I did was tell her some myths and legends...you know, sea creatures walking through the night, looking for a victim to snatch their soul so their legs don't turn back into a tail and they become human to live among us," Aidan smiled mischievously.

"That's not all! *omg*! He freaking set me up the other night, of course after he told me a scary legend about these fairy creatures that pretend to be sweet and become your friend but then attach to you, follow you around, and whisper horrible things until they literally drive you crazy. Anyways, I was taking out the trash and he hid on the side of the house and jumped out, I about peed myself!" she said and punched Aidan lightly on the shoulder when he laughed at her exaggerated recall.

"So are there a lot of scary legends like in Mexico?" Eveley asked.

"So many," Eileen replied, clearly not amused. It was ironic that Eileen loved to watch scary movies but she hated stories that were too close to home so local legends were unnerving to her.

"There are a lot of interesting ones, all the things you'd think about in Ireland, like leprechauns, fairies, sea monsters, not all are cute stories, some of them are really interesting legends," Aidan replied.

"What's your favorite?" Eveley asked.

"The nun at the Long Walk," he replied.

"Oh no, I don't want to hear that one," Eileen said and grabbed on to Eveley's arm. Aidan proceeded to tell it anyway, the entire time both girls looked fascinated by the spooky story of the sighting of this nun who everyone in town knew about. In some stories she was just a regular nun, in another she haunted people late at night. Either way they had heard enough scary stories for one night. They decided to walk back after an hour of sitting by the ocean. Jason would be home soon and they would all head into town to have dinner.

Around 5:30 pm, Jason's car pulled into the driveway, everyone greeted him when he came into the house. Jason mentioned Eveley had grown so much, he hadn't seen Eveley nor Isabel in several years.

Since they were too many for one car, they decided to drive both cars, with Eveley, Eileen, and Aidan riding with Jason to keep him company. They drove about 15 minutes into downtown Galway. They met in front of a lively pub in the center of town.

When they entered the pub, the band on stage was already starting their set, patrons were singing along, the atmosphere was cheerful. The bar was dark, with string lights through out and several levels, the walls were lined with wood paneling, the arches and roof trusses and beams were arched with thick wood.

Everyone sat down and the adults ordered a few beers and appetizers for the table. The band began a rendition of "Molly Malone", and everyone in the pub sang along. Some of the patrons stood up, eventually everyone at the O'Brien's table sang along to the chorus, including Eveley and Isabel after they caught on to the lyrics of the chorus.

Isabel and Eveley loved the atmosphere, it was cheery and spirited, and the camaraderie was palpable. Several of the O'Brien's friends stopped by to chat. Stella and Jason introduced

Eveley and Isabel to several friends and regulars who were curious about the dark-haired strangers with them. When everyone found out Eveley and Isabel were visiting and they were Mexican-American they would ask if they'd been to Mexico. Then they would usually ask them if they liked Ireland so far.

Truth be told they were both in love already. Eveley saw a wild, haunting beauty as soon as she saw the landscapes, and the people...wow she thought, just like in Mexico, were friendly and fun to be around. They felt at home, and the vibes were positive and fun.

Stella and Jason eventually got out onto the dance floor. Stella reluctantly followed Jason but they seemed to have a great time, their smiles and laughter contagious. Even Isabel danced to a few songs after a local gentleman asked her, she was hesitant but the table cheered her on.

At the end of the night which was around 1 am, (not a typical bedtime for the twins but an exception due to Eveley and Isabel visiting) Eveley excused herself to go to the restroom. When she exited the restroom, she was on the 2nd level, she walked to the balcony overlooking the band playing and leaned against the railing. She thought the band was very talented and the song they were playing was beautiful. She couldn't see the O'Brien's table from her spot. The band was really putting their all into their song. The lights were dim on this level, it seemed like a warm and inviting spot away from everyone downstairs. She thought to herself how it would be nice to have Aidan there beside her sharing this moment. She felt a pair of warm arms embrace her from behind, it startled her but she realized it was Aidan by his familiar scent, a light cologne that smelled of leather and sandalwood.

"Dia dhuit a stoirin [Hello beautiful]," he whispered softly in her ear in Irish.

He wrapped his arms around hers and intertwined his fingers with hers, he nuzzled his chin in the bend of her neck. They stood embracing for a few minutes. She closed her eyes, feeling the warmth of his body relax her. She turned her head slightly and their lips met for a gentle kiss. She felt her body floating, until she remembered she hadn't told her mother about them yet. She told herself to tell her soon. Aidan noticed the change on her face.

"What's wrong?" he said as she turned to face him.

"I still haven't told my mom about us and I'm scared she won't approve," Eveley looked down at her feet.

Aidan paused for a second, "I think your mom will be happy for us, we are growing up, it's only natural we find a person to love, and who better than someone she knows pretty well...like me." His boyish smile brimmed with confidence, she found him endearing and at the same time she could see his point.

"You're probably right," Eveley said. At that moment the band ended playing the slow song and announced a new song, "Famous Ballymote".

Aidan grabbed her by the arm, "C'mon, let's dance!" he said with a playful smile.

Eveley was not one to turn down a dance though she wasn't sure how to dance to this.

"But I don't know how to dance to this!" she whined as he pulled her down the steps.

"Don't worry, I'll teach you!"

He planted a quick kiss on her lips as they joined several other couples on the dance floor. She observed the men and women in a contra line. She got the hang of it fairly quickly, before she knew it they were spinning around locked by the arm, bobbing up and down and doing footwork that looked like fancy skips. It was exhilarating and tiring, she couldn't help laughing throughout the entire dance, by the end she felt sweaty and ready for a glass of water but it'd been so fun.

"One more?" Aidan asked before she made a bee line for their table. She didn't want to disappoint him so they waited for the next song. After the second song, they stumbled off the dance floor, sweaty and exhausted. They finally made it to their table toward the back corner.

"We were wondering where you guys were!" Eileen said loudly.

"We got caught up by the band and decided to dance a bit," Aidan admitted.

Eveley looked at her mom's expression for signs of disapproval but there was no change in her demeanor.

"I'm glad you kids are enjoying yourselves," Isabel said after taking a sip of her Guinness. Eveley had never really seen her mom drink much other than the occasional beer at the carne asada which usually was more than enough for her so she was surprised she was on her second beer.

"The band is amazing tonight," Jason said as he took a sip of his beer as well.

"I agree, they are pretty good but tonight they are really getting the crowd going huh?" Stella said to Jason.

For the next couple of songs, the O'Briens and the Lunas enjoyed the revelry of the night without any clue a dark figure was near.

CHAPTER 12

PETRICHOR

Sitting in the pub, Eveley felt a sudden heaviness in the pit of her stomach, she wasn't sure if she was nauseous or if she was overheated.

"Ma, can I step outside for some fresh air?"

"Sure, are you okay? Want me to come with you?" Isabel asked with concern in her voice.

"No, not at all, Aidan can join me...right?" She locked eyes with him.

"I can come too, three's no crowd!" Eileen chimed loudly and cheerfully, she stood up, Eveley and Aidan followed.

"What a peculiar thing to say wee girl," Stella said toward Eileen while giving her a motherly look.

"We'll be right back," Aidan said.

They stepped out into the chilly air, the perspiration and steam visible on their faces.

Eveley took a deep breath, "That feels so much better." She pulled some stray hairs off her face.

They walked further away from the pub door down the sidewalk until they reached the corner where the road intersected. Eveley looked down and found a cat by her side.

"Oh here kitty kitty," both Eileen and Eveley kneeled down and pet the little tabby. They heard loud voices in the background and the cat got spooked and ran away into the night turning the corner swiftly. Without thinking Eveley turned the corner to see where the tabby went and bumped hard into a boy of about her same age. She looked up at his hard fixed scowl. A look of pure hatred from his cool blue eyes chilled her to the bone. Yet she didn't flinch or look away, the hairs on her skin stood on end.

He was tall and imposing, dressed in all black, which matched his jet black hair. He was with three other boys about the same age.

Aidan who was still near the pub entrance tying his shoe, ran to where the girls stood when the boys started smirking and making vulgar gestures toward Eileen and Eveley.

"Watch where you're going eejit!" one of the boys shouted near Eveley's ear.

Aidan stepped in front of the girls.

"Watch your mouth before I knock your effin' teeth out!" Aidan said so ferociously the boy flinched back. It was a bit satisfying to Eveley to see him scared. Eveley had never seen Aidan so angry. He pushed both the girls back.

Eveley felt something on her lip, she licked her lips and realized it was blood from the metallic taste. She covered her nose and mouth with her hands.

"Darn it, I'm bleeding," she said as she looked down at her blood covered hands.

Aidan looked back at her, her nose was dripping with blood, staining her shirt.

The black-haired boy that scared her stepped forward in front of his friends. Eveley grabbed Aidan's hand and Eileen grabbed his shoulder.

"Aidan let's just go inside," Eileen said.

At the sound of his name the boys grinned.

"Aidan huh? You have quite a reputation." said the shortest boy with severely crooked teeth.

The black-haired boy who gave Eveley the heebie-jeebies, stared at Aidan in contempt. He stood proudly, with his head high, and chest puffed out.

"I heard you think you're the big shite around here." He spit on the ground in front of him.

"Go back inside please," Aidan said to Eileen and Eveley as he knew where this was headed.

Aidan did indeed have a reputation in his neighborhood, not a bad one by any means. He'd gotten into a few fights with several boys at the beginning that tried to bully his sister and him, especially when they found out they were from the US.

Aidan wasn't into starting fights, he was easy-going and got along with everyone. But one thing he didn't do is cower away from bullies trying to do harm to those he loved. The climactic fight and the one that gave him his reputation was when he went ballistic one day when Eileen was harassed. He came outside to Eileen in tears, screaming for help because a neighborhood bully had been harassing her as she walked their small dog. The final straw was when the boy came up to her and pulled on her skirt to scare her. Aidan ran out and as soon as he saw the boy, he ran up to him and knocked him out in one punch. The boy had to be picked off the ground by his equally cowardly friends who bullied many of the quieter teenagers that lived in the neighborhood. Word of mouth traveled fast and he made many friends due to standing up to those punks. After that knockout none of the bullies so much as looked his or Eileen's way.

"Please go inside," Aidan said to the girls.

He was not scared for himself, he just wanted Eileen and Eveley safe. It was too late for him to back out now, turning his back on a bully to walk away was a big no-no as they would often sucker punch their victims.

Eveley wouldn't leave, all of a sudden the scared feeling disappeared. She wasn't going to let a bunch of jerks hurt Aidan, even if he could hold his own.

"Leave us alone!" Eileen yelled at them as she backed up. Suddenly one of the boys, an ash-blonde boy with green eyes, jumped toward her and barely managed to grab her coat's arm and pull on it. Aidan stepped in and connected a right hook to his face. He stumbled against the wall of the building and slid down like a caricature, clearly dazed and confused.

The remaining two boys went into a frenzy. One yelling pacing back and forth, while the other made a show of taking off his jacket and ripping his shirt in half. It was a chilly night so his body turned red, which seemed funny to Aidan and made him chuckle.

He'd already sized them up and knew they weren't a threat, even two against one. The one that worried him was the black-haired boy with the icy blue eyes. He stood motionless, his demeanor serious, his gaze menacing. Aidan could tell he had some fighting experience.

Suddenly one of the boys ran full charge at him, Aidan met him with a punch and he stumbled to his knees and couldn't get back up. The much taller black-haired boy didn't help. He just moved to the side and leaned against the building, all the while making eye contact with Eveley. He propped his foot behind him against the stone wall and looked unbothered by the knockouts of his friends.

The first boy that was knocked out was now moaning and trying to stand up, pulling up on the stone wall of the building. The black-haired boy pushed him down brusquely and told him to stay down. The other boy, a boy with light brown hair and hazel eyes, yelled and came at Aidan, huffing and puffing. Eileen and Eveley were still behind Aidan.

All off a sudden the boy picked up a bike sitting on the side of the street while yelling like a maniac and threw it toward them which didn't end up hitting anyone. He ran toward Aidan and instead of going for his torso he went for Aidan's legs. While he was trying to pick up Aidan by the legs unsuccessfully, Aidan landed some punches to his sides.

The girls looked at each other knowingly, "Leave him alone!" Eileen yelled and ran and Eveley followed.

Eileen jumped on the boy's back and started pulling on his neck, while Aidan was trying to get her off so she wouldn't get hurt. Meanwhile Eveley kicked him from behind, and the boy keeled over in pain. At that moment the black-haired boy jumped from his spot and grabbed Eveley from behind. She furiously tried to push his hands away but he was too strong. He buried his face near her neck, breathing her scent in and making her uncomfortable.

"You smell like wet dirt," he said so close she could feel his lips brush her skin lightly.

Aidan pushed Eileen behind him.

"Let her go!" Aidan yelled as he saw Eveley struggle. Eveley felt something sharp poking her side, it was a knife and her insides went cold. She grimaced as she felt the tip of the knife dig into her skin. Aidan saw the knife too and knew he needed to do something quick as this had spiraled out of control.

Without warning, Eveley kicked back, right in the boy's groin and the boy released her. He keeled over with the knife still in his hand. Eveley ran to Eileen behind Aidan and hugged her.

"Go inside now! Call Gardai!" Aidan said, the girls both ran inside.

The boy started laughing as he stumbled up to standing again. He still held the knife in his hand. Blood dripped from the tip of the knife...Eveley's blood. The boy stumbled, then put the tip of the knife in his mouth, sliding it out slowly.

"Mmm, I see why you like her, she tastes like smoke and fire."

"You're sick," Aidan said.

The boy walked toward Aidan with the knife in a fight stance. He swung the knife, barely missing Aidan's chest as Aidan jumped back.

Aidan took a step forward and his right hook connected to the side of the boy's face, knocking him out cold, the knife falling out of his hand. Aidan grabbed the knife, closed it, and put it in his pocket. He walked back into the pub as his parents were rushing toward the front door, Eileen and Eveley in tears.

"Aidan! What happened?!" Jason asked.

"A few punks attacked me and the girls," Aidan said.

"I called Gardai!" Stella said as she hugged him and looked him over.

"Did they hurt any of you?!" Stella asked as she looked over the girls again.

Eveley looked at Aidan and shook her head at him to signal not to say anything. She feared if her mother knew she'd been hurt, she'd decide to go back home. She wasn't going to let some scumbag ruin the time she had left with Aidan.

They all walked outside, the only boy left there was the black-haired boy. He was at the end of the street near the corner and as soon as he saw Aidan he pointed at him.

"This isn't over!" he shouted.

"Hey! Get over here punk!" Jason yelled but the boy had already turned the corner.

Five minutes later Gardai showed up and they made a report. Other than the nose bleed, Eveley had not mentioned the knife. Neither had Eileen though she wanted to, but Eveley had whispered to her not to say anything. Plus she also knew it wouldn't make any difference in the outcome.

Eveley grabbed her side to stop the bleeding. When they arrived home, she went to the bathroom and took her blood covered shirt off. There was a one inch cut on her torso where the boy stuck the tip of the knife, it was not deep but it still hurt. She couldn't help feeling a chill through her body when she thought of his menacing eyes. Like a predator waiting for its prey, he was dangerous and he'd just proved it.

Later when she went downstairs, she found Aidan in the back garden, sitting on the steps, his face in his hands, his demeanor serious and gloomy. She sat next to him and touched his thigh.

"Hey, are you okay?" she asked as he lifted his face.

"I'm sorry," he said with a look of shame on his face.

"Sorry for what?" Eveley was confused.

"About tonight, I should have protected you and Eileen. Instead I placed you girls in danger and allowed this to happen." He pointed to her side.

"Tonight wasn't your fault, if anything you kept us from harm, thank you."

She looked at him tenderly and pushed a strand of his wavy hair away from his face. They heard footsteps and she turned to find her mother staring at them. Isabel had a look of disapproval and surprise on her face.

"Eveley, I need to talk to you, could you come to the room?" Isabel looked serious.

Eveley felt her stomach drop, it was the inevitable, they just couldn't hide their feelings from the watchful eyes of her mother. She didn't want to anymore, after tonight, she could care less if the whole world knew. Eveley followed her mother in silence to the bedroom. As soon as she shut the door, she sat on the bed, her mother sat on the opposite bed facing her.

"Now I need you to be honest with me...what's going on with you and Aidan?" Isabel waited for a response.

Eveley decided to just say whatever came to her mind first, "I love him...and he loves me."

Isabel seemed to be searching for words.

"How long have you guys been doing *this*?" Isabel said clearly upset.

"Since this summer."

"And you didn't tell me?!" Isabel said, clearly offended.

"Ma, it's not like we planned it, he was my friend until he wasn't anymore...you've always known I liked him."

Isabel stumbled, "Well, yeah, but..."

"So it shouldn't surprise you."

Isabel shook her head, "Mi niña, como has crecido [My little girl, how you have grown]."

"Lo conoces ma [You know him mom], you know he's perfect for me."

Isabel grinned, "Okay, pero no mas secretos [but no more secrets], got it?" she said sternly, Eveley nodded.

Isabel hugged her and kissed her forehead. Eveley thought this wasn't so bad, it had gone better than she had imagined it would go.

"Now you know I'm going to have to speak to Stella if I'm leaving after a week. I would like for us to be on the same page."

"Ma! Please don't make it awkward."

"Awkward? The conversation is going to happen, just consider yourself lucky you don't have to be present."

Eveley sighed.

"What are you worried about ma?"

"You know, I see how you guys look at each other. I was a teenager once...I know how teenage hormones and temptation work."

Eveley looked down at her feet as she felt her cheeks flush red. They heard a knock on the door.

"Isabel, it's Stella, are you busy?" Stella said softly.

Isabel opened the door, Stella was already in her pj's, a comfy looking tunic over baggy pants.

"Oh, Eveley you're here too, even better...I just wanted to say sorry for what happened back there." Stella's wild red hair bounced softly around her. She usually kept her hair back into a tidy ponytail or straightened, so it was different to see her with her hair down.

Isabel gave Stella a quick hug.

"No worries, you can't control what others do. I want to thank Aidan for keeping the girls safe in such a scary situation."

"Yes, unfortunately Aidan is sort of a target right now for standing up to a bully in our neighborhood a few months back. Aidan told me when the boys heard his name, they knew exactly who he was and they wanted to fight him even more," Stella said.

"That's so scary, I don't know why, but in every place there's always gotta be someone who tries to start trouble with others," Isabel said remembering when she was growing up and the bullies she encountered.

"Yes, but here it has gotten a bit out of sorts now with this incident. I told Aidan from now on he will need to drive to school. Eileen and Eveley will need to be with someone at all times." Eileen walked through the door to Stella and grabbed her arm and laid her head on her mother's shoulder.

"Mum since I'm in charge of walking the dog, does that mean I have to take Aidan with me?"

Stella shook her head.

"Eileen I don't want you to risk it, I'll walk the dog. I don't want you walking through the neighborhood for a while until we find out who the boys were from tonight."

"Okay mum." Eileen looked tired, she came over to Eveley, gave her a hug then Isabel.

"Well I'm tired, I'm going to bed, good night" Eileen said.

"Goodnight," everyone replied.

"It's late, we can talk some more tomorrow," Stella said as she looked at her watch.

"Oh yes, it's definitely late," Isabel noted.

"Ma I'm going to the bathroom," Eveley said as she walked out.

"Okay mija," Isabel replied.

Eveley walked down the hallway toward the bathroom, Aidan was just making his way up the stairs when she made it in front of the stairs.

"Hey, I'm about to go to bed...I told my mom about us," Eveley said.

Aidan raised his eyebrows, he made it up to her, and grabbed her hands softly with both hands. He seemed melancholy still, something was on his mind and she didn't know what.

"Really? What did she say?"

"You were right, she was a bit upset I hadn't told her but it wasn't as bad as I imagined."

"That's good, see?" he said and a slight grin grew on his face. He paused and looked down at her hands.

"Well, we'd both better get to bed, it's been a long night."

"Yeah," she paused, she gave him a quick kiss on the cheek, she turned to go to bathroom and Aidan pulled her hand.

"Eveley?"

"Yes?"

"Please be careful, make sure your windows are locked in your room."

"I will," she thought it was him being overprotective but she felt a dark shadow over her since her interaction with the black-haired boy. Every time she thought of him, and she tried very hard not to, her body would break out into a sweat and her heartbeat would speed up. Before she knew it she would need to distract her thoughts with other things as she started feeling paralyzed with fear.

That night she had a terrible nightmare, one in which she was transported to a dark alleyway, with a dead end behind her. She walked briskly, it was freezing cold. She could see her breath in front of her in pillowy clouds as she wrapped her arms around herself. For some reason she was in a light white robe, it was so light she could feel the chilly air right through it, and she didn't have shoes. She shivered and wrapped her arms around herself tighter as she tried to find anything familiar about the place. At the end of the alleyway, a dim light turned on, a dark figure stood still, she knew who it was... the black-haired boy with the piercing blue eyes. His breath was hot as the billowy clouds appeared all around him. She couldn't see his face in the dim light but she knew instinctively it was him and he was a predator. She stopped in her tracks, she was trapped. She thought for a second this must be a dream. She closed her eyes and wished to wake up. The hair stood on the back of her neck as she felt warm air on her skin...his breathing. Somehow he was behind her now. His arms embraced her, not in a loving way, but the way a lion might dig its claws into a gazelle and keep it down. His embrace was forceful and he squeezed her tightly, making her lose her breath.

"Don't be afraid, I won't hurt you," his words slithered out of his mouth with an underlying glee, as if he was ecstatic to have caught her. His prey drive for her disgusted her. He smelled peculiar...like dirt, blood, grass, and smoke rolled into one. It caught her off guard because it wasn't unpleasant and she'd never smelled anything like it.

"Let me go or I'll scream," she said firmly, not allowing the fear gripping her insides to come through her voice.

"There's no one here to help you."

His claws dug into the skin on her arms, deep into her arms. The tracks of blood slid down her skin. Instantly nauseous and dizzy, she tried her hardest to stay conscious but her eyelids closed slowly.

Eveley woke breathing hard and drenched in sweat. It was still dark out and her clock said 4 am. She sat up on the side of her bed in the dark. Only a slight sliver of the moonlight through her curtain touched her face and body. She took the water bottle on her bedside table and finished the entire bottle. She still felt spooked and tried to collect her thoughts.

She heard a crunching noise right outside her window. She stood quietly and walked to her window, opened the curtain a sliver and peeked out. Below her she saw a dark figure, it was very dark so she couldn't make out anything, but it was definitely a person. The figure leaped away at lightning speed, almost like an animal. Eveley rubbed her eyes, was she still dreaming? She wasn't sure of what she saw. She stood there for a few minutes to make sure the person didn't return, her eyes eventually adjusting to the dark.

"Eveley? What are you doing mija?" Isabel said as she lifted her head up and supported herself on her elbows, she turned on her lamp.

"I thought I heard a noise and saw someone outside."

"Are you sure?"

"Well no, I just had a nightmare. I guess I'm just feeling a bit paranoid right now."

"C'mon mija, come back to bed, it's only 4 am, try to get some sleep. Check the window is locked, I checked before I got into bed but check again."

"Okay ma." Eveley checked the window which was locked. She got back in bed and tried to fall asleep unsuccessfully for a long time before her fatigue finally won out and she fell asleep.

CHAPTER 13

BRUISES

The next day Stella and Isabel decided to go into town to do some shopping. Aidan had a surprise for Eveley, and asked permission to drive Eveley and Eileen with him to see the Cliffs of Moher. They drove for over 1.5 hours from their house into County Clare, a beautiful, peaceful drive.

It was a bit drizzly that day so everyone made sure to bring their raincoat.

Eveley felt at peace, she had her two best friends with her and the slow drizzle made the drive relaxing. She wondered how people could ever leave such a special place. She knew every time she would visit Mexico she had a hard time leaving and always went through culture shock and withdrawals upon her return to Dallas.

As soon as they arrived they started their hike, it was pretty early, they made it before anyone else was there. It was barely sunrise when they were already halfway through the hike.

Aidan had never taken a girl here, he'd only been there once with his family. When they first moved from Dallas to Ireland as a kid. He remembered it amplified the sadness he felt from leaving his home. Since then he'd never felt the inkling to return but now that Eveley was here, it was the first place he wanted to show her. He brought his drawing notebook and pencils, he wanted to draw while he was up there. They made it up to the cliffs and he saw Eveley's face light up when she saw the view before her.

"Wow, I could've never imagined a place like this, it's amazing," Eveley marveled.

Jagged cliffs rose out of the choppy blue waters over 700 feet tall. The uneven walls of the cliffs were dotted with green moss and striations of brown and silver through the majestic rocks. Light fog was now rising past the highest point of the cliffs barely touching them like a mysterious canopy. They felt like they were the only ones on top of this little piece of paradise looking into the misty sky with the sun rays filtering through.

Eileen laid out a waterproof blanket and sat next to Eveley, and Eveley next to Aidan. They continued to talk as Aidan drew in his notebook. After a while his drawing took shape. He'd improved quite a bit since elementary school, making it a goal to draw something, anything, no matter how small each day. This discipline had paid off as his skills improved vastly and he had won several illustration contests over the years.

It was a bit cold, so they only ended up staying for an hour. They brought thermos with hot tea and coffee plus hand warmers so they stayed pretty warm but they were starting to feel hungry and the hordes of tourists would be there soon. Having seen the cliffs in all their glory without the tourists around was special enough.

Afterward, they made it to the quaint town of Doolin, it was a short drive from the Cliffs. They found a homey café and ate a filling breakfast. After breakfast, they stopped at stores along the main road. They found a small bookstore full of vintage books, artwork depicting life in Ireland at an art gallery, a music shop selling traditional Irish instruments, and a small jewelry store.

Aidan placed something in her hand after they left the store. It was a small ring, made up of a heart made of green stone, with a crown and hands.

"It's a Claddagh ring, ladies wear it in Ireland to signal their relationship status. Since we're together you would wear it on your right hand with the crown facing toward you, that means you're in a relationship. The stone is Connemara, you can only find it here in Ireland, I thought you'd like it."

Eveley placed it on her right hand in the direction Aidan told her. She hugged him and placed a kiss on his lips, "I love it, thank you."

He also bought Eileen a set of emerald and silver earrings she gushed over in the small jewelry store. She was ecstatic when he gave them to her.

It was almost evening when they made their way back toward Galway. Stella and Isabel had checked on them through out their trip. By the time they made it near dinner time, they were tired.

They entered the front of the house, taking off their jackets and scarfs. Eveley took off her outer cardigan, she wore a short sleeve t-shirt underneath and when she removed her cardigan, Aidan grabbed her gently and turned her body toward him.

"What happened to you here?" he asked.

Eveley was confused, she tried to look in the direction he was signaling but it was out of her sight.

"What do you mean?"

"Look in the mirror."

Eveley turned her body slightly and looked in the mirror right by the front door, she gasped. There were black and blue bruises in the shapes of five fingerprints on the back of her arms, along with five bright red bloody spots, why hadn't she noticed this? she thought.

"I don't know how I did this...I didn't hit myself, maybe...the dream, but how?" she whispered the last part to herself but Aidan heard her. The look of panic in her eyes took Aidan by surprise.

"What dream?" Aidan asked.

"Sorry, I need to change." She pulled away from Aidan and practically ran upstairs.

Stella came into the hall. "Where's Eveley? I thought I heard her."

"She had to use the bathroom really bad," Aidan lied.

Isabel waved from the enclosed green room with fireplace, he waved back.

"I'm going to go change my shirt, I'll be down in a bit," he said and ran upstairs. Aidan walked down the hall to Eveley's room and stood in front of the door.

Inside Eveley wiped off as much blood as she could with wet tissue. Surprisingly, the bruising didn't hurt which is why she didn't notice it. Her mind was racing one-hundred miles a minute, she couldn't explain how this happened. And the shadow of the man she saw last night? Could it have been the boy back at the pub? She didn't know what to think.

"Eveley? Are you okay?" Aidan knocked softly on her door.

She threw the tissue in the trash and quickly put on her cardigan to cover the bruising. She opened the door and tried her hardest to act normal like nothing happened.

"Hey, yeah I'm okay, just changing."

Aidan grabbed her hands, "You don't have to act brave around me, I know what just happened downstairs scared you, did someone hurt you?"

"I don't know Aidan," she looked down, unable to put her words together.

She whispered, "Last night I had a horrible nightmare, in which the boy from the pub attacked me. He squeezed me so tight that he was digging his fingers in my arms and made me bleed. I woke up and heard a noise by my window and thought I saw someone running from my window away from the house but I don't know if I was imagining things or I was half asleep."

"Are you sure you didn't do this to yourself during the dream? Like you were squeezing your fingers into your arms during the dream?"

"I mean it's possible, that's the most logical explanation."

Aidan could see there was doubt in her face.

"Don't worry babe, I'm not going to let anyone hurt you. I'm going to keep watch tonight and every night after this. If someone is sneaking around the house, they're going to wish they hadn't." Aidan hugged her.

She felt silly, maybe she did grab her arms during the dream, causing the bruising. She still felt dread in the pit of her stomach but Aidan always made her feel protected and safe. For a moment she let her worries melt away and let herself relax in the warmth of his embrace.

"Thank you," she whispered.

The next couple of days flew by quickly. They went to several Christmas markets, attended one of Aidan's soccer games to cheer him on, and went to the movies. Regardless of the activity, Eveley had the feeling that she was being followed and observed. She told Aidan who was protective of her when they were out, and eventually, the feeling dissipated.

The day of Isabel's departure back to Dallas, Eveley mustered the courage to ask her mom about the night of her dad's disappearance. She was helping her mom look for an earring she misplaced, Eveley found it in a corner under the bed.

"Did dad give you these?" Eveley asked as she handed the earring to Isabel and sat on the bed across from her.

Isabel looked taken by surprise with the question.

"Uh yeah, when we were dating," Isabel said and looked down at the earrings.

"You still love dad a lot don't you ma?"

Isabel looked down and for a moment she didn't say anything.

"Yes mija, he was the love of my life."

"Ma, I've always wanted to ask you...are the things I remember from growing up in Dallas true? When dad disappeared?"

"I don't know mija, what do you remember?" Isabel asked hesitantly.

"I just remember something stalking us, a dark figure, a monster that was chasing all of us and wouldn't go away."

At those words, Isabel looked away, she'd struck a sensitive nerve.

"Yes mija, there was a monster, but your pa took care of it to protect us." Tears were now falling down her face.

"Ma I'm sorry, I didn't mean to make you cry. I just needed to know I wasn't imagining everything." Eveley moved next to Isabel and hugged her.

"It's okay mija, because of your dad we're both safe today."

Eveley nodded in agreement.

Later that day, everyone except Jason who had to work, joined Isabel to send her off and say their goodbyes at the airport. Eveley felt some relief she'd finally confirmed what she'd doubted all along. She couldn't admire her mother more than she already did. She'd been so brave to continue ahead after losing the love of her life.

She still missed her father, it was like a wound that never really healed. It ached like a burn at times and other times the pain dulled when she was living happy moments. But always in the back of her mind she felt a tinge of guilt and at the same time she wished she could share happy moments with him. The happy moments in her life were therefore always bittersweet. What she wouldn't do to see his face and hold his hand again, like in her childhood memories of him.

CHAPTER 14

POWER TO CONSUME

The day after Eveley's mother left for Dallas, the O'Brien family went out to do some last minute Christmas shopping. They picked a Christmas market in Dublin since they were usually very fun and festive. When they arrived to the market, they were greeted by a large stone arch with pine trees decorated in bright red and silver baubles. There was classical Christmas music playing all around them as they walked in. Once past the arch they were in a large rectangle courtyard with long rows of small wooden stands with string lights. The small stands displayed a variety of crafts, from ornaments made out of wood and glass, to jewelry, and clothing. The buildings surrounding the square were decorated with large red velvet drapes and large garlands on the windows for a festive touch. There was a merry-go-round in the center of the square carrying children on dragons decorated with garlands of red and green. The air smelled of fresh brewed coffee, mulled wine, butter, cinnamon, and bread. There was a band playing merry Christmas melodies under an open tent. The whole family strolled through the market together until the teens decided to split away and meet Stella and Jason an hour later. The market was especially full since it was nearer Christmas day and it was a weekend.

"Hey Eveley! Look!" Eileen exclaimed happily, she was full of joy especially since she'd told everyone she had a boyfriend. Apparently, Eileen kept secrets of her own and had been talking to a boy she met when they were in Mexico. A long distance romance developed over time and now they were official. Eveley and Eileen spent late nights doing what typical teenagers did...talk. When Eileen finally spilled the beans about her new boyfriend, it opened up a whole new conversation that could go on for a while between the girls. Eveley vaguely knew the boy, he was a cousin of a family friend that was invited to the quinceañera (15th Birthday party) they attended while they were down there. She couldn't believe Eileen kept this secret for so long. She knew the boy was a year older than Eileen, his family a prominent family in town. He was a nice guy as far as she knew, they'd only interacted a few times in the past and he'd always been easy going and fun to talk to, she was happy for Eileen.

Eileen was trying to get their attention after she saw the hot beverage stand. They bought some mulled wine, it was tradition after all as it helped to keep warm during the chilly weather. Despite the crowd, they took their time stopping here and there, browsing through all the different stands. So much caught their eyes, they didn't know what to buy, eventually each one of them bought a tree ornament each.

They were making their way back when snowflakes descended upon them. They all looked up in awe, including Eveley. Snow was rare for Dublin she'd been told, so she wasn't expecting it. She reached out and felt the cold flakes land on her fingertips. She looked back to say something to Aidan and Eileen and they were gone. She looked in front of her and she didn't see them either. She started calling their names, she wasn't sure if she made a wrong turn or they didn't notice she stopped walking. She made her way through the crowd, turning corner after corner, trying to find them. She figured she would run into one of them sooner or later. She kept getting the sensation she was being watched but didn't know by whom. She looked around her and didn't see anyone she recognized. She turned the corner and slammed into *him*, she jumped back in terror ...it was the black-haired boy.

"Get away from me!" she yelled as she backed up, bumping into a few people who gave her looks like she was a madwoman. He was grinning, standing so triumphantly. She realized the sensation she felt was him watching her. She turned around and ran away 30 feet before she bumped into Aidan.

"Eveley! Where did you go? We were looking all over for you. We turned around and you weren't there. Literally one second you were here then you were gone."

"I, I don't know, but look," she pointed in the direction of the boy, he was gone.

"What am I looking for?" Aidan said perplexed.

Eveley was drenched in sweat and zoned out. "It was the boy, he followed me here, I just bumped into him!" she shouted.

Aidan walked in front of her and looked to either side of where she pointed. He didn't see anyone, but he wasn't going to take any chances.

"Okay, grab on to me and don't let go, keep your eyes open, Eileen!" He called out loudly.

Eileen was a few steps in from of them.

"Oh my gosh, where the heck did you go?!" Eileen exclaimed as she came back to them.

"Eileen, the boy at the pub followed Eveley, be on alert and grab on to me."

Eileen hooked her arm around Aidan's, she started feeling dread. She hated the boy with a passion.

They almost made it back to where Stella and Jason were when Aidan made a turn and was suddenly face to face with *him*. Now Aidan was 100% sure this boy was obsessed with Eveley. They were less than a quarter mile from where they were meeting up with their parents. He pushed the girls behind him. He whispered in Eileen's ear.

"When I start running, you grab Eveley and you run toward our parents, don't stop."

Eileen looked terrified when she saw how deranged the boy looked...like a rabid animal. He was breathing hard, his hair was wild and his eyes carried a peculiar look. She couldn't figure it out at first but then she realized what is was...crazed obsession. She looked over at Eveley and she looked frozen in fear.

She whispered in Eveley's ear, "Aidan says he we need to run when he starts running, we're not going to stop for anything and don't let go of me."

Eileen grabbed Eveley's hand tightly, she was not responding. Eveley had tunnel vision, she only looked at the boy, as if she couldn't move.

"Eveley! Snap out of it girl!" she whispered to her frantically.

Aidan took off running with all his might, the boy turned around and ran off. Aidan and the boy went to the right, the girls kept running forward toward Stella and Jason. Aidan saw as the boy kept moving and swerving to the side past people. The more Aidan tried to catch up to him the further away he seemed. Aidan saw the crowds of people become more sparse, the spaces between people widening. Finally when he felt like he was almost caught up to him, the black-haired boy ran right into Gardai. Aidan stopped running immediately and walked up to them.

"Officer, this kid has been harassing me, my sister and girlfriend."

"Punk, you're the same age as me!" the boy yelled.

"What's wrong with you eh? You on something? Why are you running through all these people?" One of the officers asked, clearly not amused with the boy.

"I actually have a report of him assaulting me with a bunch of his friends a week ago. He was gone by the time you guys made it to take the report, and now he's been stalking my girlfriend."

"Is that right?" The other officer said as he kept hold of the boy's arm who seemed ready to run at any minute.

"Let me see you ID," one of them ordered.

The boy looked at Aidan with a seething look in his eyes as he grabbed his wallet and gave them his ID.

"Well we're going to give you his information and you can add it to the report now that you've found him. As for you, we're going to escort you off the premises. We don't want to see you back near... what'd you say your name was?" The officer directed his question at Aidan.

"Aidan."

"Right, and his girlfriend or his sister, find your own girl-friend," the officer said sarcastically.

He wrote down the info from the boy's ID on a business card and handed it to Aidan.

"Here you go, C'mon let's go." Both officers pulled him away from Aidan.

Aidan looked down at the card, it read:

Draven O'Connor

DOB: 10/31/1997

He finally found who this guy was, and he would let his parents know so they could press charges. He ran and found his mother and father consoling Eileen and Eveley.

"What happened Aidan?" his father asked.

"The boy from the pub showed up, he was stalking us. Here, I got lucky and he bumped into Gardaí when I was chasing him away." Aidan handed Jason the card with the boy's info.

"Goodness, I was so worried, lemme see?" Stella asked as she peeked over at the card Aidan handed Jason.

"Oh! That's what we needed to get those boys charged. Especially now, this has gotten out of control!" Stella looked livid, especially after the girls arrived scared.

"We are going to the station tomorrow and taking care of this," Jason promised.

"Let's go kids, it's getting late," Jason continued.

Aidan hugged both his sister and Eveley. He sensed something off about Eveley, like she was not herself. She was acting quiet and reserved since she saw Draven. She didn't even say much when Aidan hugged her, she was cold and distant and he didn't know why. Maybe she was still scared from the encounter or maybe she was angry at him he thought. When they were in the car, he placed his arm around her shoulder and whispered in her ear.

"Are you okay querida [darling]?"

She didn't respond, she looked blankly down at her feet.

Eileen noticed and whispered in Aidan's ear.

"She's been off since she saw the boy. I'm scared Aidan, maybe he placed a spell on her?"

He looked at his sister with a burrowed brow and Eileen shrugged. He grabbed Eveley's hand and she finally looked at him, blankly at first. Then a glimpse of recognition and her whole expression changed.

"Aidan!" she hugged him as if she hadn't seen him in ages.

"Whoa, were you in a trance?" Aidan said clearly puzzled with her behavior.

"W-what? What do you mean?" Eveley stuttered.

"It's as if you weren't here, we've been trying to talk to you and you ignored us," Eileen said.

At those words Eveley looked around confused and stuttered again.

"I, I don't know, I guess I was just frozen by fear and I don't know what happened."

Tears started falling down her cheeks.

Aidan felt bad he'd made her cry although it wasn't his intention.

"Hey hey, it's okay, you're safe now. I was just wondering because we were worried. It's okay, we found him. Gardai took his info for us, we know who he is, he's going to be in trouble now for the attack at the pub," Aidan assured her.

"Who is he?" Eveley asked wiping away her tears.

"His name is Draven O'Connor, I've never heard of him before," Aidan said.

"Draven?" Eveley said, just saying his name felt wrong.

In reality she knew exactly what happened to her, it was beyond terrifying. When she was in Draven's presence, he placed her in a trance. A tool to hold her helpless in order to get close to her. She wasn't sure why he was stalking her, she felt dread every time he was near.

When they arrived home Eveley felt fatigued and excused herself right away. Aidan was visibly worried, she was still unlike herself though she'd snapped out of whatever trance she was in.

She got in bed and fell asleep within seconds. In her sleep she sensed the boy's presence near her again. She knew she was in mortal danger, she wanted to scream, she wanted to escape, but she couldn't.

In her dream she awoke in a different world, a world full of strange creatures, barren landscapes, and the remnants of a large city. She wasn't sure where she was but it looked miserable and it made her feel the same. Even the noises in this place sounded eerie, melodic echoes would start and stop suddenly, mechanical humming increasing in intensity and speed, all of it sounded like it could drive a person mad. She looked up at a hellish sky of orange and red. A thick layer of dust covered everything making it hard to breathe.

She noticed black slithering creatures on the ground. They were like small leeches with black spikes that would flare up and down as they crawled around furiously. She quickly climbed on a rock as she didn't want to be around these things but they followed her. She saw one of the creatures crawl on her shoe and she freaked out and smacked it with her hand. Its spikes drew blood as she cried in pain, a pain that felt worse than a bee sting. The creature fell on the ground and she slammed her foot on top of it, exploding with a blue substance. When she removed her foot, she heard deep voices, forceful whispers that raised in long waves and sent shivers down her spine.

"We've been waiting for you, we can smell your fear, you belong to us," they said in unison making her panic.

At first she couldn't figure out where the voices were coming from and then she realized it was the creatures surrounding her. She already hated them, she was sure they were parasites, ready to infect others for their own survival.

She backed up urgently, trying to find any way to escape but she couldn't, there were too many of them. She ran, stomping on as many of them as she could. She didn't know where she was headed or what she was doing but she couldn't let them get on her. They followed her anyway and began to crawl on her, she smacked at them but the pain from their spikes was unbearable. They formed a massive ball at her feet. She screamed in terror not knowing what they would do to her and she awoke drenched in sweat in her room.

Eveley grabbed the bottle of water next to her and sat in her bed calming down. She didn't know why Draven set off this chain of events but she never wanted to see him again. She felt doom anytime he was around and the feelings from it would swallow her whole and freeze her mind.

The next morning Eveley woke up groggy like she was coming down with a cold. Last night was easily the worst sleep of her life. She felt extremely fatigued, she wanted to get out of bed but she felt physically weak. She tried for half an hour to get out of bed but she was too tired. Eventually she heard a soft knock on her door.

"Eveley, it's Stella, are you up sweetie?" Stella said softly.

"Uh yeah but I'm not feeling well," Eveley said.

"Can I come in love?" Stella asked.

"Yes."

Stella opened the door slowly, when she glanced at Eveley's face she became alarmed.

"Honey you look awful, do you feel feverish?"

"Just a little."

Stella walked up to her and placed her hand on her forehead.

"You feel a bit warm, do you want to stay in bed for a while? I can bring you something up here to eat if you're hungry."

Eveley shook her head.

"I don't think I could eat right now. I feel so tired, I just want to sleep," she said in a low voice.

Stella nodded. "Okay but I need to take your temperature and then I'm going to call your mom to update her."

"Okay."

"I'll be right back." Stella left the room and came back with a thermometer. She took her temp and it was normal but she still wasn't convinced.

"Well, you don't have a fever but you might be at the beginning of one since you feel hot. We'll keep an eye on your temp, I'll take it again in an hour. In the meantime go ahead and keep hydrated. Here is some water, and take as much rest as you need." Stella got up, walked out and closed her door.

As soon as she was alone Eveley used the bathroom then laid back and covered herself with her blanket. Her body felt hotter and hotter till she was sweating profusely. She didn't know what was going on but she was scared. This had to be connected to Draven. She was half asleep, teetering on the verge of total sleep when she heard his voice in her head.

"I can't stop thinking about you," he said in a deep voice. It startled her awake, she didn't see anyone in her room, she was confused.

"I don't need to be next to you to communicate with you. I just need to be close enough to you," he said.

She didn't want to have him in her head. She felt afraid, the same feeling in her dream of the slithering creatures came back.

"Don't be afraid, I won't hurt you," he lied.

She knew it was Draven who bruised her arms, she didn't know how but she was sure of it. She thought maybe if she ignored him he'd go away.

"Don't you dare ignore me!" he yelled, the rage in his voice rattled her.

"Why do you keep following me? I don't want anything to do with you," she finally said. Maybe if he sensed her disdain for him it would discourage him.

"Whether you like me or not is of no concern to me."

"Well it should, you should take no for an answer and move on, I have a boyfriend you know!" she said bluntly. She realized all this time she hadn't been speaking the words but saying them in her head. Could this monster read her thoughts she wondered? How was that even possible?

"You're amusing, this is bigger than you," he said condescendingly.

"Stop harassing me! Don't you get it through you thick skull I don't want to be anywhere near you!"

"Unfortunately for you, that's not up to you," he replied.

"What do you mean it's not up to me? It's completely up to me, leave me alone you hear me! I'm sick of you and the chaos you've caused!"

He burst into laughter, her blood was boiling now. She wanted to grab anything and throw it at him but she didn't know where he was. She stumbled out of bed to the window, she couldn't see anyone but that didn't mean he wasn't hiding somewhere. She felt so helpless and agitated by his presence she felt like screaming. She ran out of the bedroom and downstairs. Only Eileen and Aidan were home, Stella and Jason were out running errands. She ran in front of them frantically pointing.

"He's here, he's stalking me!" she shouted.

Aidan and Eileen both looked around them. Eileen screamed as she saw Draven's face in one of the windows.

"Stay here!" Aidan told them, as he ran where Eileen pointed.

He glanced out the window and saw Draven running away. He was already 30 yards or so away. He couldn't explain how he ran so far in such a short time. Aidan checked all the windows and doors were locked.

Eveley was now sobbing, partially from anger and partially from the fear of having Draven in her head. The fact he communicated with her in her head made her feel crazy and panicked.

Eileen was worried too, how did the creep find where they lived? Someone from his rat pack must have told him and he was hell-bent on stalking and scaring them.

"He was in my head. I don't know how he did it, but I could hear him talking to me. He told me he didn't have to be right in front of me to communicate with me!"

Eveley realized she sounded like a lunatic but she didn't care.

Aidan hugged her, Eileen looked at him with worry. Eveley looked physically sick and she was hot to the touch.

"Hey hey, none of us are going to let anything happen to you, I promise okay?" Aidan said.

Eveley looked at Aidan and nodded.

"Eileen can come upstairs with you so you can rest and I'll keep an eye out for Draven. I'm going to call mom and dad and let them know. We're going to go to the station in a bit to give them his info so they can arrest him."

"Arrest him?" Eveley repeated.

"Yes, most likely they're going to make him go to a detention center depending if this gets taken seriously by Gardai."

Eveley thought about what he said as Eileen tried to lead her upstairs.

"Come on Eveley, you look awful, you need some rest," Eileen said as she pulled Eveley's hand to help her.

Eveley had not been herself since the incident at the Christmas market. She looked dazed and sickly, and Eileen knew that Draven creep was the culprit. She wanted to punch the creep in the face.

Eveley reluctantly got in bed, she prayed in her head to not hear his voice again. As soon as she laid down the tiredness won because Eveley was out. Eileen walked over to her window and checked the window was locked, she stepped out softly and shut the door quietly.

She heard Aidan talking to their parents on the phone as she walked along the top of the stairs. She knew this Draven guy was out of control to be stalking them like this.

Thirty minutes later their parents returned from their errands. They needed to visit their local Gardai station to add the information to the report and hopefully have Draven detained and press formal charges. Someone needed to stay with Eveley and Eileen since she was sick. Stella and Aidan decided to go and Jason stayed behind with Eileen and Eveley.

Eileen went into the room to check on Eveley. She noticed she was breathing rapidly and decided to check her temperature since her mom asked her to before she left. Her temperature was 104 degrees. She gasped and tried to gently rouse Eveley awake, she was drenched in sweat and wouldn't wake up. Eileen ran downstairs.

"Dad! Dad!" she shouted.

"Yes Eileen? What's wrong?" Jason asked.

"Look! Eveley has a 104 degree temperature. I tried to wake her but she's drenched in sweat and won't wake up, she's also having a hard time breathing."

She handed him the thermometer.

"Okay let me call your mother, I'll find out what she wants to do," Jason said.

Jason spoke to Stella who told them to immediately call an ambulance and they would head back. They had just finished adding Draven's info to the report.

By the time Stella and Aidan returned, the ambulance had already left with Jason and Eileen riding along. Stella called Isabel, which was a very hard phone call to make. Isabel was extremely upset and wanted to get on the first flight to Ireland. Stella advised against it for now until they could find out if they could stabilize Eveley. She promised to keep her posted frequently on her condition.

As soon as Eveley arrived via ambulance to the ER, doctors started a battery of tests and attempted to stabilize her temperature as it was still rising.

Eileen cried, Jason hugged her and told her everything would be okay as they waited for Stella and Aidan to arrive.

When Stella and Aidan arrived they were led back to Eveley's room. They were surprised how bad she looked, and how quickly her illness had progressed over the course of one day. Eveley was so ill she was basically comatose from the high fever.

After the battery of tests, they determined Eveley's diagnosis was bacterial meningitis. It was serious and they started her right away on IV antibiotics. Stella couldn't believe how quickly she declined.

The first night she was admitted to the hospital, Stella stayed the night with Eveley. Both Aidan and Eileen begged to stay, but Stella thought it was unnecessary and it would serve them well to rest in their own bed. Aidan insisted his mom make sure Eveley was never alone in her hospital room, she assured him she wouldn't leave her side.

Stella spoke to Isabel over the phone and Isabel was anxious to return to Ireland. Stella convinced her to stay put and she would give her an update after the next 24 hours to see if Eveley improved.

By the next morning, Stella heard Eveley speak a few words to the nurse when she came in to check on her. By the afternoon she was speaking in full sentences and by the next day she was fully cognizant and aware of everything happening around her. She was still bed-bound due to her severe weakness but her prognosis had improved dramatically.

During the day everyone came to visit her. Aidan was so surprised again to see her change so drastically from the day prior. By the third day in the hospital she was 50% better, by the fourth day she was 60%.

The O'Briens made their own little Christmas in the hospital. They brought all their gifts and brought Eveley several gifts as well. By the sixth day she was able to walk around and her blood work and vitals were completely stable. She had to finish at least 8 days of her antibiotics to be discharged her doctor said.

On January 1st, she was finally discharged to go home. Eveley left with no lasting damage from the illness other than having lost a lot of weight and still having some weakness and fatigue. She was on antibiotics that would last a couple more weeks and she needed a few more follow-ups.

Eveley stayed another week in Ireland. Afterward, she returned to Dallas. The visit was both great and horrible. Eveley suspected Draven had something to do with her illness but she couldn't figure out how.

CHAPTER 15

COLD ABYSS

Aidan suspected Draven was the cause of Eveley's illness, it was too much of a coincidence. Since the first day he saw Eveley hooked up to all the monitors in the hospital, it was the first thought that came to his mind.

After the Gardai report was updated with Draven's information, Draven was picked up and held in detention for a day. He was already under their radar due to some other run-ins with Gardai so the O'Brien family received a protection order that could get him in bigger trouble if he tried to violate it.

While Eveley was interned in the hospital, Aidan began to stay up nights and constantly monitor the house. His dad advised against this, but Aidan was stubborn. He slept downstairs and would get up periodically and look out the windows throughout the house. Twice he noticed a dark figure stalking from afar but he couldn't prove it was Draven.

The same night Eveley's plane took off for Dallas, Aidan dreamed Eveley was taken by Draven. He awoke and looked at his clock, 3:32 am. It had been a long and emotionally draining day. Taking Eveley to the airport and saying goodbye to her, knowing he wouldn't see her again until the summer. It had been a heartfelt and bittersweet good-bye for everyone, especially for the girls who shed a few tears.

He closed his eyes, ready to go back to sleep, when he heard a sound coming from his window. He walked up to the window and saw a dark figure walking away slowly...Draven.

He didn't seem in a hurry and carried a blade in his hand as the metal reflected in the moonlight. Aidan rushed to put on his shoes. He was already wearing sweats so he grabbed his coat, a knife, and a bat he stored in his closet.

Aidan knew this guy wasn't going to stop until he did something about it. He'd been close to his sister's window which made him uneasy.

Aidan stepped out the door and followed. There was a blanket of fog which made it eerie and hard to see. He could see the faint outline of Draven's figure ahead, he was headed toward the sea.

They crossed the only street separating the last row of houses from the sea. At that point he lost sight of Draven. Aidan cautiously walked on, he couldn't see the ocean, but he felt the cold sea breeze, the air tasted and smelled of salt. His feet felt the jagged rocks under his tennis shoes as he came closer to the water's edge. He looked all around him, he feared Draven was going to ambush him, he could hear his footsteps. He felt Draven's presence like a snake, stalking and watching for the perfect moment to strike.

Aidan saw Draven appear in front of him, his silhouette slowly emerging from the heavy fog. Draven nonchalantly stood twenty feet ahead facing Aidan. His hands in his pockets with a grin on his face. Despite his portrayal of aloofness, his eyes gave him away, there was rage inside of them that betrayed him. Aidan knew he was looking for revenge. The sclera of his eyes a bright blue color he'd never seen on anyone before. Draven pulled out a long knife, flipping it over and over in his hand skillfully without taking his eyes of Aidan.

"You must be wondering why I'm here," he said as he continued to flip the knife.

"Actually, I know exactly why you're here, too bad you aren't going to get what you want," Aidan replied.

Draven chuckled, "And what is it that I want?"

"Eveley."

At the sound of her name, Draven froze and closed his eyes, his jaw flexed as he clenched his teeth and took in a deep breath.

"Are you sure about that?" he looked right at Aidan, his eyes more intense than before.

"Well considering Eveley is no longer in Ireland and is thousands of miles away I'm pretty confident," this time Aidan grinned and Draven looked enraged.

"Where is she?!"

Aidan stood silent, meeting Draven's eyes and challenging him full on.

"I don't know what the hell you are, or why you're so intent on stalking my girlfriend, but you're going to stop and you're also going to stop skulking around my house."

"You gonna stop me?"

"Yes, that's right," Aidan said confidently.

Draven turned away from Aidan, he hunched over and pulled on his face. Aidan could hear Draven's hard breathing and see the frustration in his body movements. Aidan waited for his attack, ready to defend himself at any moment. Draven turned around, his face distorted, the edges of his mouth, nose and eyes looked off, like he was wearing a mask but crooked.

"Do you know why you won't be able to stop me?" Draven said vehemently.

Aidan didn't take his eyes off Draven, "I'm listening."

"You never met the real Draven O'Connor, have you?" Draven said.

Aidan was confused, "What do you mean the 'real' Draven O'Connor?"

"If you had met him before I crossed paths with him, you would have known him to be a pretty good kid. He had a dark sense of humor, which was amusing, and he was popular at school. Too bad he always brought too much attention to himself and he happened to be a compatible host," Draven said with a grin on his face.

Aidan felt the hair on his neck raise up, Draven took small steps toward him. Aidan backed up slowly, careful not to get too close to the edge. The tide was rising with powerful waves crashing into the rocks.

"Just get to the point," Aidan said impatiently, he felt an eerie and familiar feeling around this guy.

"You look like the type of guy who doesn't run from a fight," Draven chuckled and continued toward Aidan. "You should know you're no match for me, my kind has always despised humans...so frail, so dense, so easily defeated. You're only a weak, disposable vessel until we can return to our place among the stars."

"What are you?" Aidan asked.

"I'm not from this world, but you already knew that, seems like you've run into my kind before," Draven continued.

Aidan remembered the guy from their childhood, the one that chased them in the creek...that's it! He was just like that creep.

"Let's just say I take over human bodies, and this one is brand new. That's why you were able to beat me at the pub, but now that I've gained my strength you aren't going to be lucky a second time." Draven pulled on his face and adjusted it, the skin falling back into the correct position and he grinned—a scary, demented grin.

"If it makes you feel better, I don't want to inhabit her body, even if Eveley is a compatible host. I aim to save my race from extinction, it's all about survival. Do you know how to survive Aidan? Does she? I'm going to I find her...and you're going to lead me to her."

For a second they stood in silence, neither making a move or sound. Suddenly Draven leaped toward Aidan as if he was a tiger. The sound of the bat hitting against bone was loud on this quiet night.

Aidan found himself thrust into the icy water on his back. He saw nothing, only felt the coldness enveloping him, pulling him further down, trapping him. He tried to move his body up to a swim position but he felt a bony hand tighten around his neck like a noose, the nails digging into his neck. Aidan reached into his pocket and grabbed his knife. He took the knife out and stabbed in front of him, he faintly heard the anguished cries of the parasite, and the hand released. Aidan was able to reach the top and breathe in, the icy water was brutal and made his whole body ache with pain. Aidan swam toward the shore, a strong hand pulled his ankle, yanking him underwater once more. He was pulled further and further down into the cold abyss of the ocean. He kicked with his free foot until his foot struck Draven's head, causing him to release him. He swam up as fast as he could, and broke through the surface on the verge of passing out from lack of oxygen. He swam furiously with his last ounce of energy to the shore. When he made it to the slippery rocks lining the edge, he climbed the rocks, exhausted and freezing. He noticed the bat still laying on the rocks and picked it up. He heard Draven swimming close, Aidan stood ready for another attack.

Aidan stood there for a few minutes, waiting for Draven to exit the water but he never surfaced. Aidan walked back to his house, exhausted and chilled to the bone. Once inside he changed into dry clothes. Draven was clearly able to eavesdrop and see though walls somehow. If he continued to talk to Eveley, he would figure out where she lived, he couldn't risk it. He sat up in his bed for what seemed hours and thought of a plan that would ensure he could continue to talk to Eveley...there was none. He didn't want to hurt Eveley...but he needed to keep her safe.

CHAPTER 16

EVIL ON FIRE

Aidan did the hardest thing he'd ever done...he completely stopped communicating with Eveley. Eveley was confused of course, messaging him if he was okay and why he wasn't responding to her messages. She called him, texted him, left voicemails he deleted as soon as he received them without listening to them. He told his sister she must also do the same due to Draven wanting to hurt Eveley. Eileen didn't believe Draven would be able to do anything to Eveley an ocean away so she refused to stop speaking to her best friend. Aidan repeatedly warned her to never mention Eveley's location in any of her communication with Eveley. Meanwhile, Eileen was upset with Aidan, she pleaded and begged for him to stop his so called plan to keep Eveley safe.

Naturally, Eveley was heartbroken Aidan stopped talking to her. She thought it was her fault, that her illness while in Ireland made him realize she wasn't what he wanted, that she wasn't good enough for him, or was simply tired of her. All these fears she expressed to Eileen. Eileen wanted to tell her so bad his reasoning but Aidan had made her promise to not say anything. He feared if she knew the reason she wouldn't believe him and purposely say or do something to let Draven know where she lived to "prove" him wrong.

Eileen was so upset at Aidan, even Stella and Jason noticed the annoyance from Eileen around him. They figured it was a phase, so they reminded them several times to stop the bickering. The animosity mostly came from Eileen, Aidan knew she was only reacting instinctively to Eveley's emotional pain.

Aidan was dying inside too...he missed her voice, her laughter, telling her anything and everything, from the small things in his life to the big. It was the most difficult torture he'd ever put himself through. This went on for 5 months, until one night as he laid in bed he realized what he needed to do was get far away from where Draven was. So he talked to his parents about traveling during the summer with the money he'd saved from his part-time job. They weren't too keen on it at first but once he told them this was the best time for him to travel before starting university they were more receptive and gave their blessing. Plus him and Eileen traveled each summer to visit their grandparents in Texas and this summer wouldn't be any different.

Aidan left for Japan a month later after he took his leaving certificate exam for school. He spent a week in Tokyo. The first day he touched down, he contacted Eveley, sending her a text, thinking if he could just explain why, she'd forgive him, but he did not receive a response. He tried to call her, the number went straight to voicemail, she'd blocked his number. He had really messed up he thought, he should have found a better plan, a better way. She had every right to block him from her entire life. He emailed her, still no response. He knew she might never forgive him and he figured it would be difficult to get her back but he wasn't ready to give up.

After a week in Japan, he traveled to Brazil. He stayed there a week. All the while he continued his quest to talk to her. Every day he'd send her a short email, telling her about his travels and how he felt about their relationship. He didn't specifically tell her about Draven but he hinted he was trying to keep her safe and now that he was away from home he could freely talk to her.

After Brazil he flew to Mexico City to stay for a week. While there he felt the loneliest he'd ever felt, especially since Mexico was a cherished memory of his with Eveley. This was the country where they fell in love in. To be there without her, to not be able to share it with her, it made it difficult to enjoy his time there.

After those three weeks with no luck getting a response from Eveley, he finally touched down in Texas. Eileen would arrive the coming week to spend the summer with their grandparents as well. Aidan hoped he could tell Eveley face to face what happened and reconcile with her, but all the signs so far pointed to that being a low probability. They were basically strangers at this point. Aidan couldn't even call Eveley his friend and that realization killed him inside. He didn't want Eveley to know he was in Dallas as he knew she would avoid him. He hoped eventually he'd run into Eveley at some of their events since most of their friends were mutual.

It happened that Eveley was invited by Chiquis and another friend, Valentina, or [1] Vale for short, to the same party he was invited to by his guy friends.

Aidan rode in the back of the car with Wheels sitting next to him, Julian in the front passenger seat. R.J. was driver tonight as he had just been gifted a new car by his parents for graduation and they were on their way to pick up Leo. He'd been gifted a rally blue WRX STI, which was an agile and zippy car. After they picked up Leo, they finally arrived to the neighborhood where the party was located. Aidan's hands began to sweat; he was the most nervous he'd ever been. As he got out, R.J. noticed Aidan's serious face.

"Hey bro, you alright?" R.J. asked. R.J. patted Aidan playfully on the back.

Aidan nodded, "Yeah man, just feels so different to be back in Dallas, still getting used to it," Aidan replied as they walked up to the front door and knocked on the door of the house.

"Yeah you'll get used to it alright, just wait till you see—"

---

1. Vale (Va-leh)

"R.J.!" Valentina opened the door and jumped into R.J.'s arms, almost knocking him over.

R.J. reacted by chuckling and Aidan by feeling slightly like a third wheel and taking a step to the side as she continued to gush over R.J. in his arms.

"You get prettier every time I see you babe," R. J. said.

Valentina looked at R.J. knowingly. "You're the best sweet talker, hey Aidan!" Valentina suddenly realized he was standing there.

Aidan nodded. "Hey Valentina, how are you?" Aidan said as he took a step sideways to give them even more room.

"I'm doing great! Come in! Come in guys!" Valentina motioned. By now Leo, Julian, and Wheels were also at the door looking through the doorway at the party which was already going full force.

As soon as they entered, several friends were surprised to see Aidan and came to talk to him. He noticed Valentina and R.J. walked off and he started scanning the room for Chiquis. Suddenly he saw Chiquis and their eyes met. As soon as she saw Aidan she turned away from him and walked away. Aidan walked away from the group of friends talking to him and followed Chiquis.

"Hey Chiquis! Chiquis!" Aidan said, confused she wasn't turning around. Finally he placed his hand on her shoulder and she turned around.

"Hi Aidan," she said with a nervous smile.

"Hey, is that any way to greet me? Were you trying to avoid me?" Aidan asked incredulously. She was one of his closest friends after all.

Chiquis gave him a quick hug and looked around nervously.

"I'm sorry Aidan, I don't know what went down between you and Eveley but you're like a brother to me so I'm going to advice you whatever you have planned...just don't, please don't. It's not going to end well," she said.

"C'mon, I just want a chance to tell my side of the story and apologize," Aidan said as he looked around.

"Is she here?" Aidan trailed off as he suddenly zeroed in on Eveley from across the room. She was standing next to a stairwell, a group of her friends and a few boys he didn't know stood around her. Chiquis turned to see what he was looking at.

He began to walk toward Eveley, his heart was pounding so loud, he suddenly couldn't hear the music or the chatter in the room.

"Aidan! I wouldn't do that if I were you," Chiquis said. She tried to grab his arm but he kept walking. She walked behind him in tiny, hurried steps, knowing this was a drama fest in the making.

Eveley was smiling faintly and talking with her friends when she suddenly turned her face and made eye contact with Aidan. His pulse quickened when she met his eyes. Her eyes widened in surprise and the smile fell from her face, she looked angry and hurt all at once. She turned around and walked away abruptly from her group of friends. Aidan felt his world closing in on him as he tried to catch up to her.

"Eveley!" he called her name but she refused to turn around. He finally got close enough and grabbed her arm. She turned around angrily and pulled her arm away from his hand.

"Leave me alone!" She yelled at him, her eyes suddenly went dark and her lips pursed.

"Eveley, please let me explain," Aidan implored.

"Explain what!? That you lead me to think you and me would be forever? That everything I thought about you was wrong? That everything between you and me was a lie?!" Eveley shot back.

"Nothing between us was a lie," Aidan said sternly, his feelings hurt she'd said something like that. Had she really been making herself believe all these things about their relationship in his absence he thought.

By now their exchange had drawn the attention of everyone around them. Eveley's body was tense, her breathing labored, and her face serious. He tried to get closer.

"Please let's just go talk in private..." he motioned in front of them to the backyard. She stood without saying a word. Suddenly a tall guy he'd never seen before placed himself in between them and placed his arm around Eveley's shoulder.

"Hey you heard Eveley, she doesn't want to talk to you," the guy said.

Aidan felt his anger rise. This guy looked like the jock type, tall and athletic.

"I'm talking to Eveley, can you stay out of it please..." Aidan said.

Chiquis grabbed Aidan's arm and tried to pull him back, she looked at Eveley knowingly.

Aidan tried to move to the side to see Eveley's face as the guy was blocking his view, the jock pushed Aidan back with his hand. Aidan had to use all of his willpower not to knock him out cold in the moment.

"Who's he?!" Aidan blurted at Eveley, finally fed up with this guy's intrusion.

"A friend—" Eveley said.

"Her boyfriend," the jock said at the same time, he looked at Eveley confused.

"Uh, your friend? Didn't seem like it when you let me kiss you last night," he said.

"Which obviously was a mistake," Eveley said without hesitation as she pushed her body away from the jock.

There were a few "ohs" uttered in the room as everyone looked around at each other, as if they were watching a juicy telenovela [soap opera].

"Seriously? You made out with *him*?" Aidan felt jealous but he knew he didn't have a right to be. Still, he couldn't hold back his indignation. She was his, even if she no longer was. In his mind he'd never moved on and she couldn't have either. In reality his heart was breaking knowing she'd allowed another boy to kiss her.

Eveley looked fed up with both boys.

"I'm leaving, and neither of you are going to follow me!" Eveley pushed past both boys. She grabbed Chiquis by the arm who joined her. Chiquis saw the tears fall down Eveley's face as soon as Eveley was out of view of both boys.

"Eveley, I'm sorry. I don't know what happened between you and Aidan cause you won't tell me, but maybe you should give him a chance to explain, no? He seems really sincere chica..."

Chiquis tried her best to console Eveley. Unfortunately, she had the role of being caught between two friends she loved like a brother and sister.

R.J. and Valentina came in from the backyard and saw the room hushed and people staring at Aidan and the jock who were in the middle of the room.

"Did I miss something?" R.J. said as his and Valentina's smile fell.

"I need a ride home," Aidan said.

"Valentina, I think Chiquis and Eveley might need you," R. J. pointed to the front door as he saw Chiquis by the doorway, motioning to him to get Valentina's attention.

"Oh, okay, I'll be right back baby," Valentina kissed R.J. on the lips quickly then turned to Aidan.

"I'm sorry Aidan..." Valentina said not knowing what else to say. She hurried to the front of the house to join Eveley and Chiquis who were already half-way down the front yard headed to Chiquis' car.

R.J. came up to Aidan and patted his back.

"Alright, I'll take you back home, c'mon let's go," R.J. said as they walked to the front.

Once they were outside, Aidan caught a glimpse of Eveley's face in the front seat of Chiquis' car. He saw her wiping away tears from her face...she still felt something for him. He wanted so badly to run to her and wipe away her tears, but she'd crossed him off the list of people she trusted, that he knew for sure.

The rest of the summer, especially after Eileen landed in Texas, was no different. He thought maybe his sister would help talk Eveley into giving him a chance to explain, but nothing changed. All summer was a blur of him mostly hanging out with his guy friends, as him going to any event where both boys and girls were invited meant Eveley would not attend. It was a purgatory and every time his sister went out with her girlfriends he itched to ask her how Eveley was but stopped himself.

Apparently, Eileen heard of the drama at the house party when he first arrived, and to ease his mind hinted at him that Eveley had completely cut off the jock. According to Eileen, Eveley said he'd been a mistake in the making when she allowed him to kiss her the day before Aidan showed up.

He started to consider maybe he made a rash decision, perhaps he could have found a different way to keep her safe. After all, Eileen continued to communicate with Eveley and nothing happened to Eveley. He didn't understand how that was possible but he made the decision he thought was right at the time. But now it turned out it was a stupid decision and he was paying for it in the worst way.

At the end of the summer, Aidan and Eileen returned to Galway City and started university. Aidan felt empty inside, his family kept him going and Eileen softened her stance upon their return. Still none of it mattered to him...at the end of the day he still didn't have Eveley in his life.

Worse yet, Draven was still stalking his house. The recurring nightmares that woke him in the middle of the night continued. It always made him break into a sweat when he thought of the things in his nightmares coming true. The last time he had the nightmare of Eveley being hurt by Draven, he awoke to Draven sulking by his house again. Then and there, Aidan decided it would be the last time. He was going to fight back.

He took late night walks, every night, hoping Draven would show up. Soon enough, after several weeks of doing so, Draven appeared.

That fateful night it was a full moon. By now Aidan had played so many scenarios in his head of what could happen, and what he would do, he wasn't scared anymore. Foremost on his mind was the need to get rid of Draven in order for Eveley to be safe. He wasn't human after all, the soul of the real Draven O'Connor was put out the minute Draven took over. He was just a leech—an alien parasite with no mercy on those he infected. And Aidan wasn't going to have mercy on him either.

On that night, he brought with him a long Celtic war sword. He hid it under his clothing along his outer thigh, it was at least 9 inches long and extremely sharp, he spent a lot of time sharpening it.

It was an hour of walking near his home before he came upon a large empty field. He didn't know why but he was drawn to it like a magnet. He started walking through the field with no clear plan on where he was going when suddenly Draven was there. Waiting right in the middle of the field, as always stalking, cunning, and ready to attack. Aidan stopped walking, he placed his hand on the butt of his sword, he needed to get rid of this threat in all of their lives.

Draven didn't say a word, he looked full of rage and contempt as always. They stood in their spots for what seemed hours, but it was seconds. Draven charged at him, this time he brutally tackled Aidan to the ground. Once he had Aidan on his back, he placed his hands around his neck. His strength supernatural; Aidan couldn't budge Draven's iron grip.

"I could break your neck in one move but I'm going to draw it out for you," Draven said. He tightened his grip, delighted by his physical advantage over Aidan.

Aidan grabbed his knife and in one swift move pushed the blade into Draven, right were his heart would be. Draven's eyes grew wide, his hands released Aidan. Draven kneeled on the ground and grabbed the handle of the sword, he laughed maniacally.

"You think this is going to destroy me?! You think it's going to be that easy!?" Draven shouted as he slowly pulled the blade out of his chest, blue blood leaked profusely from his wound.

Aidan saw his chance and delivered a kick that knocked Draven out. Aidan grabbed his sword, he saw Draven's blue blood pulsing on the ground as it pooled around him. Aidan pulled out a water bottle full of gasoline from his jacket and poured it over Draven. He took out the matches in his pocket, lit one match and threw it over Draven, the flames instantly came to life. The flames danced violently in hues of orange and red.

Aidan walked away, when he reached about 50 feet away, Draven came to life. He went berserk, screaming and roaring. The sounds were otherworldly, like a demon. It was too late for him to put out the flames. Aidan observed his human and alien body separating, like a full body mask Draven was pushing away. He couldn't escape his fate, there was no other host for him to inhabit. The fire caused too much damage, and although his body could regenerate to some extent, his abilities were no match for fire...eternal fire. Aidan watched as he finally slumped over and fell in the grass, the flames continuing to destroy the evil it was enveloping.

Aidan hurried home, he cleaned himself and his sword. He stood silently by his window as he saw Gardai cars and an ambulance speed past his house. Inside he felt relief...Draven O'Connor was finally dead.

Chapter 17

Unexpected Visitor

Eveley's 20th Birthday continued.

When I opened my eyes, I couldn't believe what I saw. I looked to my side, my mother held my hand with her head face down on top of her arm. On the other side...Aidan. He was asleep, leaned back on a recliner, holding my other hand.

A wave of emotion so strong came over me I couldn't process it all. Our fall out had been almost 2 years ago, a fall out excruciatingly sudden and painful. I cried every day for close to six months at the beginning. Six months after he'd put me through emotional hell he suddenly contacted me and to the day he'd never stopped contacting me, telling me he loved me forever and he wouldn't give up on us.

Even after my rejection of him in Dallas at Vale's party, he still didn't give up. By then I'd vowed to never let him hurt me again. Since then I'd never responded to him for fear of running back to him. I missed him so much I was tired of holding him away. I wanted to give in and just let him back in. Every cell in my body wanted to just forget the foolishness of our past. I was sure we'd matured since we'd been 2 love-struck teenagers.

Aidan looked tired, I wondered what was going on in his life that he had under eye circles and looked pale. I couldn't stop looking at him, thinking of some of the memories we'd made growing up together. I couldn't believe time had flown so quickly. It seemed only yesterday we were staring up at the sky and looking at stars and planets through my telescope.

Last I knew, Aidan went to university in Ireland his first year then according to Eileen had traveled all summer in between semesters. He returned to Mexico City to improve his Spanish. He sent me poems in lyrical Spanish through the mail this summer, likely inspired by the city. He even sent me flowers on my birthday, and through it all I never replied, not even a simple thank you. As cold as I may have looked on the outside, inside I was a volcano of emotions, it was hard to keep my heart closed to him.

I wanted to end my misery but something inside me always stopped me. I never understood why he cut me off so suddenly and I couldn't trust him to not hurt me again.

It hadn't always been this precarious with our relationship. There was a time when I would have sworn nothing could tear us apart, but life has a funny way of accepting challenges.

I slipped my hand out of his hand. Aidan opened his eyes slowly and before I knew it was staring back at me. For a few seconds neither of us said a thing. I don't know why I was frozen in place, this person that had known me like no one else, to make me feel so out of place. He broke the silence first.

"Eveley...how are you feeling?"

"I'm good, when did you get here?"

"I just got here an hour ago, as soon as your accident happened your mom called us in Ireland and I took the next flight out."

"I see...how have you been?"

Aidan took a pause and looked down, he didn't have any expression, he looked like he was carrying the weight of the world.

"I'm surviving I guess, but my problems don't matter, I'm here for you..."

"I didn't ask you to," I said vehemently.

He winced at my tone. I was indignant inside, he hadn't been there when I needed him and now he wanted to be here, how dare he try to be the hero now.

"I know, I was just very concerned. I didn't know if you were going to be okay and I didn't want to regret not coming to see you," Aidan said.

He looked down, his whole body barely moved as if he was afraid to. I noticed he'd lost a lot of weight. The more I observed the little details of his face and body, the more I noticed he looked like a shell of himself. I almost felt sorry for him.

"I'm sorry if I intruded...I just had to see you," his gaze toward me gave away the tenderness he still felt for me and I wanted to reciprocate but couldn't. I looked away to the side to stop myself from crying.

"*He needs you, he is going through a lot at the moment,*" the voice said interrupting my trail of thought.

I slowly turned back to Aidan. I had to fight every fiber in my being not to break down crying in front of him.

"Thank you for coming, I'm sorry if I seem rude, I'm just a little tired." This time I was almost too removed from my words. I truly didn't know how to act around him anymore.

My mother began to stir and she finally opened her eyes. When she saw me awake, she completely went into a frenzy. She hugged me and kissed my forehead several times.

"Estoy bien Ma [I'm okay Mom]," I said.

"Eveley, nunca jamas me asustes asi [never, ever, scare me like that]!" She said angrily, then turned to Aidan.

"Gracias Aidan, she just tried to run away from the hospital, can you believe it?" She looked back at me sternly with furrowed brows.

Aidan barely grinned and I wondered if he was physically sick.

"Perdoname ma, no se que me paso [Sorry mom, I don't know what got into me]," I said.

My mom softened her look and hugged me again.

"I'm just glad you're okay mija, we need to get you better so you can be discharged, life is waiting out there." She pointed to the window.

"How long are you staying Aidan?" Mom asked Aidan.

"I need to get back in three days," Aidan said.

"Oh wow, that's soon, well thank you for coming Aidan, you didn't have to by any means. Eveley is lucky to have friends like you," Mom said.

I felt the room spin again and exhaustion overcome my body, my eyes fluttered.

"Okay mija, you're still in need of rest, no more socializing. We're gonna step outside to grab some coffee so you can get some rest, c'mon mijo, let's go," Mom said.

"I don't need..."

That's all I remember, so I guess I must have dozed off almost immediately. I didn't wake again from that "nap" until the next morning. I heard a knock on the door and Aidan and my mom walked in. Aidan looked like a different person than the day before. I wasn't sure if I imagined his condition yesterday or what. He looked healthy again, his dark Auburn hair in short waves and his skin slightly tanned. He wasn't skinny like yesterday, in fact he looked like his normal self. Since Aidan played soccer he was slim but well-toned, a typical athlete's body. I didn't know what to think anymore.

"You didn't imagine it, you helped."

Helped? How did I help? I speculated in my head.

"You have the power to he-"

"Good morning Eveley," Aidan said with a bright smile. He walked to me, hugged me and gave me a kiss on each cheek like people greet in Mexico. I was confused and my mom noticed the confusion on my face.

"Good morning Aidan," I said slowly. He smelled great, like minty aftershave.

"Andale mija [c'mon my daughter], it's time to get up and going. Your nurse Janet said they decided to discharge you by this afternoon if all goes well," Mom said crossing her fingers.

"Janet has to come in one last time to take your vitals and then if you don't have any more surprises you'll be good," Mom added.

"Oh I feel so bad," I said in shame as I remembered the big chaos I caused and how crazy I acted by running away.

"Oh don't, she said she's had way worse," Mom grinned.

"You really tried to sprint out of here?" Aidan asked. There was a tone of disbelief in his voice.

"Yeah unfortunately, doesn't sound like me does it?" I said.

"Not at all, but it's okay, it's good to surprise people in your life every once in a while," he said and winked with a smile, the same smile that always got me. I was not convinced with his sudden presence in my life but I also wasn't complaining now that I'd started to let myself feel again. My heart and head were definitely still fighting internally. I just had to keep my feelings in check is all.

My mom started unpacking a large bag she brought with her, laying things on the seat by the window. Aidan stood back near the TV.

"I brought you a new outfit, soaps, lotion, and some makeup. After Janet comes in and takes your vitals, you can take a shower if you want," Mom said to me.

"Okay, I'm definitely looking forward to that," I said.

I pushed my covers to the side, stood up and stretched my arms above my head. I looked down at the burn imprinted on my chest, it was healing so quickly. It looked pink, no longer angry red, and it didn't hurt anymore. The swelling and pain in my ankle were also completely gone.

Aidan came to my side. "Need any help?"

"No, thank you. Yesterday I could've sworn I was still sore everywhere and today I feel completely pain-free, it's weird," I said to him.

"Funny, I was struggling yesterday too, it's as if something helped both of us cause I feel brand new today too."

"Hmm, weird," I shrugged. "I guess we could be worse right?" I said to him.

"Right."

He looked at me intently, he gave me that look that always caught me off guard. The same one my mother often told me she caught me giving him when I didn't realize she was watching me. Like a puppy in love for the first time. How could any man look at me like that? With my hair in a mess, and my hospital gown? The tension broke when we heard a knock.

"Oh that must be Janet, come on in!" My mom said loudly so she could hear her.

Aidan walked back to stand next to the TV as Janet came in. I couldn't believe what I saw. The roundness of her belly must have slipped my memory because I couldn't remember her being pregnant, was I that out of it?

"You helped her too."

Now I was really confused, how exactly was I helping all these people in my life?

Janet came up to me smiling, "Miss Luna, I see you're feeling much better now."

I was confused. I thought she'd be apprehensive or upset about the scene I made but she came in jolly like I was her favorite patient.

"Uh, I wanted to apologize for the other day, I don't know what came over me," I said.

Janet shook her head as she took her stethoscope off.

"Miss Luna don't even worry about it, things happen...but you aren't gonna run out on me this time right? Cause with this little tadpole adding an extra couple pounds I can't run very fast," she said as she rubbed her round belly.

"Congratulations," Aidan chimed in the background.

"Oh thank you!" Janet turned to face him then brought her attention back to me.

"Your boyfriend is such a gentleman," she said and I almost corrected her but I just grinned instead. She took her stethoscope to my chest and listened. She also took my temperature and blood pressure.

"Everything is normal, you should be out of here by noon. Just let me get all your paperwork ready, your follow-up instructions, and I'll come back in to discharge you, okay?"

"Thank goodness," I quipped.

"What?! But I thought you liked us Miss Luna," Janet said teasing.

"No offense, you guys were great putting up with me but I'm ready to get out of here," I replied.

"Oh yeah, I'm just joking with ya', totally understand."

Janet walked to my mom and hugged her, my mom was on the verge of tears.

"Your daughter is a miracle," Janet told my mom.

My mom nodded with tears in free-flow now and Janet nodded to Aidan as she walked past. "Take good care of her, she's a keeper."

"I know," Aidan replied.

Minutes later, my mother and Aidan stepped outside while I took a shower and got ready to be discharged. I had no idea of the danger we were in.

Chapter 18

JANET

When Aidan and Isabel left the room, Eveley took a quick shower. Afterwards she stepped out and changed into the outfit her mother brought her. She finished tying the shoelaces to her tennis shoes and arranged her things in the bag her mom brought.

She heard a knock and Janet's voice.

"I'm here to discharge you, ready?" Janet said with a smile as she stepped into the room.

"Yes, you don't know how happy I am to be leaving," Eveley said as she sat in a chair next to a table by the window.

"And alive, healthy, and with a loving mother and boyfriend, you are blessed beyond measure," Janet added as she sat in the opposite chair.

"I am, and I'm grateful for it every day."

Janet flipped open the papers and began to go over her discharge info.

"Okay, I just need you to sign that I went over this with you."

"Sure." Eveley signed her name.

Janet hesitated but finally mustered the courage to speak more personally.

"Uhm could I ask you a question?" Janet asked.

"Sure."

"Have you ever been told you have a healing energy by others?" Janet asked.

Eveley thought back to what the voice told her about healing people.

"Uhm not exactly but since the lightning strike I've felt a weird sensation like currents going through my body, maybe like in the movies I've gained some super powers right?" Eveley joked.

"I don't usually share personal information with my patients but I wanted to let you know you are the only patient I have ever seen heal so fast from such a bad accident, can I see?" Janet motioned to the scar on her chest, Eveley nodded. Janet moved part of her shirt collar to show the scar, the scar looked completely healed.

"Your scar was awful the first day you were brought here, it was so red, and look at it, it's basically healed," Janet paused.

"So...my husband and I have been trying for a baby for 5 years. It's been a roller coaster ride. Mainly I haven't been able to bring a baby to term. I've had 3 miscarriages. It always starts the same, I start to cramp and the bleeding starts. The morning I arrived to work before I saw you for the first time, I went to the bathroom and noticed some bleeding had started," Janet paused, tears filling her eyes, she looked down at her clasped hands.

Eveley got closer and placed her hand on her shoulder.

"I cried a lot that day knowing the inevitable was about to happen. I'd already accepted my baby's fate. I am already 6 months along but that day I barely looked pregnant, my doctor told me my baby was growth restricted. He was the size of a baby of only four months. There wasn't much hope left in me, and the bleeding was just the nail in the coffin." Janet turned and looked at Eveley.

"But then I started to care for you as my patient and something strange happened. The first time I touched your arm to give you IV fluids I felt a current of electricity or something running from your arm to my hand and after that all my symptoms went away, almost instantly," Janet continued.

"Not only did my symptoms go away but my baby thrived. The next day I woke up and noticed my belly had grown overnight and I didn't feel anymore cramping or have anymore bleeding. I was scared still. I already had an appointment scheduled for the bleeding so I went in thinking they were going to tell me bad news. It was the complete opposite, my baby was not only on target for his growth but he was a bit bigger than usual, everything checked out perfectly normal. I felt the anxiety over this pregnancy dissipate. I felt inner peace I'd never felt before, an assurance this pregnancy would be different. My body had healed, my mind too. I no longer felt anxiety or depression which I've been battling all my life. It's as if I was a brand new person...and I think it had something to do with you. You must have some kind of healing power," Janet looked at Eveley waiting for a revelation. Eveley hugged Janet tightly.

"I'm so happy for you Janet, after that lightning strike I'm still questioning a lot of things myself but I'm so happy for you."

Suddenly the voice interrupted her thoughts.

"You need to leave now, there are two men on their way to your room. They are dangerous and are here to take you away," the voice interrupted.

Eveley felt alarmed. She spoke back in her mind, "What do I do? What about my mom and Aidan?"

"Write them a note to meet you and give it to Janet to give to them, tell them I told you about the danger nearby."

"Okay."

"Janet I don't have much time to explain but I need to leave right now. I need you to give a note to my mother, please don't let anyone but her see it."

"Okay I can do that for you Miss Luna," Janet said a bit confused about her sudden rush to leave.

Eveley ripped a corner of the discharge papers and wrote on it and folded it in half. Janet looked perplexed, but took the paper in her hand. Eveley quickly gathered her purse and bag. She peeked out slowly from her door.

"Goodbye Janet," she whispered and slipped out of her room and down the hall to the stairwell.

CHAPTER 19

MEN IN SUITS

"So how has your mom, dad, and Eileen been?" Isabel asked Aidan.

Isabel knew Eileen was suffering through some health problems recently but hadn't told Eveley anything yet. Isabel knew this through Stella who she kept regularly in touch with, usually they spoke on the phone two or three times a month. Stella asked Isabel not to tell Eveley as Eileen was very clear she didn't want her friends to know.

Both moms were completely perplexed about Aidan and Eveley's sudden break up almost two years ago and to the day were still trying to figure it out.

Aidan sighed deeply, Isabel sensed it was not going well. They started walking slowly down the hallway toward the nurses desk and entrance to the wing.

"Well, just this month we received really bad news," he paused, "They said her symptoms were actually cancer, and it was really advanced." Aidan hung his head down.

Isabel felt awful, what Stella and Jason must be going through she thought. She placed her hand on his upper arm and squeezed it gently.

"I'm so sorry mijo, I really am. I'm going to pray for your sister and your entire family. I'm going to contact your mother as soon as I have a free moment and talk with her. I'm sure she needs a lot of support right now. I didn't know that Eileen had been diagnosed with cancer."

At those words Aidan perked up a bit and smiled.

"Yeah, but today I received good news from her that she felt a lot better and wasn't in any pain. That's why I can't stay very long, I don't want to be too far from her. They said she has a few months left, but I still don't want to be so far."

"Of course, thank you for coming all the way out here, I think it really helped Eveley."

"You think so? I think she still hates me," Aidan said.

"Mijo, she's never hated you, it's hard for her to trust after what happened with her dad. She just needs more time and she'll come around. I saw her looking at you, I think there's still something there..."

Aidan felt encouraged by Isabel's words, patience was all he could offer at the moment, that and emotional support.

Aidan felt tempted to ask about Eveley's dad, it would help him solve the puzzle of what happened the last couple of years between him and Eveley, but there was a lot buried he wasn't comfortable asking about.

In the past, Eveley had speculated many times about the melted-face man. Sometimes, she acted as if she believed it was an exaggeration from when they were kids, but Aidan clearly remembered that it wasn't. Now, after his own encounter with one of those things, he knew they were 100% real and suspected that Pablo's disappearance was connected to these parasites

As they turned the corner, they saw two men 50 feet in front of them standing by the nurse's station. As soon as the men caught sight they were being observed by Aidan and Isabel, they acted strange, as if they didn't expect other people in the wing besides the nurses and doctors. It could have almost been comical if it wasn't for the menacing body posture. The pair wore stiff and impeccable suits, one dark blue, the other black. Both men wore dark sunglasses which seemed ridiculous to Aidan being they were indoors. They almost reminded Aidan of a certain movie except these guys didn't seem to have a humorous bone in their body.

One nurse handed one of the men a folder with paperwork inside, her face serious. The other nurse's face had worry written all over it. Janet wasn't one of them as she was attending to patients on the floor.

The men walked toward them, they made no effort to move around them as they pushed through Aidan and Isabel without saying a simple excuse me. Aidan and Isabel looked at each other incredulously.

Isabel grabbed Aidan's arm and pulled him along, peeking around the corner to keep sight of the two men. The men inched closer to Eveley's room, Isabel was ready to run and ask what the hell they thought they were doing when she felt a tap on her shoulder. She jumped slightly and turned around. Janet stood there with a nervous look on her face. She handed her a note as she motioned with her finger to stay quiet. Aidan was also perplexed as these men inched closer to Eveley's room. Isabel opened the folded piece of paper which read:

Mom,
The voice said I'm in danger so I left, meet me where the water calls my name before sundown, make sure you are not being followed.
Eveley

Aidan peeked at the note and wondered what Eveley meant by the "voice".

Isabel knew exactly where this place was, they took daily walks in the nature sanctuary when they visited Parkville in the past. The first time Eveley joined her mother and came across the waterfall, it was full and alive. Eveley was so captivated by the waterfall that Isabel had to convince her to leave after spending an hour sitting there and playing with the water. Eveley then proclaimed loudly, "But it's calling my name mother!" Ever since then they joked of her dramatic exit from the sanctuary.

Aidan watched as the men began to open Eveley's room door. Aidan grabbed Isabel's arm and pulled her toward the exit, but not before Isabel whispered, "Thank you," to Janet and gave her a quick hug.

Aidan and Isabel walked briskly, they didn't take the time to wait for the elevator and rushed down the stairs.

"As soon as we get downstairs we need to get on a bus or go into a different building," Aidan said.

"I agree, I think I saw a bus stop around the corner," Isabel added.

Meanwhile, after Janet gave the note to Isabel, she made her way back to the nurses' station. The men came back minutes later and asked what happened to the patient in room #403. Janet told them they had already discharged the patient. The men in suits grumbled something about incompetency and walked away in a hurry. When they were out of sight, her two nurse colleagues seemed relieved.

"Who were they?" Janet asked.

"We're not sure, maybe FBI?" one of the nurses said.

"Weird, what did they want with the patient in #403?" Janet asked.

"They mentioned something about power surges among themselves and wouldn't say much else, but they brought signed court forms authorizing them access to all her medical information. It was really weird, we called the administrator, and she seemed nervous as well when we told her they were here with legal forms."

"Wow, that's so strange, they didn't smile much did they?" Janet asked.

"No they didn't."

CHAPTER 20

NEIGHBORS

Since both Isabel and Aidan came in from out of town by air, neither had a car. As soon as they reached the first floor, they both ran down the sidewalk to the main road in front and turned a corner. Luckily, the road went down a steep hill next to a multi-story garage that hid a bus stop out of view from the hospital. They were about to hide in the parking garage but they didn't have to. A bus was making its way toward their bus stop just seconds after they arrived. Their luck couldn't have come at a better time.

They boarded the bus, with plans to call an Uber from a safer spot away from the menacing men they encountered in the hospital. They looked out the window and decided to get out at the area of Union Station. They entered the grand building and sat at a small table tucked into a corner.

"What do you think that was all about?" Isabel said in a low voice.

Aidan shook his head. "I don't know but it didn't look good, does Eveley have her phone?"

"No, she said they told her the lightning strike fried it. I'm so worried mijo, we need to meet up with her asap."

"Don't worry, we'll get there," Aidan said.

Aidan hailed an Uber with the address to the nature sanctuary. Within minutes the Uber pulled up to the front entrance and they were on their way to the sanctuary. Isabel and Aidan rode in silence, both worried about Eveley and why she left so suddenly.

Isabel and Aidan were dropped off by the Uber in front of the entrance to Parkville Nature Sanctuary. The weather was now gloomy and the sky looked like it was gearing up to drench them in a light drizzle or heavy rain, it was hard to speculate on Midwest weather as it was often unpredictable.

"Okay, let's go, the waterfall is about a mile in, we'll go the clockwise direction as it's shorter," Isabel said in a low tone.

Aidan followed Isabel into the sanctuary, half-way through the sanctuary that was now showing hues of orange and red on every leaf, they saw a group of wild turkeys cross their path. They continued on until they heard the churning of the waterfall.

Eveley sat on a bench, she hid a small pair of scissors in her hand. As soon as they saw each other, Isabel and Eveley hugged. Surprisingly, Eveley also hugged Aidan, not a long hug but nonetheless.

"Are you guys okay?" Eveley said first.

"Yeah, we're fine, but what was that all about?" Isabel asked.

"Ma you saw those men right?"

"Yes."

"And they looked like they were up to no good...right?"

"That's right," Isabel answered. She touched Eveley's forehead with the back of her hand. Eveley flinched and pulled away.

"The voice told me two men were coming to take me away, it was two guys right?"

"Si mija, me dieron mal presentimiento [they gave me a bad feeling], but this voice is starting to worry me."

"That voice just saved us all from danger," Eveley protested and looked agitated.

"You don't believe me? How can you not believe me after what you just saw with your own eyes? How could I have known those men were coming for me?" Eveley added.

"I don't know Eveley, and I didn't say I didn't believe you. I just worry about this voice," Isabel continued, trying not to escalate the argument.

"Ma, that should be the least of your worries. There are two men looking for me right now, planning to do who knows what to me."

"Not while I'm around," Aidan chimed in. He was still confused about what Isabel and Eveley were talking about in reference to the "voice" but he didn't want to interrupt them.

Eveley shook her head.

"I know it's hard to believe but I'm starting to believe this is not my imagination," Eveley explained.

"Si mija, I believe you, but how do you know this being is trustworthy?"

"I don't ma, but I have no other choice but to trust it. I can't make it go away so I just have to learn to live with it."

At those words, Isabel nodded. Her daughter looked at the world in a similar way to her. She rolled with the punches, even if the punches were more like bullets.

Isabel sighed deeply. "Okay, then we need a plan. I'm sure they have all your info. They were talking to the nurses who looked nervous and handed them paperwork. If we go back to your apartment they may be waiting for you."

"Legally they can't do anything, they'd have to have suspicion you committed a crime to take you into custody. You have nothing to worry about as long as we're around," Aidan said and looked around as he heard voices.

A family with kids walked up to the waterfall and their two young kids started to play with sticks, throwing them in the water.

"Let's go," Isabel whispered.

They climbed up the embankment next to the waterfall and crossed a bridge. They continued to walk in silence, finally when they were out of the earshot of the young family, Isabel began to plan.

"Do you still have your gun?" she asked Eveley.

"Yes ma, it's in the safe."

"Do you have ammunition?"

"Always, you and dad taught me this growing up."

"Yes, but it's my job to remind you."

"Okay, this is what we're going to do. We're going to grab an Uber and ask the driver to drop us off near your place. Somewhere we can observe to make sure no one has been in your place or is hanging around," Isabel said.

"There's a small bookstore near my apartment, you can see the front door to my building from there," Eveley replied.

"Perfect, let's do that," Isabel added.

Isabel had never been to Eveley's apartment. Eveley had only been living in Missouri for three months up to that point. She started her first year of college in August at Park University which was in Parkville.

One day out of the blue right before her high school graduation, Eveley started talking about living in Missouri. At first, Isabel was suspicious since it was so random. She suspected it had to do with her father. Isabel had continued to visit Kansas City over the years to keep up with Pablo's case but it was basically a cold case at that point which deeply frustrated Eveley.

Eveley didn't know anyone in Missouri so when she continued to talk of moving to Parkville, Isabel expressed her disapproval. Eventually, Eveley confessed that indeed she wanted to come to Kansas City to find out what happened with her father. She had it in her head that being in KC full time would help the case move forward somehow. She even let it slip she planned to go hiking looking for him. The more Isabel tried to talk her out of it, the more stubborn Eveley would become, till they were arguing about it daily.

Magdalena warned Isabel that Eveley would double down if she continued to dissuade her and that's exactly what happened. One day she came home and Eveley was apologetic but didn't back down. She was leaving for Parkville, Missouri in two weeks. She had already found a job at a restaurant, been admitted to Park University, and secured an apartment in town. Isabel cried so many nights leading up to her departure.

Magdalena tried to talk to Eveley just to see where her head was at, and there was no doubt in her head Eveley wasn't going to change course. She tried to console Isabel as much as possible but eventually she advised her to get on board so she could help Eveley and keep her safe. "No use in having a fall out over something that's going to happen anyway," Magdalena told Isabel.

The first thing Isabel did was buy Eveley her first gun. Isabel and Pablo had always owned guns and educated Eveley on their proper use so she was very familiar with them. She'd been going to the shooting range with Pablo and Isabel since she was allowed at 12 years old. She'd also joined Pablo on many hunting trips so she had a lot of experience. She had access to her parent's guns in case of self-defense but she declined having a personal firearm up to that point as she didn't feel she was proficient enough to carry one full-time.

When Eveley received this gift, she looked at the gun with surprise. She had actually been thinking of buying her first gun since she would be living alone for the first time. She used all her free time testing and getting familiar with her gun at the shooting range until it was the day of her departure.

She loaded up her car, a 4-door sedan with all her clothes, small knick-knacks, and said goodbye to her family. Cesar insisted on driving to Parkville to look over her apartment and help her move, but she wouldn't allow it. If she was going to be independent, she wouldn't be a burden to her family. She knew she could take care of herself.

Eveley didn't know her grandfather made a trip to Parkville before she moved to scout everything out. He didn't let her know he was looking out for her as he admired her independence, after all, she took after him. He felt peace of mind once he saw where she would live and even met some of her neighbors. He also trusted in his granddaughter's ability to take care of herself once out there alone.

When she arrived at that small second-floor apartment on the outskirts of Parkville, she knew it was perfect for her. The apartment was in a small two story four-plex, it had a cute balcony the entire length of her living room and bedroom. She could see a large canopy of trees and the Missouri river, it felt cozy and she felt at home immediately.

It also helped that the three other tenants were awesome and looked out for each other. Across from her lived Mirabel, she was 25 and had the cutest little three-year-old son. She'd graduated 3 years ago, right before her son was born, and landed a job as an accountant. She'd lived there for five years now.

Below was Eta, a 75-year-old single senior citizen who was like their granny. She often did all the things you might imagine a nice old lady to do if you were friends with her. She baked the girls cookies and treats all the time. She looked out for all of them, she was a listening ear, gave great advice, plus she was hip and full of sass.

Across from Eta lived a 25-year-old college student who hailed from Tennessee, Annie. She was super busy with law school so they didn't see her much, but when she happened to be free; she was the friendliest and most down-to-earth girl Eveley had ever met, always helpful and nice to everyone.

Eveley had all her neighbor's contacts saved on her phone but since her phone was destroyed, she didn't remember any of their numbers by memory or else she could have asked them for information on anything suspicious at her apartment. She remembered there were some messages left for her that Janet wrote down and saved for her on a notepad. She'd thrown the notepad in her bag before she took a shower.

As they rode in the Uber, she dug into the bag she carried with her. She found the small notepad and opened it to find a dozen or so numbers and messages, a few from people she didn't even know but she found all three of her neighbors. They had always treated her like family and it made sense they tried to get in touch with her.

"Ma, can I borrow your phone?"

"Si mija, who are you calling?"

"My neighbors left me messages, maybe they know what's been going on..."

"Okay, mija, entiendo [I understand]," Isabel replied.

Eveley dialed Annie's number first, it went straight to voicemail. Next she called Eta, again voicemail. Finally, she dialed Mirabel, she'd left the sweetest message, she read it on the notepad:

Eveley,

I knew you couldn't be brought down with a lightning bolt, you're a goddess now, remember that! I'll try to visit you but they are telling me family only right now, but I've been worried for you like a big sister worries for her little sis, love you! Will try to call you later!

Mirabel

"Hello?" Mirabel sounded hesitant.

"Mirabel? It's Eveley."

"Eveley! Omg! I'm so happy to hear your voice! Oh girl, I've been worried sick for you, I've been trying to call your room all day today with no answer!"

"I was just discharged that's why," Eveley replied.

"Girl, I left you messages, algo raro pasa aqui [something weird is going on here]," Mirabel said in a low tone.

"Oh si? Como que [Oh yeah, like what]?"

"Unos hombres raros han estado vigilando nuestro edificio [Some strange men have been watching our building]."

Eveley stayed silent.

"Are you okay Eveley?"

"Oh yeah, sorry, I was just thinking."

"Girl they tried to talk to me when I was coming home. I called the cops, and Eta and Annie also refused to talk with them. We figured they were FBI or something cause when I first called the cops and they showed up they told me these guys were authorized to ask questions but wouldn't tell me what agency they were with. I told them I wasn't interested in talking to them without a court order. You should have seen their faces, they looked surprised I refused."

"Yeah I don't know why they want to talk to me, I haven't done anything wrong."

"I know you haven't...I saw a documentary that people who survive accidents related to energy sources are always under suspicion and most get questioned by FBI."

"Really? I didn't know that."

"Yeah, and I talked to Annie and Eta, Annie says you need to watch your back. These guys seem unrelenting. I've been monitoring my ring camera and I saw one of them come to your door yesterday and wiggle your doorknob."

Eveley was upset, who gave these people the right to invade her life like this? She hadn't done anything wrong.

"Eta said last night she heard footsteps in your apartment but when she looked out her door, balcony, and windows, she didn't see anyone or any suspicious cars. I think they might have tapped our phones and your apartment."

Eveley sighed, her head was spinning, she was scared for everyone in her life. She almost felt like telling Aidan to leave for Ireland and her mother to Texas but she knew they wouldn't leave.

"If you're coming home, I'd be very careful, I can text you if I see them again."

"Okay, I appreciate it, thank you so much, can you call me at this number?"

"Yes of course, keep me updated, and be careful okay?"

"Si claro, adios [Yes, of course, goodbye]."

"Cuidate, adios [Take care, goodbye]."

Chapter 21

Mr. Collins

"They tapped your apartment and phones but I destroyed their signals," the voice said.

"Thank you, what do I do now?" Eveley implored the voice in her mind.

"Do not go to your apartment yet, contact the man on your notepad named Mr. Collins, you can trust him, he will help you. Tell him everything that has happened in person, ask him to meet you at the-"

"Are you okay?" Aidan's voice interrupted her thoughts, she looked at him confused.

"Sorry I was lost in thought."

"We're here at the Parkville bookstore." Isabel pointed out as the car pulled up.

"We need to take a detour to English Landing Park. We need to meet by the boat ramp at the river," Eveley blurted out to Aidan and Isabel.

"Can you take us to English Landing Park?" Eveley asked the Uber driver, who told her to add it to her itinerary.

They drove over the same train tracks where the lightning bolt hit her and she couldn't help but wonder what really happened that night. They were dropped off near the pedestrian entrance to the park. As soon as they stepped out of the Uber, Eveley dialed Mr. Collin's number.

"Hello?" Mr. Collins answered.

"Hi, is this Mr. Collins? This is Eveley Luna."

"Eveley! I'm so relieved you are okay, my my my, I never imagined someone could be so resilient," Mr. Collins said.

Since his role in the rescue of Eveley, Mr. Collins had experienced some strange developments and often wondered if he'd ever get to speak to the young lady he helped rescue.

"Could you meet me right now?" Eveley asked.

"Right now?! Where are you?" Mr. Collins asked.

"I'm at English Landing Park, the boat ramp near the bridge. I'm with my mother and friend from out of town. There's a lot going on and I need your advice, it's urgent."

"Oh my, yes, I can be there in 15 minutes," Mr. Collins replied.

"Okay thank you."

Fifteen minutes later Mr. Collins showed up with Stanford by his side. Since he'd found Eveley on that foggy morning four days ago, his limp had completely gone away. He felt as if he'd aged backwards, every single health problem he had, completely gone. He made his way down the ramp and as he approached Eveley, before he could even make it down, Eveley walked up to him and gave him a big hug.

"Thank you Mr. Collins, thank you for not leaving me there!"

"Of course not dear, I wasn't going to leave you there if I could help it, and Stanford helped too." He signaled to Stanford.

"Oh you're such a good boy aren't you?"

Eveley crouched down and pet him as he wagged his tail. She stood, walked to Isabel and grabbed her by the shoulders.

"This is my mom Isabel," Eveley said.

Isabel approached and hugged Mr. Collins.

"Thank you so much for what you did for my daughter."

"Of course ma'am."

He proceeded to shake Aidan's hand.

"Aidan, nice to meet you," Aidan said as he shook his hand firmly.

"Irish?" Mr. Collins asked.

"Yes sir."

"It's been a while but I lived in Ireland, near Dublin back in the 80's, wonderful country."

Aidan nodded and grinned.

Eveley proceeded to tell Mr. Collins everything from the voice in her head to the two menacing men at the hospital. Afterwards, there was a long pause, his face seemed receptive. For a moment she was scared he was going to think she was crazy. But he didn't say anything, he simply looked deep in thought.

"You know back in my youth, in the 70's mind you, my friends and I from college were really into some hippie stuff. You know, the typical stuff, like believing in aliens," He chuckled.

"I went to school in New Mexico, where you know aliens are practically lore. Well, every chance we got we'd travel to all the most well known places for UFO sightings. We took up this hobby for a good two years while we were in college together.

"We really believed we could signal aliens to communicate with our minds. We believed our brain waves could somehow reach the darkest and farthest recesses of space. The gist was we would communicate by asking for aliens, any aliens, to communicate back in any way they saw fit. For about the first year we really didn't see or communicate with anything.

"We were starting to get to our breaking point especially once the hot season started. We were starting to get tired of hiking hard-to-reach canyons just to burn in the sun all day. But one day everything changed. That day six of us made the steep climb up a rugged canyon on the west side. We hiked two hours before we finally reached the peak. We split up to take our own spot along the ridge line. What we did once up there is set our own individual stations, and get into a meditative trance to communicate.

"My best friend, James, was the closest to me, he set up about 100 feet from me. I distinctly remember hearing a voice in my head. I almost thought my own mind wanted this so bad it was playing tricks on me but that wasn't the case. This voice told me to open my eyes and look in front of me. At first I didn't see anything. I thought, what a let down, I need to find a better hobby. But then a reflection in front of me caught my eye. There was an object in the shape of an octahedron, picture two pyramids joined in the middle, that's the shape. Only because I was focusing hard did I catch it in my vision when it allowed me to see it. It was a shiny blinding structure. It had hidden itself in plain sight as it mirrored the background behind it. It appeared as if it'd come to the surface of a body of water, it was truly impressive. Then in the blink of an eye, the ship shot across the sky into the distance and disappeared."

Mr. Collins took a long pause to survey the faces of his new friends. They seemed in awe and on the edge of their seats.

"What I'm about to say next is something I've never told anyone so I ask that you guys be discreet with what I say."

Everyone nodded.

"After that day, night and day I would receive messages from a voice who I can only assume was a being from that ship. This individual over time gave me information on who he was, and what his life was like.

"Eventually the ship revealed itself to some of my other friends as well, but the glimpse of the ship started a bit of unnecessary friction. When I mentioned I was communicating with this alien almost daily, some of my friends didn't believe me and one of our friends in particular, his name was Tyler became a different person.

"Eventually everyone in our group had seen the ship, every last one, yet they couldn't believe I was communicating with something inside of it. I let it go, I stopped talking with them about it except to my friend James who instead of being antagonistic, was fascinated with the things I was learning from this being.

"Unfortunately some of the background noise from my so called friends made me question myself. I doubted myself and began to ask myself if it was really true. Was I just nuts and seeing that ship set off something inside me I had no control over? So I started to go on these trips by myself and some with

James. Almost every single time we went we caught a glimpse of this ship.

"After a couple of times, James said he started to communicate with a being as well. However, this alien was in distress. It claimed all kinds of crazy things. That they were a prisoner, that they were a hybrid human, just a lot of things hard to believe.

"I warned James not to mention any of this to the other guys especially Tyler as he would just get envious. I finally asked the being I was communicating with why he only communicated with certain humans, not some of my friends and he gave me a very interesting answer. He said they only communicated with those they deemed righteous. I thought it was peculiar at the time but I understood soon enough.

"I don't remember quite the details but James somehow was talked into taking another canyon trip with our friends and I was invited. Well from the get-go it was awkward. I knew the drill, I would just pretend to not see or hear anything around these guys who were all too obsessed now with what they couldn't hear and were not satisfied with seeing the ship.

"We started on the hike, the entire time I felt a bad premonition. When we made it to the top, I thought it was strange Tyler was really friendly and nonchalant. When we took our spots, Tyler somehow convinced James to follow him to his area cause he needed help with something which was out of my line of sight."

"I began to feel uneasy, usually it took a half hour to get the ship to reveal itself, it worked most of the time anyway. I sat on the ground and began to meditate. Next thing I knew it was like an alarm went off in my head. I felt like the air was punched from my lungs, and it was hard for me to breathe. When I was finally able to speak, the first words out of my mouth were, 'Where is James?'"

He paused and his eyes got teary. His voice broke when he continued.

"Literally two seconds later, Tyler came running, shouting about how James got too close to the edge, slipped and fell. What Tyler didn't know was in that moment the alien I'd been communicating with shouted in my head that Tyler had pushed James over the canyon. I honestly didn't know what to believe. We followed Tyler to where James supposedly slipped. His body lay motionless 400 feet below. We knew he was no longer with us. No one could survive such a fall. When I saw him below I felt a seething anger build inside me. I didn't know if this alien was tricking me, if Tyler was really capable of doing such a thing. I didn't want to believe someone I knew was capable of such evil, plus how could I prove it?

"It took all day to recover James from the bottom of the canyon. I was the first person that identified him as his parents were too afraid to see him at first, though they did eventually muster the courage. It was one of the worst days of my life aside from the death of my daughter.

"That night was my last communication with the alien. I told him I wanted him to stop contacting me, that I'd had enough. But I think he was real. I've since regretted blaming it, imploring it over the years since to communicate again and it's never contacted me again. If it had been a figment of my imagination I think the voice would have returned but it never has. And as for Tyler, he disappeared under mysterious circumstances two years later, no one has been able to find out what happened to him."

"What does your gut feeling tell you now about Tyler?"

Mr. Collins looked stunned by the question posed by Isabel.

"Tyler did it, the moment I looked into his eyes, I knew he'd done it. I just didn't want to believe, it was easier to pretend the alien was lying to me," Mr. Collins said without hesitation.

"And so that's why I believe you 100%...and there's another thing. I think you may have some sort of healing power. Since the day I helped rescue you, my health has improved tremendously. Even the limp I've had since Vietnam is completely gone.

Has anyone else since the accident told you their health has improved dramatically?"

Eveley hesitated. "Well...the nurse taking care of me did."

"And me as well," Aidan added. When he heard the revelation his mind came up with an idea.

"Dear, I have to say, I don't think what you experienced on that night was exactly a lightning strike." Mr. Collins paced back and forth with his hand on his forehead, deep in thought.

"Is there any place out of the country you can go to temporarily till things die down here?"

"Out of the country?!" Eveley said with disbelief in her voice.

"Yes my dear, you're in a lot of danger. They will find you, and even if they have no right they will take you against your will. You'll be at their mercy and it will be only a matter of time before they find out about your healing abilities. You'll be their prisoner and test subject," Mr. Collins said it with so much seriousness it scared her.

"I can't just up and leave my life, won't they be more suspicious if I'm gone?"

"True, you can stay one night, but I wouldn't recommend at your apartment or anywhere they can trace you back to."

"Eveley, can I speak to you in private?" Aidan asked.

Eveley looked confused. "Sure."

She followed him to an area further down the banks of the river. "What's going on?"

"Okay, so you know that Eileen is sick right?"

"Yeah, she told me she had a few things back to back, flu and mono."

"No, Eveley, this was more than a flu, she has cancer."

Eveley looked like a deer caught in headlights.

"W-what? When did you find out? She didn't tell me anything!"

"She didn't want any of her friends and even family to know. She's very stubborn, we found out a few weeks back."

"How bad is it?" Eveley's eyes started filling with tears till the tears finally fell like a dam broken.

"They told us several months at most...she's been in a lot of pain lately," he said somberly, he looked at her intently.

"But if it's true you have healing powers you could help her, and you can also hide with us like Mr. Collins said," he added.

Eveley looked down and shook her head, "Everything is happening so fast. Of course I want to help Eileen but I don't know if I'm going to disappoint everyone. I don't want to do that to your parents most of all."

"No one has to know Eveley, I can come up with some excuse. I know! That we reconciled and wanted to visit. My mom and dad won't mind. Eileen will be upset at first because she doesn't want anyone to see her but she'll get better, I know she will. Please, I'm begging you to please help Eileen, you'll be safer with us as well."

"I can't hide forever though. I can't just give up my life all of a sudden because these jerks are after me. I need this being, Argh! I need to give him a name or ask him his name, but I need to have a talk with him. To ask him the million questions I have about all that's happening, including the lightning strike. Not to mention my mom thinks he's a bad omen or something."

Eveley was talking a mile a minute, her head was spinning from all of the latest developments. Aidan simply hugged her, for a moment she wanted to resist but she didn't. She embraced him back and placed her face on his chest. She felt the weight of the world a little lighter when he was there.

"I know it's a lot placed on your shoulders, but we all support you and we've got your back." Aidan stepped back and held on to her arms.

"You can do this, we can do this, right?" He looked at her with hopeful eyes.

"Right, yes, I can do this, *we* can do this, okay let's go tell them."

Aidan and Eveley walked back to Mr. Collins and Isabel.

"Okay, so I have a place I can stay for a while. I'll be leaving with Aidan tomorrow, how long do I need to be away?" Eveley asked.

"At least a few weeks if possible. Once their interest dies down you can return, but you'll need to move to a new place discreetly after your return."

Eveley sighed, this had become more of a dilemma than she signed up for. "Okay, I'll do that."

"But Eveley, you cannot travel under your identity. I need your ID to give you a new one," he whispered.

"What do you mean?" Isabel asked, afraid for Eveley.

"She'll need to travel a bit differently...she'll need to book the flight last minute, at the airport right before the plane boards."

Isabel shook her head in concern.

"Before you leave, come to my address. There will be an envelope with everything you need under my doormat. Burn your credit cards, get all your cash out now, you cannot use them or your phone, time to get a new one."

Eveley took out her ID and handed it to Mr. Collins.

"Are you sure this will work and this is safe?" Isabel looked around.

"It's the only and safest option she has right now. As for you Isabel, I'm pretty sure they'll be investigating everything about you and any other person they realize is helping Eveley," Mr. Collins said.

Isabel hugged Eveley tightly, here was her daughter thrown into another serious situation, sometimes she wondered if her family was cursed since so many tragedies had fallen upon them.

"Don't worry, I'll keep you safe. You can return to your apartment tonight, I'll be watching over you," the voice said.

"I'm going to go back to my apartment tonight, we all are. I'm not going to be a fugitive tonight when I haven't done anything wrong," Eveley said.

Mr. Collins sighed. "Okay but be very careful, they're most likely watching you."

"Okay, will do," Eveley said.

Mr. Collins wrote down his address on a card and handed it to her.

After their meeting, they took an Uber back to her place. There didn't seem to be anyone near the front of her four-plex. They made it to the entry and up the stairs to her apartment.

Eveley opened the door, the inside looked okay except for a few things she noticed were moved out of their spot. She was a very organized person and had a spot for everything. She knew at first glance someone had been in her place, rummaging through her things and moving stuff around carelessly.

"I guess they really are serious about talking to you mija." Isabel noticed the concern on Eveley's face.

"But while I'm here and so is Aidan, we aren't going to let anyone harm you," Isabel pulled out a gun from under her clothing. This whole time she'd been carrying and Eveley should have known but didn't think about it.

"Ma! How did you get it on the plane?!"

"Don't worry about it mija."

Eveley shook her head in disbelief.

"You're all I have, and you may be grown and on your own, but you're still my little girl. If anyone wants to take you away they're going to have to do it over my dead body."

Eveley hugged her mom tightly, "Ma, no digas esas cosas [Mom, don't say those things], nothing's going to happen."

"Mija, if it does, I'm prepared."

"He's watching over me, he said he'd keep me safe," Eveley said.

"You trust him that much?"

"Si ma, I do, he's earned my trust, he's only kept me safe so far. You heard Mr. Collins, you need to go back to Texas as soon as possible or they will try to come after you as well."

"I'm not leaving your side until you're on that plane safely."

CHAPTER 22

REALIGN

For the next hour, Isabel and Eveley packed Eveley's clothing into one large backpack.

After they were done, Aidan decided he'd sleep on the couch but before he could take the couch he noticed Isabel had fallen asleep on it. Eveley grabbed a blanket and covered her mom.

She walked barefoot to her balcony, she stood pondering and looking at the view in front of her. She was at a crossroads, she knew her life as she knew it was never to be again.

Aidan walked to the balcony and stood beside her.

"I like it here, it's very peaceful," he said in a raspy voice, the cool Autumn air having an effect on him.

"Yes, it's pretty special, I'm going to miss it," Eveley said softly.

"You know...I regret every day we've been apart," Aidan said as he looked ahead.

For a while Eveley didn't say a thing, she didn't want to remember the past, *their* past.

"You hurt me...a lot," is all she said as her eyes filled with tears.

"I know, and I hate myself every day for it, but I had no choice, I had to keep you safe."

Eveley looked at him confused. "Safe from what?"

He knew she deserved an explanation, it may not make her trust him but it would make everything make sense.

"I know you don't want to admit it. I know you're just protecting yourself from the memory of your dad, and of that monster lurking in the shadows, but you know it was all real."

At those words Eveley felt agitated, "Don't you dare bring my dad into this! My dad disappeared, as kids we all had big imaginations, we made stuff up."

"Eveley, you know it was real, don't lie to yourself."

Eveley breathed harder but didn't say a word. She wanted to keep lying to herself that all those "dreams" were just an overactive imagination, but she knew it wasn't.

"Okay, and what does that have to do with us? You left my life, you gave me no explanation. You simply stopped being there for me. How do you think I felt?" Her pain spilled into every word as her voice shook from holding tears back.

Aidan wanted so bad to embrace her and cure her of her pain but how could he do that when he was the cause of it and she would recoil at his attempt.

"The monster you tried so hard to forget from your mind? Well he wasn't the only one of his kind...you remember Draven O'Connor?"

"Yeah, how could I forget that jerk."

"He was one of them... and he was after you. You remember how crazy you felt and how sick you got right after he came into the picture and started stalking you? Eveley, they take over human bodies, they are parasites. They look for compatible hosts, but he wasn't looking for you as a host, he wanted you as his mate."

Eveley shuddered at the revelation.

"How do you know he was one of them?" Eveley asked.

She remembered the eerie feeling she'd felt on several occasions since the encounter at the pub. She also had a distant memory of him speaking to her telepathically although her illness immediately after clouded that memory.

"After you left, he came around again. I guess he'd gotten stronger. He told me he'd recently inhabited the body he was in, and now that he'd built up his strength I was no match for him. Luckily for us, you'd already left the country. He went ballistic when he found out you were gone. Of course he pledged to find you, that he was going to use me to find you. I couldn't let that happen, I had to protect you at all costs until I could get rid of him."

"What did you do Aidan?"

"What I had to...to keep you safe."

"Which means what?"

"Don't worry about it, he's no longer a threat."

Eveley looked ahead, Aidan came to her and turned her head gently to look at him.

"I'm sorry, I didn't want to hurt you. If I would have told you at the time, you wouldn't have believed me and it would have been worse because it would have led him to you. Can't you see? I loved you so much I was willing to never see you again in order to keep you safe? Why do you think I traveled so much? It was the only way I could get away to where he couldn't see where you were if I contacted you. By the time I figured out I could communicate with you that way, it was too late, you had shut me out completely."

Eveley looked into his eyes for truth, he'd never lied to her before.

"I had to close my heart to you in order to protect myself and move on. After you stopped talking to me, I thought the worst. I thought maybe you realized I wasn't good enough for you, but it never made sense."

"Good enough?! You are more than enough, more than anything I could have ever dreamed of. I suffered too...there hasn't been a day I haven't thought of you and wished you were by my side. That I haven't thought of all our memories, of your face, your smile, your voice—" he sounded frantic, running his hands over her hair then face, he couldn't help himself now that she was allowing him in again.

She placed her hands softly on his face. She leaned closer, looked into his eyes, letting her vulnerability come through in her gaze.

"Don't hurt me like that ever again," the words barely escaped her lips in a whisper as tears streamed down her face. "I don't think my heart could take it."

"Never, I promise," he whispered between kisses on her forehead, eyes, cheeks, and finally her lips. Afterwards they embraced for a long time, there was no need for more explaining. It was as if their world shifted yet again...equilibrium, hope, joy, was once again possible for the both of them. It was like taking a big breath right after a desperate swim to the surface.

Later that evening she went to Mirabel's apartment where all three of her neighbors were waiting for her. She wrote down Mr. Collin's info, she gave them her keys and money for them to pay for her apartment until she could return and move. She told them she couldn't say where she was headed. They would let Mr. Collins know what was going on so he was aware. They hugged and wished her well, there were a lot of tears. Eveley thought of all the things she was leaving behind...friends, school, stability, her job, basically her life as she knew it.

When she came back Aidan was on her bed, he'd tried hard to stay awake but the exhaustion won. He'd fallen asleep on her queen size bed, one arm behind his head, part of his leg sticking over the edge of her bed. He'd at least managed to take off his shoes, he was wearing jeans and a long-sleeved shirt.

Eveley stood by the doorway and simply watched him for a minute. He was here in her life again, it was surreal and it was the happiest she had felt in a long time. She gently pushed his leg on top of the mattress, and moved his arm to a more comfortable position by his side. She got in bed, her bedroom didn't have a door. She snuggled up to his side and breathed his scent in, she fell asleep by his side almost immediately.

"I have so many questions for you, first of all what do I call you, what is your name?"

"My name? I don't have a name, we are simply known, down to the last cell."

"Well that doesn't help me, here on earth we have names."

"Then you may give me a name of your choosing if that will help you."

"Yes, it would, I will think of something. Can you tell when people are lying?"

"Yes, I can."

"Did anyone lie to me today?"

"No."

Eveley felt relief, in her sleep she was having a perfect conversation with the voice, finally able to ask all the questions she'd wanted to ask all day.

"What did you mean when you said I was helping everyone earlier?"

"You are able to heal people."

"You mean like wounds?"

"Yes, both physical and psychological."

"But how? What really happened to me the night I was hit by lightning?"

Silence.

"Hello, are you still there?"

"Yes, you weren't hit by lightning, in a way, yes it was lightning but it wasn't a natural phenomenon."

"It was you wasn't it?"

"Yes."

"How could you do that to me?"

"It wasn't planned."

"How is it you are supposed to be so advanced but this wasn't in your plan?"

"We are advanced, not perfect."

"So what happened and what are you? I need to know everything about you."

"What would you like to know?"

"Well, where do you come from and why were you at the train tracks that night and why do I have healing powers? Why was I feeling your presence physically through my body when I tried to run away from my hospital room?"

"When they introduced the needle your instincts woke up. It's a survival mechanism since your blood has a different signature than before."

"But why could I feel you?"

"I was trying to help you gain your strength by lending you some of my energy."

"I didn't like that feeling, it felt highly invasive and my mind was confused."

"I know, I had to do it to help you gain strength."

"So...what happens when the people I heal touch others? Are my powers contagious?"

"Yes, but in others they have to gain their powers over time, it takes them weeks to increase."

"Does it always work to heal others no matter how badly they are sick or hurt?"

"Yes, unless their heart has already stopped, once their heart has stopped there is no hope."

"And what did you mean by psychological?"

"It heals the mind as well...any anxiety, depression, mania, trauma, gone. Reasoning and self-control at its peak, it makes you pacifists, it makes you a version of yourself without the trauma, pain, and hardships of the past having an effect."

"What about those that are evil?"

"It heals them too, any impulses they had prior will be healed immediately."

Eveley felt the immensity of what the alien just revealed. She literally held the antidote to so many things plaguing the world.

"Why were you here?"

"I left my world voluntarily, I wanted to know what existed outside of my world."

"What is your world called?"

"You wouldn't understand our language, we really don't communicate the way your species does."

"Okay, and how far away is your world then?"

"Light years away."

"Why were you so curious about other worlds, were you not happy in yours?"

"We don't understand human emotions such as what you call happiness, but I was feeling, what would be closest to an emotion humans call curiosity. That night I experienced a malfunction as I was entering your atmosphere. When you saw me I was within detectable distance to you. I was still not physically there as I can be far but still within distance to communicate with you. Physically you would never be able to touch me or even be in my presence, my energy is too strong. Luckily, it wasn't me that touched you, just an arc from my energy field.

"Eveley, there are billions of worlds and species out there. It's only a few species that have advanced to the capacity to have contact with other species, we are one of them. However, our species forbids us from contact with humans."

"So why did you go against that rule? Why did you decide to visit our galaxy?"

"I felt a curiosity about your species...after all we are distantly related."

"What?!"

"Yes, we split away at some point, many eons ago. We are so different now we have nothing in common, but in a way you carry some of the same DNA. I guess it explains you ability to survive my arc and gaining your powers. It also explains why our species bans contact with your kind."

"So why are we so different now?"

"I would hypothesize it has to do with our ability to obey the laws placed forth for us. We've been rewarded for our loyalty and faithfulness, allowing our race to advance to this point."

"So what do you look like?"

"Like you but we are pure energy. We can't be very close as our energy would damage your cells, or worse."

"So are you near me now?"

"Not particularly, I can be as far as another galaxy and still communicate with you."

"So what's gonna happen now? Will my powers heal the world?"

"Yes, but there will always be a small minority that will resist. One percent of the world population will always resist because they will be made to believe it will kill them. They will run, fight, and never surrender."

"But doesn't that mean world peace? People doing the right thing?"

"Yes but my species is looking for me. It's only a matter of time before they find me. If they find out what happened they will destroy your species."

"What?! why?!"

"Because it would mean you would quickly advance just like our species. They don't trust humans, and they especially don't want a mixing of hybrid species. It would taint our inherited advantage. You would be considered an abomination in their eyes. The only way you could save your planet is if you left earth."

"Left earth!? Are you insane, how? This surely must be a crazy dream."

"This is a dream but you are also still consciously communicating with me."

"But why me? Why can't you just leave? Wouldn't they never find me if you're gone and they don't follow you here?"

"I wish it were that easy. Unfortunately, now that you have these powers and I visited your planet, your signature would be perceived by them and evident to them on your planet as they pass by. If I somehow backtrack to a different location and you go along with me, you will remove that signature that will tip them off near your planet."

"But wouldn't it tip them off on the new planet?"

"Not if I take you to a planet that masks your presence."

"Wouldn't they still sense the others I gift my powers to on earth?"

"No, the changes in their body are much more subtle than yours. They would not be perceptible to them unless they landed and observed for a while or took a blood specimen, which there is very low probability of them doing."

"But, where would I go? How would I even survive leaving my world? How would I get there? Won't they still know what is going on and how everyone is healing?"

"No, only you, the original, will be detectable. You have to leave."

"Hold on hold on, I can't believe I'm talking to an alien about leaving this planet. I must be going insane."

"You are very far from it," he assured her.

"I know...but that's not how it feels. Wait a minute, my mom keeps telling me I shouldn't just trust you. How do I know you're trustworthy?"

"I will prove it to you, just not yet."

"Not yet? I mean I can't continue to talk to you."

"I can tell you everything about the alien that was after you."

Eveley became silent. She shuddered when she thought of Draven's intense eyes.

"Okay, why have those things been after my family since I was a kid?"

"You're one of the few compatible hosts. You attract them just like a mosquito is attracted to a blood meal."

"What are they called and how many of these things are there?"

"They are the lowest of the low so you may call them VERMIN. There's a couple thousand of them. Lucky for your species, when they hitchhiked to your planet, it turned out there weren't many humans compatible with them. Their race is dying out quite quickly due to this impediment."

"Just my luck I would be one of the compatible humans."

"And your mother too."

"No! I hate those things. I think they are the reason my dad never made it back to us."

"They are just a primitive species. Surviving is all they know, yet they believe they are superior at the same time, nothing more dangerous."

"How did they come here to earth and how long have they been here?"

"They have been here almost from the beginning. They destroyed their own world with their imprudence and ended up traveling an empty black journey through space until they crossed paths with earth."

"What happens if I touch one of them?"

"You must not touch them Eveley. They will only become stronger. You must be careful not to run into them. They will be more frantic to infect you when they sense you have a special power that can amplify their strength. Your gift will not heal them in any way."

"How do I know when someone is infected by them? What happens to those they inhabit?"

"The minute one of them infects a human, that human ceases to exist, like the lights have turned off. Their physical body will no longer live if the parasite leaves the host. You will only know if they are infected if you can look them in the eyes closely. They have an ocular occlusion like a busted vein in the white of their eyes, but instead of it being red like in a human it is blue in color. Their pupil is also scalloped, not round."

"I'm not sure I can do this, everyone I love will be at risk."

"They will be at risk regardless. I can help you, your family and everyone of your species. After all, we are distant relatives."

"Is that your bad attempt at a joke?"

"I guess."

"Okay, but I'm not going anywhere with you."

"We don't have much time Eveley. Six months tops before they find your galaxy."

CHAPTER 23

EVENT HORIZON

The next morning before the sun came up, Eveley, Isabel, and Aidan walked out the back door of her apartment. They walked the mile to Mr. Collin's address. In front of his door was an envelope. Eveley opened it, inside was a passport, IDs, along with a data sheet of every conceivable thing about the person on the passport.

Eveley felt a knot in her stomach. Is this what she had been reduced to? Running away with a passport that belonged to Mr. Collin's deceased daughter and hoping she didn't end up in federal prison? Her hands felt clammy, she felt lightheaded. Aidan squeezed her hand and looked at her.

"Don't worry, it'll be okay," Aidan said.

Isabel was just as worried as Eveley but she didn't let it show. She didn't want Eveley to feel worse when it was imperative she pulled this off. At that moment Isabel received a text message from Magdalena. Strange men in cars were patrolling their house and asking around for Isabel.

"Mija, you'll be fine once you make it overseas."

They walked quickly to the local coffee shop that had opened for the day although the sun was still not out. They hailed a taxi there and paid cash. They planned to buy two airplane tickets to get to Atlanta, then finally to Dublin. Isabel would get on a plane to head back to Dallas.

Isabel figured there would be strange men waiting for her somewhere in the Dallas airport or her home.

At the airport, Eveley and Isabel said their tearful goodbyes in the taxi before they separated and exited the taxi. Eveley gave her mom an envelope to open on the plane. It contained a letter she wrote about the VERMIN. She had to warn her mother of the danger she was in due to her compatibility with them.

When Eveley stepped out of the taxi, her heartbeat started racing. It was getting very serious and scary but she had to keep a poker face and confront this challenge without rousing suspicion.

When they made it to the counter of the airline, it took less than ten minutes to set up their flight. They paid cash just like they were instructed.

Meanwhile, Isabel planned to get a burner phone once she touched down in Dallas, to communicate with Eveley without leaving a trace.

Once Eveley and Aidan made it onto the plane and it took off from the runway, she looked at Aidan with an exhausted look on her face. She felt relief she'd made it that far. She was still nervous, unable to relax as she felt she must surely be leaving traces of her presence everywhere. Regardless, she still dozed off, her head falling softly on Aidan's shoulder.

He was tired too, but didn't want to fall asleep as well. He hoped they were doing the right thing, although at times it felt very wrong and surreal.

They arrived to their layover in Atlanta, as soon as the plane touched ground, Eveley woke up. Her anxiety shot up when they started to deboard and one of the airport policemen stood by the door. Aidan looked over at her and could see she was anxious, he squeezed her hand. She had on sunglasses, and a baseball cap.

"Let's go," Aidan said as he stood and grabbed their backpacks. He walked in front of her, holding her hand behind him. As they walked closer to the front exit, the cop who was chatting with the flight attendant, took on a serious face and looked at them intently.

Eveley's heart started beating like crazy, she was sure this was it—she was going to get caught.

Just as Aidan was in front of the cop, the policeman placed his hand on Aidan's shoulder and stopped him.

Inside Eveley felt like fainting, she wanted to run away from this situation. She was glad she wore sunglasses or it'd be obvious how nervous she was. For now she was hiding her discomfort perfectly, not fidgeting, acting like a typical stone-faced traveler, but inside she was screaming. Aidan squeezed her hand again, letting her know it was all okay.

The policeman pointed behind him.

"Looks like you're forgetting something," the cop said motioning with his head.

Aidan looked back, Eveley's jacket was on top of her seat.

"Aw, man, you scared me, thought you were gonna arrest me or sumthin," Aidan joked.

For a minute the cop continued with a serious face, suddenly the policeman burst into laughter.

"The look works every time, doesn't it?!" he said.

Aidan smiled and kept his cool, playing along.

Eveley walked back quickly and grabbed her jacket. Aidan stayed put until she was back next to him and grabbed his hand.

"See ya officer, have a nice day," Aidan said.

"Have a nice day man!" the officer said loudly in between chuckles.

Once they made it past the airplane taxi and into the crowds of people, Eveley felt some relief.

Aidan looked at her with admiration, she'd done so well, he was proud of her. He grabbed her by the shoulder, pulled her toward him and planted a kiss on her cheek.

"You did great *bunny*," Aidan said using his pet name for her.

"I thought I was going to die of a heart attack back there."

"But you didn't, you're my partner in crime now," he said grinning.

"I'm glad this has been enjoyable for you *ducky*," she said sarcastically.

"Who doesn't love a troublemaker? Especially when she's beautiful as well."

She grinned at his compliment. She didn't feel ashamed of what she was doing. She was left with no other choice, they pushed her into a corner. No one was going to experiment on her because of something given to her to give to humanity.

She had been thinking of everything she'd learned since her conversation with the voice. She tried to tell Aidan some of it but the day was rushed and full of danger, so she'd only managed to tell him tidbits of it.

She couldn't get the thought out of her head that she was given a gift which could better mankind. It was such a huge responsibility, something she needed to protect at all costs. She had made up her mind, she was willing to do anything to protect this gift. No one but God, would be allowed to take it from her.

This gift could bring peace. It could bring people to understand each other, to almost wipe out all suffering, violence, deceit, sadness, trauma, and sickness. People would act with responsibility and kindness, no one would go hungry or be left behind. The haves and have-nots would no longer exist. Everyone would help each other out because it was the right thing to do, not because they were forced to. It would be a revolution, not a revolution set in violence, but one set in personal healing for each person.

She thought of how it had already been set in motion and people she'd barely touched days ago had their lives changed for the better. Janet would hopefully be holding a little one in a few months. The healing coming full circle as she looked into those little eyes that held hope, joy, and possibilities. Mr. Collins who suffered scars from his tours in Vietnam healed, the pain of his friend's murder eased, his limp healed. She hoped her touch would heal her mother's pain. The one that set in since her father's disappearance. She hoped her touch would ease Aidan's fears, his anxiety over Eileen. And most of all she hoped she could truly help Eileen get better. That was the ultimate test in her mind. If she could bring her best friend back from the brink of death, it would be the final proof her powers were truly what the voice claimed.

Their flight to Dublin was uneventful, they slept the majority of the flight. After they deboarded at the Dublin airport, they walked to the lot where Aidan left his car parked. The drive to Galway was always relaxing for Eveley, she usually fell asleep, especially if there was a dreary drizzle. She always felt at ease in Ireland, like a part of her belonged there.

"Will your mom be upset I show up all of a sudden without notice?" Eveley asked, anxious she would upset Stella although she wasn't the type of person to react negatively.

"My mom? Nah, she's gonna be happy you came to visit. She'll be curious of course why so suddenly since we've been broken up for a while. She tried her hardest to be detective and find out why we broke up. She really wanted us to get back together again, she said we were perfect for each other. She said whenever you and me were in the same room, she always noticed how I looked at you, like you were the only person in the room."

"And is it true?"

"What?"

"That you still look at me like I'm the only one in the room?"

Aidan grabbed her hand and kissed it tenderly.

"I can't help it," he admitted without shame.

Eveley grinned sheepishly.

As the drive progressed, she began praying in her head. She didn't want her power to fail her, not with Eileen. She was so scared to see her best friend. She was still a bit hurt she hadn't told her about her illness. She could have lost her at any time and she would've been none the wiser. But she understood Eileen didn't want to be seen like she was. She was selfless like that, always thinking of others before her own well-being. But Eveley wasn't going to let her sacrifice herself anymore. Eileen needed everyone's support, and she was going to cure her if it was the last thing she did.

They arrived a bit past 5 pm, it was still daylight when Aidan pulled into the driveway. Both his parent's cars were parked in the driveway.

"Ready?" Aidan looked at Eveley's anxious face.

"Yes," she replied as she took a deep breath.

They walked to the front door, Aidan opened it with his key.

"Hello!" Aidan called out from the entryway.

His mother and father were in the kitchen. Stella dropped her coffee cup and her eyes grew big like saucers. Jason looked speechless.

"Oh my goodness! Aidan! Eveley! What a wonderful surprise!" Stella exclaimed.

"Yes indeed!" Jason said as both he and Stella walked up to them and hugged Aidan, then Eveley.

"My oh my, what an awesome surprise! I'm sure Eileen will be super happy..."

Jason trailed off as they heard footsteps down the stairs. Stella ran toward the staircase. She made it just in time as Eileen lost her grip.

"Wee girl, what are you doing darlin'? You should be in bed!" Stella said as she grabbed her by the elbows.

"Mum I thought I heard Aidan and Eveley's voi—" she struggled to speak as she almost collapsed.

Jason, Eveley, and Aidan were now next to Eileen as well and Eveley managed to grab a hold of Eileen's tiny wrist. She couldn't waste any time giving her a chance. They all supported her small body.

Eveley was almost in tears now as she saw Eileen's condition. She was very thin, about 70 lbs, her face gaunt, and her hair mostly gone. She seemed delirious but when she saw Aidan she livened up.

"Aidan! You're back h—" Her chest rose desperately trying to grasp more air.

Jason picked her up in his arms.

"I'm taking your sister back upstairs, Stella can you come help me tuck her in?" Jason asked.

"Yes darlin'." Stella looked mentally drained as she followed Jason and Eileen upstairs.

Eveley walked into the kitchen, Aidan followed behind her. Tears streamed down her face, she didn't expect Eileen to look so sick. She turned to Aidan and dug her face in his chest as he embraced her. Her muffled sobs were the only sounds echoing in the house.

Aidan realized his sister either lied or downplayed how bad she'd gotten since he left which was a few days ago. He couldn't bear the thought of losing his twin sister. The shock from seeing Eileen so sick made him feel in despair. She was too close to death's door.

Later, Stella and Jason returned downstairs for a few minutes. Eileen had fallen asleep but not before asking to see Aidan and Eveley. Stella promised she'd send them upstairs in a bit but she needed to rest first.

"I'm going to go back up there in a few minutes," Stella said as she sighed and closed her bloodshot eyes.

"Eveley, I'm sorry she didn't say anything. She didn't want anyone to know," Stella said.

"I understand, she never liked people to pity her," Eveley said.

"You know her very well." Stella hesitated, "Aidan, when you left she really took a turn for the worse, we think tonight or tomorrow." Tears started falling like waterfalls from Stella's eyes.

Aidan went to his mom and hugged her as she sobbed, tears were streaming down his face too.

"Can we go talk to her mum?"

"Yes, but she's in and out of delirium so just keep that in mind."

Eveley and Aidan walked to the second floor, they knocked softly on the door. Aidan opened the door slowly. His sister was struggling to breathe, he could see the short and labored breaths she took as her chest rose and fell. Aidan sat next to her first and gently grabbed her hand with both of his, he kissed her hand. Eveley sat on the other side of Eileen and also grabbed her hand, she prayed this would work.

"C'mon little sis, you have to get better," he said to himself in a low voice.

Eileen stirred and barely opened her eyes halfway, she managed to smile.

"You're both here, I missed you both," she barely whispered.

Eveley squeezed her hand, "I've missed you too chica. It's been a while, but you don't have to say anything. Just rest a while, we'll stay here by your side."

Stella made Eileen's room super cozy, adding dim lights and aromatherapy as well as soothing music. Jason and Stella's routine consisted of taking turns staying by her side round-the-clock. They helped her with everything since she was too weak to do anything for herself anymore. They were told by their oncologist once she got to this stage there was nothing to do but make her comfortable if she was in pain. Eileen denied being in pain the last couple of days which was a relief for everyone. Regardless of her being pain-free, she was still weak and had trouble breathing the night before.

After a while, Eveley stood and sat next to Aidan, she rested her head on Aidan's shoulder as they continued to hold Eileen's hands. Eveley rubbed her fingers over her hand, letting her know she was still there. She was so nervous this miracle wouldn't happen. They sat by her side listening to the soothing music for at least an hour, until Stella came in to take over and sent them downstairs to eat something.

The mood in the house was naturally somber. They sat quietly, no one ate much. After about another hour, Stella came downstairs and Jason went upstairs to keep Eileen company.

That night they all slept in Eileen's bedroom.

Stella got in the bed with Eileen and held her. Stella felt like she was in a dream. She couldn't face the future. Her world was breaking apart and there was nothing she could do to stop it. She thought back to the first time she held her after being born. After being in the NICU for almost a week and waiting so long to hold her for the first time. She remembered holding her fragile little body and snuggling up to her.

She couldn't believe this could be the last day she'd ever see those beautiful eyes open or hold her in a warm embrace. It was the hardest thing she'd ever faced and she wasn't sure if she was strong enough to endure the pain.

Jason pulled a recliner next to the bed and fell asleep. Eveley used the sofa bed next to the bed, and Aidan fell asleep in Eileen's desk chair. The hours passed painfully slow.

The next morning, Eveley could've sworn she heard Eileen's voice. She opened her eyes, the room was flooded with sunlight, she was unsure what time it was. She looked around the room, no one was there, she panicked. She stood up and rubbed her eyes, she was so confused, where was everyone? Was Eileen okay? Oh no what if she'd passed during the night?! Eveley ran down the hall and down the stairs.

"Aidan?! Stella?! Eil—"

"Whoa whoa, we're all in here," she bumped into Eileen. She looked completely different than yesterday, like she'd never been sick except for her hair.

"Eileen you're feeling better?!" Eveley exclaimed in surprise.

"Never felt better," Eileen said nonchalantly and they gave each other a long heartfelt hug. Tears started streaming down both their faces. Everyone else was around the kitchen counter with tears down their faces too.

Eveley shook her head, it worked, by God's grace it worked! She was shocked, she was shaken in a good way, but most important of all, she was a believer now.

"Sit down, I helped mom make french toast for everyone," Eileen walked into the kitchen pointing at the food.

Stella was wiping off tears as she took another piece of toast and placed it on a plate.

"We didn't want to wake you, you looked so tired," Stella said.

Eveley nodded and walked to Aidan. He hugged her, she wiped a tear off his cheek.

"Thank you baby," he whispered in her ear.

She smiled softly at him. The gratefulness she felt at that moment in her heart, it was so full she thought she'd burst. She was infinitely grateful for this gift. There was no way she was allowing anyone, not the FBI, CIA, parasite, nor monster to take it from her.

Everyone sat around the breakfast table. Stella and Jason were naturally still scared. They kept insisting Eileen rest in the house at least for that day but Eileen was not cooperating. She was anxious to go outdoors. She wanted to go for a hike, smell the fresh ocean breeze, see nature up close again after being sick for so many months.

Eveley and Aidan didn't discourage her since they knew she would only improve. She'd already improved by leaps and bounds since last night. But fear was stubborn, and it still gripped Stella and Jason.

"Hey Eileen, why don't you listen to mum and dad? At least for today? We can make it fun, eat tons of snacks, watch movies in our pj's. If tomorrow you still feel the same, with mum and dad's permission we can take you somewhere, what do you say?" Aidan said in front of everyone.

"Okay, can we watch a scary movie?!" she exclaimed as she voraciously dug into her food. She'd been unable to eat much for the last couple of weeks so it was a welcome sight.

"I'm down," Aidan said as he stood from his seat and walked to the living room.

"Do you want to see something in particular? Something you've already seen or something new?" Aidan shouted.

Eileen practically ran to where Aidan was and started looking for a movie in their DVD collection.

"I know which one you're looking for," Aidan said, amused she'd ran there so fast, with a mouthful of food at that.

Eveley also couldn't believe her improvement. It hadn't just been a small or even moderate improvement but a total transformation.

Stella looked worried, she was confused and still afraid this was just a dream. Jason looked less worried and more willing to go with the flow. Eveley wished she could explain to them what was happening, to ease their fears so they could relax, to let them know Eileen was saved.

"They are very suspicious of her recovery, they might think your visit had something to do with it," the voice said.

She was taken by surprise and she wondered why he'd been absent so long, she was starting to worry about him.

"But how could they suspect anything about me?" she spoke to the voice in her mind.

"They can't put their finger on it but since you touched them, you have already given them clues by their healing. They know the common denominator is you."

Eveley sighed, she needed to have a conversation with Stella fast.

That evening, they all watched Eileen's movie of choice.

Stella made them homemade Bailey's cheesecake, homemade pizza, and a salad. When the movie was over Eveley excused herself to go to the bathroom. She found Stella in the kitchen and stopped to talk to her about what was going on.

"Hey, do you need me to help with anything?" Eveley didn't wait for an answer and picked up a dirty plate and started scrubbing it.

"Oh no honey, thank you, you've always been such a kind girl. I'm so glad Eileen has such a good best friend," Stella said smiling warmly.

Eveley continued to scrub the plate in her hand, trying to get the nerve to talk to her more seriously.

"Thank you, she is such a good best friend too, I don't know that my life would have been as fun without her."

At those words, she noticed Stella got a worried look on her face.

"But it's amazing how much she has improved. She will only get better, I'm sure of it," Eveley continued.

"I wish I had your optimism, I really do. I just can't let go of this fear gripping me. Fear is all we've known since Eileen's diagnosis. I'm so used to it, I'm so afraid to enjoy it only for things to take a turn for the worse." Stella looked like she was on the verge of tears.

"Oh I'm sorry, I didn't mean to upset you. She'll be okay, I know it."

"Do you sweetie? How?"

The question caught Eveley off guard.

"W-well, I think the amount of improvement she experienced is a miracle, no other explanation."

At that, it was like the clouds lifted and Stella's pained expression softened.

"You're right, I can't believe I didn't believe before. I've prayed long and hard enough, why not us? Why not Eileen?"

Stella seemed happy and finally able to compose herself.

"Tomorrow we are going to go on that hike Eileen wanted to do so much and we're never going to look back," Stella said.

Eveley nodded in agreement. The cheerfulness in Stella's voice made Eveley feel relieved she helped ease her distress.

"Hey Stella?"

"Yes darlin'?"

"Do you think you could refrain from talking about me with my mom or anyone at all when you're emailing and talking?"

Stella looked perplexed.

"What's wrong? Are you okay, is everything okay at home?"

"Yes, yes of course! I'm just...I've been dealing with a stalker, and I, well, I need to make sure they don't know I'm here. I mean not that they would follow me all the way here, of course not, but I just need my stay here to be as private as possible. I'm contacting my mom through a different phone than mine since my recovery from the accident."

"My goodness! I've been so loopy lately. I haven't even asked you how you feel. I'm such a terrible person. My dear, don't worry about it. I can't believe someone is harassing you like that, especially when you're in recovery."

"Thank you."

"How did you convince your mom to let you out of her sight with someone harassing you plus your accident?"

"Aidan...she trusts him and felt a lot better he was with me. Plus she thought I should see Eileen after Aidan told me she wasn't well. I actually feel completely normal, except for this scar, I'm pretty much back to normal."

She lowered the neck of her shirt to reveal the scar. The scar was no longer angry and red like it was at the hospital. It was a uniquely shaped scar that usually made people gasp. Not only because it was large, but because there was a violent beauty to it that intrigued people. Her neighbors certainly expressed fascination with it when she showed it to them.

"Oh my goodness! That must've been painful, you're a miracle sweetie!" Stella said as she hugged her.

Eveley felt relieved by their conversation. She decided to go upstairs and call her mom. She laid on the bed Stella made for her in the guest bedroom. She talked to her mom for about 10 minutes letting her know she was doing okay and she planned to stay there until her neighbors back home told her the heat had died down. She hung up the phone, Aidan knocked on the door softly.

"Come in."

Aidan opened the door and left it wide open.

"Hey, how are you feeling?" he laid down on the bed facing Eveley.

"Good, I just spoke to my mom, she said Mr. Collins already sent her messages. He's been watching my place, my neighbors too, and they're still trying to find me."

"As long as you're here with us, no one is going to lay a finger on you, I promise you," he said with confidence.

Eveley sighed, the scar on her collarbone caught his attention. He ran his fingers lightly along the raised ridges and intricate branches.

"There's a reason you lived through this and I'm not going to let anyone take this from you if I can help it," Aidan said.

Aidan always said the right thing at the right time. It was as if he could sense all her fears, doubts, and anxiety and ease all of it. She placed her hands over his hand touching her shoulder and looked at him with a dreamy look in her eyes. He was like a quilt on a cold night...warm and safe. They laid there for a bit, lost in their own little world, just being themselves, talking and connecting. Before they knew it an hour had passed. When they realized how much time passed, they quickly stood and hurried downstairs to join everyone else.

Chapter 24

SCOTLAND

The next day, they took a small hike near their house, it was just short enough to give Stella and Jason reassurance and long enough to satisfy Eileen.

Jason surprised them that night and told them to pack, he was taking them on a trip to Edinburgh and Loch Ness. Eileen had always wanted to go and this was the perfect occasion to take her.

Eileen was ecstatic when her father told her the sudden news. She ran to her room and started packing before he was even done telling her the details. She came running back downstairs and hugged both Stella and Jason.

"Thank you mum, thank you dad!" she said happily and ran upstairs.

That night Eveley and Eileen had a sleepover like old times. They did their nails, ate too many snacks, and stayed up way too late, but it was great to have the opportunity to spend those moments together. Moments that were not even possible a day ago. Eveley would still get emotional when she thought of it that way. She'd find herself getting teary-eyed and feel a lump in her throat. She'd quickly gather her thoughts and try to focus on the present so that Eileen didn't see her getting emotional.

That night Eveley dreamed only a short conversation.

"I think I figured out a name for you."

"Really? What is it?"

"LAR...it's an acronym, it stands for Luminescent Advanced Race."

"Has a good ring to it, I guess now I have a name on earth."

"Yes you do."

The next morning they woke up at the crack of dawn. Eileen was most excited of all. She woke up as if she hadn't missed a beat and wasn't running on four hours of sleep. Ironically, Eveley also woke up feeling refreshed. They both started their routine, making their beds, and cleaning up quickly.

Eveley was the first to exit the bedroom toward the bathroom. When she was almost at the bathroom door, Aidan opened the door to exit. He made his way to her in the dim hallway light, he lightly placed his hand on her forearm and tenderly squeezed her arm.

"How'd you sleep sunshine?" he said in his raspy morning voice which made Eveley get a dopey smile on her face.

He didn't know it, but little things like the sound of his voice in the morning, the way he looked at her, the way his body would brush up on her, even his scent, would sometimes make her lose herself a little. Maybe it was infatuation, or maybe it was just another component of what made her fall head over heels in love. After all, these little bursts of joy only left her wanting more.

"I slept well, you?" she replied softly, looking demurely up at him. She noticed the tiny specks of green in the inner part of his iris.

"I slept pretty well," he moved closer, until he lightly pushed her chin up with his fingers and planted a gentle kiss on the tip of her nose.

"You can leave the suitcases outside your door and dad and me will bring them down for you girls, okay?"

"Okay tiger."

She snapped out of her dream and entered the bathroom. She closed the door behind her and for a few seconds she felt giddy like a little kid.

The road trip from Dublin to Edinburgh was about eight hours long, they made it to their hotel a little after check-in time. Jason reserved two rooms in the heart of Edinburgh, right on Victoria Street which he knew Eileen would love. As soon as they pulled up to the hotel, Eileen's face lit up. She'd been raving the whole drive into town how beautiful it all looked and no one in their group had ever been, so everyone marveled at the new sights. It was simply a beautiful, enchanting city with airs of mystery and amazing architecture.

Eileen thanked and hugged Jason and Stella when they stepped out of the car. Stella looked teary-eyed when Eileen let her go from the big bear hugs she was used to giving her family and friends. Eveley noticed the emotion on Stella's face when she turned and wiped her face quickly emerging with a nervous smile. She wished again she could reassure her everything would be okay, but she could see Stella looked much more relaxed than the days prior. It was good to see her improving and Jason too. It also made Eveley happy to see Eileen and Aidan being carefree siblings again, playfully teasing each other like they were used to.

The first place they explored was Edinburgh Castle, a stone behemoth that stood as a long-time witness to the history of the area. Eveley thought it was so amazing to be able to walk over the same ground as kings, queens, and prisoners even. She could imagine the echoes of the people who once inhabited its rooms and how time had passed while its stone walls stayed the same.

Next, they hiked through Arthur's seat, a large mound in the center of town that showed them the full majesty of Edinburgh from its summit.

Then they walked through the narrow, winding brick roads of Dean Village. Stone buildings hugged the river that cut through town in cascading levels giving it a fairy tale aura.

They also strolled through the Royal Mile. Tall, slender buildings towered over them. They explored many of the "closes" or small courtyards that branched off the main road.

They randomly picked pubs to eat in while on their explorations which was fun to do. Before they knew it, four days had passed and it was check-out day. It was time to drive to their next destination, Loch Ness.

Eveley was first to wake up the next day. She shared the room with Eileen and Stella while Jason and Aidan shared the second room.

After showering, she changed and organized her things in her suitcase. She texted Aidan as it was past 8:30 am and she knew he'd be awake. They would head downstairs to meet for breakfast then return to gather their suitcases and check out.

After Stella and Eileen were ready, they made their way down to the restaurant inside the hotel. When the girls arrived Jason was already waiting at a table. They all greeted and Eveley looked around.

"Where's Aidan?" Eveley asked.

"Oh, he went down the street to buy a charger for his phone, his stopped working and our phones don't have the same one," Jason said quickly.

"Oh, don't they sell chargers here in the hotel?" Eileen asked.

"Oh, I don't know, but he should be here soon, you girls go ahead and get your breakfast now," Jason said signaling for them to head to the food.

"Huh, okay," Eileen muttered as the girls set their purses on a seat and walked to the breakfast spread.

Ten minutes later Aidan showed up, he carried a bag, he greeted everyone and kissed Eveley.

"Hey handsome, what are you up to?" Eveley looked at him with curious eyes.

Aidan cleared his throat, "What do you mean?"

Eveley smiled, "I don't know, you seem different."

"Really? Hmm, I feel the same," Aidan chuckled.

Eveley observed him, trying to pinpoint the change, without success.

After a hearty breakfast, they checked out and they took the 3.5 hour drive to their next destination.

They stayed in Drumnadrochit for 2 days, visiting the small towns surrounding the Loch Ness. Their trip was relaxed but they still had plenty to do, like their tour of Urquhart Castle and their day cruise down the Loch which made them feel even more captivated by the beautiful scenery. The area exuded a peaceful aura that at the same time held an unsettling edge due to the legends of the waterways.

On their last day before returning to Ireland, they took a hike on a clear and sunny day to Meall Fuar-mhonaidh. It was a good hike with everyone in great spirits. When they made it to the top of the hill, they were graced with a majestic view. The effort of the steep climb immediately forgotten, everyone stood in awe. The length of the entire Loch was visible to them as well as dozens of hilltops in varying heights hugging the Loch. Rays of sunlight filtered through the fluffy clouds. Eveley stood between Eileen and Aidan, she placed her arm around Eileen's shoulder. Stella and Jason stood next to Eileen.

Aidan turned to face Eveley directly. He looked at her tenderly, hugged her, and placed a kiss on her forehead. He took her hands in his.

"You know when I thought I was losing you, along with my sister, those were the darkest days of my life. I didn't know what I was going to do with my life without you girls...and by some miracle, everything changed overnight..." he paused and looked at the sky briefly.

"And I realized life is too short to not spend it with those you love, those you would give your all to, including your life. I realized since we've been back together there will never be another woman that makes me as happy as you, that's as perfect for me as you, and I know you feel the same way about me." He paused, reached in his pocket and pulled out a small box, he kneeled on one knee. Everyone gasped, including Eveley who was completely caught by surprise.

"I know this is sudden, but I know the timing is always right when two people truly love each other. Eveley, will you grant me the honor of being my wife?" Aidan said, his eyes full of optimism.

Eveley stood wide-mouthed for a second, she burst into a smile.

"Yes! Yes I will!"

Aidan smiled and looked relieved, he placed the blue sapphire and diamond ring on her finger, it was dainty and elegant. He stood up and they embraced and kissed while everyone clapped. Afterwards, everyone congratulated them and hugged them. Stella was teary-eyed and so was Eileen.

Jason made a proposition. "I think this calls for a perfect ending to our trip and I'd like to take us out for a celebratory dinner tonight, to celebrate the new fiancées, and health," he said. He put his arm over Eileen's shoulder, and gave her a little squeeze.

"Yes, that sounds wonderful!" Stella added, and everyone agreed.

That night, they all dressed up. Aidan wore a nice suit and Eveley wore a sequined white dress, they were especially glowy together. Stella looked at them and it was evident they were so in love. Though she worried they were a little young for marriage and surely Isabel would be surprised by this development, she didn't want to burst their happiness with talk of a long engagement. She figured they were mature enough to figure out what was best for their life together. After dinner they went to a sophisticated club and danced the night away. Eveley and Aidan were inseparable after their engagement. This was one of the best days of their lives, one they would remember forever, a day in which their happiness seemed endless.

CHAPTER 25

BLUE STARS

Mexico 1.5 months later.

It wasn't long after their engagement that Eveley and Aidan snapped back to reality and realized Eveley couldn't stay in Ireland forever. The entire time, Eveley's grandparents plus her mom sent several money transfers although Stella and Jason never asked for a penny from her the two weeks she was in Ireland.

Fortunately, Eveley reached out to friends in Mexico who ran in the same circle as Eileen's Mexican boyfriend, Andres. They were more than gracious when they invited them to stay with them in Mexico for a month.

Eveley figured going to Mexico then back to the States after more time had passed would be the safest thing to do. Aidan decided he wanted to go with Eveley, and naturally Eileen did too. They asked permission from Stella and Jason to join Eveley in Mexico, and they reluctantly agreed. They left at different times, with Eileen joining them three weeks after they left.

The day after Eileen landed in Mexico, Eveley, Aidan, and their group of friends decided to go to a dance club which Eveley looked forward to as they hadn't gone dancing since their engagement night.

She still felt a bit paranoid at times that someone would be watching them from afar and ready to grab her at any moment, whether the men in suits or a VERMIN. However, the moments she was with Aidan she felt completely at ease. It was hard to put into words how secure he made her feel, like she was untouchable.

They were staying at their friend Miguel's house, his girlfriend Liliana also lived with him. Their friend Alex was visiting who was well know around the city for DJ events and house parties. It was already close to 11 pm.

The guys were waiting for the girls to finish getting ready, they sat in the living room talking and watching TV. They set up bowls of chips with Valentina sauce, lime, and sodas on the coffee table.

Liliana was in the bathroom, finishing the last part of her hair. Eveley knocked on the door and asked her if she'd like help and she replied yes. Eveley entered and took the curling iron and finished curling the last couple strands in the back of Liliana's head. Liliana's hair was long, almost past her lower back, full of beachy light brown waves.

Liliana hadn't exactly probed regarding Eveley's hasty arrival to town, but Eveley did tell her not to tell anyone or post anything on social media. Liliana agreed not to say anything, she was like a little sister and Eveley knew she'd never do anything to place her in danger. She also told Alex and Miguel, which ironically they both made jokes about being wanted by the FBI. Eveley played along but it left her nervous they saw the worry on her face. Though she knew they were trustworthy, she knew it was easy for things meant to be kept secret to casually slip from people's lips. She didn't want to burden any of them.

Eileen and her boyfriend, Andres, were on their way there as well. Eileen left with Andres earlier in the day, they went to dinner at his house and met his parents. A milestone that made her nervous and anxious in the days leading up to it.

When Eileen and Andres returned, Eileen knocked on the door of the bathroom. She was let in by Eveley. Eileen looked ecstatic as she hugged and greeted each of the girls.

"So by the look on your face I assume things went well?" Eveley said to her.

"They went more than well, they went great! His family is so nice and everyone is so chill and funny, it was amazing. I like him even more now that I've met his family, our families would get along so well."

"I'm so happy for you!" Eveley said.

"You know Andres' parents are really well liked by everyone in town that knows them, they're really good people," Liliana added.

Eileen looked giddy and like she would burst from happiness. Eveley knew her so well, she knew she was in the best possible mood. Liliana glanced at her phone.

"We'd better get going, I think the guys might end up getting too comfortable and not wanna go if we don't leave soon," she said as they stepped out of the bathroom.

"Listas chicas [Ready girls]?" Andres asked, relieved they were finally out of the bathroom.

"Claro [Of course], let's go!" Liliana said as she walked confidently to Miguel and grabbed his arm.

Everyone stood up and started out the door. They took two cars, Andres' car and Miguel's car. Eileen, Andres, Eveley, and Aidan rode in the same car. They drove about ten minutes to an area on the eclectic side of town; hip coffee shops, posh stores, and designer brands lined the modern streets. They arrived to the biggest club in the city, it was known for having some of the best music and DJs. The place was already full of people and it was so packed they had trouble walking through.

The dance club theme was futuristic and they played a good mix of reggaeton, pop, and EDM. They stayed together in their own little group, dancing and socializing for a couple hours. It was almost 2:30 am when Liliana asked them if they were down for going to her place out in the country where they typically hosted their family events. It was like a second vacation home but they typically used it for parties as well. They all agreed and they left close to 3 am. They followed Miguel's car, it took about 20 minutes and they were on the outskirts of the city, overlooking the valley in all its majesty.

The property was well hidden, tucked away between treed slopes, the private drive leading up to the property was almost a mile long.

When they arrived the house was lit but Liliana told them there wouldn't be anyone home. The house was fully stocked for them and service staff had cleaned the home just in case they used it that evening.

The house blended in with its surroundings, modern but unassuming, it contained a long rectangular pool offering an impressive view of the city below. The pool was even heated for chilly nights since it wasn't always scorching hot as many people assumed in those parts.

Liliana kicked off her shoes and walked barefoot, she stood next to the pool, Miguel took off his shoes as well.

"Wanna have a pool party!?" Liliana asked eagerly. Before anyone could answer Miguel grabbed her, carried her in his arms, and jumped in the pool as she screamed.

Andres looked at Eileen with a devilish grin.

"Oh no! don't get that look in your eyes!" Eileen shouted playfully as she ran around the pool. Andres acted as if he was going to run after her but stopped. She was across from him on the other side of the pool next to Aidan and Eveley, Aidan pushed her in the pool.

"Traitor! I'm gonna get you later!" Eileen said as she swam to the edge. "It's so nice! C'mon guys get in!" she motioned with her arm to get in.

"Get us some drinks and snacks first no?" Liliana asked.

Eveley signaled behind her, "Want me to go?"

"Sure, there's snacks on the counter and drinks, also towels on the sofa for us."

Eveley and Aidan went inside, they found an array of snacks on the kitchen island, along with a fully stocked fridge of drinks. They brought as much as they could carry.

The night felt so nice, hot during the day and cool and pleasant now that it was nightfall, although the heated pool was still necessary for comfort in the mild night weather.

Everyone grabbed a drink and Aidan and Eveley stripped down to their underwear. They hadn't been as spontaneous as everyone else who'd jumped in with their clothes and were now peeling off their wet clothes down to their underwear. They entered the pool to join everyone else.

The group of friends played music on a large speaker mounted in a corner of the yard. They laughed, joked, and talked till they saw the sun barely start to ascend over the horizon.

Liliana's house boasted eight large bedrooms since it was a house meant for big events and entertaining. She also let them use some of the clean pjs they kept for guests to get out of the wet clothes they were in. She typically kept a few pjs for people since during parties, friends and extended family would stay the night for convenience and safety. It was almost like a hotel experience.

Eveley and Aidan literally crashed in the bed in their bedroom and fell asleep within minutes, it'd been an epic night but they were exhausted.

The next day, they heard a soft knocking on their door, it was Miguel. Eveley woke first and looked at the time on her phone, it was 1 pm. She stood up and opened the door slightly.

"Hey Miguel."

"Hey, sorry to wake you guys up, but Liliana said there's brunch downstairs if you guys wanna join us."

"Sure, let me just get Aidan up and we'll come down."

Eveley returned to the bed and nudged Aidan softly, bright rays of sunlight were on his face, he opened his eyes and squinted.

"Hi love."

"Hi handsome, there's brunch downstairs, Miguel just told me."

"Awesome, I'm starving."

They quickly used the bathroom, tidied up and went downstairs. Liliana and Miguel were walking around the kitchen while Eileen, Andres, Alex, and a friend he'd ran into at the club, Dalia, were seated at the table.

"Rise and shine lovebirds!" Liliana said from across the kitchen, there was an older lady helping set up some dishes. The spread consisted of chilaquiles verdes, pan dulce, fresh coffee, fresh-squeezed oj, steaming-hot tamales, french toast, fresh fruit, avocado salad, fresh tortillas, and a few salsas.

"You're our designated party host from now on," Aidan joked at Liliana.

"It's the least I can do after making you guys wait an extra hour last night." She was referring to her getting ready before the club.

Liliana came a from a well-to-do family, the reason her and Andres ran in the same circles and she knew his family well. They went to the same private school as kids and their families still socialized regularly.

"Hey, the guys have a great idea. Have you ever gone hiking and four-wheeling in Dunas del Diablo [Devil's Dunes]?" Liliana asked.

"No, that sounds like fun," Aidan replied.

"Well if you guys are up for it, we could go, it's not far from here and we have several 4x4s here at the house."

"Really?" Eileen asked, her face beaming.

"Yeah, a big group of our friends are already arriving..." Liliana looked at her watch, "Yep, they're probably arriving as we speak."

Aidan looked at Eveley and nodded to ask her opinion, "What you say?"

"I'm down if you are," Eveley said.

"You know I'm in," He placed a kiss on her cheek.

"Awesome, what about you guys?" Liliana asked Dalia and Alex.

"Yeah, we're in, I feel like I'm on vacation," Dalia said and everyone nodded.

"Okay, then it's settled," Liliana said.

After everyone finished brunch, Liliana took the group to a large "shed" that was more like a house-sized garage and pointed to the several vehicles they owned for off-roading. They owned 2 side-by-sides, one for four people, one for two, and two large ATVs. Eileen and Andres went in the side-by-side for two, Alex, Dalia, Liliana, and Miguel went in the four person side-by-side, and Aidan and Eveley each took an ATV. They followed Liliana and Miguel's vehicle directly from her house down the trail that took them all the way where the edge of the dunes started.

It was supposed to be a big gathering of about 50 or so people according to Liliana. She asked her staff to bring a UTV full of drinks and food. There was always a large array of food as everyone pitched in to ensure there was enough food for everyone. It took them about 30 minutes to ride down the trail to a large area that was a mix of canyons, valleys, along with a large area with sand dunes. They rode along the top crest that overlooked the sand dunes below. There were already many people gathered and Liliana seemed to know everyone.

They made it to the spot where everyone was grilling carne asada and enjoying drinks. Liliana introduced them to some of her closest friends.

They decided to drive through one of the most popular, but easiest trails. It consisted of a few areas that were wet and bumpy and other areas where they could crank up the speed without fear of falling easily as it was mostly flat ground.

They rode among a group of about 10 other vehicles, there was music blasting, lots of laughter, and friendly competition. By the time they made it back to the food area, more people had arrived, it was closer to 80 people now.

They decided to explore a different part of the dunes, where the trails were shaped like shallow valleys. The exhilarating part was the turns, where the vehicles gripped the sand walls of the valleys and sent torrents of sand flying behind them.

After that trail, they followed a different group to watch the most experienced drivers conquer the hardest parts of the expert trail. Everyone was friendly and sociable, the vibe was fun, and they all made new friends easily.

After watching the top riders conquer those trails, they followed a different group that was shooting a short video. Since they were wearing helmets covering their faces, it wasn't a big deal.

Once the sun set, everyone turned on their neon lights and did a nighttime group ride. It was unbelievable no one crashed as some went lightning-fast while others went at a slower pace. Eveley and Aidan watched from the top, he turned on the lights to his ATV which was a bigger version of hers.

"Wanna ride together?" He offered as he walked up to her and stood close enough for their arms to touch.

"Sure."

He hopped on his ATV, and she hopped on behind him, wrapping her arms firmly around his waist. At first, he joined the large group of vehicles slowly, but once he found his rhythm, he really kicked up speed. He was fearless and it felt exhilarating for them both. Eveley's adrenaline kicked in, and she squeezed him tighter. He gently told her not to be afraid. She wasn't worried; she knew she was in good hands. His confidence was always the deciding factor, and she never doubted him.

They rode for a good half hour before they returned back to the food area. Eveley took off her helmet, and Aidan playfully pulled her off the ATV and swung her around as she laughed.

There was now a big bonfire and they sat around next to their friends, laughing and talking till late into the night. It was 1 am before they drove back to Liliana's house. They watched a movie and then everyone went to sleep.

The next day they enjoyed another delicious breakfast at Liliana's house before they finally returned to Miguel's house.

It was their last day there. Everyone was sad, especially Eileen since she decided to stay a few more days with Andre's family, then she'd be returning to Ireland.

Eveley and Aidan would be going somewhere just the two of them, it was bittersweet to leave. Their friends made their stay so wonderful they really didn't want to leave, but they promised to return soon.

"They are getting closer Eveley, they are not giving up just yet. They have an idea you are on the run but they have no proof."

"I don't understand why they want to find me so bad...why LAR?"

"It is not your fault you do not understand, your species has been ignorant of your planet's true history due to worldwide government involvement. Those governments will always keep the truth about what is beyond your world hidden from you. They have been trying to find, replicate, and master technologies that do not originate from the human consciousness for many years. You are just another mystery or possibility they want to learn from, but they do not care who or what they destroy in the process of this mission."

"Well they're not going to succeed, they're not going to do what they please with me."

"Eveley, I was serious about you leaving this world, we do not have a lot of time. They will eventually find you, and me, and your whole species will be in danger."

"I don't know if I want to believe you."

Eveley paused, she wasn't ready to leave her home.

"I can't yet, I have more I need to do."

"Please reconsider."

The next day, Aidan and Eveley set off on a bus in the morning, the trip would take 9 or so hours for them to arrive to her rancho in Chihuahua. There they would stay on her mother's property for a few weeks or more depending on how things went. Her tia

Lupe and tio Gerardo were already expecting them. She made the calls from Liliana's house prior to her departure.

When they made it to Chihuahua in the evening, they got off the bus and took an Uber to their final destination close to 8 pm, her tia was waiting for them with a few dishes of food ready for them. They ate quickly, then settled their things in their bedroom in the main part of the house.

When Eveley arrived, she instantly felt at ease, if there was anywhere she felt free and content, it was there. Despite how late it was, Aidan and Eveley walked to the horse stalls. There were several beautiful horses her tios took care of for her mom. Eveley rode Chispa [Spark], a silvery-colored Aztec horse, and Aidan rode Trueno [Thunder], an Onyx-colored Aztec horse. They rode to the same spot next to the river and laid down on a blanket, they held hands and looked up at the star-studded sky, there was no light pollution there, it was as if they were the only ones in the world.

"You remember when we used to look up at the sky as kids?" Aidan reminisced.

"Yes, how could I forget, it was my favorite thing to do each day," she said softly.

"Well, I could look at this all night," Aidan finally said.

Eveley nodded, a few tears building up in her eyes as she looked at the wide expanse, the stars beautiful, yet terrifying at the same time. She turned her head toward Aidan.

"There's something I have to tell you."

"Okay," he said with a worried expression.

"I might have to leave this world soon."

"What do you mean?" Aidan didn't have a clue what she was talking about.

"LAR told me his race are looking for him, he's in hiding right now. Aidan, what he did was forbidden, to have contact with humans, it's like the worst thing he could have done. They are looking for him and it's only a matter of time before they also find me. When they find out what I've become, they will not only destroy me but they will destroy every human on earth."

"But why?"

"They do not trust us with their knowledge, with their inherited advantage, and since I'm an abomination in their eyes, they will destroy me and my species. The only solution is for me to leave this world according to LAR."

Aidan couldn't believe what she'd just told him, he was not aware so much was going on he didn't know about.

"And go where? How? When? Do you even trust him?" Aidan looked flustered, as if the earth stopped spinning.

"I know this is a lot to take in, and I don't know all the details yet but my gut feeling is I can trust him and he's telling me the truth," she sighed.

"As cruel and ugly as this world can be, there is also so much beauty, and love, and wonder. I don't want to leave my home, but I also don't want everyone I love to perish," she added and a tear slid down her cheek.

Aidan thought for a few seconds of the immense responsibility placed on Eveley's shoulders, what would he have done in the same situation?

He squeezed her hand, and gave her a look of determination.

"If you must leave, if you must make this sacrifice, I will help you along the way. I will not leave your side till you're safe and your mission is complete."

Eveley burst into tears. She knew he was selfless, the best man she had ever known and loved besides her father. He was too good, she would never be able to thank him enough for everything he had done for her. He rubbed her shoulders as she buried her face in his chest and sobbed softly.

CHAPTER 26

TRUST AND REVELATION

They both left Mexico grateful for all the great memories they made. Eveley found a profound appreciation for her extended family in Mexico who treated her so well the entire month she was there with Aidan.

Things had finally died down in the States so she thought it was time for her life to go back to normal. Her mother was able to gather her things discreetly one weekend from her apartment in Parkville, and move them to a storage facility in Kansas City. She knew Eveley would have to make the decision whether she would return to Missouri or stay in Texas permanently.

The night Eveley and Aidan touched down in Dallas, LAR spoke to her again, this time more insistent they were running out of time.

Lately there were whispers of a profound change all around the world, a sharp decline in crime, mental illness, and general malaise in the population. In the States, there were vast discussions on the declining crime rate. Things were starting to change and the change was starting to snowball as more people were touched by the healing that touched so many others.

Eveley did not intend to ignore LAR but she still wanted to leave on her own terms, she just wasn't ready yet to say goodbye yet. She also wanted more proof this was the path she needed to take and that he was trustworthy.

That night she talked to him in her dream. It was hazy and hard to remember in the morning, the first time she'd ever experienced trouble remembering any of their conversation, but she could remember his faint voice in her head...

"I know where your father's remains are."

She felt chills run through her body as she made the realization of this memory. How could he know this? And why was his voice so faint and hard to remember? Was he farther away from her? Was he serious about what he claimed to know? She felt an almost frantic energy, and pretty soon she felt nauseous and dizzy. She laid back down, her eyes wide open. Was he telling her the truth?

That day she waited and waited for him to make his presence known again, to no avail. This went on for a whole torturous week, she was afraid something happened to him. She told Aidan and he tried to ease her fears by telling her LAR had always returned before.

Isabel noticed something was weighing on Eveley's mind, but Eveley couldn't tell her mother. She couldn't get her mom's hopes up, she couldn't let her know until she was 100% sure.

"You must leave now!" LAR bellowed one day as she was getting ready to help her mother with dinner. It startled her, and her mother noticed.

"Que pasa [What's happening] Eveley?"

"Ma, me tengo que ir [Mom I have to leave], LAR is telling me they're after me again, they're on their way. I need to grab some clothes and head out."

"What?! Just like that?!" Isabel exclaimed.

"Si ama, he's not lying, they must be pretty close."

"They will be there within an hour, you must leave now," LAR informed her.

"He said they will be here within an hour, mom I need your help."

"Okay mija, look, I'll gather some things and give you some cash. Once you're able to get somewhere safe we can figure out the next step."

Aidan walked into the kitchen since he was over for dinner that day. They both turned to look at him.

"What's going on?" he asked noticing the tension in the room.

"Eveley has to leave now, she got a warning from LAR they're on their way to pick her up," Isabel updated him.

Aidan looked pissed.

"Okay, let's gather some things and get going then." Aidan never missed a beat.

He'd been so happy since being in Dallas, mainly due to seeing his little old grandparents again. He hadn't seen them in a year, and they were beginning to get a bit more elderly so he enjoyed helping them a lot since being back. He helped them fix a few things around their house, helped drive them to their doctor appointments, and helped his grandma in her garden. But the greatest joy came from gifting them the healing that had already become apparent in their lives. It was so easy and beautiful, and every time someone's life was literally touched by this gift, it was the most incredible act of love a human could gift another human.

Since Aidan's return to Dallas, his grandparents had reversed their aging by 30 years; in the way they moved, their cognition, their ability to care for themselves.

One day they surprised Aidan and gifted him a vintage Harley his grandfather owned. A sentimental gift his grandfather kept for one of his sons, Levi, who died shortly after his 15th birthday in a car accident. His mom Stella was greatly affected by her younger brother's death, which happened when she was only 17. Over the years, Stella told their family many stories of them growing up making Aidan feel like he knew his uncle Levi personally.

After Levi's death, his grandfather was a shell of himself for a few years, hating everything that reminded him of his son's untapped potential and what could have been. Everyone in the family thought he got rid of the motorcycle he bought shortly before Levi's death and was never able to gift him. No one ever saw the motorcycle again after Levi's death, relegated to an old locked up shed along with all of Levi's trophies and other things.

When Aidan received the keys, and his grandfather calmly told him of the significance of the bike, Aidan couldn't help but get a little emotional at his grandpa's gesture. His grandfather had finally let go, and giving Aidan the motorcycle was like coming full circle in that endeavor. And so this motorcycle meant for his uncle, was now his.

That same day, Aidan bought helmets for him and Eveley and invited her to ride with him. He eased his motorcycle to a stop under the silvery moonlight in front of Eveley's house. She ran out wearing jean shorts, a flowy crop top, hoop earrings, and her long hair in loose waves. He couldn't help feeling captivated by her beauty and energy. He flashed her a playful smile as he revved the engine lightly.

"Hop on love." He offered his hand to her.

Eveley placed her hand in his and Aidan pulled her close, wrapping his arm behind her. She giggled as she looked down at him with a sparkle in her eyes. Her scent, of citrus and tropical flowers intoxicated him. She brought her hands to his face and leaned in for a kiss. It was like nothing else mattered in that moment, just them, under twilight, lost in each other's touch.

That night they rode without a destination in mind, just vibes, they lost track of time and they only stopped because they got hungry. They found a hole in the wall restaurant called "Midnight Taco" and had the best tacos, afterwards he returned her home safe.

It became their favorite thing to do. Endless nights riding together, exploring different parts of Dallas, and stopping along the way to all the interesting sights, and late night food spots.

They were both helping Isabel at the café during the day but as soon as they finished their shift they would ride. They found so many interesting things along the way they would've missed riding in a car.

And so it was meant to be they would also be on the run on this motorcycle. That they would once again say goodbye to the city that saw their friendship bloom and their dreams and imagination reach the skies above them.

As soon as Aidan and Eveley said goodbye to Isabel in her garage, they took off quickly. They packed light, only a backpack each, they would ride to Aidan's grandparents so he could say goodbye and then to her grandparents to do the same. Eveley knew her mother was tough like a tank but she still worried about her and asked her abuelo and abuela to keep an eye out for her mom. Her grandfather suspected why she was leaving in a rush but hadn't made a fuss or tried to stop her. He'd long ago learned his granddaughter was strong-willed like he was and he wouldn't be able to stop her. He slipped a stack of bills in her hand when he hugged her goodbye.

"Cuidate mijita [take care of yourself my granddaughter]," he said with a worried expression.

Once they were on the road toward New Mexico, the farther they rode away from Dallas, the more uneasy Eveley felt. She was tired of running, of hiding, but they were left with no other choice. Mr. Collins, as well as LAR, had made it clear nothing good would come from turning herself in to these government agents. They could keep her under custody indefinitely and no one could stop them.

When they crossed into New Mexico, they found a state park close to the highway. They paid for a small cabin inside the park to stay in for the night. That evening they cooked their dinner on the outdoor grill next to their cabin and sat on the stairs of their porch looking at the sunset. Eveley laid her head on Aidan's shoulder, he wrapped his arm around her and kissed the top of her head. He turned to face her and lifted her chin gently to look at him.

"What do you think about us getting married tomorrow?" Aidan said out of the blue, his eyes full of hope.

Eveley was taken aback by his sudden idea, it was the last thing she guessed was on his mind. But she didn't have to think twice, she smiled.

"I'd love to amor," and kissed him playfully.

He picked her up, lifting her off the ground in his arms as she wrapped her arms around his shoulders and they kissed once more.

In a way, they were both thinking of what the future held for their relationship with a looming separation, which they both knew could be forever. They wanted to live in the moment and have every milestone and core memory as a couple ingrained in their minds. Perhaps this would make their separation even more difficult but they didn't care. They loved each other and they weren't going to compromise on their love.

Afterward, they found firewood to add to the firepit and sat around the fire cuddled up under the warm blankets from their cabin. They didn't have a telescope but they looked at the constellations which were very easy to see under the dark skies of New Mexico. It was like going back to their childhood, a time that was simple, and less fraught with peril.

Despite the high of their impending nuptials, that night Eveley couldn't sleep. She drifted in and out of nightmares of the parasite from her childhood returning, of infecting her while she was asleep. She called on LAR to talk to her that night but he was nowhere to be found. She'd gotten used to the fact that he would show up when she least expected him and she was alone for now, unsure of what to do.

The next morning, rays of sunshine peaked through a gap in the curtains, they landed on Eveley's face, rousing her awake with their warmth. She awoke slowly, squinting at the sun in her eyes. She noticed Aidan wasn't next to her, she found him outside, checking his motorcycle.

"Hey beautiful," he said as he looked up at her and Eveley stepped out the door of the cabin. He was kneeling down, messing with his bike's tire.

Eveley wrapped the blanket around her body as it was still a bit chilly.

"Buenos dias amor [Good morning my love], what are you doing?"

"Just checking a few things on the motorcycle, making sure it's good, you ready to go?" Aidan asked.

"Yeah, let me get ready real quick."

Once they checked out, they found a place to have a hearty breakfast and good coffee, then they went to city hall and obtained their marriage license. Afterward, they started calling around trying to find an officiant to marry them. Two hours later, they finally found an officiant able to meet them later that day where they wanted to have the ceremony.

Eveley found a public telephone to call her mother and Aidan's parents. Aidan didn't tell them the full truth, just told them they were on a small road trip, but they suspected something was up because their tone was skeptical. When Aidan hung up he looked conflicted, it was hard for him to not be completely honest with his parents, but their safety was foremost on his mind.

CHAPTER 27

SANDIA CREST

That evening the officiant arrived just before sunset to the lookout point he suggested due to it being away from the main areas and more private for the ceremony.

Eveley and Aidan were waiting, they'd been quietly sitting, knowing they were making a major life decision without their families present. This reality gnawed at them, but overall they tried not to let it dampen their happiness.

They sat holding hands, Eveley rested her head on Aidan's shoulder as they observed the view from high above the city. The sky was starting its beautiful metamorphosis into a prism of colors. Eveley tried to dress in the spirit of the moment, she intentionally wore a white shirt plus jeans and boots. Aidan surprised her earlier by coming back to the hotel with pompom Dahlias he found somehow. Instead of a bouquet she made them into a flower crown she wore. They also found a jewelry store that made custom jewelry on the spot and they had their bands made within an hour.

"Hello, Eveley and Aidan?" the officiant, Abraham Turin called out when he saw Aidan and Eveley sitting at the lookout.

He was a peculiar looking man, he looked to be in his sixties and looked like a skinny Santa Claus. His all white beard was long but neat, and his long silver hair was held back in a low pony tail. He wore a black and beige bowling shirt and black slacks. Next to him was his wife and his grown daughter. His wife was also silver-haired, and also had a jolly appearance just like you would imagine Mrs. Claus to have. Her face was youthful and round for a sixty year old woman, her cheeks flushed a rosy color, her eyes hazel. Her daughter looked to be in her twenties, she had long wavy golden hair, and looked like the younger version of her mother.

"Oh hi! Yes I'm Eveley" Eveley stood up and turned to face him. He walked up to Eveley and shook her hand then Aidan's hand. Mr. Turin's wife and daughter also shook hands with them.

"I'm Aidan, thank you for coming on such short notice," Aidan said.

"Of course, well I'm so glad I could help you guys. It's not often I get a call needing an elopement on such short notice but I'm happy I happened to be open today. Now I will have you guys stand right there at a slight angle, you guys will be facing each other but also able to see the view of the sunset. Luckily, the weather has been lovely today so the heavens have graced you with a wonderful backdrop for this moment." He pointed where they should stand.

"My wife and daughter will be your witnesses and they can record and take pictures for you with your phones," Mr. Turin said.

Eveley was so glad he offered, she hadn't even thought of this detail. Aidan and Eveley nodded and thanked them as they handed each of the women their phones.

They moved to the spot where Mr. Turin signaled again. They held each other's hands facing each other. Aidan smiled then took a deep breath as the gravity of the moment became real. He didn't want to screw up, he had memorized short but meaningful vows. He noticed Eveley also seemed nervous, he squeezed her hands and looked at her tenderly.

"I'm nervous too corazon [my heart]," he reassured her.

She nodded, smiled, and squeezed his hands in return.

"Okay, you guys have your own vows correct?" Mr. Turin asked.

"Yes," both Aidan and Eveley answered.

"Okay I will begin and I will cue when you will exchange rings and say your vows, then I will finish by declaring you husband and wife."

Aidan and Eveley nodded in acknowledgment.

"I always like to start any ceremony at Sandia Crest by giving couples a few minutes to simply feel the moment. I'd like for you to remain as you are, holding hands, and look at each other. Try to think of your journey as a couple, remember all the emotions and experiences that connected you together and made your relationship stronger. All the tribulations, the fears, the joys, and highs that brought you to this point and made you who you are today...when you are ready to begin just say okay," Mr. Turin clasped his hands, took a step back and let the silence take over.

Eveley and Aidan looked at each other, *really* looked at each other...their flaws, their strengths, the highs and lows of their love story.

Eveley thought back to their childhood, how they were play-mates then friends before they ever felt more and it made her smile. She'd had the love of her life by her side all along. It made her heart feel full and grateful. Those nights in the treehouse by his side looking up at the sky, and the adventures they got into. They shared so many everyday moments together, moments that seemed insignificant and ordinary but had slowly built their bond. She always felt accepted and seen by him. She thought of how many times Aidan had protected her, had eased her fears and pain, always there when she needed him. He'd always been the one from the beginning. Her eyes glistened with gratitude and love for him.

Aidan looked into Eveley's eyes, soft and tender. He'd given their nuptials a lot more thought than he let on when he sprung the idea on Eveley. He hated the thought that he didn't know what the future held and soon they might have no control over their fates. He loved her way before he ever expressed it openly. He thought about the crush he developed on her when they were kids, the year he gave her the stone and drawing. They were so carefree and happy then. Now there was peril at every corner, but even with danger looming over them, their love grew. He had to protect her, keep her safe at all costs, and he knew he couldn't fail her. She'd always been a beam of light in his life. Even when there was conflict in their lives, the clouds could never block the light. He knew she was the one he wanted to be next to for the rest of his life. And this moment was them writing it into history. He didn't know where they were headed, and frankly it didn't make much difference as long as she was his. He noticed the expressions on her face change. There was so much trust and vulnerability in her eyes. He hurt her badly once, but he'd never do it again. He smiled at her and she smiled back. Aidan turned back to Mr. Turin.

"Okay, we're ready now," Aidan said.

Mr. Turin's speech was short and sweet, he prompted Aidan to say his vows.

Aidan looked at Eveley's warm honey eyes. They were especially striking under the sunset, like liquid gold, they shimmered softly.

"Eveley, mo stoirín [my darling], it seems only yesterday we were small kids, gazing at the moon and stars together. Since then, we've been through so much to get to this point. We don't know what tomorrow brings, and we may be out of time and that's frightening, what the unknown brings for us...but this, being here with you, holding hands, and vowing to love each other forever, that's not an unknown, it's reality. I promise to always cherish you, keep you safe, and do everything within my power to make you happy. I will love you till my blood runs dry, that's set in stone, and will never change."

Eveley hung on his every word.

Mr. Turin didn't have to prompt Eveley. She took a step closer; she looked up into Aidan's sky-blue eyes. She felt her heartbeat speed up as she became lost in his gaze.

"Aidan, mi amor [my love], you've been a part of my life since before I can remember, since we could barely walk as toddlers. I've been waiting for this moment all my life. I've been waiting on you my entire life, yet in one way or other you've been next to me all along. I want you to know that no matter where life takes us...where fate forces me to go, I will be loyal, true, and faithful to you. And you're right that the unknown is terrifying, but it won't stop me. It won't stop me from living, from loving you, and I plan to live in the now for as long as destiny allows. That is enough for me, all of you, with me today and always."

Eveley felt like they were on the precipice of the unknown, ready to jump eyes closed, hand in hand, into the deep end. She wanted it all and she wasn't willing to compromise.

Mr. Turin prompted them to exchange rings, they calmly and slowly placed the rings on each other's hands.

"It is my honor to pronounce you husband and wife. You may kiss the bride."

Aidan placed his hand behind her neck, gently pulling Eveley into him. Eveley felt a rush as he did so and felt her body floating when their lips met. For that moment time stood still, and everything around them faded away.

After their kiss, they signed their marriage license and Mr. Turin and his wife and daughter congratulated them. Mrs. Turin had tears running down her face, she felt touched by Aidan and Eveley's vows. She could tell they were going to be a forever couple by the way they treated each other and how they looked at one another.

Eveley and Aidan were grateful for the pictures and video.

After Mr. Turin and his family left, Aidan and Eveley sat on the edge of the ridge, observing the view again. By now the sunset was at its climax. It was the most beautiful sky they'd ever seen, a kaleidoscope of sherbet orange, pink, and blue. The city lights twinkled below them, as if to say congratulations. They forgot for a while their lives were in peril and they would soon be apart. Sitting there among the clouds, all was perfect in their world, if only for a short while.

CHAPTER 28

ESCAPE VELOCITY

The next morning, the newlyweds took to the road again. They noticed right away they were being trailed by a dark SUV. They purposely made three turns in the same direction to prove it. Aidan sped up as the SUV weaved through lanes to keep up. That's when they changed plans from going toward Nevada, to Mexico across the border where they would have no jurisdiction to pull them over. The problem was they were several hours away from the border and would likely run into lookouts or an apprehension order at the border. They would have to find a way across no one else used.

Aidan made one final attempt to lose the SUV trailing them. He had to go faster than he'd like, but he got off an exit and quickly took cover in an underground parking garage. He'd lost them for now, but they would return. They waited it out for an hour before they exited and took the south direction toward the Mexican border.

Once on the road again, LAR spoke to Eveley, she instantly felt relief. LAR told her they were tracking everyone in their lives now. They had lost them for now, but they would soon find them again and they couldn't pass through the regular border crossing. He told her in an almost frantic voice his race was closer than he'd thought. He had no choice but to travel further away from her galaxy therefore she wouldn't be able to communicate with him for a while.

LAR emphasized there wasn't much time left, he needed her to leave earth soon.

She couldn't give him an answer yet, she knew it was inevitable but she just couldn't picture it...leaving earth. And her father...she couldn't leave without returning to his final resting place.

Later that afternoon, LAR told her how to get to the area on the border where they could easily cross into Mexico and evade officials. They were on their own though as LAR stopped communicating after he told her how to get there.

Eveley wanted Aidan to stop and hide till dark again. They stopped at an old motel on the way to the border, paid in cash, hid their motorcycle away from the road, and took turns napping while the other watched outside.

They were ready when nightfall finally came. They gathered their things quickly and took off again. They were two hours from the border and made their way as fast as they could. For an hour and a half nothing happened as they continued to make their way toward the border.

They came to an intersection on the highway that was a four-way stop. As Aidan was pulling to the stop, he noticed four black SUVS to their right, perpendicular to them. He prayed silently it wasn't them, but as soon as he crossed and they turned behind him, he knew.

The nearest SUV was coming on their tail fast as if it wanted to run them off the road and Aidan increased his speed. The SUV turned on red and blue emergency lights but Aidan ignored them. If he could just get past the border they'd have a chance. Unfortunately, this time they weren't willing to let them escape. The SUV sped up to match their speed and Aidan was almost sure they would run him off the road.

Finally, they turned onto the desolate road LAR told them to take. They needed to drive until they saw a small bridge. They had to get off and push their motorcycle across otherwise it would be too dangerous and the bridge might break under the weight of both their bodies and motorcycle. They dismounted and turned off the lights to the motorcycle, Aidan urged Eveley to go in front of him. They made it onto the bridge over the water, the current didn't look strong but in the dark it was hard to say for sure. Aidan started to push the motorcycle across the bridge. Behind them, high beams from several SUVS turned on, pointed right at them. Ten or so vehicles blocked them from behind, border patrol made up half of them, while the other vehicles were unmarked.

"Go, don't stop Eveley!" Aidan shouted, as he pushed the motorcycle.

The wood and metal bridge looked like it was used as a temporary crossing by some entity trying to sneak in. It was dilapidated so it was difficult to push the motorcycle down the rickety and dangerous segments. Some of the boards were missing and on the verge of falling apart. They made it halfway when bright lights appeared in front of them. Eveley stopped and backed up, brushing up against Aidan.

"If someone comes from that direction you run, I will keep them from taking you, got it?"

"What if I can't get past the—"

"Hey you guys stop right there!" a border patrol agent yelled behind them.

At the same time two men in suits appeared in front of them, their guns pointed at them from the end of the bridge. Aidan pulled Eveley behind him protected by the motorcycle as they realized they were trapped from both ends.

"Put your guns down, we're not a threat, we're unarmed!" Aidan yelled at them.

A helicopter appeared above them, Eveley felt panic, she knew this wasn't going to end well.

One of the border patrol agents ran behind her. He almost grabbed her except she ducked and Aidan reacted just in time, pulling Eveley behind him and pushing the man back hard.

Three more agents ran toward Aidan trying to subdue him, punching him as Aidan tried to defend himself by punching back.

The men in suits inched further onto the bridge, then realized it wouldn't hold their weight, and backed off again.

Eveley was thrown to the ground during the scuffle. One agent grabbed her ankle trying to restrain her, she kicked the man in the shoulder and backed away from him. Aidan punched him in the face and knocked him out cold. The remaining three agents continued their mission to stop him. They punched and kicked Aidan mercilessly. Eveley screamed as they all piled on Aidan and continued to give him blows. They finally placed him in handcuffs as he groaned on the ground in pain.

She frantically scooted away from them, the men at the other end still pointed their guns at her. The border agents pulled Aidan off the ground brusquely, he was barely able to stand. Aidan's eyes were black and swollen, blood dripped from his nose and mouth. Despite his condition he was able to utter two words when he faced Eveley's direction.

"Run Eveley!" Aidan shouted.

She cried in anger and helplessness, she wished she could destroy them all. As they brought their attention back on her, and dragged Aidan off the bridge, she realized she couldn't get past them. She frantically clawed and climbed to the top of the rickety bridge railing, she took one last look at Aidan being dragged away...then jumped.

"Dammit! Get all teams and eyes on her now!" one of the men in suits shouted behind him.

Eveley was already floating with the current, it was fast, making it difficult to swim across. The helicopter above focused its bright light on her, making her disoriented. She would have to swim underwater if she wanted to lose them. She was carried down about half a mile when she dove under, struggling against the current as she swam across and finally touched land. She was exhausted and for a few seconds laid on the ground catching her breath. Thankfully, the helicopter was still searching for her in the water. She slowly crouched and managed to get under some large brush. She needed to wait it out till the helicopter moved along.

She heard vehicles with their sirens and lights speed by. She couldn't get the picture out of her mind of Aidan. She knew if they were willing to beat him the way they did just to catch her they would do worse to him while in their custody. She stood up and walked back toward the bridge, defeated. She knew this needed to end.

She walked for about 1/4 mile before the helicopter came back around and hovered above her. She stopped and looked up as the wind from the helicopter created a dust storm around her. Within seconds she was surrounded by a dozen unmarked SUVS, several men ran to her and pulled her toward one of the SUVS. They placed her in the back, which was divided by a partition to the rest of the interior, not allowing her to see the front seats. They didn't place her in handcuffs which she found odd.

As soon as the car started moving, large partitions came down which blocked out the windows so she wasn't aware where she was going. She was scared, and all she wanted to know was where Aidan was. He didn't deserve the beating they gave him, all he was trying to do was protect her.

After an hour, against her best efforts she fell asleep. The drive felt like it went on for hours but she wasn't sure. She finally woke up groggy and unable to explain why she fell asleep when she wasn't sleepy when she was placed inside the SUV. She felt the car turning and for a moment go downhill. Someone finally opened the door, it looked like a concrete parking garage, she suspected it was underground since there were no windows.

They grabbed each of her arms and led her through four security entrances, each one with its own protocol. She finally made it into a large concrete complex, everything from the ceilings to floor were concrete and they seemed to go on for miles. Immediately she knew this complex was designed to be confusing as all the hallways were identical with no signage. She saw no clues anywhere to what it was for or where she was. Finally they walked her in front of a doorway, this entire time no one spoke a word to her and she hadn't spoken either as she didn't feel it would help her.

They scanned several of their badges and the door automatically opened. Inside it looked like a regular apartment, except there were no windows, just fake window frames, with idyllic pictures of panoramas as if to drive the point further that those inside would never see the light of day.

"Please Miss Luna, you may enter. There is a small meal ready for you there and clothing to change into, we will return in an hour."

She looked at them incredulously, they thought this was perfectly okay, to kidnap people and throw them in concrete boxes. Unfortunately, she had no choice, she entered slowly and they shut the door behind her, locking it manually. She looked around, there was a small kitchen off the living room, and finally a bedroom and bathroom down a small hallway. The rooms besides the essentials, were barren. Ironically, there was a TV and DVDs. The kitchen didn't have any cooking mechanism but there was a small sink and fridge. On the countertop was a small meal container and a sports drink. She opened the meal container, inside was a meal of chicken and veggies. On the bed was a change of clothing; a generic white t-shirt, dark blue sweatpants, socks, slippers, and a bath towel.

Eveley grabbed the clothing and ran the shirt between her fingers. How did I get here? she thought. Why did it go south so quick and where was he? Where was Aidan? Where was LAR?

LAR had kept Aidan and her safe till this point and now she was alone. No one in the world knew where she was, not even she knew where she was. She let out a sigh and sat on the bed, resting her head in exhaustion and frustration in both hands.

She prayed, the only thing that made sense when there was no hope left.

She started to feel a weird sensation, something bothering her senses, a high-pitched sound rang in her ears and she felt the worst headache she'd ever experienced. Like a switch turned on, the pain became unbearable. Her head felt like it was going to explode from the pain and pressure. She ran to the front door and banged furiously on the solid metal door.

"Hey! What are you doing to me?! Let me out! Stop it! You hear me?! Stop it!" Eveley pounded till her palms were bright red and her knuckles were bleeding from the punches she landed on the steel door. The pain didn't even register. Her head hurt so badly, if someone had offered her a way to end it she would have taken it. She finally collapsed in front of the door as her body couldn't bear anymore.

Eveley's eyes fluttered open, everything looked hazy, she could see bright rectangular lights above, moving cold lights. She wondered why the lights were moving but her body wasn't. She felt weak and sore like her body had been torn apart. Her head throbbed with pain, she could barely remember what happened, as if she'd been in a dream. She tried to move her neck, and she realized she was being carried. A dark suit and the poker face of one of the agents was all she could see when she managed to turn her head slightly. She felt tired of fighting until she remembered what they did to her...they used some type of weapon on her to agitate her or confuse her. She wanted to fight back with all her might but at the moment she was too weak. Her throat and lips felt so dry, she felt hot like she had a fever.

She felt her body slump on a couch in a small barren room. The agent simply placed her there without a word and left, closing the door behind him. A room with only a table, a half-full glass of water, a couch which was uncomfortable and scratchy on her skin, and a large mirror she was sure was a two-way mirror.

She could barely keep her head up, she felt a sensation of something down her nose, she wiped with her hand and saw a bright streak of blood. She noticed her clothing had been changed, her hair and skin felt different, someone had showered her and changed her clothing. Who or how, she wasn't sure.

Her engagement and wedding band remained on her finger, she noticed a small tattoo on her wrist that hadn't been there before. Upon seeing it she felt a big wave of heat over her entire body and her mouth felt parched. She began hyper-ventilating and managed to stand up, she took the glass on the table and chugged it all. She sat down on the couch again trying to keep herself from feeling worse.

She started to calm down when a tall, imposing agent entered the room. He didn't address her, he merely glanced in her direction before sitting down in the chair on the other side of the table.

"Will you please sit down Miss Luna?" he motioned to the chair across from him.

Eveley gave him a look that could kill.

"Where's Aidan?!" she hissed.

The agent looked unbothered.

"We will get to that Miss Luna."

Eveley managed to stand up.

"No! We will get to that right now! Where is he?! You have no right to keep me or him locked up like this! And you had no right to do this to me!"

She pushed her arm out with her wrist showing the tattoo that made her sick every time she looked at it.

"Please calm down Eveley, Aidan is fine, and that will fade away within three days."

"Calm down?! You beat my husband to a pulp almost killing him, when he didn't do anything, *we* didn't do anything. I want to call my lawyer."

Eveley started feeling a sudden calm come over her, like the sensation of relaxation from a hot tub. She found she'd sat down in the chair without any further prompting.

"Looks like it's finally taking effect."

Eveley faintly heard the agent's words.

"What was in that gla…" her voice trailed off as her brain failed to make the connection. Her eyes fluttered with sedation.

"Eveley, Eveley, Eveley," she heard the agent's voice repeating her name.

"Eveley!"

Eveley heard her name loud and clear, not from the agent, but from LAR. She startled to attention facing the agent. With eyes wide open she challenged him to the truth. She needed to restrain herself because internally she was jumping for joy LAR was there with her again.

"I know what you're doing, and it isn't going to work. I won't say another word until you tell me where Aidan is and I have my lawyer in the room with me." Eveley fell silent.

"Eveley, all we want is your cooperation, this is a matter of national security. We need vital information and we think you may know all of the answers, don't you want to help your country? Don't you want to keep your loved ones safe?" the agent countered.

"Eveley, do not speak to them. I will help you escape, just hang in there, I can help you get to Aidan."

Eveley spoke to LAR as quickly as she could in her mind, "I can't do that anymore, I can't keep running. I have to beat them at this the legal way or they'll continue to chase me and think they have justification to do so forever."

"Okay, but I'm in grave danger, you are in grave danger, we don't have much time, it has to be soon Eveley."

"We know you survived a lightning strike several months ago." The agent motioned quotes with his fingers when he said lightning strike.

"Now, all we want to know is how your recovery has been over the last couple of months. Could you tell me more about what happened that night? Anything you can remember?"

Eveley looked at him blankly, there was nothing that was going to make her speak. She folded her arms and didn't respond, the agent tapped his pen on his notepad. He sighed.

"Look Eveley, I just want to help you. We know you've had a very troubled childhood. Your mom becoming a widow, you losing your father at such a young age."

Eveley seethed inside, how dare he try to use her past against her. To use it as a cheap tactic to get her to talk. She stood up, walked to the scratchy couch, and laid down, arms crossed. She placed her feet up on the couch and acted as if she had no care in the world although she wanted to knock him out. He stood up and left the room exasperated by her behavior.

Two hours later another agent walked in. His demeanor was more "normal", meaning he didn't seem like a cold robot. His voice was warmer, more natural, like any person you'd meet out in the real world. Yet she still knew it was all a game. He tried for an hour to get her to talk, she was at the point where she knew she was doing everything right. They were going to try to beat her down with this routine until they thought they could break her.

Whenever she wanted to toy with the agents she'd periodically walk around the room, stretch her arms in front of them, and act like something they said suddenly touched a nerve. Mostly when they would bring up eerily accurate details of her childhood they dug up. She'd turn up the emotions on her face and really played into their hope she'd break. And just when it looked like she would burst into tears and spill all the beans, she'd look up at them with dead cold eyes and repeat "I want my lawyer". They'd get a look of contempt on their faces to the point she almost thought they'd use violence to get their answers, but luckily for her they never crossed that line. This routine went on for a grueling 24 hours, she finally took a nap during one of the breaks the agents took. She was prepared to endure another 24 hours, and another and another if she needed to. She was tired but she wasn't defeated yet.

What kept her going was LAR reassuring her Aidan was okay and she would see him again.

CHAPTER 29

RIDING INTO THE SUNSET

Aidan was put through a grueling and intense interrogation, but after he'd been as uncooperative as Eveley, and he'd threatened to get Ireland's embassy involved, they finally let him go. Albeit with a lot of warning on how they suspected he aided and abetted Eveley in traveling somewhere with a different identity which they clearly couldn't prove since they released him.

After he was let go, he was dropped off at a hospital near the border where they were arrested. He received a pretty bad beating while in custody but luckily he didn't need to go to the hospital. He walked right out of there and took an Uber to the spot near the river. He needed to find clues on where Eveley was, if she'd made it to Mexico, if they'd caught her.

Aidan was dropped off near a main road, he found the desolate road they'd tried to escape from. He walked down the road as quickly as he could, the pain in his side coming and going as he walked further. He came upon the river, luckily no border patrols were near at that time as he saw a few stragglers making their way across. They nodded, looking at his condition and deciding staying far way was the smartest thing to do.

When Aidan arrived to the area where he was arrested, he saw the remnants of the bridge, it had been cut, straggling pieces of the bridge hung from the opposite side. The current wasn't especially strong today, and the tide was much lower.

In the corner of his eye, under some brush, he caught the small reflection of a piece of metal. He walked as fast as he could toward it. He leaned down and touched the side, realizing it was his motorcycle. He pulled on it, struggling initially as the pain in his body turned on all at once like a light bulb. It took him a while of pulling, then digging some of the mud and brush around it before he was able to get it out. He sat next to his motorcycle for a few seconds, marveling at his luck.

He didn't turn the motorcycle on as it could damage it further, he simply pushed it along the dirt road. Surprisingly, he'd been given back his phone, wedding band, and wallet with everything in it, he was sure with some extra tracking abilities of course. He pushed his motorcycle forward slowly, he hoped he wouldn't run into any border patrols or cops as he was sure they'd stop him.

He pushed his motorcycle along for two hours before he saw a more populated area. He looked to see if he could find a mechanic and by chance came upon one small shop. The mechanic was an older gentlemen, looked about 65 years old, his demeanor was of an old Texan cowboy with a Southern twang for an accent. Aidan asked the man if he could help with his motorcycle.

The man didn't seem alarmed at the slight Irish accent and the nonsensical details...a man who looked beat to a pulp, a waterlogged motorcycle, near the border in an area known for border crossings.

The man introduced himself as Bill. Bill told Aidan it would be a while before he could get to his motorcycle. It was only him and one of his mechanics that day and the day was fully booked. But he sensed this young man needed help so he didn't refuse.

Aidan sat in the shop lobby, a small TV in a corner was playing news, unusual news: news of sharp declines in crime, decline in homelessness, politicians doing the right thing for once.

He'd been in the waiting room for an hour when Bill went to the deli next door to grab a quick bite. Bill returned five minutes later through the front door in the lobby and handed Aidan a sandwich and soda can. Aidan thanked him and devoured the sandwich in less than a minute, he'd been given no food nor water while he was in custody.

Finally when the shop was an hour from closing Bill was able to work on Aidan's motorcycle. It needed a few spark plugs but other than that, the water hadn't done any damage. When he came in and handed Aidan the keys, Aidan looked on in disbelief.

"Done," Bill said.

"Thank you! How much do I owe you?" Aidan asked.

Bill shook his head, "No charge, didn't need much."

Aidan looked at him incredulously, "Seriously? Thanks man."

"No problem," Bill said as he saw the gratitude on Aidan's face.

"Hey Bill, can I ask you a question?"

"Sure," Bill replied.

"How come you didn't seem surprised by my appearance or ask questions?" Aidan asked.

"I figured you were just a man in need of a helping hand, we've all been there at one point." Bill began to clean his hands with a rag then stopped and added.

"And in these parts unfortunately I've seen worse, things that would shock most...you learn not to ask too many questions."

Aidan didn't probe more.

"Well thank you again Bill."

"Anytime lad," Bill said with a grin.

Aidan stepped outside and looked at his motorcycle, scratched and a few small dents but nothing major. When he inserted the key in the ignition it started right up like nothing ever happened.

Now he just needed to find Eveley...his sole mission now was to find her. He tried calling her phone several times but it went straight to voicemail. He wasn't sure where she was but he figured she hadn't made it into Mexico since she never tried to call him, which is what she would've done. He feared the worst, that she was in custody and who knows what lengths they took to get answers to their questions. He knew if LAR returned, he'd help her but he had no way of knowing. The uncertainty was gnawing at him, he needed to find a way to find her.

He tried to call FBI headquarters and talk to anyone that would tell him where she was, but no one would say. He called Eveley's family, Isabel was extremely upset. Aidan didn't give her all the details, omitting the way they were caught and how they beat him up several times. Isabel would have worried herself sick thinking the same was happening to Eveley.

Isabel told Aidan she would have Cesar call him immediately. When Cesar spoke to Aidan five minutes later he seemed to already know Aidan had been hurt, since he asked him right away if they'd hurt him too bad. He also wanted to know if anyone had hurt Eveley. Aidan made Cesar understand his phone was most likely bugged and he couldn't say much over the phone in so many words. Cesar was aware this was a probability.

Cesar told Aidan exactly where to go, there was only one place he knew in New Mexico with a top secret area near Aidan's location, Roswell. Cesar told Aidan he couldn't get anywhere near the complex but he could find a cheap motel in town, and wait till Cesar and his family found a lawyer to pressure the release of Eveley from custody. Aidan agreed to the plan and set out to Roswell.

It took Aidan a few hours to get to Roswell. He was surprised how extensively the area was commercialized for tourism but then again everything became a tourist attraction in America, especially aliens. He found a nondescript motel in the area Cesar told him. As soon as he entered his room he tried to call Eveley's phone once more, again it went to voicemail, he left her a voicemail telling her he was safe and to call him. He laid back on the bed, despite his efforts to stay awake, he dozed off.

Meanwhile, Eveley was escorted back to her room, aka cell. They kept her in the dark, gave her no info on when she'd be released or when she'd be able to call her lawyer or family. She had survived 24 hours of intense and manipulative interrogations. They were running out of patience with her but so was she with them.

She was convinced they had used weapons on her, like the glass of water that contained a substance that made her lose her resolve to remain silent until LAR spoke to her. Plus the high-pitched sound in her room that propelled her blackout, she was sure it was a sonar weapon.

There were cameras in all the rooms in her cell, she knew they were watching everything. She laid on the bed, exhausted, thirsty and hungry, despite all this she refused to drink or eat anything they gave her for fear of it being tampered with. She held her stone necklace with both hands, her eyes shut slowly, and as she fell asleep she started to ask LAR questions.

"Where did you go? I was worried something happened to you."

"I had to get further from your galaxy again, my race was close enough they would have detected my presence, I couldn't risk it Eveley."

"I figured that's why you were gone."

"Eveley, we don't have much time, you must leave in five days or we will miss our opportunity."

Eveley said nothing, five days? That's all she could give her loved ones? Five more days and she was locked up in a concrete box.

"Will I ever be able to return?"

"Perhaps, it's a possibility. Eveley...I don't want you to get your hopes up. It is likely you will not be able to return for many years."

Eveley's eyes filled with tears, she needed to know for sure...the last test.

"My father...you said you knew."

"Yes Eveley, when you leave this place, I will lead you to the exact place."

"I also need to find Aidan, I need to see my family, if I only have five days left."

"You will be released this morning, they are already discussing it. They have no proof of any of the things they suspect. They have no choice but to release you."

"Thank goodness! I was starting to think they would never let me go."

"They will let you go but they will continue to track you. They took blood samples when you were blacked out and it is only a matter of time before they realize your blood has a different signature and try to get you in their custody again. You must get rid of your phone as soon as you get in touch with Aidan, both your phones need to be discarded."

"Okay understood...I need to know, where are you taking me? How will I even be able to survive up there?"

"There are an infinite amount of places Eveley, our universe is vast, and the good thing for you is you can survive in most of them, you will see with your own eyes."

Eveley wanted to know so much more but she felt herself waking slowly.

"Don't worry Eveley, I have disabled all their weapons against you and the cameras, they won't hurt you again."

Next thing she knew, she was wide awake looking at the ceiling. She heard the door opening to her cell, she sat up and looked at the doorway to the bedroom which had no door, two agents stood there. They did not look happy and looked around the room.

"Miss Luna we'll have you know it's a federal offense to tamper with federal property, one of which are those cameras installed for your safety."

Eveley looked puzzled and shook her head.

"I haven't touched anything. I've been asleep this whole time."

The agents didn't respond.

"Please come with us Miss Luna."

She stood, both agents grabbed each of her arms. Just like her entrance to this complex she was escorted out and placed inside a SUV. Again the partitions came down so she couldn't see outside or to the front seats. She wasn't sure if they were using weapons on her again because she felt suspiciously tired and sleepy as soon as she entered the SUV. Within minutes she was asleep and didn't wake until the last 30 minutes of the trip. She wasn't sure how long she'd been asleep or how long the trip had really been. They came to a stop and the front partition opened, one of the agents handed her a bag.

"You're free to go," he said coldly as the doors unlocked and the partition to the front closed again.

Eveley opened the door slowly, the sun made her wince, she hadn't seen daylight at all in custody. She was in front of an emergency room to a hospital she'd never been to. As soon as she stepped out and closed the door behind her, the SUV sped away. She opened the bag they gave her, inside were her wallet and phone, her purse and backpack were not returned.

She turned on her phone, only 5% battery left and dozens of missed calls. She ran into the hospital and found a charging station. She hooked up her phone and looked at her missed calls, the first ones were from Aidan. She was relieved, he must have been set free. She called his number and when Aidan saw her name on his phone screen he instantly felt relief.

"Eveley!?"

"Aidan! Oh my god, I was so worried baby, are you okay?!" the worry and excitement was palpable in Eveley's voice. She sounded happy but also on the verge of tears as her voice trembled.

"Yes, I'm okay, are you okay? Did they hurt you?"

"No, did they hurt you?"

"Not too bad, I need to know where you are, I'm coming to get you."

"In what?"

"I got my motorcycle back."

"What? Really?! I can't believe it, how?!"

"I went back to the bridge looking for you and it was under water but I managed to see one of the mirrors sticking out. I got it out then walked it two hours to a mechanic shop where they checked it over and it was fine."

"Wow, I can't believe your luck."

"Yeah me neither...so where are you so I can come get you?"

"Hold on let me check."

Eveley found her location on her phone's map feature with GPS and texted it to Aidan.

"I'm 20 minutes away from you, your family knows what happened, I called them and told them. They have been calling the FBI to get you released. Actually your grandfather told me to come to Roswell since he was pretty sure this is where they had you in custody."

"I guess he was pretty spot on."

"Yeah he was. Alright, I'll be there in 20 minutes amor [love]."

"Okay, I'll be out front by the ER entrance."

"Okay, I love you." Aidan said.

"I love you too."

Eveley dialed her mother, her mother was frantic, crying, and upset. She'd been calling and demanding different government offices to know where Eveley was being held all day. Her grandparents were on their way to meet with their state representative and a lawyer alongside Isabel.

Once Eveley told her mother everything that happened and how they beat up Aidan, Isabel became angry and indignant. Eveley told her mom not to worry about that for now, they had bigger issues to worry about in their immediate future. She needed to meet her right away in Kansas City, she didn't have much time to explain but it had to be in Kansas City. LAR made it clear she must to return to Missouri to show her what he promised.

Eveley took her phone from the charger and stepped outside, it was five more minutes before she saw Aidan pull up. He still wore the same clothing he wore the night they were ambushed. His t-shirt was splattered in red and brown blood, lots of of it, and it was muddy. His jeans were muddy and torn, his face bruised, his eyes no longer black but shades of purple and blue. She could tell he was beaten again by the mix of fresh and old bruises on his torso. She ran up to him and hugged him tightly, tears streaming down her face.

"All that matters is you're here with me again," she whispered, her voice breaking with emotion.

His eyes filled with tears as he hugged her tightly. He placed his hand behind her head holding her against his body, he kissed the top of her head, his tears spilling onto her hair. They remained in this embrace without letting go for a solid minute. They felt the pain, both physical and emotional of what happened to them but their reunion made everything right again.

"I love you," he whispered.

"I love you too," she whispered back.

If they could stay in this moment forever, they would. He pulled slightly away to look at her face, she looked up at him intently. He cradled her face in both hands and gently wiped away her tears with his thumbs. She touched his face in return and wiped away a few of his own. He leaned closer as he held her face in his hands and kissed her on the lips, it was the first joyful moment since they'd been ripped away from each other.

They ended their kiss and embraced again, they didn't want to ever let go. Aidan finally pulled away, he was ready to leave this place behind.

"Okay, let's go back to the motel. On the way we'll grab something to eat, buy a change of clothes, we can shower and change back at the motel. I want us to get the hell out of here as soon as possible."

Eveley nodded, they hopped on his motorcycle quickly. She wrapped her arms around his midsection, Aidan placed his hand over her arm to reassure her. She rested her head on his back, grateful to God for the chance to touch him and speak to him again. The cool breeze felt amazing on their skin as they rode. Maybe the phrase "riding into the sunset" was a cheesy scene in a movie but she realized it was really a feeling. A fleeting moment...but the happiest moment, one she desperately wanted to hold unto for eternity.

The barren desert landscape suddenly made her feel melancholy. As soon as she realized she was complete and happy being by his side, she realized this would end in five short days. Her life would be just as barren as the landscape in front of her. She would have to live with the empty existence she felt when she was in that cold concrete box below ground. That feeling which made time slow down, the world stop making sense or matter, and the feeling of longing...eternally longing for his presence. She was not prepared to go through that hell again, she didn't know how she would survive it.

She knew how it felt to lose a loved one, to live in limbo, living but not truly living. She lived that with the loss of her dad.

In a real sense it'd be like they were dead to each other, although their love would still exist. She held him tighter, took a deep breath, and vowed to stop thinking these thoughts or she'd drive herself crazy. She vowed to simply live in the moment for the next few days.

After they purchased a few basics, and grabbed a quick bite, they finally made it to the motel. Eveley was exhausted, and while Aidan showered and changed, she fell asleep, then it was her turn to shower. After they both cleaned up and changed, they sat on the two beds facing each other talking. She finally found a moment to tell him the news she was going to leave very soon, he was stunned and in silence, his expression pained. He suddenly perked up.

"What if I go with you?" Aidan looked hopeful.

Eveley looked at him for a moment and for a second she wanted to accept his offer happily but she thought of his family when suddenly LAR spoke to her.

"*He cannot go with you.*"

Her heart sank, she asked why in her mind.

"Aidan, you can't, what about your family? They would be devastated," she said trying to convince him.

"*I cannot secure passage for both of you, it's impossible.*"

"LAR is also telling me he can't get both of us out, it's impossible."

Aidan looked defeated. He grabbed both her hands and kissed the top of one of her hands.

"Will we ever see each other again?" Aidan asked.

Eveley felt her heartbeat go crazy, her palms started sweating and she looked him in the eyes.

"I don't know, LAR tells me there is a possibility but I think he just doesn't want to tell me the truth that we'll never see each other again." Eveley looked down at the floor, tears fell softly on top of her feet.

Aidan lifted her face gently by her chin, "Eveley, esta bien corazon, mirame...te amo [it's okay sweetheart, look at me...I love you]."

Eveley loved when Aidan spoke Spanish to her, his words somehow conveyed a much deeper meaning.

"How many days do we have?"

"Five days."

"Five days?! Dammit! I didn't know you meant so soon!"

Aidan sighed and looked ahead as if he couldn't quite put his thoughts together.

"I'm not going to lose hope you'll make your way back to me. I have to hold unto that hope in order to continue breathing.

Promise me you'll also hold unto that hope, that we'll see each other again...I need you to promise me," Aidan implored.

"I promise, a thousand times I promise!" Eveley declared as she fell to the floor on her knees, embraced him and sobbed as she rested her head on his chest. She looked up at him, she ran her fingertips gently over his bruising, careful not to cause him pain. She felt deep resentment this is what they went through, especially him on the last days of their journey together. Her hands slowly made their way down his face to his shoulders, then softly over his chest.

"Just help me forget, I don't want to think about it. I don't know if I'm strong enough to do this. I know I must be, but right now I just can't see it." She looked up at him with pleading eyes.

Aidan rubbed her shoulders, his fingertips moved slowly along the contour of her neck to their final resting place on either side of her chin, cupping her face gently, he leaned down and kissed her, There was so much emotion communicated in their kiss...angst, passion, tenderness, and longing. The hours continued to pass, the sands of time in their hourglass continued to fall, their doomsday countdown. And yet in those hours in that motel room, they made each other forget with their tenderness, leaving nothing unsaid, or untouched. For a moment they were together forever as one.

CLIFF DRIVE

Eveley and Aidan left the motel a few hours later, arriving in Missouri after 12 hours on 'Fragarach', as Aidan had affectionately named his motorcycle, a fitting name for the resilient hunk of steel. He'd sped through most of the way, making up precious time. They arrived tired to the bone, still recovering from the events of the previous days.

Eveley's mom arrived in Kansas City first, and secured a hotel room downtown. Eveley and Aidan arrived around 1 am, they both fell asleep in one bed, while Isabel slept in the other bed.

Eveley wanted to thank Mr. Collins before her departure, so they woke up around 8 am and made their way to Mr. Collin's place. They parked in the parking lot behind his apartment. They knocked on his door and he answered with a look of surprise on his face.

"Oh my goodness, come right in!" He shut the door behind them and they all hugged him, especially Eveley, she gave him a long hug.

"You were right, they weren't going to stop till they found us, it took them four months but they got us." Eveley pointed at Aidan and all his bruises.

"Damn them! They shouldn't have done that to you son," Mr. Collins patted him on the shoulder.

"It's okay, I didn't break, I didn't give them anything," Aidan said proudly.

Mr. Collins shook his head and spoke to Eveley, "And did they hurt you sweetie?"

"No, but they tried using weapons on me, some type of drug in my drink and a sonar weapon that made me blackout. I gave the alien a name...LAR. LAR told me they took blood samples and it would tip them off I'm different once they get the results back. We threw away our old phones and bought new ones but they're going to start looking for me. I just came to say goodbye."

Mr. Collins looked perplexed.

"I have to leave this planet in four days..." Eveley trailed off as she hadn't told anyone except Aidan.

Eveley's mom looked surprised, she went to Eveley and hugged her tight.

"You didn't tell me this mija!" Isabel got teary eyed, "But why? How?"

"I can't be here ma, LAR's race is getting closer and if they see I'm here they will land and upon seeing what has happened they will destroy me along with our entire race or subjugate us. I can't let that happen, I can't let the ones I love perish."

"Mr. Collins, I just wanted to come to say thank you for everything you did for us and to say goodbye," Eveley continued and gave Mr. Collins another hug.

"We must go now, as we don't have much time. Take care Mr. Collins, and by the way, LAR told me Tyler did it. Tyler was captured by that alien you spoke of, which by the way their race are called EDEN."

Mr. Collin's eyes got big and he looked relieved.

"I always worried he was out there hurting more people. That's such a big worry off my chest, but it's devastating to know he was capable of such evil."

"Yes, but at least he can't hurt anyone else now."

"Yes, you're right."

After this, everyone hugged again and they left. Once they were in the car, Eveley felt the big weight of what was to come.

"I'm ready to lead you there."

"Ma, tengo algo que decirte [Mom, I have something to tell you]."

"Okay, que es [what is it]?"

"The reason why I had to meet you in Kansas City is because LAR knows where dad's remains are."

Eveley observed her mothers face, it was as if it didn't register. Isabel was speechless. After what seemed like minutes but was only ten seconds Isabel spoke.

"Uh, what? I don't understand."

"Ma, he's an alien from a different galaxy, with different abilities, and technology. He told me he knows exactly where dad's remains are, and he's going to show us."

"But how? How could he know?!" Isabel's mom seemed confused and anxious.

"Ma, it's going to be okay. I'm going to be right by your side." Eveley grabbed her mom's hand and squeezed it.

Isabel sighed deeply as she fixated on Eveley's hand. Isabel grabbed and raised Eveley's hand, she looked back and forth at Eveley and Aidan. She clearly noticed the addition of the wedding band on Eveley's finger.

"What's this?! Don't tell me this is what I think it is!"

"Yes suegra [mother-in-law], we eloped. We didn't want to put it off any longer in case something happened."

"I knew you guys looked a little suspicious," Isabel said with a slight grin and hugged Eveley. She grabbed Aidan's hand and squeezed it.

"Congratulations! I'm so happy for you guys, now you take good care of my princesa [princess] you hear?"

"Of course, she's mine to protect and love always." Aidan smiled, locking eyes with Eveley through the rear-view mirror as he spoke.

"Turn here Aidan," Eveley instructed as he continued to drive toward a place LAR told her was called Cliff Drive.

Eveley noticed her mother's face was pale in comparison to before she told her their purpose in driving to Cliff Drive. Eveley grabbed Isabel's hand and squeezed it with both of her hands.

"It'll be okay ma, don't worry, I'm anxious too but we need to find out. We're going to finally find his remains and give him a dignified resting place and this will also prove LAR is trustworthy so you can stop worrying for me."

"Okay mija, let's go," Isabel said quietly.

The entire drive to Cliff Drive took about 15 minutes, they parked along the street. The city skyline peaked through the blooming trees. The area around the entrance was graced by large turn-of-the-century mansions...beautiful stone palaces of yesteryear. The pinnacle was the KC Museum which used to be the home of a lumber baron in the early 1900's.

They got out of the car and walked toward the entrance to Cliff Drive which boasted large whimsical wrought iron gates, there was an open door for pedestrians to use.

It was an unusually warm and sunny day, 70 degrees outside. A few people were walking down Cliff Drive with their dogs.

Eveley felt her heart rate increase, her mom looked terrified. Aidan looked somber, this wasn't what anyone wanted to do on a beautiful, sunny day. They walked slowly about 1/3 of a mile into Cliff Drive which was a scenic byway closed to cars. They walked along the middle of the road, now empty of other pedestrians. They stopped where Eveley signaled.

"We need to go down this bluff," Eveley said.

They found a small clearing in the brush, they could see the train tracks several hundred feet below. They made their way to where LAR instructed Eveley, slowly, as to not slip and fall. Once they were at the correct spot, Eveley stood and took a deep breath. Her mother stood on one side of her and Aidan on the other. They waited for Eveley's cue.

"It's here...his remains will be around this area, we may have to dig," Eveley said.

Isabel closed her eyes, sighed deeply, her hands were trembling, Eveley noticed and grabbed her mother's hand.

"It's okay ma, I'm here with you, you're not alone," Eveley said gently.

Isabel still looked afraid but she nodded and looked around. Something caught her eye, a small reflection in the ground. She kneeled down and tried to uncover it, she realized it was gold, a wedding ring...his wedding ring. It was unmistakable, a custom symbol she had engraved still visible on the band of the ring. She burst into sobs as she frantically dug around the ring. Eveley kneeled down next to her mother and helped her dig in the mud. A skeletal hand emerged, they both gasped but continued digging as they could feel there were more bones.

Aidan started to dig near the same area and found a gun, he picked it up.

"Eveley, suegra, look."

"Pablo's gun!" Isabel exclaimed.

She grabbed it, wiped the mud off with her fingers and looked closer. Pablo engraved his initials on every one of his guns. She found his initials and knew it was his. She set Pablo's gun in front of her and squeezed his wedding band in her fist as tears streamed down her face.

More and more of his skeletal remains were uncovered by all three of them, until they found the skull and Isabel looked like she would faint.

Aidan found a Mora knife a few feet away from Pablo's remains and he wondered if it was how Pablo died. He looked for more clues though he guessed it was another parasite that stalked Pablo and his family, since Isabel and Eveley were compatible hosts.

Eveley hugged her mom and cried with her. They dug up as much as they could and when they were done, Isabel called the detective in charge of Pablo's case.

Isabel couldn't believe it'd been over a decade since he'd gone missing. Ten long years his remains laid in this spot, it hurt Isabel to know that.

The detective came to the area immediately and closed Cliff Drive to gather evidence. Isabel kept his ring but everything else was collected by the forensic team that descended on the area. The investigator on his case would have forensic analysis made of his dentals, and an autopsy would be performed within 24 hours to determine cause of death. If the remains did in fact confirm their suspicions, Isabel would be given the remaining skeletal remains for burial.

After such a brutal day they all returned to the hotel. Isabel collapsed on the bed in exhaustion, she sobbed and Eveley stayed with her mom and consoled her. She sat next to her mom and brushed her hair out of her face. It reminded her of her mom returning from KC the first time she went looking for her dad and how'd she'd almost fainted from the pain of realizing he wasn't coming home. She knew it was gut-wrenching for her mother, and it was painful for her as well. There hadn't been a day she'd stopped missing her father and wishing he'd been in their lives. Eventually Isabel cried herself to sleep. Eveley quietly got into the bed and hugged her, eventually falling asleep as well.

The next morning they met with the KC police investigator. He'd received the results, the dental records and skull matched positive for Pablo. The autopsy revealed a few deep cut marks on the inner ribs closest to his heart which along with the blade they found, would indicate he was fatally stabbed. They found a few bullet casings which were in process of being matched to his gun but if the police department's theory was correct it indicated he tried to shoot someone or something in self-defense but they couldn't be sure. With all the given facts in the case they classified Pablo's death as homicide. They would keep the case open but it would be difficult to solve given the time passed.

Isabel would be able to pick up his remains and transport them with her back to Dallas. Later that day she picked up the heavy box of his remains, placed them in the trunk of her car and made the journey back to Texas.

They arrived to Isabel's house close to 2 am in the morning. They were exhausted and slept till the next morning when Isabel took the remains to the crematory. Isabel and Pablo's parents arrived shortly after Isabel called them that same morning and told them the unfolding of events. She decided to cremate his remains and plant a tree in their backyard with his ashes and have a small ceremony with just her parents and his. By that afternoon his ashes were ready and that evening they planted the tree, the entire family mourned and said their peace at this small ceremony.

Eveley still couldn't believe her dad had been gone from her life for over a decade. She couldn't comprehend how she'd endured the pain when she introspected. Yet, she barely had time to reflect with the days till her departure dwindling. Two days remained with her loved ones...every minute was precious.

CHAPTER 31

VERMIN AMONG US

That night there was a cathartic thunderstorm, the violent thunder and lightning somehow lulled Eveley to sleep in Aidan's arms.

She awoke at 6 am, the outside world was still dark, the thunderstorm had slowed to a light mist. She walked through the dark hallway to the front living room, she peeked out the front window and felt she was being watched again. She walked back to her bedroom and grabbed her gun from the night stand. She returned to the front window and peeked out, she wasn't sure what was going on but the hairs on the back of her neck stood up and her heart rate sped up. She felt sweat beading on her temples, she walked back to her bedroom and softly nudged Aidan, he stirred and opened his eyes.

"What's going on cariño [darling]?"

"Something's wrong Aidan, I can feel it," she whispered and tightened her grip on his arm. He stood up immediately, grabbed his gun from the nightstand and followed Eveley to the front room. They both looked out the window, the pavement was wet, the street lamps were dim under the constant drizzle of the rain. Aidan's eyes took a few seconds to adjust to the darkness, he squinted and Eveley held her breath.

"Did LAR tell you anything?"

"No, he hasn't communicated with me since he helped me find my dad's remains."

"Okay, stay back." He stood in front of Eveley as they observed the street, she peeked her head from the side of his torso. They saw a dark figure leap across from the corner of the house to the other side. Eveley screamed and fell back, Aidan caught her before she fell on the floor. Isabel heard the scream and came running to the front living room.

"Eveley! Aidan! Are you guys okay?"

Eveley hugged her mom as if she was a little girl who'd lost sight of her for a second, panicking and feeling the sweet relief of finding her once again.

"Ma, esta uno de esos monstruos afuera, los que mataron a papa [Mom, one of those monsters that killed dad is out there]," she said trembling.

Isabel held her gun in her hand too. She knew Eveley's mind was heavy with the realization Isabel was also a compatible host and she was scared for her once she left this planet. Isabel knew it was imperative she showed strength and bravery. She wanted Eveley to feel the same confidence and bravery to face the upcoming days.

"Mija, we need to find out the location from where you'll be leaving earth and get you there, has LAR given you this information?"

"No ma, he hasn't talked to me since he helped us find dad's remains."

"Okay, you keep trying, as soon as you find out we need to start heading there, we don't have time to lose."

"But ma, what about you? What if that monster keeps trying to go after you when I'm gone?"

"Mija, no te preocupes [don't worry], I'm still here after all these years, nothing is going to happen to me."

"You don't know that!" Eveley was acting beside herself, she was not the kind to dwell on the worst case scenario but the stress from everything recently was finally making her break. She was thinking of what LAR told her, that she must not touch them as her power would only make them stronger, she needed to stay as far away from them as possible.

"We need to leave soon Eveley, we're sitting ducks here," Aidan said as he felt the stalking presence of the monster near the house. He knew it was just like Draven O'Connor, but this parasite seemed more desperate than the one he encountered in Draven.

The rest of the early morning, everyone was on alert inside the house, with their guns ready. Eveley desperately tried to communicated with LAR until 10 am, when she finally heard his voice.

"You must leave now, I will direct you to the location you need to go. There is not a lot of time, you must go west. The FBI is being dispatched right now to come find you. They have the results back and they have obtained a court order to give them jurisdiction to hold you in custody indefinitely, you must not let them catch you."

Eveley told Aidan and Isabel what LAR told her and his instructions. All three quickly packed some clothes in a backpack each. They took Isabel's car, Aidan drove the ten minutes to Eveley's grandparents house. Isabel and Eveley went in quickly to say their goodbyes. Eveley told her grandparents she would probably never see them again, which prompted many tears as they embraced. They wanted to know more but she told them she had no time, she was under great danger and so was Isabel and Aidan. After the emotional goodbye, they headed west like LAR told them.

Aidan drove the first couple hours of the journey, he was careful to keep an eye out for anyone following them. After driving for about six hours, Isabel decided to take over to give him a rest. Eveley gave her mother directions to Gila National Forest.

The first hour of Isabel driving was uneventful, they were in the middle of nowhere after filling up the gas tank again. Just as the drive seemed like it was going better than expected, their tire busted. Isabel was going 55 mph so the car swerved a bit but she was able to keep control of the car. She pulled over to the shoulder of the desolate road. Luckily, Isabel carried a spare tire and the tools to change it. Aidan and Eveley woke from their sleep.

"Flat tire?" Eveley asked.

"Yeah I think so, not sure why, my tires are almost brand new," Isabel said.

"Okay, I'll take a look, you have a spare?" Aidan asked.

"Yeah in the trunk."

"Ma, no podemos estar mucho tiempo aqui [we can't be out here for long]." Eveley moved her phone from side to side looking for a good signal. "What? No signal."

"Yeah these areas are spotty when it comes to cell signal," Aidan said as he felt around for the obvious spot on the flat tire. He found a big gash on the tire, the tire had almost 90% tread so it shouldn't have busted.

The road they were on went on for miles in each direction, there were no cars in sight. It was only barren desert with dark stormy clouds in the distance. The sun was starting to make its slow descent, they needed to get the tire swapped out as quickly as possible to get back on their way.

Aidan took out the spare tire and jack, he pushed the jack under the car quickly. He furiously pumped the handle until the tire was off the ground. He worked on removing the lug nuts with a wrench, he was on the last lug nut which was giving him trouble when he caught a car approaching from a distance.

"Hey, there's a car coming our way, be alert, stay back from the road and be ready," Aidan said to Eveley and Isabel.

"I see it," Isabel said, all three of them were carrying a gun. Eveley and Isabel on their hips under their shirts, and Aidan carried one on his hip and ankle as well. Of course he'd been a big fan of guns while growing up in the States, especially Texas.

He bought a gun as soon as he was old enough and kept it stored with his grandparents when he wasn't in the States.

He kept an eye on the approaching car as he continued to struggle with the lug nut until it finally turned. He took the tire off and placed the new one on. The car was now 50 yards away and he was praying it wasn't anyone out to get them.

The car sported dark tinted windows, it slowed down as it came closer and came to a stop a little ahead of their car. Aidan stood up and gently pushed Isabel and Eveley back. The car passenger window lowered down, inside were two men. Aidan got a bad feeling as soon as he saw their faces, his gut feeling told him they were up to no good. He kept his hand in ready position to grab his gun. Eveley walked to his side and Isabel to his other side.

Eveley felt the eerie feeling from her childhood return. She remembered LAR's words about their eyes...she took a step forward and Aidan grabbed her arm to stop her.

"They are VERMIN! Do not let them touch you!" LAR bellowed.

The one in the passenger seat pulled off his sunglasses and she saw the blue color in his eyes and the irregular iris. She stepped back just as the driver reached over desperately and tried to grab her.

"Get back! It's one of those parasites! Shoot them!" Aidan shouted as all three unholstered their guns and shot directly into the VERMIN. They heard growls and beastly screams as several shots hit the parasites and they sped off.

"We need to leave now!" Isabel shouted after she squeezed the trigger one last time.

Aidan tightened the lug nuts as quickly as he could and all three hurried back into the car. He took off driving, they needed to get to their destination before the VERMIN returned. The parasites had obviously been trailing them.

"Somehow you and your mom in the same area has amplified your scent and these VERMIN are catching it wherever you go. These were not the same ones from Dallas. You must hurry as quickly as possible

to your destination and try not to stop along the way as it will only attract them at this point," LAR told Eveley.

They knew the FBI was nearby since they removed a tracking device from the car before they left Dallas. LAR told them it was placed there at some point since their return from Mexico. They were tracking everyone in Eveley's life.

She was one step ahead of them for now, but the tire blowout wasted precious time they didn't have. She had to make it or it'd be a catastrophe if the VERMIN touched her or worst yet were able to inhabit her body. As they sped away, she turned around and she could see the reflection of another car way off in the distance.

"They are close, you must hurry or they will catch up to you," LAR informed Eveley.

"How are they finding where we are?" Eveley asked LAR.

"They have an entire team of agents on you, you are their biggest case this year. Due to all the world changes in such a small span of time, they have data suggesting something changed on earth the night you obtained your abilities. From government agencies like the FBI, military, to politicians and their overlords, they have all been worried. Fortunately, they have been slowly healed but there are still many that have not been and so they are committed to capturing you."

"Damn it! Why didn't you tell me this earlier?"

"It would not have made a difference in the outcome and would have only made you worry, I was trying to save you from that."

Eveley was upset but she knew in the end it didn't matter. There was no time to fret about it for long.

They were still driving through an isolated area and nightfall was upon them. She was so worried they wouldn't make it in time. Ahead they saw blinking lights, as they got closer they recognized the car from earlier blocking the road, there was also a fire on the side of the road. Aidan was still driving and he slowed down to go around the car on the opposite side. He was still not letting his speed go too low as he didn't want anyone to jump out at them.

"We're gonna go around so hold on in case anything happens."

Aidan sped up again and he turned on his high beams, he couldn't see anything moving but he knew it was a trap.

As he approached, something hit his side of the car, causing the car to swerve to the shoulder of the road and almost hit the raging fire. Aidan was able to get the car under control again and avoid the flames. He looked through his side mirror and saw one of the VERMIN attached to the side of the car. A second VERMIN had hooked himself onto the other side, near Isabel. The one on Isabel's side shattered the window and reached his hand in to grab her, she shot him in the chest, it yelped and fell on the road, thrashing in pain. Eveley pointed her gun and shot the second parasite from her side, it was difficult to hit accurately while the car was in motion. She was successful as he saw the parasite fall on the pavement behind them without moving.

Once they drove past them, Aidan picked up speed, they were less than two hours away from the canyon he needed to take Eveley. They drove for an hour before they made it to Las Cruces, New Mexico. They felt some relief though they weren't in the clear yet. They drove through the center of town until they made it to the edge of the city. They had to pull over to get gas as their tank was near empty. Aidan noticed a suspicious SUV in the corner of his eye and waited impatiently until the tank was full. As soon as he pulled away the SUV got behind them and turned on red and blue lights. Aidan had no choice, he wasn't going to let them take Eveley again. He sped up, several more SUVs got behind them, he was now entering the highway approaching 90 mph. Eveley knew if the FBI caught her, it would be the end, she'd lose her chance to save everyone.

"Don't worry Eveley, tell Aidan to continue as fast as possible, I will help you up ahead."

"LAR said he will help us, we need to keep our speed up. Don't let them catch up and run us off the road, keep going as fast as you can," Eveley said quickly.

"Okay, we are only 30 minutes away from the canyon, suegra are you okay?"

"Yes, just keep your eyes on the road," Isabel held onto the car door with one hand and Eveley's arm with the other.

The SUVs sped up and closed some of the distance, luckily there weren't many cars on the highway.

"Go! Go! They're gaining on us!" Eveley shouted as she saw five SUVS getting closer and closer to them. Ahead was a fork in the road, the side they were headed to would lead them to the isolated canyon where the ship would be waiting for Eveley. The SUV closest to them was just a car space away and gaining on them even at 110 mph.

"You must have more distance between the cars chasing you in order for this to work. Aidan must go faster at least momentarily until there are at least three car spaces between you."

"LAR says you must go faster Aidan, there has to be more space between our car and theirs for him to be able to help us," Eveley said frantically.

"Okay, I'm on it, hold tight as this might be a bit unsafe."

He pressed the accelerator until they were almost at 130 mph. As soon as the SUVs and car gained distance from each other they saw a bright light that blinded them temporarily accompanied by a sonic boom that jolted their entire car. Aidan was barely able to keep control of the car. When they looked back, they saw all the SUVS stalled behind them. Several of the agents got out of their SUVS and threw their hands up in the air in frustration that their cars were fried. Eveley felt relief, but they still needed to get to the spot LAR told her.

"You only have about 30 minutes before they will catch up, more VERMIN are tracking you as well, you need to be careful as they are desperate."

Aidan drove about ten more minutes before they took the exit LAR told them to take. They got out of the car and used flashlights to see as they climbed the trail quickly and quietly. The air was cool and dry and Eveley wrapped her arms around herself. She couldn't believe what was about to happen, she knew it was the end and she dreaded it with every cell in her body. Internally she panicked but kept it together by sheer will.

They broke a sweat despite the cool weather, after 20 minutes they finally made it to the top and Eveley saw the rock jutting out from the edge. They stopped and everyone stood in silence. They had to wait until LAR gave the signal. Eveley allowed the tears to fall down her face silently, she hugged her mom tightly and told her she loved her, she'd miss her, and would try to come back as soon as possible. She then turned to Aidan and they hugged tightly.

"Don't forget me please," Eveley said.

"I could never forget you. Come back to me as soon as you can, I'll be waiting," he said, and they kissed.

"I love you so much," Eveley said as she pulled away from their kiss.

"I love you forever," Aidan said as he held her without wanting to let go.

"Please don't let anything happen to my mom after I get on that ship," she pleaded. They heard growling from VERMIN in the distance.

"I won't let anything happen to her," Aidan said.

LAR let her know the ship was in front of her and she reluctantly let go of Aidan.

"I have to go now," she said, her hands trembled and her chest hurt as she turned to face the ship.

"Where? I don't see it LAR," she said in her mind.

The ship blended into the sky behind it, it was a large mirror, until it wasn't. The slight reflection when it moved sideways is what finally caught their eye. A portal opened in front of them, inside it looked like a long hallway of diffused blue. Eveley couldn't move, she was frozen. They heard sirens in the background and the fever pitch of VERMIN in the distance.

Eveley's heart broke inside as she took one slow step after another in front of her. She walked to the edge of the rock sticking out above the canyon. She looked behind her at Aidan and her mother standing still. She closed her eyes, took a deep breath and etched their image in her mind one last time. Facing the ship, she somehow felt recognition, as if she'd been inside it before. She stood very still and as soon as she made the conscious decision to enter the ship she was on it, she hadn't moved a muscle after her decision. Yet she found herself in a dream-like state inside an ivory white cocoon, only conscious for a fraction of a second before she crossed into a deep sleep.

CHAPTER 32

AEVEN

When Eveley awoke, she was slow to come to consciousness, she wasn't sure how much time had passed. She opened her eyes and noticed she was in a type of pod, a white pod. She pushed the ceiling and it opened without much effort, it was darker in the room she was in than inside her pod which had been brightly lit with some type of artificial light. The room she awoke in was dark, full of containers, it looked like a large holding warehouse for shipments. She stood up, her legs gave out from under her, she wondered how long she'd been inside.

"*Everything is okay Eveley, take some time to acclimate your legs. Take small steps and keep doing it over and over again. I will guide you where you need to go, do not speak to anyone.*"

"Where am I? What is this place called?"

"*There's no time for that right now Eveley, please leave out the door to your right when you are able to walk.*"

Eveley looked to her right and saw a small exit sign dimly lit above a doorway. She walked to the doorway, hesitating before opening the door. She stepped out onto an expansive parking lot. The outside took her breath away, LAR interrupted her trance.

"*Eveley, please hurry, you can't be out in the open, you must keep moving.*"

Eveley continued on the sidewalk surrounding the warehouse and made her way around the building. She saw large machinery systematically moving around all types of large shipping containers. She didn't see any people and she walked briskly where LAR told her to go. She couldn't help looking up at the sky once more as it took her breath away. The sky was a beautiful turquoise color, and the clouds were lower than she remembered on earth, but the most beautiful part of the sky was the slightly orange tinted moon, she thought it must be at least double the size of the moon on earth.

For a second her heart sank, she was no longer on earth. So many questions were flying around in her head coupled with the new sights and feelings on this planet.

From her first breath, she felt lighter, her mind fired on all cylinders and at one point she felt like an outsider looking in on her thoughts. This surprised her as that had only happened when LAR tried to get her attention the first time he made his appearance in her life.

As soon as these thoughts went through her mind she realized it smelled different on this planet too. It smelled like right after a heavy rainfall, yet there was nothing wet around her. She saw drones fly above her, she picked up her pace as she realized there had to be a reason LAR didn't want her out in the open.

She finally made it to the edge of the parking lot, she could see a highway and a road running parallel to it, she walked along the fence to where she saw an entry point for vehicles. She saw there was an automated system for entries and exits, she slipped under the bar preventing cars from entering and exiting. As soon as she made it to the road, LAR instructed her to walk along the road for a mile until she reached a bridge.

She saw houses and cars ahead, the cars on this planet had the styling of cars from the 1930's-1950's on earth, except more modern, and very quiet. As she got closer to the bridge, traffic increased, she noticed the people outside, a school bus dropping off children. The children's laughter was so clear even though she could see them from a distance. It was all at once startling when she realized their laughter sounded as if she was standing next to them. She saw several people outside working in their gardens, and again she could hear some of what they said as if they were next to her. People seemed friendly, everyone that noticed her had a puzzled look on their face, yet they still eventually smiled and waved. Eveley knew it was because her clothing made her stand out since she was dressed very different than them.

The people on this planet dressed formal. The styles were a mix of what people would have worn on earth from the 1920's to 1950's but it also was its own style, sleeker, with cleaner lines. Even the children that exited the school bus were impeccably dressed, the little girls had the same school uniform consisting of formal dresses in varying colors with matching ribbons in their hair and the boys wore suits with hats. The colors they used in their clothing were saturated and eye catching. Vivid teal, apricot, scarlet, emerald blue among many others. Everyone looked so proper and well-dressed.

Once she arrived to the bridge, her mouth fell open. The bridge was something she'd never seen before, it seemed to go on forever without stopping. From her perspective, the alabaster white floating bridge never seemed to touch pillars or connect to the ground, she was over what seemed like a large lake but on either side there were walls of waterfalls. The water below was so clear she could see to the bottom, a large array of bright colored fish swam at the bottom. It was mesmerizing and she realized the air smelled like rain because the waterfalls churned this water into the air nonstop. She stood there and took a deep breath in, enjoying the refreshing and energizing mist from the waterfalls.

She made her way over the bridge down the wide sidewalk which was relaxing. Since the cars here were quiet, the only noise was the churning of the waterfalls. It took a mile for her to cross the bridge. By the time she crossed, the traffic had picked up, must be rush hour she thought.

She was able to decipher people spoke a language very similar to English. There were only a few words she didn't understand.

This seemed unlikely on another planet completely different than earth.

When she made it to the end of the bridge, she noticed the city below. She was on a hill and the skyline sparkled before her. She noticed most of the buildings were white and contained terraces and gardens, their glass façades gleamed in the sunlight. She started noticing small details such as how every house seemed to have some sort of garden and their design was minimalist but they used plants and terraces to make every house look unique. One thing for sure is people on this planet loved nature and incorporated it easily into their homes. She saw so many exotic plants and flowers she'd never seen before, she felt like she was walking in a dream, a beautiful dream full of new sights, sounds, and smells.

"How long was I in that pod LAR?"

"I will explain all this later, right now I need you to find the final address. You must get there before sundown as it will be easier to be detected if you're walking around at night."

"Okay LAR, I'm going as fast as I can," Eveley replied.

It took Eveley another 45 minutes to arrive to a neighborhood near the skyline she was just dazzled by. The neighborhood was made up of much larger houses than the smaller houses in the neighborhood across the bridge. He led her to a large house on top of a hill. It was a little different from the rest of the homes, it was still a large mansion, but its façade had an older world feel than the ultra modern homes around it. She walked to the front door and rang the bell, a few seconds later an older woman answered the door.

"Well hello, are you Eveley?"

"Yes, hi, I'm sorry to bother you," Eveley replied.

"Well come right in Eveley, I've been expecting you, and your friend told me you'd be coming. My name is Lyra Venus, but you may call me Miss Venus for now."

"Nice to meet you, how do you know LAR?"

Eveley was feeling a bit out of sorts, she wanted to know where she was, how long she'd been on the ship.

"Oh, you gave him a name? How sweet, I love it. Well, that's a long story my dear."

"I have all the time in the world," Eveley replied. She felt anxious for answers to all the questions swirling around in her head.

"Well let's just say many of us in the higher echelons of society have always had access to knowledge the lower classes don't. We've known for years his species existed, now getting one of their kind to communicate back is a whole other story."

Miss Venus led her down the expansive hallway to a large sitting area, she motioned for her to sit. Eveley took a seat on a plush sectional.

"Now when he asked me if I could help you, and he told me your story I was completely fascinated and of course agreed. The deal was I'd help you blend in, I'd give you a place to live and cover your expenses, in exchange for the simple privilege of hearing your story."

Eveley felt a bit uncomfortable, she fidgeted in her seat but spoke up.

"Look, I really appreciate what you and LAR are doing for me but I'm not a zoo animal. The things I went through are not something I want to talk to anyone about right now, especially with a stranger."

"Oh you have the wrong idea about me dear, of course I don't see you as a zoo animal or you being here for my entertainment. I don't doubt you are going through a lot right now, having left your home and those you love. I just want to offer a listening ear...when you're ready of course. I also want to help you stay safe, and help you fit into our society for however long you need."

Eveley looked around and sighed, "Thank you, can you tell me more about this place? How I got here and where I am? LAR tends to never give me the whole story."

"Oh, yes, of course. LAR told me your galaxy is pretty far from us, but the EDEN ship managed to reach your solar system easily through a wormhole. Our planet does not bar communication with other species but we are not allowed physical contact nor excursions to their planets and vice versa. I believe our solar system is in the realm of possibility for parallel theory but since no one is allowed to live on other planets or bring others in we've never confirmed it. Maybe you'll be the first pioneer to confirm it.

"Anyways, our planet is called [1] Aeven. We have territories that are just for general purposes since people are allowed to move about freely. There are over 200 territories all under one government. Our territory's name is [2] Orai and we are in the city of Araven. We are considered a fairly primitive race in comparison to those like EDEN or your LAR, but we are still much more civilized than others that exist out there.

"We do have fairly advanced technology and we are free of most violent crime, extreme poverty, and disease but we are not a utopia. We have a lot of conditions placed on our personal freedoms in order to keep our society as orderly as you see," Miss Venus said.

"I could tell you were far more advanced than my planet just walking through the neighborhoods. I can't believe we truly thought we were the only ones in the universe." Eveley shook her head in amazement.

Miss Venus nodded her head in agreement.

"Oh how rude of me! I haven't even offered you anything to eat or drink, are you hungry?"

"Oh no, I'm not at all, I am a little tired though."

---

1. Aeven (A-venn)

2. Orai (O-rye)

"Well say no more, let me show you to your room. Tomorrow we can get you all the things you need."

"Okay, thank you."

Eveley stood and followed Miss Venus to the second floor. She led her to the end of the hall, in the front part of the house. She opened the door to a large bedroom with floor to ceiling windows on one side overlooking the city skyline. Eveley's jaw dropped.

"Wow, this is beautiful," Eveley said.

"Yes, the front part of the second floor has these large windows. Don't worry, they are mirrored so even though you can see outside perfectly fine, those outside and the drones can't see inside," Miss Venus said nonchalantly. It didn't seem like much impressed her being so wealthy.

"Well if you need anything please let me know," Miss Venus said and smiled.

"Thank you Miss Venus," Eveley said.

She looked at the skyline in front of her. The horizon was dominated by glass and alabaster white skyscrapers with exotic terraces and sleek trains passing through the center of downtown.

"No problem," Miss Venus replied and turned around to leave. "Sweetie, I hope you feel much better tomorrow," she added.

"Thank you, I hope so too," Eveley answered.

Miss Venus stepped into the hall and closed the door behind her.

Eveley sat on the large bed for a few seconds, she finally let her body fall back on the bed and closed her eyes. She opened her eyes and looked at the ceiling, she was alone...to start anew, without her family or husband. She missed them so much already it hurt. She closed her eyes and played the last image of them in her mind. When she opened her eyes again, hot tears ran along the edges of her eyes down the temples of her face. She tried to imagine herself waking from a terrible dream, but her eyes only confirmed it was all too real and she was stuck in this new world. She wanted to scream, she wanted to hit something, how was she going to learn to live without everyone she loved?

CHAPTER 33

SUPERPOSITION

The first week on Aeven, Eveley was a walking zombie. She could barely function, she was tormented by worry for her mom and the pain of missing Aidan which was all-consuming. She barely slept, barely ate, and she couldn't find joy in anything.

Miss Venus was naturally concerned but very understanding of Eveley's situation. She gently encouraged her every day to go outside in the garden and pool on her property in hopes it would help Eveley feel better.

Eveley tried to think of ways, any, to feel better and keep hope for the future but almost every night without fail, the reality of her situation drove her to cry herself to sleep.

Eventually Miss Venus began to push her to accompany her to her studio downtown. She wanted to get Eveley fitted for clothing she would need to wear to fit into society. She also thought the more she began to participate in society the more she'd slowly improve her mental state.

For the next couple of weeks, Eveley distracted herself from her emotional pain by learning as much as she could about Aeven through books. She also learned a lot more about her benefactor Miss Venus. Miss Venus turned out to be a gracious and generous host, always lending a listening ear. She was not how Eveley perceived at the beginning, out of touch with normal people and stuck up, elitist even. In fact, Miss Venus had a lot of compassion for the less fortunate.

She held a peculiar view of the world and rejected most modern technology. She was one of the few people in her neighborhood who didn't use robots or humanoids in her house, everything was done the old-school way.

Eveley also soon found out her powers on Aeven didn't work. This detail perplexed Eveley but Miss Venus told her it was nothing out of the ordinary. Aeven was a completely different galaxy with different "vibrations" than her own planet which might have something to do with her powers not working.

Eveley asked Miss Venus a million more questions regarding humans and how people on Aeven could reach other species. Miss Venus explained they regularly communicated with them, but very rarely did they ever communicate back. Eveley thought maybe she could use their methods to contact her loved ones on Earth.

Unfortunately Miss Venus did not find anything cataloged that even matched closely to Eveley's galaxy, they were simply too far away. The wormholes other species used and how to access them were hidden to Aeven.

Eveley soon fell into a routine, she worked for Miss Venus downtown in her clothing design studio. Miss Venus taught her all the dos and don'ts to stay undetected by the humanoid robots she would encounter in almost every place in the outside world. She would need to avoid looking directly into any of the robot's faces and wear sunglasses for the most part to prevent facial recognition and iris scans.

Miss Venus offered to take her every morning with her to work but Miss Venus woke up at 5 am, she usually made it to her office by 6 am. Eveley was definitely not a morning person, more of a night owl so she decided to go in at the normal time and take the train every morning. It was by chance one day she walked by a cozy coffee shop and it became her morning routine before catching the train downtown.

In her quiet corner of the café Eveley sipped her coffee, she looked around, observing the small details in people's faces, the elegant way they dressed. Men dressed in suits and women in formal knee-length dresses. It reminded her of the 1930's at the peak of the art deco era. She herself was dressed by Miss Venus' design assistants. Miss Venus told her she had to fit in so it was imperative she dressed the part. Miss Venus had her assistants give Eveley many of her designs left over from her collections as well as a few vintage pieces.

Eveley was dressed in a silk white blouse, and matching pencil skirt. Her long chestnut hair was perfectly styled in vintage waves, her red lipstick was classic, she wore a necklace of pearls. Her heels were nude and made her legs seem like they went on for miles. She decided to wear delicate lace gloves today and one of the formal hats she saw all women wear here. Her hat was a deep royal blue that looked amazing against her golden skin. It was undeniable that dressing formal made her feel confident and helped her fit in.

She took a small sip of her coffee when she saw him enter the café...her heart felt like it would explode, her breathing stopped, her hand trembled and she immediately put her cup down. In front of her, she couldn't believe it, she blinked a few times as she thought surely it was her imagination. There in a suit...Aidan.

She tried to control her breathing and calm down. How could it be? It was impossible. She observed his every move. He ordered coffee and sat at a table on the opposite side of the café, directly facing her. She dropped her gaze immediately. He opened a book and sipped his coffee. She raised her gaze and he his, their eyes met, his eyes filled with curiosity and she quickly lowered her gaze again.

When their eyes met, Eveley felt as if she would faint, she felt the warm rush of adrenaline through her veins. She didn't see recognition in his eyes, could it be possible another Aidan existed on Aeven? Why hadn't LAR told her this? And did this mean another of her also existed on Aeven? Is this what Miss Venus meant by parallel theory?

She felt a jolt of energy run down her neck and along her spine. She tried to keep her gaze down at her own book. Eventually, her gaze was drawn to him again, he glanced at his watch, then like a magnet he raised his gaze and met her eyes, he grinned at her. She instantly felt dizzy and the rest of the time she kept her gaze down.

Every morning since that day, she woke up with a newfound happiness in her heart, anticipating watching him from afar for a few minutes each morning. This little routine continued for several days. Every day was a new roller coaster of emotion seeing his face in person. In moments she would reflect and try to reel in her feelings, but in the moment, when her eyes fell upon his face and especially when his eyes met hers all that went out the window. Like a tsunami, she would willingly drown in that wave of emotion, she couldn't help it.

Unfortunately, LAR had disappeared again, not letting her know for sure what was happening on Aeven. But one thing she knew for sure is he didn't recognize her. By the third day it had turned into a coy little game she wasn't trying to play on purpose.

She watched him closely like every morning before. This time however, he stood up and started walking toward her table. As soon as she saw him headed her way she panicked and abruptly grabbed her purse and ran out the door closest to her. She'd have to skip a few days of this she thought, it was too much of a close call.

Even though she knew she needed to avoid him, every cell in her body wanted to be in his presence. She only lasted three days. On Monday she decided to resume her routine. She walked down the few blocks to the café, this morning it was another perfect day, 75 degrees and sunny. The weather was beautiful almost every day on this location of Aeven.

She dressed in a skin hugging knee-length dress that showed off her décolleté. Her waist-length hair fell around her in big shiny waves. She wore black stilettos, black lace gloves, and a red hat.

She planned to get to the office a little later than usual which meant she would spend more time at the café before leaving. She ordered her usual coffee, and sat in a different spot than usual, tucked away in a corner. She sipped her coffee leisurely and it wasn't ten minutes later before he showed up. Her stomach felt butterflies and she lowered her gaze and buried her face in her book.

She noticed he hadn't seen her yet and sat down in his usual spot, he sipped his coffee and scanned the room.

This Aidan seemed so different, he wore a sleek business suit, expensive watch, clean-cut, and looked much more mature and serious than her Aidan, except for the mischievous gleam in his eyes when he'd catch her looking his way and the boyish grin. She knew she was walking in dangerous territory, why did LAR bring her to a parallel planet and not tell her? She only knew he would take her somewhere she could physically survive but not this. Eveley was so busy hiding behind the book in front of her face she didn't notice when he made his way to her table giving her no time to make her escape.

"Excuse me miss..."

Eveley jumped slightly, first she noticed his nice leather shoes as her eyes looked down beyond the border of her book, her eyes peeked from the top of her book at him.

"Sorry to bother you, I think this might be yours."

He held out a delicate black lace glove.

"Oh, thank you!" Eveley noticed the one glove on her table. She reached for her glove, her fingers brushed the palm of his hand and a slight shock ran through her arm.

"So I don't want to come across as forward but you and I have been playing a little staring contest the last couple of days. I wanted to officially introduce myself...that is before you run out the door," he smiled knowingly.

She felt her face get hot.

"I'm [1] Cian O'Brien, nice to meet you."

He held out his hand, she placed her hand reluctantly in his and shook hands. She noticed the small birth mark on his ear, the same one Aidan had.

"Nice to meet you Cian, I'm Eveley, Eveley Luna."

He smiled at her introduction, Eveley thought how captivating his smile was, just like Aidan's.

Her mind and body were fighting internally, she just couldn't believe when she was with Cian that he wasn't her husband. She soon realized as soon as they talked the first time, that even their personalities were the same. Over the next week, Cian would come and sit with her every morning and they'd talk about their lives.

Many times she reminded herself she couldn't be completely honest with him and tell him everything she wanted to say. He wasn't her husband, he'd never lived the memories etched in her mind. He'd never known the sacrifice, he'd never known how much they fought to stay together, he'd never known every beauty mark on her body, but oh how she wanted to show him and give in to her desires. The labyrinth they were in was getting more intricate and complex the longer they were getting to know each other and she was starting to feel a gnawing guilt every time her heart skipped a beat upon seeing his face.

Cian told her about his work, he worked at his father's company, a large aerospace company, Rogue Enterprises, where he was set to take over the family business as CEO in a few years.

---

1. Cian (Key-in)

He had a sister, [2] Aisling, and she was married to his best friend from college, R.J. and they had a young baby boy, Midas. He showed her a picture of his sister with her small family, exactly like Eileen and R.J. on earth, it couldn't be a coincidence. He casually mentioned his mother and father's name and she was sure this was something LAR should have warned her about. She couldn't help but notice how easy it was to talk to him, despite having to be careful not to inadvertently talk to him as if he was her husband.

The third week of them talking almost every day, Cian invited Eveley to the premier of a new launch for Rogue Enterprises, it was a fancy gala event. He mentioned he knew her benefactor, Miss Venus, and invited her as well. Eveley accepted his invitation, she was going on her own, not his date so it was okay she thought. When she arrived home she told Miss Venus and they took a trip back to her design studio downtown to go through her archive of vintage dresses. Eveley found a perfectly fitting red ball gown, with delicate lace and sequins, strapless with a sweetheart neckline and a beautiful sheer train in matching red that fell elegantly from her lower back like a sea of red all around her, she looked captivating.

The night of the gala, Cian sent a limousine to pick them up. When she arrived, she could feel all eyes on her. She caught Cian's eyes from across the room, he looked at her the same way Aidan would look at her from across the room. She wanted to run to him, embrace him, and tell him everything she'd wanted to tell Aidan since she last saw him, but she couldn't. She looked

---

2. Aisling (Ash-ling)

shyly away, his intimate gaze made her feel so vulnerable, he looked at her like she was his muse.

Cian walked toward her, little did Eveley know, Cian was fully aware she was who he'd love and lose, but she'd come back to him again in a way. Every dream told him this story over and over again, and he'd wondered for years why. All he knew was her name would be Eveley and she would break his heart. She was always the silhouette of a beautiful woman with long hair in his dream. She was always in a perfect sleep...a sleeping beauty in a pod of some sort. He could never see her features but the first time he saw her in the café, somehow he knew it was her before she ever spoke her name.

"Hi Eveley," he said as he handed her a glass of champagne.

"Hi Aida—Cian." She accepted the glass from his hand.

"You look beautiful," he said with sincerity in his voice.

She felt her cheeks flushing red, "Thank you, you look very handsome as well."

She really thought so, on earth Aidan was the boy next door, literally, and was rugged and masculine. On Aeven, the Cian version was just as masculine but he was so dapper and clean-cut. His classy style gave him an air of refinement and mystery that was irresistible. When he came into the room, he'd command esteem and admiration, she could see it in the way women melted around him and men respected him.

Meanwhile, Cian could see right through Eveley, he knew she was intrigued, he sensed she was hesitant for a reason unknown to him but he wanted to find out why. He wanted to pull her to him even if he knew eventually she would pull away.

The gala event invited many of the cities' most important people, from politicians, entrepreneurs, and moguls. Eveley felt so out of place, during the event Miss Venus introduced her to so many people and most of them were very gracious but she was not the kind to enjoy parties like these. She'd rather be at home curled up on the couch reading a good book, especially history books about Aeven. It was fascinating to learn about a new planet...how many things were exactly the same on this planet and how many things were so different, which only led her down rabbit hole after rabbit hole.

The gala event was to debut new technology which allowed farther travel than ever before in the history of Aeven, at least further into the authorized zone, and the expansion of the company to other areas of Aeven. Cian's dad, Jason, made the presentation and Cian assisted with a speech. Cian was the newest face of the company, and was expected to slowly take the reins at company events.

The gala was sophisticated, there were cocktails, a four-course dinner, performers, dancing, and music. The gala was held at the large Astra Museum which had captivated Eveley even before the limo pulled up to the building. The museum loomed over the city on the highest peak of [3] Vathlevi Mountain which stood majestically on the edge of the city. From almost any location inside the city of Araven you could always find the monolith on that peak. At night, a large blue light danced like a flame upwards into the heavens from the top of the museum adding to its intrigue.

The building was on a beautiful part of the mountain, even the drive was scenic, there was lush foliage and beautiful arches of trees along many parts of the uphill climb to the top. Many of the foliage had bioluminescence making for a spectacle of glowing colors along the drive. Once at the apex, they had a bird's eye view of the city below. The building, an enormous reflective monolith stood in omnipresence over its beautiful setting. The monolith loomed so large over them, there was a spiritual, poetic aura to it. It stood in front of vast, shallow pools, reflecting entire swaths of the sky above, giving the illusion of being in the heavens among the birds. Various exotic-looking birds walked about the grounds lazily, opening their plumage

---

3. Vathlevi (Bath-levee)

in full display from time to time. Other birds swam leisurely in the pools, dipping their heads in the water and preening and rousing their feathers.

Eveley fell more in love as soon as she stepped inside. The building, instead of being several floors, stood in beautiful harmony with the sky above. There was only one floor, the walls in the main atrium climbed so high it was hard for her to understand the architecture and how it was possible. The top of the ceiling was an open skylight with pieces of reflective stones around the rim that produced a prism of colors to dance down the length of the walls which were made of smooth white stone and marble. On the ground, the floors and walls were all marble.

Eveley stood talking to several friends of Miss Venus when Cian approached her and asked for a dance. She blushed a little as she placed her hand in his and they approached the dance floor. The song playing was a beautiful slow melody with instruments closely resembling violins but more ethereal in sound. He placed one hand on her lower back, and took her other hand in his as she placed her hand on his shoulder.

Other couples were already waltzing down the large marble dance floor. Cian skillfully lead their dance, she felt like she was in a fairy tale as he twirled her around the dance floor and she felt everyone's eyes focus on her and Cian.

"Are you enjoying the party?" he said near her ear.

She nodded, she caught his cologne, it was something she'd never smelled before, it smelled deep and sultry yet bright and fresh at the same time.

"Yes, you guys threw an amazing party, how often do you host these events?" Eveley asked.

"We only throw gala events twice a year but we do a few smaller events for our employees every month."

"Oh, nice, well I'm impressed," Eveley said.

"I'm glad to hear that...I wanted to ask you if you had any plans for tomorrow?" Cian asked.

"No, why?"

"I was wondering if you'd like to join me at our beachfront property, we have a large estate on the coast we escape to sometimes, perhaps you need some relaxation, a break from big city life?" Cian said.

He spun her around and she smiled. It was hard to say no.

"I guess I could use some relaxation..."

"Okay how about I pick you up tomorrow at 8 at your house?"

"Okay, I'll be ready."

Later that night, Cian walked Eveley and Miss Venus to their limo when they were ready to go home.

In the limo, Miss Venus looked at her mischievously.

"Okay, spill the beans!" Miss Venus said.

"What do you mean?" Eveley said.

"I saw how he looked at you, he's definitely into you, every girl in that room wanted to be you."

"Lyra, I'm going to tell you something amazing but you can't tell anyone."

"Oh my! What is it?"

"That's my husband."

Her mouth fell open. "What do you mean?"

"It's him, down to his birth mark, his personality, his way of talking to me and looking at me. This is a parallel planet to earth and he's Aidan."

"Oh my goodness! Oh my dear! I couldn't have predicted this was going to get so complicated!"

"Yeah well...I'm not sure I should be seeing him, he isn't *my* Aidan after all." Eveley looked down at her hands as she fiddled with her purse.

"Oh sweetheart, you must be in so much turmoil, yeah this is quite a jam, my goodness, poor girl," Miss Venus said and hugged Eveley.

That night Eveley prayed to God LAR would appear again so he could explain to her what was happening and she prayed she could return back to earth and see Aidan and her family again.

As much as Cian was easing her pain, she wanted to be in front of her husband, the one who knew everything about her.

Chapter 34

OCEAN EYES

Eveley woke early the next morning, prepared a beach bag and sat in the living room waiting for Cian. He arrived five minutes early and came to the door, before he could ring the bell she opened the door.

"Well hi, good morning," he said dashing his handsome smile.

"Good morning Cian."

Cian was dressed more casually than usual, he wore a pair of light blue slacks and a white linen shirt. Eveley also dressed more casual given they were going to his beach house. The weather in Araven was still cool in the mornings, but along the coast where they were headed it was quite warm. The drive was two hours long.

He carried her beach bag and opened the car door for her. She got in and smoothed the hem of her short dress. He placed her bag in the back seat and got in.

"Ready?" he asked, he sensed her nervousness.

She cleared her throat before speaking, "Uhum," was all she could get out.

This situation made her nervous, being alone with him, not because she feared for her safety but because being alone with him eliminated all the distractions usually around them. She couldn't avoid feeling like she'd start falling into a tunnel of sorts, where only he mattered.

Cian took off, they opened the windows, turned on music in the background, and right away fell into an easy and comfortable conversation, why wouldn't they she thought. He was Aidan, she knew his personality and it was effortless.

They laughed so much on the way to his estate, she felt relaxed as they arrived to the coast and drove along the highway beside the ocean. She felt like this was just a continuation of a chapter in her life with Aidan, it wouldn't be difficult to just wake up the next day with this version of him. She knew his likes, dislikes, despite their different lives on two very different planets, she felt the same when she talked to him, she felt the same affection, and he looked at her and treated her exactly like her husband did. But then she stopped herself when she realized she was letting herself get carried away.

When they finally arrived to the beachfront mansion, Eveley couldn't believe how beautiful their estate was, it was a minimalist modern home, directly beach side. The mansion was a combination of white limestone and earthy Chukum walls. What it lacked in ornamental value due to its minimalism, it made up in greenery and sheer size. The one story house had 20 foot ceilings and the perfectly pruned palm trees and exotic plants all around them created a tropical oasis. It was impossible to feel stressed on their estate.

Several of his friends were already there as well as his family, he introduced her to everyone. Eveley couldn't believe how everyone was a perfect copy of those she knew back on earth.

Eveley began to talk to the parallel of Eileen, Aisling, and they quickly hit it off just like back on earth. Her son, Midas, was so precious and motherhood looked great on her, she was an attentive, devoted mother which didn't surprise Eveley. Stella was exactly the same except for her hair being dyed a blonde color and Jason was also the same. R.J. who was Aisling's husband was also a carbon copy of R.J. on earth.

The estate had several pools, with the main one being an enormous infinity pool that seemed to blend right into the turquoise-colored ocean. She walked toward the sandy beach between the pool and ocean, she placed a towel on top of the white sand and sat down. She admired the perfect view, Cian sauntered up to her.

"May I?" he asked pointing to the spot beside her.

"Sure" she said as she adjusted her sunglasses.

He sat beside her.

She couldn't help looking at his profile from the edge of her sunglasses. Her eyes skimmed his eyes, lips, arms...she knew she needed to stop.

"So how did you end up in Araven?"

Eveley choked on the lemonade she'd started sipping. She coughed for several seconds.

"Are you okay?" Cian asked concerned.

Eveley raised her arm and nodded her head.

"Yup, just went down the wrong way."

Cian patted her lightly on the back and she smiled sheepishly. Once her coughing fit was done, she hoped he'd forgotten his question but he continued.

"I figured you aren't from around here, your accent is a little different. The whole time I've known you I haven't even asked you where you're from...so are you from Dravo, Navaray?" Cian asked.

Eveley realized he was talking about a different territory of Aeven and she felt relief.

"Oh no, I'm not from any of those places—"

"Cian! Eveley!" Aisling shouted from the infinity pool behind them.

Both Eveley and Cian turned to look at her.

"What are you waiting for? C'mon! Join us in the pool!" Aisling shouted.

Cian simply nodded and looked at Eveley.

"Wanna join us?" He asked.

"Sure, why not." Eveley stood and followed Cian back to the main pool area.

"There's a bathroom here on the side of the pool if you need to change into your swimsuit," Aisling said. She carried baby Midas in her arms as she walked past Eveley.

"R.J. I'll be right back, I'm going to feed Midas real quick and put him down for a nap," Aisling shouted to R.J.

R.J. nodded. They were in the middle of a game of pool volleyball.

Eveley took her dress off, she wore a one piece swimsuit underneath.

She watched as Cian entered the pool by diving head first into the deep end, he looked agile and strong. Eveley was not complaining about his fit physique on full display. He surfaced on the opposite side then made his return underwater and popped up in front of her extending his hand to her.

"Here, I'll help you in," Cian said.

Eveley placed her hand in his and jumped in the water, she surfaced near him and he placed his hands on her arm and lower back to steady her.

"You good?" Cian asked with a chuckle.

She nodded. She felt so clumsy, or maybe it was the effect he was having on her she thought. Just him touching her innocently made her heartbeat quicken. She placed her hands on his arms to steady herself. Before she knew it she realized his ocean eyes were looking at her with such intensity she felt bare and powerless. Their bodies were inching closer, he literally left her breathless. Everything about him was electric, the voltage from his touch ran down her skin and her face flushed red.

"Ahem!" R.J. stood behind them, both Eveley and Cian snapped out of the little trance they were in.

"You guys wanna join us and play?" R.J. asked with a slight grin.

"Yeah, c'mon, you wanna play?" Cian turned to Eveley who was a few feet away from him now.

"Sure! Why not." Eveley made a little silent o with her lips to control her exhale without Cian noticing as he swam behind her.

The rest of the day was fun, they enjoyed food and drinks, more swimming, and pool games.

Close to 10 pm, Cian and Eveley left to drive back to Araven. She got Aisling's number to communicate via phone so she was ecstatic to see her best friend again in a sense.

Phones on Aeven were peculiar, they had several types. Some were directly implanted in the user's brain as a chip that integrated virtual reality and allowed the user to type with their mind and open things in their "phone". This is what the majority of citizens on Aeven used. A smaller number used discreet glasses that also worked the same way. And even smaller still were physical phones like the ones Cian and his entire family used as well as Miss Venus. They were phones in the traditional sense but they were made of an indestructible clear material that was also flexible.

Eveley noticed that in every room and even in their cars, both Miss Venus and the O'Brien family placed their phones inside small boxes made of a type of stone. Miss Venus explained to her that this was for privacy reasons and it blocked signals from the phones that constantly listened to everything around them.

When they arrived to her house, Cian helped her out of the car and walked her to her front door.

"Thank you for inviting me to your family's beach house, it was a lot of fun," Eveley said.

"You're welcome, I was going to ask you if you're able to, maybe we can have lunch together tomorrow?"

She thought about it, perhaps it would be okay.

"Okay, sure, I take lunch at noon, meet you in the lobby?"

"Yes, I'll be there." Cian grinned at her.

She looked back at him and smiled as she stepped into the house and started closing the door.

"Goodnight Cian, drive safe."

"I will, goodnight Eveley."

She walked to her bedroom and plopped down on her bed. She tried not to think about Cian, she knew it was wrong. She suddenly felt a wave of nausea come over her. She wondered if maybe it was the food and drink again, as delicious and exotic as the food was, it still took her body a while to adapt to the new air, water, and food. She drank a bit of tea and her stomach settled. She finally got in bed, and prayed again this was all just a dream. Despite the futility of it all, she still held hope that she'd be in Aidan's arms again when she awoke.

CHAPTER 35

UNFORESEEN

The next morning, Eveley made her usual way downtown to Miss Venus' office. Her posh office was in one of the top floors of the tallest skyscraper of the city. In fact, Cian's company headquarters was also in this building, about 20 floors down. He'd offered to take her every morning when he found out she worked in the same building but she preferred to take the train and enjoy the view. Plus she felt like she needed some distance between them or she'd give in to her desires. They ran into each other at work occasionally, and when they did, she'd grace him with a demure smile and he would flash her his mischievous smile in return.

Miss Venus owned a prestigious clothing designer brand and she'd given Eveley work there as her assistant. Eveley arrived later in the day as her job position was really just a decoy to keep her busy and fit into society, but she did have responsibilities, they were just very flexible.

All day Eveley was nervous, her stomach felt terrible again which she thought was strange. When it was 11:55 am, Eveley made her descent down to the lobby where they would meet. Cian was already there, dressed nicely as ever, in a tan suit.

"Hi," he said flashing his captivating smile.

"Hi, were you waiting a long time?"

"No, actually I just arrived, ready?"

"Yeah, let's go."

"What do you think of going next door then eating in the park?" Cian proposed.

"Sure, that sounds nice."

They walked next door to an entertainment district attached to their building containing a multitude of restaurants. They picked a casual spot specializing in gourmet sandwiches. After they ordered, Cian paid, even though Eveley tried to pay for her own food.

It was a sunny, warm day, they crossed the street into a large, modern eco park. The focal point, a large lake, was filled with row boats and surrounded by large trees that swayed in the breeze. People were out walking their dogs and running. Children played in the distance on a playground. Nearby, a group of friends practiced music on a peculiar guitar-like instrument pleasant to the ear.

They found a large tree providing shade and Cian placed his jacket on the ground for Eveley to sit on. He rolled up his sleeves and sat next to her. They ate the light meal while talking and laughing. After they finished eating, Cian leaned back against the tree with his arms crossed behind his head and they talked and people watched. They sat in a moment of silence after but it wasn't awkward at all, it was peaceful. She felt his hand inadvertently brush up against her and she felt a knot in her stomach.

"You know it's strange, but I feel like I've known you in another life or in my childhood," he said as his blue eyes gleamed in the sun. She couldn't help but feel captive to his gaze, so much was communicated by the subtle way they held their gaze just a little too long, like lovers watching each other from across a crowded room.

He turned to her and pushed a strand of hair out of her face looking at her tenderly, she knew what was coming and she needed to once and for all decide if she was going to cross that line or not. Suddenly her stomach felt awful and she felt the biggest wave of nausea, she stood up abruptly and apologized.

"I'm sorry, I don't feel good."

She ran across the street into the nearest café and into the bathroom, her entire meal came back up with no effort. After she cleaned herself up and looked in the mirror she started to think something was seriously off. She realized she'd been late for her period since she'd already been on this planet five weeks without any period. Could it be? She couldn't believe it, she rubbed her stomach and looked at it sideways in the mirror. A multitude of emotions came over her, from joy, fear, hope, shame, excitement, to guilt. It was definitely possible, she looked down at her belly, she needed to get back to earth. If it was the last thing she did, she needed to get back to Aidan.

She took a quick detour to the nearest pharmacy and purchased a test, she took it back to the office. She was nervous as she took the test. She looked at the lines on the stick and cried tears of joy and sadness. Sadness she couldn't share it with Aidan.

She went back to her desk, passing by Miss Venus. Miss Venus noticed the tears and rushed to her concerned if everything was alright. Eveley nodded and told her she'd tell her everything when they were back home.

That evening she arranged for Cian to drive her home. When she saw him waiting for her in the parking garage, he looked as handsome as ever leaning against his car. She felt sadness come over her, her affection for him was undeniable but also an impossibility.

He noticed the sadness in her eyes because he immediately looked concerned.

"Are you okay?"

"No, I'm sorry about earlier, I didn't mean to leave so abruptly but I was nauseous."

"I figured, don't worry about it, but is that the only thing bothering you? You seem like you've been crying."

"Yes, I have been crying Cian."

"Why?"

"Cian, can I trust you?"

"Of course you can, what's going on?"

"Let's get in your car first."

Cian opened her car door and she sat in the passenger side, he got in the drivers side and shut the door.

"Okay, I'm all ears Eveley."

Eveley looked down at her hands.

"I'm pregnant."

After she said those words there was silence between them. After a few seconds Cian spoke.

"I don't understand..."

"Cian, I'm married, this is my husband's child."

Cian looked disappointed for a second.

"Why didn't you tell me?"

"It's not like what it sounds Cian, if I give you the full explanation you may not believe me."

"Tell me."

"I'm not from your planet...I arrived only what I think five weeks ago. I come from a different galaxy than yours. In our solar system my planet is called Earth. I was forcefully exiled due to an alien I named LAR transferring healing powers to me on earth that claimed his species would find me and destroy my species if they found out what I'd become. He has a habit of disappearing since he's on the run."

Cian seemed fascinated by what she was saying.

"Shortly before I left earth I was married to my childhood sweetheart, Aidan. We consummated our marriage days before I left, and so I had no clue until today in the park, when you were about to kiss me that I was pregnant. I took a test after and it was positive."

"Wow, that's not what I was expecting you to say. I was thinking you were just going to tell me I wasn't your type," Cian said and looked surprised.

"That's not all Cian." Eveley cleared her throat.

"This planet, Aeven, is a parallel planet to Earth, and you are the parallel Aidan on this planet, so in a way you are my husband."

Cian looked speechless and for a while he was. Eveley took her purse and took out a picture of her and Aidan, the one she'd placed in her pocket along with the one with her mom and dad. She handed it to him.

"See...you are him, and he is you, down to your birthmark." She touched the small birthmark on his ear.

"And so, I'm naturally attracted to you, like a moth to a flame, because you're him, and for a while the pain of being exiled from my planet, and not knowing if I'd ever see him again clouded my thinking. But now...now that I know I'm carrying his child, I can't cross that line, as much as I want to." She held her stomach gently. Cian still looked surprised and she wasn't sure what was going through his head.

"Wow, this is so much to process," he said.

He held the picture in his hand, now he knew why he had the recurring dreams all his adult life. He handed her the picture back.

"I understand, and I'm sorry I've made your life more difficult. I promise I won't interfere anymore, but I'd like you to always consider me a faithful friend. If your destiny wasn't back on Earth, it would surely be with me." He grinned, grabbed her hand and kissed the top of it, she grinned faintly.

He drove her home and when they arrived, Eveley already felt better knowing Cian knew the truth and he'd understood, she looked at him before leaving the car.

"Thank you for being you," Eveley said.

Cian's eyes lit up when she spoke, and she gave him a quick kiss on the cheek before she exited his car.

CHAPTER 36

VIGIL

As soon as Eveley made it through the door, Miss Venus came rushing toward her.

"Child, you had me worried all day, what's going on sweetheart?"

"You're going to have to sit down for this Lyra."

Miss Venus' eyes grew wide.

"Okay, well let's go to the living room, c'mon sit down. I'll get you something to drink."

Eveley waved and shook her head.

"Oh no Lyra, I couldn't right now, I'm not feeling well right now."

"Oh goodness, is it the food again? The water? I tell you our government claims we have the pures—"

"I'm pregnant."

Miss Venus stopped mid-sentence and burrowed her eyebrows in confusion.

"Say what?"

"I'm pregnant."

"My goodness, you and your husband before your exile?"

"Yes, I didn't know till today. I'm probably at least a month, well LAR still hasn't shown up to tell me how long I was in transit here but I assume I'm about a week late."

"Goodness! Oh my," Miss Venus said with a panicked look on her face.

"What?! What?! Why are you freaking out?!"

"Well I was going to tell you but remember how I told you about the conditions placed on citizens?"

Eveley nodded her head, she had noticed many of the differences and also read a lot about Aeven's history. For one, it seemed Aeven was about 100 years further in its technological advancement than Earth.

They completely manipulated their climate. 98% of the energy produced was renewable. Robots were integrated into every day life. Residents were required to be more self-sufficient and cut down on their footprint. They were required to provide 40% of their food supply via gardens hence why Eveley saw a garden on every property. The other 40% of their plant food was grown inside buildings via hydroponics. Even the skyscrapers here contained gardened terraces and were required to grow produce.

Most diseases had been eradicated, aging had been slowed down significantly, organs had long been able to be grown in labs to replace them in humans. People who had accidents could have surgery to walk again. Lifespan according to Miss Venus was close to 200. Due to the longer lifespan, families in cities had to abide by population control. Citizens that wanted to have more than two children had to live in less populated areas surrounding the city. Extreme poverty had been mostly eradicated, there were a few small pockets throughout the world but it was by choice. They were people who completely rejected technology and modern medicine. They had something similar to social media but streamlined and impossible to post anonymously or under a fake account as the accounts could not be hacked or created like on earth.

But like Miss Venus had emphasized time and time again, they were not an utopia. One of the biggest indicators of this was the monitoring system in place over the entire planet. The system, Virtual Intelligence Governing & Interdiction Liege, or VIGIL, integrated artificial intelligence with private and public surveillance systems. VIGIL took in so much data there were entire artificial cities to house the data on the outskirts of the city. VIGIL had an autocratic relationship with the people, it had been autonomous for several decades now, meaning humans didn't control VIGIL at all, instead he controlled every aspect of society. How he came to be autonomous and have absolute power over citizens was a mystery only a few dissenters had tried to solve since the transition of power. Another hallmark of VIGIL was his ability to detect when "homeostasis" was disrupted. Since Eveley's arrival to Aeven, VIGIL had picked up the disruption but it hadn't found the culprit yet.

There were many specialized robots she encountered since her arrival. Eveley found a creepiness in most of the humanoids used in every day settings such as public transport and restaurants, most were indistinguishable from humans. However, over time she had learned to spot the very subtle differences. The dead, emotionless eyes, their cold "skin", and their identifier which was on their forearm. She avoided interacting with humanoids as much as possible as Miss Venus warned her they ran as much data as possible on the individual they were interacting with.

But the worst thing about Aeven, was what Miss Venus revealed to Eveley next.

"Your pregnancy places you in a precarious situation sweetie, if they found out about your condition they would most likely exile you. And...there's another thing Eveley, they require all residents to give a blood sample every year to be analyzed by VIGIL. If you refuse, they take you in by force and take the sample against your will. Every year it's a surprise announcement and we are given a week to comply.

"Now, theoretically VIGIL gets plenty of our blood samples from medical procedures but he also uses it as a litmus test to gauge citizen's loyalty and willingness to the status quo. There are ways around it if you know the right people but even then it is only delaying the inevitable as VIGIL will eventually figure out you are in violation and send a warrant for you arrest. It just buys you time, that's all. Once your blood has been cataloged in the system you will be monitored and traceable forever. This is why I said we are not an idyllic society.

"Lucky for you, you're not in the system, but we have to keep it that way so you'll need to hide and be extra careful around the time they begin their campaigns and reminders to comply. Also, there are always riots around that time from those that have rejected the technology and decree since inception. It's always so sad, the media tries to paint them as uncivilized and backwards, but I think they should be able to have a choice. Unfortunately, it's too late for the rest of us to refuse, we've accepted the technology and the majority of us rationalize the high quality of life and these monitoring efforts for our own good—"

"So that's why you shun robots so much and don't keep them!" Eveley exclaimed.

"I hate the little gremlins! They're all spies for VIGIL. From the domestic machines to the humanoids, they're constantly running data and looking for inconsistencies in the algorithm."

"So why is there so much need for monitoring? What is VIGIL afraid of?" Eveley asked.

"Oh honey, it's afraid of itself, of how weak he is compared to other species in our universe. It knows there are much more powerful beings in our universe. Plus the truth is you can manufacture and make people believe their world and society is this perfect place aided by technological advancements but at the same time something dies in humans when technology takes over unimpeded.

"VIGIL knows sooner or later, human nature will win, human curiosity is a strong survival instinct, a drive we've inherited from our wild ancestors. Technology has lulled those instincts for the time being, but VIGIL knows our true nature will eventually re-awaken. And when human nature finally wins it's going to be like a star imploding. Society has to have change, sometimes it's peaceful, sometimes it's not.

"VIGIL is always monitoring the ebb and flow that would indicate something is brewing in society. Since he thinks he has accounted for all the possible factors that would make humans lash out and rebel against him, his big fear is other species will hybridize with us or we will bring other species in.

"He fears these species will instigate violent change, and disrupt our society. He does not want to lose control to more advanced races although if you think about it, if they are more advanced it wouldn't take much for them to take over if they really wanted to. The key word is wanted to, obviously they don't want to as they see us as primitive and flawed like our friend LAR and the EDEN race."

Miss Venus kept a book on her coffee table, a vintage book on philosophy. She picked it up and opened it, she pointed to a quote:

> "A man can trade humanity for technology and be doomed to the coldness of that void" - Ilex Regen.

"I've been wanting to read that book, it looks so interesting," Eveley said.

"Amazing book, the author is one of the biggest opponents to our current technology. His books are extremely rare to find, most of them have been banned and burned. Definitely read it when you can."

Eveley nodded, she was so intrigued by these new revelations.

"The longer we are under VIGIL, the more we lose what makes us human."

Miss Venus' eyes looked like she wasn't there, she sighed, clearly dejected.

"LAR told me they have been given their abilities based on their obedience to a creator. I'm assuming he meant God." Eveley said.

"That's a convenient theory considering LAR and EDEN do not like to engage with the more primitive species such as humans or perhaps they are forbidden by the creator since they are closer to him in some way. They definitely have an advantage, they seem to be infinitely more advanced and knowledgeable than us, so we must have done something wrong at some point."

"So if they find me they will know by my blood sample that I'm not from this planet?" Eveley asked.

"Exactly and they will arrest you or worse. People who stick out disappear all the time. VIGIL initiates their arrest and we never find out what really happens to them. Usually the "official" story is these people are exiled whatever that means, we don't have prisons after all, he calls that transparency."

"I want nothing more than to return to Earth but if LAR is gone it means he's still on the run. I can't be sure it's safe to go back to earth yet. I need to get back to my husband and family though, I'd give anything to be able to return," Eveley said.

"Well LAR needs to return and in the meantime we can't let VIGIL and his steel servants find you. As your guardian I'm going to do everything in my power to prevent that. So here is what we're going to do. Depending on how long it takes LAR to return we may have to go to extremes to keep you and your baby safe," Miss Venus said.

Eveley nodded.

"First thing is we will need to keep you out of the public eye. I'm sorry dear but you will need to stay home from now on. There are humanoids that can detect when you're carrying a child and they are more vigilant when they find a woman is expecting. They run your credentials because they want to ensure the child gets registered under VIGIL when it's born and has a valid pedigree. So being out in public is out of the question. Next we need to find someone that can give you basic prenatal care here in our house."

"Cian's sister is an ob/gyn nurse," Eveley said.

"Perfect! I will contact her, you cannot tell her anything about this on any electronic device. I will invite her to the house to discuss. I will do my best to keep you occupied. I can bring some of my work for you to work on if you want. Of course you can use the pool, the garden, any area outside. The outdoor areas have technological blocking systems in place, so any drones outdoors cannot record or trespass. We will get through this, you'll see." Miss Venus took Eveley's hand and squeezed it.

"Yes, I have to," Eveley said in a voice barely above a whisper.

Eveley looked unsure but hopeful. Being all alone in such a big house was not something she looked forward to but she had to keep herself and her baby safe. She knew if there was a more pivotal moment and journey in her life, it was this one. Becoming a mother in the midst of a society that wanted nothing more than to dehumanize her and submit her to their rule. She was not about to let that happen.

CHAPTER 37

CHRYSALIS

Later that week Miss Venus invited Aisling over, she instructed her to leave any electronic devices in her car.

All three sat in the living room, Aisling spoke first.

"What's this all about? You guys are scaring me."

Eveley and Miss Venus told her the entire story, from beginning to end and finally how Eveley was pregnant.

"I wouldn't be asking you unless it was necessary. I need someone to provide discreet prenatal care for Eveley," Miss Venus said.

Aisling sat in silence for a few seconds.

"I know it's a risk but I would never let a pregnant woman who needs my help do this alone, especially one I admire so much." Aisling grabbed Eveley's hands.

"So yes, I will help you, and I'll come monitor you more than the standard schedule since we are having to use old-school tech."

"Thank you! Thank you!" Eveley hugged Aisling and felt some semblance of relief.

Afterward, Aisling took her vitals, and although it was too soon to listen to the baby's heart rate with a stethoscope, she took another urine test which confirmed her status.

"Eveley, when you took your test did you take one of the digital tests?" Aisling asked.

Eveley shook her head.

"Whew! Okay good, cause VIGIL monitors those too. I tell you big brother is always watching."

"What's going to happen when they start to do the yearly blood samples?" Eveley asked.

"Well, let's hope you aren't here by then, luckily we just had one about 2 months back so it shouldn't be a danger at least for about a year, but we'll see." Aisling gave her a hug.

"Okay, I will come back next week, same routine, take good care of yourself, and by the way Cian says hi."

Eveley smiled, she had missed him since she started being cooped up in the large house. She often thought of him and wondered if he still thought of her.

Over the next couple months, other than the occasional loneliness Eveley experienced, she was doing well.

She had taken up several hobbies to occupy her time. Miss Venus was happy to indulge Eveley whenever she mentioned anything that she fancied. The first such occasion of this was when Eveley mentioned wanting to learn to paint. Miss Venus had a delivery several days later of canvases and every color imaginable of the highest quality paints for her. Eveley learned from books the different painting techniques she would use. Eventually she had the courage to send Aisling and Cian pictures of her paintings via phone. Miss Venus proudly displayed some of Eveley's paintings on the walls of her mansion.

Eveley also took up knitting and although it took her a while to learn, she made several pieces for the baby.

She loved the garden and added new plants and tended to them as time progressed.

She also loved to bake and she would learn to make at least one complex recipe each week.

What Eveley had to fight was the feeling of loneliness she sometimes felt and dwelling on thoughts of missing her family and Aidan. Thoughts which would still bring her to tears weekly.

She was also thinking of her baby, she believed that her emotions during her pregnancy were important. She didn't want to expose her baby to only tears and sadness even if sometimes she couldn't help it. She told herself that she would focus on small things that brought her joy. Like the joys of escaping in a book, a good cup of coffee, watching her plants grow tall, of eating bread she made with her own hands, and seeing her creations on canvas. It wasn't anything earth-shattering but it made a huge difference over time adopting this mindset.

Before long, she was entering her 5th month of pregnancy. Aisling came over to give her a checkup, this time she brought her infant son, Midas. Miss Venus carried him about the house joyfully, showing him her knick-knacks and playing on the floor with him while Eveley was checked over.

This time Aisling was able to hear a strong fetal heartbeat, she let Eveley listen and Eveley's eyes glistened with tears. It was becoming more and more real, her small protruding belly was a daily reminder, each week it was growing larger and larger.

Aisling measured her stomach, everything was right on target which gave Eveley relief.

As she was about to leave Aisling turned around. "My brother wanted to come by and see you if that's okay?"

Eveley was surprised, other than texting, her and Cian had not talked on the phone or seen each other in person since the last time she told him she was pregnant with Aidan's baby.

"Sure, how come he didn't ask me?" Eveley asked.

"He said he didn't want you to feel pressured, plus for your safety."

Eveley was very careful not to mention her pregnancy in any messages to him, so their texts were pretty vague. It would be nice to truly catch up she thought and agreed to have him visit her whenever he had a chance.

The next day, Cian took time off work to come see her, he left his phone in his car as he knew it was imperative for Eveley's safety.

Eveley couldn't understand how they could stand so much monitoring of their activities in everything. No wonder crime was extremely rare, it'd be near impossible to get away with anything on Aeven.

Eveley opened the door when the doorbell rang, careful to hide behind the door as to not allow neighbors or drones to potentially see her stomach.

"Hi, how are you doing?" Cian asked as soon as she opened the door.

Cian looked nicely dressed as always in a dark blue suit, he shut the door behind him.

"I'm doing great, and you?" Eveley replied.

She gave him a quick hug, he carried a gift bag.

"Good, you look beautiful, glowing really."

Eveley smiled shyly, why did Cian also have a way with words? It was truly unfair that even on Aeven she couldn't escape his charm.

"I thought I'd bring you some things to make your day."

He handed her the gift bag and she gracefully took it. The gift bag contained chocolates and books.

"Thank you!" She gave him another hug, she noticed his pleasant scent, sandalwood and Tonka bean. She'd missed everything about him. She wanted to just enjoy every single moment from seeing him, hearing his voice, and getting to touch him like this. Even if there could never be anything more between them, she enjoyed his company greatly.

"C'mon let's go out to the garden, it's beautiful today!" Eveley said with enthusiasm, she grabbed his arm and led him toward the back of the house.

"Yes it is, I like your clothing by the way, it looks very comfortable." Cian complimented Eveley.

She was dressed casually in a long tunic and leggings, albeit with luxurious and expensive materials. It was an outfit she'd asked Miss Venus to design for her, something women didn't wear on Aeven, as it was too informal.

"Oh thank you, this is something Lyra made for me at my request, we wear this style on earth."

He followed her out to the expansive back part of the house, where there was a huge garden and large pool.

She walked barefoot, and leaned back on a oversized outdoor daybed she typically relaxed in and often times fell asleep in due to how comfy it was.

Cian sat next to her, admiring her features for a second. He noticed her dewy sun-kissed skin, her apricot cheeks, her small freckles visible in the sun, her sparkling honey eyes, and her long shiny brown hair. Motherhood looked beautiful on her.

She crossed her legs in front of her, her little belly sticking out. She took the books out from the gift bag he brought her. He knew how much she loved to read and now that she was unable to be out in public, he knew she needed something to occupy her time.

"Your books came just in time. I was running out of books to read believe it or not."

"I believe you," he said and continued to observe her.

Cian felt a need to protect her fiercely. He knew she was in more danger than Miss Venus let on. What Miss Venus didn't know that he did, was if Eveley was caught, they wouldn't just exile her, they would destroy her after experimenting on her.

Since he was part of the aerospace industry he'd been privy to many things ordinary citizens wouldn't know. The so called transparency policy regarding those committing crimes was elimination. No one was exiled to another place. Instead, they were cruelly sent out into the vacuum of space to an excruciating death...the reason no one ever returned.

He knew Eveley was unique and they would try to experiment on her or the baby and he wasn't going to let that happen. He'd been worried the minute she told him she was pregnant.

Pregnancies were highly monitored on Aeven. There was a system in place that made all females infertile from birth. Only when married couples applied and were approved for conception were women given the antidote to restart their reproductive abilities. Couples were required to prove they were worthy to reproduce based on rigorous standards and psychological tests. This in theory ensured children were legitimate, and born into stable, loving homes.

So when a baby was born that wasn't authorized which was extremely rare, it was very big news. Usually government officials would fuss and act like they cared about the well-being of the baby but the baby would be cruelly taken away and given to a wealthy family where a wife did not want to go through the rigors of a pregnancy and labor.

"You know I can come keep you company each week if you'd like," Cian said.

"Oh no, you don't have to do that, I wouldn't want to be a burden," Eveley replied.

"You're not a burden, you're a dear friend and I want to." Cian sounded sincere.

"Okay, if you want to come visit me I'd like that," Eveley said.

Cian smiled and wondered if LAR had returned.

"Has LAR appeared yet?"

"Nope, he needs to though. Lyra told me once they start the blood sampling I'll need to be even more careful. No matter what, I need to leave this planet, it's not safe for me and my baby."

She grabbed her stomach and he gently placed his hand on top of her hands.

"May I?"

Eveley was surprised Cian wanted to touch her belly. She nodded and moved her hands to her sides. His hand was fully over her belly, he smiled.

"Women's bodies are amazing, to be able to bring forth life." He moved his hand.

"I will do my best to continue to help you Eveley, if I can help you get back to Earth I will. You'll be safer there, although I will miss you quite a bit."

"I will miss you too," she said sincerely. He'd been the best part of Aeven. She tried not to see him as intensely as before when she was obsessed with him.

After talking for an hour Cian left, with the promise to return in a few days to see her again and keep her company. This little routine happened for the next couple of months, Cian visiting her twice a week, sometimes more if his workload allowed. He usually brought thoughtful gifts that made her day, but what she looked forward to the most was simply his company, she always looked forward to his company.

Aisling had also taken the time to visit her more than just for the prenatal check-ups, she sometimes brought Midas with her which was great practice for Eveley. He was a beautiful baby boy, with a cheerful personality and an eagerness to explore. He was starting to crawl and try to pull up on furniture. He had the cutest infectious laugh whenever he'd find something he fancied or anyone played peek-a-boo with him.

Eveley was infinitely grateful for the attention Cian and Aisling devoted to her, to keep her sane, to have others to talk to and exercise her mind. They made the time fly much faster than if she had been locked inside without anyone visiting her. Of course in the evenings she had Miss Venus to talk to, but as much as Miss Venus was a great motherly figure in her life, she missed her own mother immensely. Especially now that she was going to be a mother herself, she needed her mother desperately. She sometimes felt consumed by the worry of leaving her mother behind with VERMIN still after her. She felt guilt, she felt regret, and she tried not to think about it too long, she just prayed her mother was okay.

CHAPTER 38

HAVEN

According to Aisling, Eveley measured right on target on the day she turned 40 weeks pregnant.

"You know baby could come any day now," Aisling said to Eveley as she lowered her shirt back over Eveley's large belly.

Eveley's face beamed.

"Really? I'm getting so excited but also anxious, about everything, labor...the pain, the danger I'm in..." Eveley suddenly didn't look so excited.

"Hey, everything will be fine, there's no way we're going to let anything hurt you or the baby."

Aisling said it so confidently, she was always so sure of the future. She never seemed anxious, or fretful, or maybe she hid it better than her Eveley thought.

It suddenly hit Eveley how hard of a journey it had been. The isolation, missing her family and husband, worrying about her pregnancy and the impending birth, worrying about being detected.

Later that day, Eveley went out to the garden as usual, she started to let herself feel relief she was almost at the finish line. But the other big worry on her mind was LAR. She wasn't sure where he was or what happened to him. She desperately needed his help.

She laid on the daybed for a minute, and realized she was having regular contractions which made her worry. She decided she would continue to monitor their interval for the next couple hours and if they began to get closer she'd contact Aisling.

In the meantime, Eveley decided to take a quick dip in the pool. What she didn't realize as she entered the pool, was there was an extra pair of eyes observing her.

Eveley swam in the warm water for 20 minutes, she loved swimming as it was great exercise and low impact. Low impact was essential since now even reaching her shoes or walking tired her.

An almost invisible net above blocked the abilities of the random drones and cameras that monitored the city from recording, scanning or entering in the open areas of the house.

She felt apprehension being outdoors at first, but Miss Venus insisted it was completely safe since the technology blocked all their signals and the near invisible net created another layer of protection. Miss Venus had an unspoken agreement with the local city government just like other wealthy residents to have extra privacy in their open areas. They weren't bound to any official agreement but generally the wealthy enjoyed more privileges than those in the lower classes.

Eveley decided to end her swim with five laps. She swam leisurely to the end. She tried to pick up the pace every lap. She still felt like something was off as she swam but she just couldn't put her finger on it. She finally began her last lap. She swam half the length above water then dove underwater the remaining length of her lap. When she was near the end furthest from the house, she came up for air, she opened her eyes and screamed. Directly in front of her was a drone in the corner of the property. It looked like there was a small part of the net that was ripped by falling debris or maybe deliberately.

Eveley got out frantically, she wasn't sure how long the drone had been observing her, but she knew this wasn't good. She ran into the house and locked the door. She closed all the shades and called Miss Venus' office. She told her in so many words they knew and she wasn't safe, Miss Venus agreed she was no longer safe in her house. She told Eveley to pack her things and she'd have a friend pick her up.

Eveley stuffed her few possessions in a bag and peeked out the window, there didn't seem to be any more drones than usual. Thirty minutes later Eveley saw an unrecognizable car come into the garage. Her blood pressure shot up as she heard a car's door shut. Cian burst through the door, she ran to him relieved it was him and hugged him.

"Shhh, don't talk too loud, the drones outside are listening, we must whisper. I'm going to take you somewhere safe okay? How are you feeling?" Cian placed his hand on her belly.

"I'm having contractions, I think the baby is going to be here soon, Cian I'm scared."

"It's okay, I'm not going to let anything happen to you. I'm going to get you in the car, try to stay as low as possible. We're going to change cars midway. Then I'm going to take you to our family home, you'll be safe there and Aisling can continue to help you. C'mon, I'll help you."

Cian grabbed her bag, and held her arm gently. He opened the door to his car, helped her in and helped put on her seatbelt. As soon as they opened the garage door there were drones approaching the back of Cian's car. Eveley ducked as low as possible so they couldn't detect her in the car. Cian pulled out of the driveway, hitting one of the drones.

They drove for a good 45 minutes, finally, they entered a private underground garage in the middle of nowhere. At this point, there was no indication any drones had followed them. However, the drones had most likely already scanned the car's info. Fortunately, Cian had always had access to technology that could block their signals. This technology would have jammed the signals upon scanning his license plate, which was false, as he usually had a decoy cover as a precaution. His father Jason, had always had a distrust of VIGIL and with his immense wealth, had prepared a Plan B for the day when he said things could go awry and their family could be targeted.

Once they were safely underground, Cian helped Eveley move from one car to another. He took off again and it took another hour to arrive to a large stone Gothic mansion deep in a deciduous forest. The architecture surprised Eveley since she hadn't seen anything similar to the architecture on earth until then. Once they arrived he pulled the car into the large underground garage. He helped her once more to exit the car and carry her bag. Once inside the large house, Aisling popped out from the living room and rushed to Eveley and hugged her.

"Oh my god! What happened?! How did it happen?!" Aisling asked.

"I don't know, I was swimming, and the next thing I knew there was a drone right in front of me. I don't know how long it had been observing me," Eveley said.

"Well I'm glad you're here, you'll be safe here. They're going to start looking for you everywhere but it will be a while before they make it out here. Plus hopefully by then you'll be back on your planet Earth," Aisling said and Eveley nodded.

"Make yourself at home. Aisling can you take Eveley to one of the guest bedrooms?" Cian motioned upstairs.

"Sure, c'mon," Aisling said.

Aisling grabbed Eveley by the arm and helped her upstairs. They made it to the second floor and entered the guest bedroom closest to the stairs, Eveley suddenly keeled over in pain.

"Are you okay?! What's wrong?!" Aisling helped her back up and helped her sit on the bed.

"Here lay down, I'll check you, let me get my supplies."

Aisling returned and gave her an exam.

"Your water has already broken somehow, you're having this baby tonight. I'm going to send my brother to grab some more supplies, I'll be right back."

Aisling had been a nurse for a few years so she wasn't exactly new but she had only assisted the doctor during labor of her patients not done it alone. Eveley was progressing quickly and she was sure the baby was coming that night. Aisling got halfway down the large main staircase when she saw her brother in the open study.

"Cian, she's having the baby tonight. I need you to grab me a bunch of towels!"

"Tonight? Are you sure?!" Cian looked surprised.

"Yes, I just checked her, she's moving along quite fast."

"Okay, I'll go get the towels, anything else you need me to grab?"

"Yes, grab my tool bag on your way up."

"Okay."

That night it rained hard, the shutters on the house shook from the strong winds. This was the first day Eveley saw such "bad" weather since she'd arrived. She actually loved rainstorms but in this situation it just added to the anxiety of not knowing if she and her baby would be safe for long.

The intense pain from the worst contractions came when the clock passed midnight. She thought maybe she couldn't do it as the pain intensified, she went within herself as the pain came to its climax. She had no knowledge of what or who was in her room at that point.

Cian stayed outside the room since he didn't feel it was respectful for him to be in there. He pulled up a chair outside the room in case Aisling needed anything.

His mother and father came over around 1 am, his mother made a beeline straight to the room to help Aisling. She'd also been a nurse before she retired so it was a welcome sight for Aisling who respected her mother's experience.

Eveley was so thankful to have these two strong, knowledgeable women helping her, and they were women she trusted and loved dearly as friends back on earth.

Eveley pulled through the pain stoically and at 2 am, a new life was born.

"It's a boy!" Aisling exclaimed as she held the baby boy.

The baby boy let out a hefty cry, she handed him to Eveley and covered them both with a blanket. Eveley looked at him for the first time and fell in love. As soon as he was skin-to-skin with her his cries ceased and he looked around the room and in her direction. The tears were already flowing and she couldn't help but hold him gently against her and thank God he was here.

Eveley was well taken care of by Aisling and Stella, she was able to bond with her baby boy for several hours after the birth.

Aisling felt so relieved, everything went well regardless of the stress of it all. Mom and baby were happy and healthy and that's all she could ask for. Now it was just a matter of keeping them safe and LAR returning to help get them back to earth.

Aisling stepped out into the hallway, Cian was walking back from getting a bite to eat from the kitchen. He brought some food for Eveley and Aisling which he set on the chair outside the door.

"You can come and visit with Eveley and baby if you want."

Cian nodded, but seemed reluctant, as if he was doing something he didn't want to do.

"Hey, are you okay?" Aisling grabbed his arm and stopped him from going in.

He shook his head, "Ever since I found out there is another me on another planet and Eveley is the person I've been dreaming of since I can't remember when, I've felt off, like something is missing...I'm also scared to see the baby, in a way I'm seeing my own child although it isn't."

"Hey, don't do mental gymnastics with this, this is her and Aidan's baby. Just like you, I know now there is another me on earth, it's a lot to take in but we are still here living our own lives. You're still Cian, living your own reality, remember that."

Cian nodded and knocked, Eveley answered and he stepped inside the room. Eveley was holding her baby boy in her arms, he walked up to her and leaned down and hugged her.

"Congratulations." He managed a smile, and she smiled back. He looked over the little baby, and touched his little fist.

"He's a handsome little fella isn't he?"

"Yes he is," Eveley said proudly.

"He has a good set of lungs on him too doesn't he? I heard him from way out there."

Eveley chuckled, "Yes, he does."

Eveley observed Cian's expression as he held his little fist, his expression seemed that of a loving father gazing upon his firstborn. It took her breath away and at the same time it was the strangest feeling. She saw Cian's eyes tear up, he let go of the baby's hand gently then abruptly backed up, as if he wanted to create distance between him and the wife and child that wasn't his. Cian sat down and tried to become more detached.

"Have you picked out a name for him yet?"

"No, I wanted to wait till I'm back on earth and give Aidan a chance to help name him," Eveley replied.

"That's understandable, how are you feeling?" Cian continued.

"Really good actually, that was the most painful thing I've ever gone through, not gonna lie. Fighting through the pain was excruciating, but it was definitely worth it," she said it as she looked lovingly at her baby.

"Well the saying goes anything worth having is worth fighting for...so mission accomplished." Cian looked at her with sad eyes, he stood.

"Well, I'll let you rest Eveley, anything you need just let one of us know. I might need to go into the office today but Aisling and my mom will be here at all times."

"Okay, I will."

Cian started walking toward the door.

"Cian?"

"Yes?" Cian turned his head to look at her.

"If it hadn't been for you I don't know if I would be here right now...thank you."

Cian smiled faintly.

"Thank you for giving me the chance to do this for you," and he left and closed the door gently behind him.

Eveley finally let the tears flow she'd held back when he was in the room. Cian collected his thoughts outside the door, every muscle in his body was telling him to go back in there and take her in his arms, throw caution to the wind, and just give in to his desire to love her, but he didn't. It was the hardest thing he'd ever done...stop himself from loving her. She belonged to another version of himself, it was the most incomprehensible mental prison he'd ever been in.

CHAPTER 39

BLOOD AND TIME

That night Eveley saw on the news that Miss Venus was taken in for questioning, it worried her to no end what would happen to her. Cian and Aisling reassured her they would never do anything to such a public figure as it would look bad.

It surprised Eveley how the news, worldwide news at that, were only focused on this one story of an "unauthorized pregnant woman on the run". Being unauthorized meant neither iris scan nor facial recognition returned a profile, which meant their DNA was not cataloged in VIGIL. Which lead to speculation the culprit was a different species.

The fear mongering started immediately, fear mongering was the biggest strategy for compliance, they also employed technology. VIGIL sent daily updates on this story to each individual citizen...ways to report suspicious people and any changes in their routine. How unauthorized people especially a pregnant woman were a threat to society and the privileges citizens enjoyed. Government manipulated Aeven's people to tell on their neighbors, their loved ones, and even themselves, it was absolute control.

The O'Briens usually hired waitstaff for all their homes, but at this house they didn't, which was another vacation home they kept for privacy reasons as it was in such a desolate area. Fortunately, this detail ensured no one but the O'Brien family knew their whereabouts.

Typically, it was rare for them to see drones in this area. In the 20 years they'd owned the house, they had only once found a drone on their property which Jason shot down, prompting a court case he fought bitterly and lost. He'd never been conformist and VIGIL categorized Jason as a "low risk" threat, hence why he was to give the reins to Cian. VIGIL believed Cian was more "emotionally balanced" and would be easier to control than Jason.

Eveley was getting more anxious as the hours passed, she needed to get off this planet before they found her and her baby. She struggled to fall asleep, Aisling brought her a small cup of tea before bed to help her sleep. The baby had been fed and was safely next to her, she finally drifted to sleep.

"Eveley I can't speak very long. I'm still being pursued. I'm sorry I wasn't able to return sooner."

"LAR! Where have you been?! We are in so much danger, I need to return to earth!"

"I know Eveley, that's why I returned to help."

"We don't have a lot of time, they're looking for me."

"I know, and I will help you return to earth."

"How soon?"

"I can get you on the ship in four days, right outside this house."

"Okay," she paused for a moment, "LAR?"

"Yes Eveley."

"How long was I on the ship that brought me here?

"It was a matter of hours."

"How is that possible?"

"The ship traveled through a wormhole."

"Unbelievable, I could've never imagined."

"Eveley there is something else I need to tell you..."

"Oh boy, this doesn't sound good."

"About you returning back to earth, keep in mind this galaxy and this solar system are different than yours. Due to the difference in time dilation, time flows differently here than on earth."

"What do you mean LAR?"

"Time here is slower, for every month here it is a year on earth."
Eveley was dumbfounded, she'd been on Aeven nearly a year.
"You mean to tell me on earth it's been almost 10 years?!"
"Yes."
"LAR how could you keep this from me? How could you do this to me?! I trusted you!"
"Eveley, this was the only place I could bring you that was safe and quickest to get to. There are other galaxies with a larger time dilation, 1 year equals 20, 30, 40 years."
Eveley felt like she was drowning under a large tide, it'd been 10 long years on earth for Aidan. For all she knew he'd long forgotten about her and moved on. No, she expected him to be fully moved on from her, no matter how great their relationship had been. She felt so aggravated at LAR, he'd left her in the dark this whole time while time was ticking away.
"I can't believe you."
"I'm sorry Eveley, I know all this was because of me, but I never intended to hurt you."
"I know LAR, but it's time for me to return, your race is no longer looking for you in my galaxy, my baby and I are no longer safe here."
"That is correct, but you are not safe on earth either, VERMIN are dying and doomed to extinction, they will be frantic to reach you when you return."
"I will deal with them when I get to that point. I need you to promise me you'll get me back."
"I promise, just be ready and do not go outside this house."
"I won't."

The next day Eveley was having dinner with Stella and Aisling when Cian joined them toward the end of the meal. He looked worried, and it roused Eveley's suspicions there was something they weren't telling her.

After dinner, she went to their sunroom, she placed her baby in a small bassinet Aisling brought her from her house.

Cian joined Eveley and sat across from her. He took his phone and placed it into one of the boxes the family kept in every room of their house to block all signals.

"Is everything okay? You look worried," Eveley said.

Cian seemed distracted, he nodded.

"How was work today?" Eveley asked.

"It was a rough day for sure," Cian replied.

"I'm sorry to hear that," Eveley said.

Eveley was becoming more anxious as she realized Cian was keeping things from her as to avoid worrying her. She could always tell just like with Aidan, when he was trying to protect her.

Aisling walked into the room and stood by the baby, who was awake and cooing.

"May I?" Aisling motioned to the baby.

"Sure," Eveley said.

Aisling picked up the baby and rocked him in her arms, she spoke softly to him and smiled.

"Eveley, the mandate for blood samples came in today unexpectedly. In this case because of the fervor over VIGIL looking for you, they have made the deadline shorter, three days. After the deadline expires they are going to start going door-to-door. We know they have technology to verify and confirm who is inside of each dwelling, riots have already started since the announcement." Cian looked defeated.

Aisling continued for him, "This has never happened in the history of Aeven, they are very desperate. Usually they allow those in the upper classes to buy more time but there are no exceptions this time. We're pretty sure they are going to go to any lengths to find you. Is there any way LAR can help you board the ship faster than four days? The longer you're here the more dangerous it is for you and baby."

Cian looked off into the distance, he seemed so deep in thought that it was concerning to Eveley. He hadn't been worried at all when he rescued her from Lyra's house, but had he now lost hope? She shuddered at the thought of how dangerous it really was if he was worried.

"LAR did you hear? Can you help me leave sooner?"

"*I cannot Eveley, that is the soonest I can get a ship to you, but I will keep trying.*"

"He says it's impossible, four days is the soonest he can find me passage," Eveley said.

Cian and Aisling looked worried.

"Okay let us think of a plan, in the meantime just continue to stay inside, okay?" Aisling said.

"Yes, of course." Eveley took the baby upstairs to her room.

Aisling came by later to say goodbye before she left to return home to her family. Cian would stay the night to keep her and the baby safe.

"Aisling, how do you feel here on Aeven?" Eveley said.

"What do you mean?" Aisling replied confused with the question.

"Well how do you feel as far as all the monitoring? Like you can never keep a secret, even if you wanted to."

"I don't know, I guess since I've never known any different.. .it's just a meh feeling."

"You've given up?" Eveley asked boldly.

"Futile, hopeless, defeated, sure in a sense all those words fit the bill. But at the end of the day, I have my family, and I see how happy they are despite our limitations, and the sting doesn't feel as soul-killing anymore."

Eveley nodded, "I see."

Eveley felt sad for them in a way. Lyra really meant what she said about Aeven looking like a perfect society and, in many ways functioning like one, but beneath the surface, VIGIL kept a stronghold on Aeven's citizens. Like a snake that slithers its way onto its prey and squeezes with no chance of escape, it was tightly coiled around the throats of its citizens.

Eveley grabbed a piece of paper from her table, she handed it to Aisling. Aisling unfolded it, and looked at the page.

"Eveley what's this?"

"You know what it is, when I leave Aeven I want you to do this for me."

"I don't know Eveley, are you sure you want me to do this?"

"Yes, I do."

"Okay, consider it done," Aisling said.

Eveley managed to grin, even though her heart hurt just thinking about it.

Chapter 40

CATASTROPHE

The next day, Stella came over in the morning to stay with Eveley. Everyone else had to work. Stella made her breakfast which Eveley appreciated. Eveley remembered how good of a cook she was back on earth. She wondered what the Stella on earth was doing at this moment.

"Sweetie, after breakfast I'm going to tidy up a bit, I can do your laundry."

"Oh no Stella, I wouldn't want to be a bother," Eveley said.

Stella looked at her like really.

"Okay, first rule of being a new mom, when someone offers to help you, take the help sweetie," she said grinning.

"Noted." Eveley chuckled.

Stella stuck around until Cian and Aisling arrived. Cian came to her room and knocked. He'd seen so many horrible things happening around him since the announcement, things his wealthy family was immune to in many ways. It often made him feel guilty he didn't suffer any of the same consequences. Maybe he was a coward he told himself, there were people out there right now willing to die to oppose VIGIL, but he was happy to go along, to keep his wealth, his comforts, and his family safe.

Though in secret some of the programs Rogue Enterprises developed were not disclosed to VIGIL, excursions to look for suitable planets to move to, he still felt the guilt deep down.

Those excursions were risky and could end badly for him and his family.

"Hi Eveley, how's your day been with the little fella?"

"Hi Cian, it's been pretty peaceful and laid-back today, we are really getting into a little routine, plus your mom has been so helpful."

"I'm glad to hear that." He walked to her and gave her a quick hug.

Eveley was folding her clothes, the few pieces of clothing she'd managed to bring with her in the rush to escape Miss Venus' house. The baby laid on her bed, bundled up and asleep.

"I wanted to talk to you...I think things are going to get worse in the next couple of days. There are riots everywhere since the announcement, even near the city which is unheard of. I never knew there were so many people who opposed VIGIL and were part of the Helix Rebellion. They call themselves Helixes, in inside circles they just call them agitators but they're not," Cian said.

"Lyra mentioned something about a group of people who opposed VIGIL, I didn't know they had a name," Eveley said.

"That's because even talking about them is a good way to get VIGIL hyper-focused on you. He wants them to be unthinkable, like they don't exist, but they're an ever-persistent thorn in his side," Cian said.

Eveley shook her head, it dawned on her she was in the midst of a very complex and tumultuous time in Aeven's history. It was such a contrast to the enchantment she felt upon laying eyes on Aeven's sky for the first time almost a year ago.

"But you know what? I'm glad they exist, because the Helixes are right about VIGIL. He has no right to demand in essence a blood sacrifice each year, and they shouldn't be forced to provide it. They've never negotiated on that stance and every year they're punished for it," Cian said.

"How are they punished?"

"Well, from the few leaked videos I was able to get my hands on, it seems they generally take into custody any Helixes that are openly so. There are also towns around the major cities closed off to normal citizens. That's where they force the Helixes to segregate themselves from society. But I know there's so much more they don't allow us to see behind the veil, and it makes me question everything I've ever lived here."

Eveley felt surprise all these feelings were expressed by Cian. She felt bad for him, he was starting to come to terms with the depraved system in place on Aeven. She placed her hand on his shoulder. He turned and looked at her, she saw a mix of regret, shame, and uncertainty in his eyes.

"You can be a part of the solution though Cian, you can do something about it, you don't have to follow the current."

Cian nodded, "And that's precisely why they aren't taking you, they're not going to hurt you, and they're certainly not going to destroy you, not while I'm around."

"Cian what are you planning?" Eveley asked.

"Starting tonight I want to take you to a secret hiding place in our house. It's fully soundproof, the walls are a foot and a half of thick concrete to block out any of their technology. We will not allow anyone to harm you Eveley."

"Okay, underground?"

"Yes, if you want to start gathering your things. I'll take you there and Aisling will help you get settled, we have to make it 24 more hours and you'll be back on earth."

Eveley continued to fold her clothes which weren't many, she placed them in a small bag. Aisling made it upstairs and helped her gather the bassinet and the baby's things. Cian and Aisling carried all her things downstairs.

In the garage, a portion of the floor opened when Cian placed his hand over a specific spot on the garage floor. An opening in the floor automatically opened up, measuring about four feet by four feet. It revealed long stairs which descended two stories below, it was well lit and Cian entered first, followed by Eveley, then Aisling. Once the stairs ended, the room was a large 12×12 concrete room, there was a small separate bathroom in one corner, barely large enough for a toilet and sink. There was a bed in one corner, a bedside table, a small dresser, and a shelf with an array of books.

"What did you guys use this for?" Eveley asked.

"Our dad insisted all our houses should have a secret hiding room below ground. I guess he knew something we didn't," Cian said.

Aisling set the things she carried on the floor next to the bed. They heard the doorbell ring upstairs which was unusual. Cian and Aisling weren't expecting their parents so they knew this was troubling.

"Aisling you stay with Eveley, keep the door closed no matter what," Cian said.

"Okay," Aisling said. Aisling's eyes looked heavy with worry.

Cian ran up the steps, he closed the secret entrance in the concrete floor. He ran into another secret room in the middle of the first floor. He grabbed his great-grandfather's vintage gun and hid it in his waist under his shirt.

Aeven had disarmed all of its citizens long ago. However, vintage guns were allowed, the technology deemed too unreliable, weak, and low threat. VIGIL made it a policy to never show citizens being hurt by government agents on any media. But Cian knew better, he knew what VIGIL was capable of.

As soon as he made it to the main lobby, he heard the loud banging on the door. He took a deep breath and opened the door. As soon as he unlocked it, it flew open hitting the wall, at least 20 humanoids in riot gear and large rail guns entered his lobby. Cian took a few steps back.

"Hey! You have no authorization to enter this house!" Cian yelled.

The main humanoid, the captain, stepped forward. Cian could tell because his uniform was different from the others. The captain threw papers in Cian's direction.

Cian had never encountered humanoids like these before, militant humanoids that treated citizens with such despotism. VIGIL made it a policy to never show violence on media, all media was government controlled so that was easy enough. And it was mostly unnecessary as most of Aeven's citizens were submissive and followed all the laws and conditions placed on them. But in every society there are people who eventually stick out, and those people usually disappeared on Aeven.

A few clips posted by Helixes escaped over the years, usually they would be scrubbed right away never to be found, and rumors would start. Citizens would receive reminders their society was a peaceful one and any media showing such violence was a plant to cause division and were fake. All these leaked clips showing questionable behavior were always involving force used against the Helix Rebellion. The only ones who had rejected Aeven's decree on blood sampling from inception, which now in retrospect, made Cian feel ashamed he never cared about their struggle before. Most citizens were taught to think of these people as troublemakers.

Cian picked up the paper from the floor, the highest seal from VIGIL was stamped on it. They possessed the authority to search his whole house.

"Please proceed to remove yourself from the premises," the captain said.

"What?"

"Leave now, or we will use force," the humanoid said coldly.

Cian wasn't leaving, he wasn't leaving his sister and Eveley at their mercy. He backed up, if only he could make it back to the room where he'd just grabbed his gun, he might have a chance.

Behind the humanoid, two drones flew in and scanned each room. The humanoids stood in perfect lines waiting for commands which came from the captain who was receiving orders in real time as he walked into each room. As soon as one room was cleared they moved to the next room.

Cian backed up slowly, when he cleared enough distance between himself and the robots, he took off running. Without hesitation one of the humanoids shot in his direction, luckily none of the shots hit Cian.

He barely made it to the secret room and locked himself inside, he set up as many vintage weapons as he could. The humanoids systematically looked for him. Cian knew it was only a matter of time before they found him.

Cian texted his dad the situation in their house and asked him to come to the house right away. Jason replied he'd be there in fifteen minutes as he was already on his way having decided to check on everyone that night. He told Cian to hold out on them as long as possible.

Cian grabbed his great-grandfather's old rifle which contained armor piercing rounds, he'd need them if he was going to destroy any of them. Slowly and quietly, he slipped out a different hidden door than he came in and made his way down the dark hallway. He could hear the heavy footsteps of the humanoids upstairs. He stood hidden in the shadows, he thought maybe if they made it through every room, they'd just leave but he wasn't counting on it.

Jason texted he was five minutes away, Cian heard them make their way downstairs and enter the garage. Cian's heart rate sped up, he couldn't let them find the spot in the floor although it was perfectly hidden. Jason pulled up and all of a sudden he heard his voice.

"I'm the owner of this house, Jason O'Brien, you have no authority to be here—"

Could it be?! Cian heard the sound of their weapons, he heard the unmistakable sound of the vintage gun his dad kept in their other house. Cian ran to the area where the humanoids stood facing the front door with their guns drawn. Cian shot at them as they turned their attention back on him, he managed to hit several of them. He couldn't believe they'd shot his father without provocation.

Jason was wounded, a humanoid grabbed Jason and hurled him against the wall. He fell to the ground unconscious. Cian saw the wound on Jason's leg bleeding profusely. A second humanoid started to place Jason in handcuffs. Jason came to and struggled with him but he was no match for the humanoid who was much stronger. He placed his heavy metal foot on Jason's back and finished placing handcuffs on him.

Cian continued to shoot and take cover, knowing in all possibility he could be cornered easily as there were too many of them. One of the drones flew up behind him and shot a non-lethal which hit him in the back, a second projectile from the drone knocked him out.

When Cian came to 10 seconds later, he saw his dad across the room from him. Cian was handcuffed and two humanoids forced Cian to his feet. He could barely stand as the projectiles the drones shot at him where one level below lethal. The jolt from the projectile alone made Cian's body jerk, he felt as if a boulder had fallen on him. But he stood with unsteady feet in defiance of VIGIL's agents.

For a second it seemed like the search was over. They dragged Jason first, then Cian. Just when they were headed to the front door and Cian thought at least the girls and the baby were safe below, the humanoids made a sharp turn and made a beeline to the garage. Cian had never felt more fear in his life than at that moment, being helpless to protect those he loved from evil. In his mind, he repeated to himself he couldn't fail them; he had to protect them.

Once everyone entered the garage, the captain walked up to Cian and spoke.

"We have reason to believe you have a fugitive hidden in this house, in a hidden room. We know there is an entrance somewhere in this room, give us the code to enter."

Cian shook his head, "I don't know what you're talking about. I don't know where you got you intel but you're wrong."

The humanoid didn't look amused. He grabbed Cian and threw him on the concrete floor, he placed his heavy metal foot on top of his back.

"This is your last chance to tell us where it is."

Cian didn't say a word. The humanoid, seeing Cian's resolve to stay silent, grabbed his face and slammed it hard against the concrete floor.

Jason yelled expletives at them. One humanoid grabbed Cian roughly from the floor and released his handcuffs. They placed each arm in front of him with his hands laying flat. The humanoid stood in front of him, placing his heavy metal feet on top of each of his hands, placing increasing pressure on them. He grabbed Cian and slammed his face into the concrete floor one more time causing him to lose consciousness.

Jason tried to get up and they slammed him back down too.

The captain grabbed Cian by the back of his shirt and dragged him methodically in a straight line up and down the concrete floor, while another humanoid kept his hands flat on the surface of the concrete, they did this throughout the entire floor.

Jason prayed the system wouldn't catch his print. In the very last corner his hand scanned and opened the hatch.

"Bingo," the captain said.

Several humanoids entered, single file line down the narrow stairs.

Eveley and Aisling were completely silent. The room was completely soundproof, but the fact Cian did not return right away confirmed to Aisling something serious was happening.

As soon as she heard the commotion and heard the footsteps down the stairs she was ready.

Aisling begged Eveley to implore LAR to help them, if this was VIGIL's army it would be almost impossible to escape them. Eveley and the baby hid under the bed, the only spot with any cover in the room. Aisling waited next to the steps. As soon as she heard the footsteps get closer, she stuck her weapon into the first humanoid and discharged an electrical charge that fried his system, it fell to the floor. Before she could get the next humanoid, one of them slammed her hard into the dresser, she fell on the floor disoriented and unable to stand up. The room filled with several of the humanoids. One of them walked to the bed and turned it around forcefully, slamming it against the wall. Eveley shielded her baby protectively.

Two humanoids picked Aisling off the ground and dragged her up the stairs by her arms, she yelled all the way up as she saw they'd discovered Eveley.

Eveley was frantically imploring LAR to help her if he was near. The humanoids grabbed her, making her stand still, and scanned her face.

"Negative on the scan, it's her," the humanoid communicated.

By now Eveley was frantic inside, one of the humanoids reached for the baby, and Eveley pulled away. The humanoid grabbed her by the throat and picked her off the ground, her feet barely an inch off the ground. She noticed the small rectangular window on the humanoids arm, inside the window was a purple light that when scanned held a unique identifier. This is how VIGIL kept track of all humanoids and allowed confirmation by humans it was a machine. This was due to how human-like they were and some people's inability to distinguish machine from man.

Eveley, Cian, and the rest of his family agreed the eyes of humanoids gave them away. Their irises and pupils were void of any human emotion, it was very subtle to pick up on. Perhaps an evolutionary survival mechanism only some humans possessed.

Eveley saw the humanoid's empty eyes and the lenses opening and closing as it zeroed in on her face. Eveley tried to scream, but her windpipe was being crushed by his metal hand, she knew if she stayed in this position long she'd pass out and drop the baby.

Eveley was desperate as she felt her lungs struggle to bring in air. The captain walked into the room and motioned to the humanoid holding her up to put her down. A different humanoid snatched the baby from her arms. The one holding her up released her to fall on the ground just as she was on the verge of passing out.

As soon as she landed on the ground and saw her baby in the humanoid's arms, she became extremely agitated.

"Give him back to me!" she yelled in tears. She tried to run toward the humanoid holding her baby and another held her back. She fought with all her might. She could hear Aisling, Jason, and Cian yelling upstairs as they heard but couldn't see what was happening.

Eveley saw the weapon Aisling used on the first humanoid from the corner of her eye. She reached for it and managed to grab it and discharge it on the humanoid holding her back which fell to the ground. A drone flew into the room and discharged a projectile that hit her mid-back, she doubled over in pain on the ground. She tried to crawl on her hands and knees toward her baby who was now crying. She reached for him with one arm as she tried to ignore the pain. One of the humanoids grabbed her arm and dragged her up the steps, she kicked and screamed, reaching out for her baby still. The rest of the humanoids followed behind.

When Cian, Jason, and Aisling saw Eveley being dragged up the stairs and the humanoid holding the baby boy, they felt the most utter despair and helplessness.

"Stop this insanity right now! What you're doing is wrong and against the law!" Jason yelled.

Cian was seething inside, when they survived this ordeal, he vowed to destroy VIGIL and his agents. Aisling was crying, she looked at Eveley who looked terrified.

The humanoid threw Eveley in the middle of the lobby. "Say hello to your friends," he said.

The captain seemed to be getting orders and motioned to the humanoid holding the baby. "The infant can be removed for analysis in the lab."

The humanoid nodded in confirmation and began to walk away toward the front door.

Eveley's eyes grew wide. "No! Don't! Stop!"

Eveley stood and ran toward the baby and right when her hand managed to touch his skin, a bright ball of light blinded her and everyone around her. Eveley landed safely on the floor with the baby in her arms. She opened her eyes and saw every single humanoid destroyed to pieces. Jason, Aisling, and Cian were still there, alive, and disoriented as well.

"Eveley! The ship will be there in 10 minutes, you must leave now, they will send more humanoids to finish the job."

"Was that you just now?"

"Yes, I am sorry it took me so long to get to you. I was trying my hardest to return when I heard your call for help."

Eveley looked down at her baby boy, who'd stopped crying. He looked to be okay, but her body still trembled from shock. The blast disabled the handcuffs on everyone and opened. Eveley stood and rushed to their spot, she fell on her knees in front of them, they embraced her, relieved she and her baby were safe.

"The ship will be here in 10 minutes according to LAR. I have to get on it, they're sending more humanoids," Eveley said.

It was evident from the numerous drones beginning to congregate outside the property there were more reinforcements on the way.

"Okay, we will cover for you," Cian said.

Cian, Jason, and Aisling grabbed weapons from their secret room and walked toward the back of the house, they surrounded her and shot down the drones before they could dispatch their projectiles.

Eveley made her way to the edge of the property, overlooking a small clearing below. Cian, Aisling, and Jason had shot all of the drones by that point. Eveley turned to all of them, thanking them for their help, knowing she would probably never see them again. Cian came up to her and kissed her forehead as well as the baby's, Aisling and Jason gave her and the baby a heartfelt hug.

Eveley finally turned to find the ship just like before, again she saw the slight reflection of it, the portal opened, and she knew as soon as she made the choice she'd be back toward her home. On the ship, she laid asleep with her baby boy nestled safely beside her, in her mind her body floated peacefully through beautiful clouds, yet she was traveling at the speed of light back to Earth.

CHAPTER 41

HEAVEN ON EARTH

Eveley's 22nd Birthday

Eveley found herself face to face with Aidan again, she carried the sleeping baby boy in her arms...their baby boy. She couldn't believe she was here in front of him again. His face instantly recognized her, and she recognized him. How could she forget him? The last time they were face to face she was 21 and now upon her return he was 33.

He was still as handsome as she remembered him, he looked more mature of course, more distinguished. He looked at her for a second, his gaze followed to their son, she noticed confusion in his eyes. Nonetheless, he ran to her and hugged her and she held unto him tightly as well, as tightly as ever without squeezing the baby between them.

So many nights she'd dreamed of this moment. She'd seen him in her dreams longing for her just as much as she did for him, except for him it'd been 10 long years. Aidan tenderly touched her face and shook his head.

"I thought I'd never see you again...you came back to me," he said. His eyes looked at her with such love.

Her heart was beating so fast, she felt unable to catch her breath. Her voice shook slightly when she spoke.

"I've been trying to make my way back to you since I landed over there, every night I prayed to see you and my family again," she said.

He continued to hold her and caress the side of her face with his fingers. He looked down at the baby's face. He was small, with tiny little features, a soft nest of delicate, reddish hair on his tiny head.

"Who's the little guy?" Aidan asked as he touched his little hand gently. She sighed and looked at him.

"Your son." She watched his face more confused than ever.

"I- I don't understand, how could that be possible? You left 10 years ago."

"I can explain, do you notice anything different about my appearance since you last saw me?"

"No, you look the same."

"Exactly, the planet I was taken to, Aeven, has a different time dilation than earth. For every year that passes on Aeven, it equals 12 years on earth."

It took Aidan a second to understand but the aha moment made him grin faintly. He looked down at his son and leaned down and caressed his little cheek, then gave him a kiss on the forehead. His eyes welled with tears and he hugged both of them and told them how much he loved them.

"I'm an old man now compared to you, 10 long years, wow, even I can't believe it's been that long, may I?"

Aidan motioned if he could hold their son. Eveley handed the still-sleeping boy to him. He was a natural, he scooped him up and rocked him in his arms, looking so proud. She loved him even more seeing him with their son and how he'd accepted him without doubting her or needing more convincing. She knew their trust was infallible, which is why she woke up from her stupor, the weakness Cian made her feel on Aeven.

After ten years passed on earth, she was prepared to find Aidan married to someone else with his own family, she had mentally prepared for it. She didn't expect him to be here waiting for her return. She actually wanted him to find love and happiness. Ten years was an unreasonable amount of time to expect him to wait for her. She had prepared to accept he had moved on, but here they were...both holding out for their love, and they had been rewarded with the sweetest reunion.

She read so much devotion and adoration in his eyes when he looked at her, and she felt the same way, there was no one above him, even another Aidan on another planet. Every time he came close to her or touched her, her skin came alive and her heart sped up. It was the best of both worlds, the wonder and aliveness of young love from their past, and the depth of a blue ocean of emotion between them. Their son was the culmination of their love, and it was beautiful to share this moment together.

CHAPTER 42

CONFESSION

That night her mother kept their son in her room. Eveley felt nervous anticipation, they were in her old bedroom. Aidan took a shower first, then Eveley. She came out and changed into an oversized t-shirt. A soft orange glow came from the lamp next to her bed, slow music played in the background. It felt nice to be so casual, even little details like a beat up oversized t-shirt compared to the fastidiousness of her routine on Aeven felt familiar and comforting.

Aidan sat on the side of the bed in long sweats and no shirt. It was all so strange to be in her room again, with her husband, who looked at her like a Goddess as she walked up to him and stood in front of him.

He'd gotten several tattoos since she last saw him. She ran her fingers over their designs on his forearms, biceps, and shoulders. He'd also grown a beard and mustache which made him look more mature.

Aidan asked a lot of questions about life on her new planet, which fascinated him. Eveley told Aidan about the parallel theory, and VIGIL. Finally, she got the courage to tell Aidan about Cian. How she started to feel tempted to be with him, in every sense, emotionally and physically. The pain of Aidan being far from her almost broke her but she recovered her focus when she found out she was carrying their son.

Aidan listened sympathetically. Eveley felt scared he'd be upset she just admitted to almost cheating on him with himself if that made sense. Even though they didn't know at the time if they'd ever see each other again.

He took both her hands in his, "It would have been understandable you felt that way, it was me after all. If another Eveley had appeared in front of me I probably would have reacted the same, but for you it was only a year." He grinned and winked, she was really surprised.

"You're not mad at me?" she asked.

He pulled her closer, he rested his head on her stomach as he wrapped his arms around her hips and thighs. He looked up at her lovingly.

"No, I think it's sort of comical, but I'm sorry it was so painful for you. That you were by yourself while you went through pregnancy and birthing our son. I wish I could have been there to support you." He always knew how to ease her pain, and let her know she was appreciated and special.

"You're so strong, thank you for our son," he said tenderly.

"Thank you," she said as she dimmed the lights further.

"For what?"

"For never giving up on us, for waiting for me even though it was such a long wait."

"You're worth it," he said. "Sometimes I still can't believe you're here in front of me again. I feel like it's a dream, I have to pinch myself. You're the best thing that's ever happened to me," Aidan said.

They kissed...a tender, yet passionate kiss, his hands slid slowly up her legs. That night was a night full of discovery...of everything they missed for so long and yearned for in their dreams of each other.

The next morning, Eveley woke up feeling the happiest she'd ever felt. She opened her eyes to Aidan sleeping peacefully by her side. She stood and put on her robe. She went into her mom's bedroom. Isabel was rocking her grandson in her arms.

"Hola mami, como estuvo el bebe [Hi mom, how was the baby]?"

"Fue un angelito mija, y tu como dormiste cariño [He was an angel, how did you sleep sweetie]?" her mom raised her eyebrows, Eveley smiled.

"Dormi muy bien [I slept well]" Eveley replied, they both chuckled knowingly.

"Creo que vas a tener una hermanita muy pronto mijo [I think you're going to have a little sister soon my grandson]." Isabel said to her grandson.

CHAPTER 43

CITLALLI

She entered the lobby of the tallest high-rise downtown, she'd never made her way into the city before, isolating herself like the many other Helixes on the outskirts of the city. Her parents fought and died trying to protect her from VIGIL, from forcing the blood sacrifice from her as a newborn. It made her sick to think of it in that way, but that was how she was taught to think of it, since they had no choice in the matter.

It was strange that now she was here, in this shiny, beautiful city rotten at the core. She had one mission and it was serendipity this opportunity fell into her lap. An opportunity with Rogue Enterprises, she was sure this was her way in, to infiltrate and destroy. Her past followed her, so she had to make an effort to blend in, for once she dressed like the poor lambs around her. She knew as soon as she opened her mouth, she'd give herself away so she planned to speak little except for yes or no if possible.

She waited in the lobby, facing the expansive four-story-tall glass windows overlooking the street. She watched society move along, a society she never wanted to be a part of. Everything was a façade, if these people knew what really happened in the dark on this ground, they'd shudder.

She stood there, feeling her insides recoil in hate, she tried her hardest not to feel it, to not let it take over, after all her enemy was invisible, yet he was everywhere, and everyone helped him stay in power.

She felt a light tap on her shoulder, she turned around. She was faced with a tall handsome man, dark auburn hair, light blue eyes, and he looked at her with confusion.

"Eveley?"

"No, my name is [1] Citlalli."

"Oh, I'm sorry about that, I'm Cian O'Brien, you'll be interviewing with me today."

He smiled but looked taken aback which confused her, had he recognized her? Was her cover blown completely? She vowed to remain calm. He extended his hand and they shook hands.

"Follow me," he said.

Her presence definitely made him act off kilter.

When Cian saw her face, the same exact face of Eveley's, her parallel, his mind and body went to war with each other. He was sure his sister had something to do with this...this was no coincidence, perhaps Eveley asked her to? He wasn't sure but inside he didn't know how to feel. He felt happy, he felt curious, he felt bewildered, all these feelings were fighting for control as they made their way up the elevator to his floor, and into his expansive office.

She sat down, he sat down, for a second he couldn't help staring at her, noticing the same iris freckle in one of her eyes as Eveley's. It'd been a month he hadn't seen Eveley's face except in his dreams of her at night, and in his nightmares. He snapped out of it when he realized he was staring and she was staring right back without breaking eye contact. She was intense and unafraid, her bold and mysterious eyes told him a much different story than Eveley's.

"So, it's Citlalli Luna?"

"Yes."

---

1. Citlalli (Seat-lah-lee)

"Well I need to know what your true intentions are Citlalli."

Citlalli felt exposed...but she didn't care anymore and took out a piece of paper. Aisling had told her that her brother was looking for someone unorthodox, that he was ready to rid himself of this weight on his back. She wrote on the paper, and slid the paper to him, watching him intently. He saw smoldering fire in her eyes. Cian took the paper and read it:

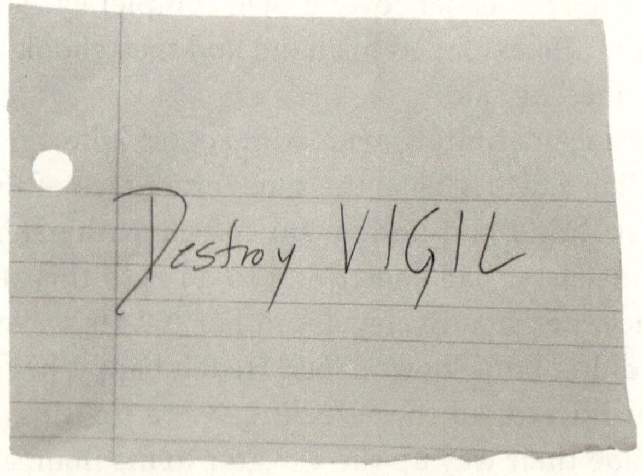

Chapter 44

SLITHER

On foreign soil, the vulnerable larval form of VERMIN was an unwanted passenger on the EDEN ship. Instead of taking over Eveley's body, it slithered its way into Aeven's soil, waiting, adapting to the air, water, and soil quickly and growing slowly at first. This planet was the perfect environment, it no longer needed human hosts. The soil provided everything it needed to grow stronger and bigger. There would be a day when these humans would understand the power of a species stronger, better, and more vicious than them...

EPILOGUE

Day 1 without her- Today was hell, no other way to describe it. After the FBI took me and Isabel in for questioning, I was ready for another beating. This time I would have welcomed it to wake me up from how numb I made myself to the pain. Yet they didn't, they were surprisingly cordial and civil this time. After Eveley entered the ship, which was the coolest thing I've ever seen by the way, we were surrounded by VERMIN. Literally seconds after the EDEN ship disappeared from the sky, the first VERMIN jumped out at us from the shadows.

Man oh man am I grateful for my gun. If I didn't have it I don't know if I'd still be here, or been able to keep my promise to protect Eveley's mom. There must have been at least 15 parasites by the time the FBI showed up and joined the fight. Not against us, but helping us, which surprised me. It took all their manpower to destroy most of the VERMIN. They ended up killing all except one, which they wounded and took into custody. After the craziness of that fight I was ready for more. I hadn't even had time to process Eveley being gone although I knew it inside and it fueled my anger during the battle. Now the guys are trying to get me to talk. I'm still not sure if I should say anything, I may have to in order to keep Isabel safe though.

Day 2 without her- Today I had an Agent Eiserman talk to me. He told me that they knew that Eveley had healing abilities. He said crime around the world had decreased by 50% which was unprecedented and unheard of. They knew she had something

to do with it and these VERMIN were also related. They wanted
to know where she was. I told them if I knew I'd be there, not
rotting here in a concrete box. I haven't seen Eveley's mom since
they took us in separately. I've asked them several times to let
me call my family and talk to Isabel but so far they haven't
allowed me to make any calls. I'm starting to get really sick of
their tactics. The stupid games they play and the way they've
treated us like criminals is what stops me from giving them the
info they want.

Day 3 without her- It finally hit me, like a freight train crashing
into me. It dawned on me that I might never see her face again.
Her face has haunted my dreams since she left but today I realized it's my reality. I wonder sometimes how much a human can
endure. I'm weary and I don't know how much longer I will have
to bear this misery. Sometimes I want to scream and punch the
wall, the pain gets so overwhelming. I stop myself only because I
made us promise each other to keep hope. Hope...the only thing
that keeps me breathing.

Day 4 without her-Today they sent Agent Eiserman to talk to
me again. He told me that in exchange for my cooperation they
would protect Isabel from the VERMIN. They started a program
to eradicate these things and wanted me to lead it. I told him
I'd need it all in writing and I'd need a lawyer to look it over
before I signed anything or told them more. I also wanted to
be let go immediately to be with my family. Surprisingly, they
agreed. Maybe the healing that affected those around Eveley is
finally making its way to the FBI. They're acting reasonable and
didn't beat me up this time. I guess the bar was set pretty low
on their ethics but it's an improvement.

Day 10 without her-I can't believe how much has changed
in ten days. I have barely had time to process Eveley's departure and I'm already back in FBI headquarters. Now, not as a
prisoner but as the leader of a newly formed team whose sole
mission is to hunt, and destroy the estimated 3,000 VERMIN
left. Did I really want to upend my whole life to do this? I can't

say that with my depression over Eveley leaving I'd be much use anywhere else. This gives me purpose, it gives me hope. Every dark emotion I can pour into this mission instead of letting it consume me. A mission that, at its core, is still about Eveley. I may not be able to bring her back but I can ensure that when she returns to me, her world will be a safe one, free of these parasites.

ABOUT THE AUTHOR

Roxana, is a bilingual author originating from Chihuahua, Mexico who resides in the Midwest. She aims to transport you to new worlds with endless possibilities. Her overarching message is to convey the value of humanity in a technological world. She is a lover of travel, music, miniatures, pickleball, and new experiences.

Please don't forget to leave your review for Luna's Edge on Amazon.com

Reviews are the best way to support independent authors.

Thank you for your support!

OTHER WORKS

- Luna's Fury, the 2nd book in the Luna's Edge Trilogy.

- Luna's Dawn, the 3rd book in the Luna's Edge Trilogy.

For updates on new releases please sign up to receive newsletter at roxanamacias.com

PLAYLIST

A curated list of songs I listened to while writing Luna's Edge

- "Nebula" Melezz

- "Shadows" The Midnight

- "Kings of Summer" Ayokay

- "Crush" Yuna

- "Stellar" Incubus

- "My Blood" Twenty One Pilots

- "The Core" Chris Tilton

- "Above me" LEISURE

- "We Are The People" Empire of the Sun

- "Can You Feel It?" Cannons

- "Amorcito Corazon" Lupita Infante

- "Soledad y Mar" Natalia Lafourcade

- "Beckoning" Melodysheep

- "Edge of Night" MALINDA

- "Solitude-Felsmann+Tiley Reinterpretation" M83
- "BLEED" The Kid Laroi
- "Como Respirar???" Humbe
- "Moving On" Melezz
- "Cuando" Ruzzi
- "Those Eyes" New West
- "Stand Still" Sabrina Claudio
- "Hasta La Raiz" Natalia Lafourcade
- "Moonlight" Kali Uchis
- "Memories" The Midnight
- "Galaxy" Paperwhite
- "Everything Everywhere Always" Elijah Woods
- "A Race Against Time" PYLOT
- "Sky over Tokyo" RADWIMPS
- "Skywards" Christian Reindl
- "Drown Inside it" Icarus
- "Visions of You" LEISURE
- "Think of You" Estereomance
- "Drift" Alina Baraz
- "Back in Love" LEISURE

- "Spells" Cannons

- "Place" Lucy Rose

- "Go Back" John Summit

- "Empire of Steel" Essenger

- "Right Back to You" Electric Youth

- "Frozen" Sabrina Claudio

- "Static" Timecop1983

- "Blood Moon" Essenger

www.ingramcontent.com/pod-product-compliance
Lightning Source LLC
Chambersburg PA
CBHW031842310726
48972CB00005B/1372